D1207428

THE SWAMP OF DEATH

REBECCA GOWERS

THE
SWAMP
OF
DEATH

A TRUE TALE OF VICTORIAN
LIES AND MURDER

HAMISH HAMILTON
an imprint of
PENGUIN BOOKS

HAMISH HAMILTON LTD

Published by the Penguin Group
Penguin Books Ltd, 80 Strand, London WC2R ORL, England
Penguin Group (USA), Inc., 375 Hudson Street, New York, New York 10014, USA
Penguin Books Australia Ltd, 250 Camberwell Road, Camberwell, Victoria 3124, Australia
Penguin Books Canada Ltd, 10 Alcorn Avenue, Toronto, Ontario, Canada M4V 3B2
Penguin Books India (P) Ltd, 11 Community Centre, Panchsheel Park, New Delhi – 110 017, India
Penguin Group (NZ), Cnr Airborne and Rosedale Roads, Albany, Auckland 1310, New Zealand
Penguin Books (South Africa) (Pty) Ltd, 24 Sturdee Avenue, Rosebank 2196, South Africa

Penguin Books Ltd, Registered Offices: 80 Strand, London WC2R ORL

www.penguin.com

First published 2004
1

Copyright © Rebecca Gowers, 2004

The moral right of the author has been asserted

All rights reserved.
Without limiting the rights under copyright
reserved above, no part of this publication may be
reproduced, stored in or introduced into a retrieval system,
or transmitted, in any form or by any means (electronic, mechanical,
photocopying, recording or otherwise), without the prior
written permission of both the copyright owner and
the above publisher of this book

Set in 12/14.75 pt Monotype Bembo
Typeset by Rowland Phototypesetting Ltd, Bury St Edmunds, Suffolk
Printed in Great Britain by Clays Ltd, St Ives plc

A CIP catalogue record for this book is available from the British Library

ISBN 0–241–14168–0

To my mother and father
whose music has fed me
as I've grown up

Contents

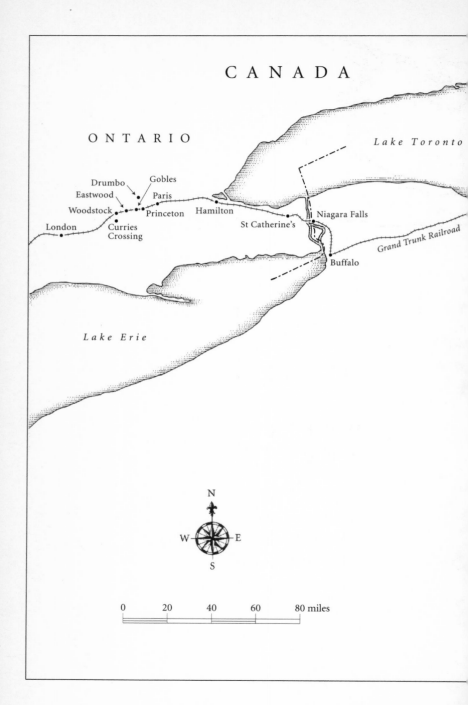

CANADA

ONTARIO

Lake Toronto

Drumbo
Gobles
Eastwood
Paris
Woodstock
Princeton
Hamilton
London
Curries
Crossing
St Catherine's
Niagara Falls

Grand Trunk Railroad

Buffalo

Lake Erie

N
W   E
S

0   20   40   60   80 miles

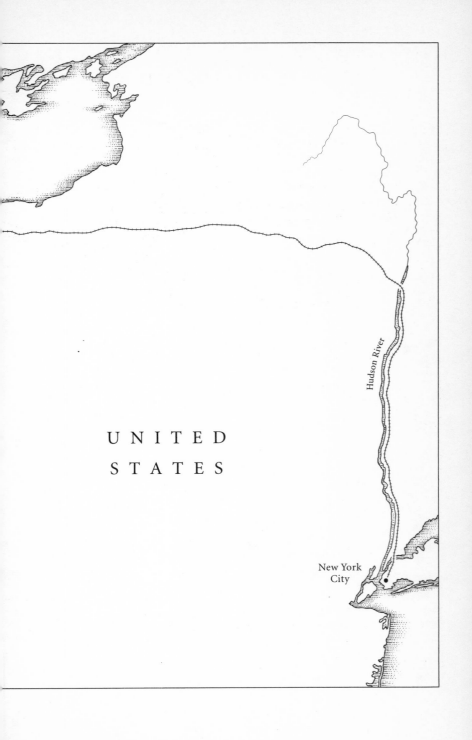

'Shan't I feel a fool if all
this proves to be only imagination'

Preface

On the morning of Friday, 21 February 1890, two Canadian backwoodsmen, brothers called George and Joseph Elvidge, went out in bitter weather to cut saplings in a swamp near the small township of Blenheim, Ontario. A short way from the nearest road, draped across a pile of saplings, they found a young man lying face upwards, dead. The harsh conditions had caused both the corpse and the boggy ground to freeze.

The dead man lay with one leg dropped down, the other raised on a stump, and his left arm bent up against a branch. This had allowed the sleeve of his waterproof overcoat to fill with rain or slush, which had also frozen solid. His clothes were disarranged, any valuables had clearly been taken from his turned-out pockets, and his shirt front had been left exposed. The shirt's collar had been ripped right off and lay nearby, along with the dead man's necktie and crumpled bowler hat. There was a nasty wound, possibly from a bullet, behind one of his ears, and on the saplings below, underneath a layer of snowfall, were a few frozen drops of blood. George Elvidge stood guard while his brother fetched local officials to the scene. In order to remove the body to the undertaker's premises in the village of Princeton, three miles away, the dead man's left foot had to be hacked out of the frozen quagmire with an axe. When he was lifted up, it became clear that all the name tags had been snipped out of his clothing.

That afternoon, the local coroner, Dr McLay, opened an

inquest at Dake's Hotel, Princeton. Joseph Elvidge described how there had been snow on the victim and a little blood under his head, but no sign of any conflict round about. There had also been footprints leading away from the corpse, and witnesses agreed that these seemed to have been left by flat-soled footwear, possibly worn-out overshoes, or moccasins. William Crosby, a Justice of the Peace, stated that 'the appearance of the body was that it had been placed there by other hands than his own'. He also mentioned that the 'face was of a dark colour' as if the victim 'had been dead some time'. Others ventured that 'leaving out the question of the dark colour of the skin,' the dead man's features were 'strikingly Indian'. One press reporter explained that 'the forehead recedes considerably, the nose is Roman and rather prominent and the upper lip very thick and projecting. His eyes were of a greyish–blue tint and his hair black.'

The next day, the local newspapers devoted numerous columns to the story. 'The deceased,' noted one, had been 'more than usually fine dressed' in what seemed to be English and French clothing. His jacket was black and white check, his trousers were black with grey stripes, and his tie had been made from a green silk with white spots. Only one slight clue to his identity had been found: the back of his silver–set pearl cuff buttons bore the maker's stamp, 'W. West'. Reporters went into considerable detail about the distribution of the footprints around the corpse, which witnesses believed must have been made before the most recent fall of snow:

The foot marks indicate that the man after depositing his ghastly burden had been careful to leave as little and as unreliable a record of his course as possible. The steps were not in a straight line nor were they at all regular. He appears to have jumped from hillock to hillock, stepping in the snow only where it was absolutely necessary for him to do so.

Those who had seen the dead man *in situ* all judged from his position that he 'could not possibly have taken his own life and lain down to die'. No 'implement of destruction' was found.

1. A Sort of Travelling Gentleman Farmer

Many gentlemen have gone to New Zealand and Australia, and many more to Canada, preferring a life of honourable industry and eventual abundance in a new country to hollow and pretentious penury at home.

W. R. Greg, *Why are Women Redundant?*, 1869

Throughout his childhood Douglas Pelly longed to become a soldier. Early in 1882, at the age of seventeen, he was duly gazetted lieutenant in the Third Volunteer Battalion of the Essex Regiment; but any hopes he might have cherished that this would lead to professional employment were soon crushed. His grandfather, who was a banker, kept a tight hold on the family purse strings, and let it be known that if his grandson ever attempted to shape his military pursuits into a bona fide career, his allowance would cease. This prohibition remained in force even after the old man died, in June 1886, just as Pelly graduated from Cambridge with a mediocre degree in law. Six idle and indecisive months later, with Pelly still perplexed by what he called the 'burning question difficult to solve' of his future course, his father walked into the family drawing room in Saffron Walden one evening and said to him without preamble, 'Your fate is sealed. You are to be an underwriter.' Pelly had no idea what an underwriter was.

His name, he discovered, had been 'given' to an old chap called Bullen, who was an active underwriting member at Lloyd's. Pelly was to be Bullen's apprentice, learning the ropes

over a minimum period of seven years, at a guaranteed profit
to Pelly of one hundred pounds per annum. In a brief account
of these events, Pelly failed to mention that in 1886, after
tortuous vetting procedures, a new Lloyd's underwriter was
required to provide the company with an entrance fee of two
hundred pounds and a minimum deposit of five thousand.

He should perhaps have been undilutedly grateful for the
opportunity that his family had delivered to him, but when
Pelly understood that he had been consigned to an office job,
he was dismayed. This was not simply because he found the
prospect uncongenial. The Lloyd's arrangement completely
overlooked the fact that, having suffered serious illnesses in
adolescence, he was under medical orders to avoid a sedentary
career. Even by Victorian standards, the working conditions
for Lloyd's names were notoriously unpleasant. Pelly and
Bullen spent the first and last part of each day crammed
together in Bullen's little office, while the five or so hours in
between were passed on the first floor of the Royal Exchange,
amid a crush of aged members, in an atmosphere that was
evilly airless. It was said that no one could endure more than
five years of this toxic drudgery without falling sick. Pelly
succumbed in under twelve months. He developed an abscess
under his left shoulder and severe tonsillitis; and while his
tonsils were removed without ill effect, albeit during an operation that was conducted without anaesthetic while Pelly sat
up in a chair, the operation to remove the abscess left him
with a wound that would not heal. Pelly languished for many
weeks, until at last, in the manner of the times, his doctor
suggested he recuperate by taking a long voyage somewhere
warm.

So it was that on 14 March 1888 Pelly found himself on the
RMS *Garth Castle* bound for Cape Town. The journey lasted

Douglas Pelly as a student at Cambridge.

three happy weeks, time enough for him to indulge in a carefree flirtation with a girl going out to Africa to be married. They parted when he took a smaller ship up the coast to Durban, before travelling six weeks inland by river boat to the mission station, Blantyre, in what was then called East Central Africa. Pelly amused himself on this journey by spotting the gravestones of dead colonists up the river banks, and by shooting wild animals, including a hippopotamus that 'promptly sank in deep water'. At the same time, the mosquitoes were 'awfully bad', so that he was pleased when he reach Blantyre at last. He was also boyishly delighted to discover when he got there that he had put himself seven hundred miles from the nearest telegraph station and a thousand from the nearest shop.

Almost the moment he arrived, Pelly collapsed with malaria, spending his first two days completely unconscious; but between continuing fevers, he found it marvellous fun to be amongst the missionaries, diplomats, leopards, scorpions, native chiefs and hunter boys of the region. He wrote full of naive enthusiasm to his parents: 'If you could come here you would never look down on the "poor negro" again. He is just as fine a man as a white, and far more of a gentleman in most cases. You <u>can</u> only be very fond of them.' His letters thrum with details of slave raiders, native wars, outlandish meals and poison drinking; with tricks for surviving puff adders and elephant charges; with curious aspects of lockjaw, and of the amputations that his new mission friends frequently performed upon the local supply of lepers. Despite a few close brushes with death, as when he swam, against advice, in a river choked with crocodiles, the five months Pelly passed in Africa drew to a close long before he had exhausted his appetite for its excitements.

Fortunately, his meandering journey home again also delivered the kinds of adventures that Pelly seems most to have enjoyed. Straight away his ship was blown six hundred miles off course into the South Polar regions, losing most of its sails in the process. Conditions were so bad that for days it was possible to get about on deck only by digging narrow alleyways through piles of snow, and passengers and crew became badly bruised through the vessel's endless lunging. When at last better weather prevailed Pelly was able to stop off for a short spell in New Zealand, characteristically imperilling himself on a mishandled bush trip outside Napier; but temporary starvation failed to dim his spirits, and he went on to Australia, where in the seas at St Kilda, Melbourne, unexpectedly strong currents caused him to swim to the point of exhaustion. It was his good fortune that a stranger saved him from drowning. Even this near-fatal exploit seemed preferable to his confined life in the Old Country, but when the time came to go home he made the best of this too, choosing a ship that had dancing on deck every night of the voyage from Sydney to Tilbury docks. Pelly later calculated that his convalescence had taken place over a distance of thirty-seven thousand miles.

Back in England, and returned to the pink of health, he felt compelled to take another crack at Lloyd's, but the dismal influence of its offices soon caused him to fall sick again. He became an inactive member, and once more quit the sedentary life. As the weeks drifted by Pelly re-immersed himself in his work as a volunteer officer with the Essex Regiment, surprised and pleased to be promoted to major. Yet, however agreeable he found his military pursuits, they were necessarily only a pastime, and he spent almost the whole of 1889, the year he turned twenty-four, anxiously wondering what he ought to do next to support himself in the world.

By the late nineteenth century it was standard practice for genteel English lads who had failed to make a go of it at home to venture out to the colonies with a couple of bags, a couple of names and addresses, and not that much money. The well-to-do stripling sailing away to make his fortune through hard graft in Natal or New South Wales was also a stock figure in Victorian fiction, so conveniently could he be made to dis-appear or reappear, ruined or rich beyond belief, at critical moments in a plot. Any young man of good family who took this path in real life would inevitably have had in mind visions of annihilating failure to set beside any hope of a doughty and toilsome success.

Life in the colonies was cheaper than at home, but this did not make it more secure, and many of those young emigrants who wished to become farmers knew nothing about agricul-ture. Various shady firms in London exploited this difficulty by promoting a system for learning on the job known as 'farm pupilage'. The farm–pupil agencies not only charged a large fee for their services, but also required the pupils to provide their own passage out to the colonies and, once there, to pay for board, lodging and instruction for a fixed term, undertaken at a recommended farm from the local agent's list. When a pupil had acquired some knowledge of prevailing agricultural practice, the reward of his labours, with family help, was supposed ultimately to be sufficient capital for him to be able to buy and stock his own farm. In a superior version of this arrangement, the pupil would invest a sum of money in the farm where he studied, receiving, in return, a percentage share of the farm's profits, though, once again, the eventual aim would be to set up on his own. Naturally, neither system guaranteed a pupil against the total loss of his funds.

Pelly's father, Revd Raymond Pelly, was well connected, with even a sprinkling of titled relatives, but he was also a priest with eight children to support. It was because Pelly was the oldest son that he had been given the great if unwelcome privilege of a start at Lloyd's. His apportioned lot of family money would now be tied up in the company for years, and with a military career vetoed, Pelly's father hadn't the resources to finance any other suitable outdoor life for his son at home. In the circumstances, it is not surprising that when Pelly turned his back on the insurance business for a second time, it occurred to him to appeal to his parents for permission to pursue colonial farming. The plan may have been a sensible one, but from a worldly perspective Pelly's change of direction constituted a blow to his standing. The archetypal Victorian image of the gentlemanly emigrant farmer was that of a second or younger son, with only a very limited ration of family money given over to establishing his livelihood. Pelly had in effect demoted himself. For his new adventure he would have little more to draw on than two hundred pounds.

As the end of the nineteenth century approached, the potential hazards of the farm pupilage system were sufficiently well understood for Pelly later to write that he had been 'shy of the many advertisements of that life' to be found in the newspapers; but if he really wanted to farm, he did need instruction. At first he considered returning to Africa. After contracting malaria at Blantyre, he had written to his parents that the doctor treating him there had told him 'that in a year or two, when I am a little older, I should quite do for an African traveller, as my constitution is fitted for it. Bother the fever!!!' Now that a year had passed, Pelly's first realistic plan was to return to the part of the world for which his constitution had been pronounced fit, to set up as a coffee planter. Even so, months continued to drift by, and he made no concrete move towards this end.

It was not until early in December of 1889 that Pelly finally took steps to settle his future for himself. In the columns of the *Standard*, he lit on an advertisement, placed by a Mr Mellersh of Cheltenham, that spoke in favourable terms of a position on a farm in America. What drew Pelly to this particular advertisement he never said, but he armed himself with paper and pen and wrote for further details. Mellersh wrote back and proposed a day and an hour for them to meet at the Constitutional Club in London. Pelly kept the appointment but Mellersh failed to appear. When Pelly wrote for an explanation, Mellersh failed to reply. Pelly's maiden step towards settling his own destiny seemed, at first, to have led nowhere.

Some days later, however, a letter came from a man who signed himself J. R. Burchell, to say that Mellersh had passed on Pelly's details as being someone who wished to make an outdoor life for himself in the New World. Reginald Birchall, as his name was properly spelled, claimed to have just the kind of opening Pelly sought. He said that he owned a farm at Niagara Falls, on the Canadian side, that he had for some time been running jointly with his brother, but added that since his brother had now moved west, buying himself a farm in Manitoba, Birchall was in need of a new partner. He was looking in particular for a gentleman. Pelly wrote to ask for more information. Birchall replied as follows:

Bainbridge
Maberley Road
Upper Norwood
S.E.

Dear Sir,

   I received your note in answer to mine about farming. I have a farm of some 120 acres, with English house and buildings upon it, and also two branch farms in the country. I have a fair amount of general produce yearly, and make a general crop on all, but also make a speciality of Horses; I am a very good judge of horseflesh, and I found that this combined with the general farming (so as to produce one's own feed for horses) was by far the most paying business to adopt. I have some very good contracts with the Railway & other Cos. for their supply; and have an agent in New York for the sale of any horses that I may send down there. In this line considerable profits are made; & I am desirous, as I said of getting a gentleman to take the place of my brother in the business, as it is too large for me to superintend singly, and I desire to have a Gentleman, as my wife is an English lady; & we do not associate with the ordinary class of farmers. I have no family.

What I would propose is that you should live with me for a time & get an insight into the general routine & then you could either be managing the branches, or I might, & you at the farm or vice-versa. I desire to extend the business as much as I can, & at present we have a splendid connection all round Niagara & further up Country. The climate is very healthy, and the Country beautiful. You would <u>not</u> of course do any common manual labour such as ploughing &c. That should always be done by the hired labourers & it would take us most of our time superintending & attending sales &c &c. The terms I would propose are that according to amount invested you should have a share of the profits & of course Board lodging & expenses given in. Capital is not so much a consideration as a desirable man. If you could invest £500; (under your own supervision) I could give you Board lodging expenses &c & what we might call a good Salary or you might take a fair share of the profits which are large as during the 1st 6 months of this year I made over £800 clear profit on horses alone. We live in English style & have English servants &c &C. Of course it would be very nice for me to have a University man for a partner, I should prefer that above anything else. However I think if I could see you, we could discuss matters & terms very much better & no doubt make terms to suit one another. If you could run up to Town, & see me, or I could meet you anywhere or I would run down to Saffron Walden (a place I know very well) I should be glad to do either. I propose returning shortly, so shall be glad to hear from you at yr Earliest Convenience— of course I shall be glad to give you many and excellent references—

I am Sir
very truly yours
J. R. Burchell

If Pelly had even the slightest sense of the social isolation that a well-to-do Old Country immigrant could experience in frontier territory, then this letter must have been especially reassuring. He later said that he had understood he was being offered the chance to become 'a sort of travelling gentleman farmer'.

Birchall's picture of relative ease did not square with official attempts at encouraging 'temperate and moral' British farmers to the Niagara area. Government propaganda in the 1890s expressly declared:

The Ontario farmer is himself a worker, and in this respect is very different from the large British landowner, who rides around merely to oversee the work of his men. Of landed gentry there are none, and the 'squire' and the manorial system are not found in Ontario.

A sense of gentry was exactly what Birchall was promoting. He also happily implied that his brother had been able to earn enough from their joint business to move on to a farm of his own. At any rate, as a result of this letter, both Pelly and his father thought it would be sensible to arrange a meeting, so they invited Birchall to visit them at home in Saffron Walden. Although he agreed to come straight away, Birchall broke his first appointment, and it was only on 18 December, after several reorganizing letters and wires, that he did finally appear.

Birchall was a charming, self-possessed and persuasive individual, and he set about making his Canadian affairs sound as secure as possible. He himself, he explained, had started out as a farm pupil, and was a good example of the system working to best advantage. He told the Pellys that he was successful enough to have been back and forth to Canada many times over a span of eight years, a claim that would have supported the impression he gave most people that he was about thirty years old, though he was in fact only twenty-three. As it stood now, he said, his business was mainly to buy horses in the rough, to clip, groom and feed them up, and sell them on at a profit. He said he had about two hundred acres of land and a large, gaslit farmhouse, as well as extensive stabling. One of his stables was made from brick in the latest English style, and all were lit by electricity. As to his branch establishments, he spoke particularly of one in Woodstock that was something like a livery stable with an attached sale yard. He said he had a part interest in this place, or had recently bought it out, or intended to: Pelly did not quite grasp the particulars. Meanwhile, Birchall re-emphasized that Pelly would do no manual work except possibly at harvest time. There were two hired men, brothers called Peacock, who managed the main farm, while a local farmer, an old Scotsman called Macdonald, oversaw the whole of the business. Birchall's servants, he said, were English, and included the man who had been his scout when he was a student at Oxford. There were plenty of other English people at the Falls, and he himself had helped to set up a very pleasant English club there. Finally, Birchall noted that he retained his New York agent, Mr Maloney, on an annual salary, with the result that any friends could expect to be well looked after when they passed through that city. Birchall was seeking an agreeable companion to fit into a well-established business.

The outdoor rigours and challenges of Canadian horse dealing, plus the promise of congenial English society, must have sounded to Pelly like a near-ideal combination; but if this talk raised Pelly's expectations of what Canadian farming life could be like, he knew that he himself must drastically lower Birchall's expectations as to the amount of money available on the Pelly side for investment in such a project – about a third only of the five hundred pounds that Birchall had speculatively asked for. On the other hand, if capital was not so much a consideration as a desirable man, Pelly was beyond question a gentleman, and a University man, fully in the English style. Birchall himself certainly seemed enthusiastic about their joint prospects, and the two of them separated on the understanding that with all speed Birchall would send a letter to Pelly that included a definite plan. Some days after it was expected, this letter arrived:

Bainbridge
Maberley Road
Upper Norwood
S. E.

Dec 29th 1889

Dear Mr Pelly,

Pray excuse my delay in writing, but my mails were very late in arriving—I told you I think that my brother (who has been my partner hitherto) has left me to go into business for himself. I have now settled all my arrangements with him, & paid him his share. He is going to take with him 4 horses which were of great service to me, & I shall have to replace them immediately. I have bought two very good ones to take partly their place & I wish to buy two more. The two I have bought cost £312; & I do not wish to expend much more until the sales come on. I have now myself 37 very fair animals in stock, & these of course will sell at the first sale—of course the two I have got are thoro'breds and they go on Saturday next, so as to be comfortably housed when I arrive at the end of January. Now I thought a fair arrangement would be as follows. That you should live with us for a year, of course including all travelling expenses (which in a year are considerable) horse for yourself, board, lodging &c &c and receive 22½% of the sale price—, & that you should invest now £170, to be repaid in the event of your not caring to stay, an agreement to be drawn up to that effect. If you would do this, I would also spend another £170, & this would enable me to get a couple of splendid animals out of which considerable profit can be made. I feel that you would get on well in the business, & be invaluable in many ways—, & I am sure we should get on well, of course if you did not stay, a fair rate of interest to be paid with the principal at time of leaving— Please let me know what you think about the matter. Of course I [*sic*] all the other little things, machinery &c that my brother had, I have replaced without considerable expense, & everything is in good working order now. The weather there is good and sleighing in first rate order—I have renewed my contracts with the Railway for 2 more years—of course I shall be pleased to give you numerous references to gentlemen, who know me well on both sides of the water if you wish, & shall be very glad to see you if you would come up to town any day.

 I hope you had a good Xmas.

  Kind regards.

   Yours very truly,

    J. R. Burchell

P. S. Don't hesitate to criticise my arrangement.

With its hard information on stock numbers and contracts, on payments, percentages and profits, not to mention Birchall's persuasively reassuring use, six times over, of the phrase 'of course', this letter was enough to convince Pelly that he had hit on just the opening he desired. It only remained to pursue the question of Birchall's references, and if they were fair, to regularize the arrangement.

Pelly kept a detailed diary of this exciting new phase in his life which later helped him to reconstruct a brief, day–by–day account not only of how events began to go awry, but of how he came to place himself in grave danger. From this account it is plain that during the initial meshing together of his and Birchall's interests, Pelly was affected by only a mild sense of annoyance at Birchall's undependable behaviour. In the letter of 29 December, for example, Birchall had offered for a second time to provide numerous references 'if you wish', though without actually doing so. Pelly replied with sufficient enthusiasm for Birchall to take steps to press their partnership forward. On 6 January he wrote to Pelly once again asking him to visit his home in Upper Norwood, in order, it seems, to play down the separate issue of testimonials. Even so, the point did come when Birchall was forced to supply some names. 'You need not have troubled to send me references,' he wrote to Pelly. 'I was perfectly satisfied without. I enclose you one or two for formality's sake, of course if you come down you can judge for yourself.'

Pelly was not completely reckless. He checked at least two of the four references that Birchall sent him. 'As far as I could hear from them,' he later noted, 'Burchell seemed entirely satisfactory.' Besides these proofs, there was a more general kind of endorsement implicit in the excellent public standing of Birchall's father-in-law, David Stevenson. Stevenson was goods traffic manager of the massive London and North

Western Railway Company, a company he had served, in various guises, for over fifty years – from the very beginning, in fact, of the commercial railway system. As a guarantor of Birchall's respectability he was beyond reproach. The Upper Norwood address on Birchall's letters, where he and his wife Florence were then living, turned out to be Stevenson's home.

On 10 January Pelly went to pay a call on the Birchalls, as he had been urged to do, and the encounter passed off without a hitch. Florence Birchall was an attractive and attentive woman. One of her sisters also appeared, and the four of them took afternoon tea together. Birchall asked his wife to fetch out a photograph album that included a picture of them both close to the upper suspension bridge in Niagara. He explained where their farm lay relative to the area shown in the photograph, placing it about a mile and a half above the Falls on the Canadian side. The two young men discussed further details of how their joint venture might work and found them satisfactory, and it was now that Pelly made the firm decision, as Birchall had hoped he would, that he wanted to be in on the deal.

On 14 January Birchall sent Pelly a letter that laid out the brass tacks of the agreement they had been discussing. Enclosed were two copies of a contract, one signed by himself and one for Pelly to sign. 'I don't suppose we shall ever want them,' wrote Birchall, 'but of course it's business like—.' He also wrote, in apparent haste: 'Will you please make out the cheque to my order but <u>don't</u> cross it, as my bank is the Imperial Bank of Canada, and all cheques have to pass through their Bank & causes delay—.'

It was anything but businesslike that the agreements were made out in Birchall's own handwriting, bore no notary's stamp, and had slightly different wording one from the other. Pelly was worried by this. On advice he had the copy with

Mr and Mrs Birchall in a studio shot with watery backdrop.

Birchall's signature on it stamped, then signed the other copy himself and sent this one back to Birchall unstamped. Pelly also sent, as asked, an uncrossed cheque for the full amount of his investment in Birchall's business. His disquiet at Birchall's amateur paperwork grew as the days passed by and no acknowledgement came that the valuable packet had reached Upper Norwood. Pelly finally felt driven to telegraph to find out what was happening. Birchall wrote back an apology and said that he had been off hunting: 'Pray excuse my delay but I have been away in the country.' The packet was safely sitting in Norwood: all was well. At the same time that this response reached Pelly, his bank returned him his pass book. From a glance at its entries, he made the troubling discovery that Birchall had cashed the hundred and seventy pound cheque the day after Pelly sent it to him. Faced with this inconsistency, Pelly persuaded himself that Birchall 'simply had given a false excuse to hide his forgetfulness'.

Across the whole month of their initial relations with each other, Pelly was annoyed most by Birchall's prevarication and plan changing, but he also continued to be perturbed by small obscurities in the descriptions Birchall gave of his interests. Exactly how many acres did he own in Canada? How many branch establishments did he have altogether? Did he fully own these branch establishments or not? Despite their discussions, the answers remained oddly opaque. Furthermore, Pelly balked at what he felt to be an insinuating side to Birchall's manner. Birchall had repeatedly talked about getting people 'fixed up', Pelly afterwards wrote, and

a very constant expression of Burchell's was, 'We'll question so and so about his business and find out what they know.' Another expression of the same sort was, 'What he knows may be valuable, but I know more,' or 'but he could tell it all in two minutes.' All these expressions and many others he used simply ad nauseam.

This kind of talk may have irritated Pelly; nevertheless, as the planning went on, and with his whole future in the balance, he clearly started to delude himself about Birchall's integrity almost as capably as he was misled by anyone else.

On 29 December Birchall's stated aim had been to reach Ontario by the end of January, but delay crept in. It was then

settled that he, his wife and Pelly would leave Liverpool on
1 February by a ship called the *Umbria*. Once again the days
ticked noticeably by with no word arriving at Saffron Walden
to confirm these departure plans. Once again Pelly felt driven
to wire Birchall to ask exactly what was happening. Birchall
replied carelessly that as he had been expecting some foreign
mails that had been delayed by rough weather, he had put off
their journey by a few more days. Negotiations continued in
this irksome manner until at last Birchall announced to Pelly
that they would leave London for Liverpool on Tuesday
4 February, sailing on the *City of Paris*. Pelly undertook to
come to town from Saffron Walden the day before, and
Birchall promised to meet him at Liverpool Street Station.

On Monday 3 February Pelly stepped off his train into a
dense London fog. Birchall was nowhere to be seen. Pelly sent
a wire to a friend, put some of his bags in at the baggage office
and then walked about the platforms. When Birchall did
emerge out of the miasma he claimed that he had been on
time to meet the train, but that somehow he and Pelly had
failed to spot each other. The two partners now agreed to
wander around town together on various last-minute errands.
Birchall took Pelly to the house of a doctor who was out and
never came in, and then to the office of an effusive American
colonel. This man had invented a new kind of railway truck
which he was attempting to promote in Europe. Birchall told
the colonel that he had fixed matters so that at any time the
colonel wished, he could arrange for an interview with Mr
Stevenson. After the colonel had taken Pelly into a back
office to explain the mechanics of his truck, Birchall proposed
meeting Pelly the next afternoon at four o'clock at Euston
Station, from where, with Mrs Birchall, they would at last set
off for Liverpool and the New World. That evening, as far as

he knew the last he would spend in London for a very long time, Pelly gave a talk to a missionary meeting and then played billiards with a friend.

The next morning Birchall wired Pelly to say that he might reach Euston late. Pelly arrived at the station half an hour ahead of time anyway. The Birchalls were duly late. Birchall claimed airily that his father-in-law's London office in the Gresham Buildings had been on fire, that Mr Stevenson lay ill in bed, and that in consequence he, Birchall, had had to stand in for Mr Stevenson supervising matters in town. He also mentioned that as a result of some mistake about the tickets, they would not after all be travelling on the *City of Paris*, but on the White Star steamer, *Britannic*. Pelly, still more exasperated than concerned by the unreliability of all arrangements, wired his family to let them know the new details.

After supper in the station, the party of three boarded a train not due to reach Liverpool until half past midnight. Only when they were actually in transit did Birchall inform Pelly that another young man would be going out with them as far as New York. This fellow, Birchall said, had previously been in New Zealand, so Pelly could question him about it and 'find out how much he knew'. Unfortunately, this unheralded extra traveller was 'not much of a man to meet and would not be a very delightful companion', but Birchall was taking charge of him as a favour to the young man's father. His name was Frederick Benwell.

As they journeyed north through the darkness, Birchall, without preliminaries, put a hand into his back pocket and pulled out a revolver. Pelly later recorded that

he asked me if I was in the habit of carrying one, and I told him that since I had taken to travelling I always had one in my kit, but I did not often carry it on my person. He told me he always had his with him and on his person.

Pelly felt highly disquieted by this exchange with his new partner. What he didn't know, and couldn't have guessed, was how very soon he himself would be stashing his revolver in an outside pocket, ready for immediate use.

2. A Greater Nuisance

He had a good deal of money with him, I understand, and he had already paid a hundred pounds to a firm in England that had agreed to place him on a farm in America. Of course, now that the money had been paid, there was no use in telling the young man he had been a fool. He would find that out soon enough.

Robert Barr, *In a Steamer Chair*, 1892

If Pelly had doubts about Birchall, he was also deeply unimpressed, when they reached their hotel in Liverpool that night, to discover that Mrs Birchall drank:

As soon as our rooms were allotted to us Mrs. Burchell retired. Burchell and I went to the smoking room and had whiskeys and soda, Burchell at the same time ordering a long brandy and soda to be sent up to his wife. This struck me at the time as a very curious thing for a so-called lady and made me wonder what sort of people they were that I had run against.

It is true that Pelly had had a strongly religious upbringing. Before the move to Saffron Walden, his father had been the vicar in a slum parish in the East End of London, and the whole family had helped with Sunday school classes, Mission services and other improving activities. On his mother's side Pelly was directly descended from Elizabeth Fry, the great Quaker reformer, and as a child holidaying with the maternal branch of the family had regularly included being made to thrust fistfuls of pious tracts on unwilling passers-by. Pelly's disapproval of Florence Birchall may have reflected this background, but she would certainly have been aware that drinking spirits alone laid her open to being thought indelicate and fast.

After a late breakfast the next morning, and a visit to a barber, Birchall and Pelly went to find Frederick Benwell at his hotel. Benwell at once made a bad impression on Pelly, who concluded then and there, 'I could never be on very friendly terms with him. He was short, very dark, very sallow and had a most disagreeable manner.' The three young men had drinks together in the smoking room, then idled away the hours performing an array of little errands, which included Benwell having a pair of glasses made, until at last it was time to reconnoitre with Mrs Birchall. Finally the moment came when they could gather up all their kit and sail out to board the *Britannic*, which departed for Ireland at seven o'clock.

Pelly registered from the start that the Birchalls appeared to be making a concerted effort to ensure that he and Benwell never spoke to each other alone. If the four of them fell into pairs, Mrs Birchall stuck to Pelly, and Birchall always stuck to Benwell. Pelly also noticed that both the Birchalls 'constantly made slighting remarks' about Benwell, while Pelly himself found increasingly that his unexpected travelling companion was 'very dictatorial and a man in whose company one could not be long without almost quarrelling'. Indeed, in his later record of these events, Pelly was keen to note that the dislike he formed for Benwell would have been equally intense whether the Birchalls had encouraged it or not.

Numerous aspects of Victorian life were altered by the use of steam power, until the English language itself began to reflect the change. In the middle of the nineteenth century, for example, it became possible for people to think of themselves as 'getting up steam', or 'letting off steam', and amongst the more conspicuous novelties to usher in this development were the earliest steam-powered crossings of the Atlantic. These took place in the 1830s, and at once reduced by around two thirds the journey time of a ship under sail. This dramatic advance sparked an era of aggressive competition amongst all the different shipping lines that vied for the Anglo-American trade in emigrants and mail. As the liners themselves began to resemble marvellous hotels, pleasure travel also became a lucrative trade; but if the luxuriousness of the steamers played its part in company rivalries, the real competition, for many decades, continued to focus on speed.

The ever-faster transatlantic crossings facilitated illegal business as well as any other kind. A criminal in the 1840s running an operation that required him to travel between Liverpool and New York would have had to calculate his profits based on spending about a month just getting back and forth across the water. By the 1880s this time had halved, while in 1889 the *City of Paris* had become the first steamer ever to complete the west-bound crossing in under six days. There is no doubt that Birchall was drawn to the fanciest vessels, and the *Britannic* was in her own way no less spectacular. Pelly knew her by the tag 'The Greyhound of the Atlantic', and though it had been a decade and a half since she, too, as a newly minted vessel, had beaten every other ship on the seas, later improvements meant that she actually made her fastest-ever crossing in 1890. None of this implied that nineteenth-century liners were safe. Seven weeks after the Birchall party sailed out of Liverpool, the *City of Paris* suffered a mechanical failure at top speed on the open seas that left her

The Britannic *crash, 19 May 1887.*

engines 'shattered almost to pieces'. The *Britannic* herself had
also recently survived a near-catastrophic collision with a sister
ship, the *Celtic*, in heavy fog two days out of New York.
Grimly, the *Celtic* had struck several times, breaking the
Britannic wide open on the port side and killing several passengers. Some months later, as though to prove that she was back
on form, the *Britannic* had cut in half a brig called the *Czarowitz*
while sailing across Liverpool Bay.

There had been 'terrific weather' in the Atlantic in January
1890, and February saw no improvement. After the *Britannic*
left the Irish coast, the seas were rough for much of the
journey to New York. During the crossing the passengers had
impressive icebergs to contemplate, but they were also obliged
to endure a terrible gale. As was still usual with ocean steamers,
the *Britannic* carried sails in case of need, so that when Pelly
described the effect of twenty degrees of frost, he wrote, 'every

rope, and the masts and yards were covered with frozen spray nearly an inch thick, and when the gale was over and the sun came out the ship looked very lovely'. Almost the whole way to America, Birchall shut himself in his cabin, complaining that he felt unwell.

Despite the efforts of the Birchalls to keep Pelly and Benwell from talking freely, Pelly had found occasion, while they were still in Liverpool, to tell Benwell the nature of his business in going out to Canada. He was greatly surprised during the voyage, therefore, when Benwell, whom Pelly felt otherwise unnecessarily 'shunned' him, described his own business with Birchall in not dissimilar terms. Benwell seemed to believe that he was going out expressly to take a look at Birchall's farming interests, and that if after three months he was satisfied with what he found, he and Birchall would be going into partnership with each other. This conversation left Pelly greatly disturbed. When he had heard Benwell out, he rushed down to Birchall's cabin where he breathlessly demanded to know

on what terms Benwell was really travelling, as, if he was going to become his partner, I certainly did not wish to remain with him any longer, but would like to part at once. Burchell agreed with me when I said I considered Benwell a great nuisance and a man who would make a very objectionable business companion.

These 'objectionable' characteristics, whether real or imaginary, were the main reason Pelly had omitted to discuss his doubts about Birchall with Benwell himself, and at this point Benwell's flaws also gave Birchall perfect grounds on which to start to undo the damage Benwell had just wreaked. Birchall told Pelly that he had never had any intention whatsoever of going into partnership with such a person as the young man in question. Furthermore, 'if possible,' Birchall said, he was finding Benwell to be even 'a greater nuisance' than he had 'at first expected'. Benwell was completely deluded about a prospective partnership. Birchall did have a piece of unwanted land that Benwell might conveniently buy if he wished to set up his own farm, but otherwise Birchall intended to place him on some other farm without delay and that would be the end of it. On board ship, Benwell had become friendly with a lawyer from London, Ontario, called Hellmuth. If Birchall couldn't settle Benwell himself, he said, perhaps Hellmuth could. Birchall told Pelly frankly, what Pelly could very well believe, that he 'intended to get rid of Benwell as quickly as possible'.

Pelly did raise this subject with Birchall several times more, but 'after all talks with Burchell I had the unsatisfactory feeling that I knew little if any more than I had known to begin with'. In one such conversation Birchall managed to tell Pelly that Benwell's father was a colonel; that one of his own neighbours at Niagara Falls was a French lady who was a very good shot with a revolver; that another near neighbour, an Englishman called Pickthall, had shabbily charged his sisters for their board when they came out to live with him; that in consequence these girls had quarrelled with Pickthall, and unfortunately were very likely to have returned home again; that most of his own horses were just then stabled in Toronto; that his New York agent, Maloney, was otherwise a steamer runner; that he might well leave Benwell with his own overseer, Macdonald, who would 'give him lots to eat' until he inevitably got bored with farm life and went back home to England; and that it would probably be for the best if, while he, Birchall, took Benwell to Niagara to get rid of him, Pelly stayed behind with Mrs Birchall in New York. Pelly, desperate to reach

Canada and start his new life, was deeply opposed to any question of being left behind, and said so.

Pelly not only found both the Birchalls to be erratic and unsatisfactory, but considered them hypocrites as well:

Mrs. Burchell, when a few minutes before she had been saying all sorts of things about Benwell's disagreeable manner and disagreeable behaviour, would sit with him and make herself excessively agreeable in every way. Burchell acted in very much the same manner.

Despite Birchall's earlier assurances to Pelly that everything on the Niagara farm was 'in good working order now', he one day mentioned that he had not informed the people there of his imminent return, his given reason for this being that he intended to surprise them in order to find out how well they had been working without his supervision. Pelly absorbed this peculiar news with dismay, and began to suspect that when he finally reached Niagara, he would find Birchall's businesses to be 'in no particular as good as he had made out'.

The travellers reached New York on Friday 14 February: Valentine's day. The view, which Pelly had expected to be dominated by the Statue of Liberty, was a veil of rain. The cobbled streets were wet and muddy. Their hotel, the Metropolitan, seemed second rate; and at Niblo's burlesque theatre that night, the entertainment, *Bluebeard Junior*, was 'most unexciting'. Mrs Birchall left early saying she was tired, but after Birchall had seen her to her room, he reappeared at the theatre to maintain watch over his two charges. The three of them eventually retired to the writing room of the Metropolitan for a smoke, before themselves turning in. Pelly and Benwell had refused to share a room.

The next day the young men set out on business around town. First they had to exchange money in order to pay for their railway tickets. Birchall warned Pelly that the American banking system was so defective that the safest way to move large sums about from now on would be to sew any surplus money into their clothes. He and Mrs Birchall, he said, had shifted a thousand dollars by this means in 1889, when they had last travelled out of the country. As Birchall was telling him this, Pelly remembered two other stories with exactly the opposite import that Birchall had recently related. In a different context he had described how at a moment's notice he had been able to arrange for funds to be cabled internationally overnight, from England to Canada in one instance, and from Canada to America in another. 'These last two stories,' Pelly felt, 'made the first sound so improbable that I was more suspicious of him than ever.' The longer Pelly spent with Birchall, the less he found Birchall took the trouble to be consistent in what he said about almost anything.

Mr Maloney, who worked at the docks, and whom Birchall had described to Pelly as his employee, had helped the party pass their luggage through customs on arrival the day before, excepting two large cases that Benwell had sent direct to the Falls in bond. Now they went to Maloney again for their railway tickets. Birchall insisted, inexplicably, that they take the train only as far as Buffalo; but at least Pelly was able successfully to oppose all plans that would have left him and Mrs Birchall behind in New York.

There were various further errands to be completed that day. Benwell had to deliver a packet of photographs to a business address. Pelly had to leave a book and a fancy iron bracket at the Fifth Avenue house of a friend of his mother's, and needed to match some buttons. Back at the Metropolitan,

Mrs Birchall announced that she was sure she had seen Pick-thall, the man who maltreated his sisters, on the stairs. Birchall immediately said that Pickthall must be down in New York on a spree, and that they were very likely to find themselves travelling with him to Buffalo.

That evening they caught a ferry to Jersey City and then took a carriage to the Erie depot where they waited for their overnight train. Birchall now suggested for the first time that they spend the following night in Buffalo, arguing that it would be awkward to arrive at the Falls on a Sunday. Pelly was infuriated by the thought of yet another delay so close to the Canadian border, but agreed to wait and see whether they made it to Buffalo in good time or not. As it transpired, after an uncomfortable night on the rails, they did face an unscheduled wait while they switched trains at breakfast the next morning. On the last stretch of the ride to Buffalo the young men left Mrs Birchall and went to sit together in the smoking car. Pelly had the strong sense on this occasion that Birchall's apparent favouritism was operating the wrong way round:

from several remarks which Benwell made, I felt most sure that Burchell had been saying slighting things to Benwell about me and had been trying to make me at any rate of very small account in Benwell's eyes.

Even at this new pass, Pelly did not attempt to negotiate a way out of his ever more worrying situation.

They arrived in Buffalo at noon, late enough for Birchall to insist that they stay. He took them to the Stafford House, an institution Pelly described as 'the most dirty and altogether worst hotel I ever saw, which is saying a good deal'. He suspected that Birchall had chosen it simply because it was cheap. After lunch, Birchall, Benwell and Pelly drifted about town together, to another hotel, to the river and to the Barracks, a form of time-wasting at which they were becoming accomplished. Birchall pressed forward a plan that required Pelly to stay behind in Buffalo the next morning with Mrs Birchall, while he and Benwell passed over into Canada together. They would visit his farm, surprise the people there and make sure the place was in good shape. Benwell was delighted at the thought of escaping the Stafford House, which he, like Pelly, found dreadful. Pelly, for his part, 'demurred' as far as possible without fussing, and pointed out that if he and Mrs Birchall couldn't go to the farm at once, they might nevertheless just as well while away the hours at the Falls as in Buffalo. Birchall replied that he wanted Pelly to stay behind the next morning to manage their luggage and the hotel bill. Most probably, he said, he would telegraph Pelly to tell him which train to catch a little later in the day.

In the Stafford House writing room after dinner that night, Birchall came up with an idea to inject a little fun into proceedings:

Burchell began showing his skill in varying his handwriting, and got Benwell to see how well they could copy each other's signatures. With Benwell's help Burchell was soon able to copy the former's signature extremely well. He asked to have a try at mine. Of course I refused.

When the opportunity arose for a private word with Pelly, Birchall mollified him by explaining that the real reason he wished to take Benwell alone the next morning was that he meant to concentrate on getting him permanently 'fixed up'. He was looking to place Benwell on a farm 'fairly out of the way'. Birchall's idea, he told Pelly, was to be absolutely sure that Benwell was 'not in a position to interfere with our business any longer'.

The next morning, Monday 17 February, some time after five o'clock, Birchall went to Benwell's room to rouse him. Pelly, whose room was only one away, called out that he, too, was awake. Birchall came into Pelly's room, lit the gas, sat on the end of Pelly's bed and had a brief talk with him. He showed Pelly that he was wearing country garb: a dark-blue jacket and waistcoat, a black astrakhan cap, heavy field boots, and a pair of gloves that he managed to leave behind on Pelly's bed. He told Pelly to be on the lookout for a telegram, and promised to be in touch by two that afternoon at the latest. If he did not himself return to Buffalo, any last details about a final departure from the Stafford House would, he said, be clarified by Mrs Birchall. He added that he had made sure she had the money for their bill.

That morning Pelly also exchanged a few words with Benwell, though he did not see him properly out in the darkness of the corridor. Their conversation was brief. All Pelly remembered of it afterwards was that he had asked Benwell, should he be leaving any spare items of luggage behind, to take them down to the hotel office rather than leave them in his room, in case he, like Birchall, did not return.

3. The Unfortunate Unknown

LA MORGUE. Formerly near the Bridge of St. Michel, on the quay du Marché Neuf, where it was built in 1825 – now stands on the east of Notre Dame, near the Seine. On slabs prepared for the purpose lie the bodies of those found dead in the river or elsewhere for identification. Ofttimes four or five bodies may be seen there at the same time.

Henry Gaze, *Paris, how to see it for five guineas*, 1867

Three hours after Birchall and Benwell set off that Monday morning for Niagara, Pelly and Mrs Birchall met for breakfast in the dining room of the Stafford House. When she revealed that, after all, her husband had failed to provide funds for paying the hotel bill, it crossed Pelly's mind to wonder whether the Birchalls had any real money left. Mrs Birchall also admitted that she, too, regretted having been left behind in Buffalo, and 'all this day,' Pelly later wrote, she 'was in an extraordinarily nervous state, and quite unable to keep still'. It would appear unlikely that either she or Pelly expected to take much pleasure in each other's company.

Once they had eaten, they went to their rooms to pack so that they would be ready to leave at short notice. After this they were reduced to pacing the streets together. Pelly bought gloves. Mrs Birchall bought galoshes. She then said that the furniture at the farm was growing old and might need replacing, so they wandered off to look at various house-fitting stores. What most concerned her about the farm besides its furniture was the state of the wallpaper, so they also looked at wallpaper samples. From time to time Pelly popped back to their hotel in the hope that he would find the promised telegram from Birchall instructing them to proceed to Niagara; but no telegram came. Not until eight thirty that night did Pelly discover that a wire addressed to 'Petty' had been turned away by the hotel. This was such a common mistranscription of his name that he went straight to the nearby telegraph office, where he found out that the telegram in question had indeed come from Birchall. It instructed Pelly to remain with Mrs Birchall in Buffalo for yet another night.

Almost as soon as Pelly got back to the hotel, Birchall himself walked in. Mrs Birchall at once retired upstairs. Birchall went after her briefly, but then came back down to drink with Pelly at the bar. Birchall had three or four glasses of 'lager beer', exclaiming that he was exceptionally thirsty. Pelly had one. He asked Birchall what had caused the great delay. Birchall responded by asking if Pelly had not received a telegram. Pelly replied that he had only just tracked it down. Birchall said that besides sending the telegram, he had also telephoned from Niagara at about midday. If so, said Pelly, it was inexplicable that the hotel had failed to pass on the message. Birchall had no explanation.

At least he had come back without Benwell. As Pelly saw it, 'This was of course no surprise after what both he and Burchell had said.' Birchall described how he had taken Benwell to the farm and had introduced him to Macdonald, but said that Benwell had been sulky all day, refusing to eat breakfast on the train or lunch at the farm, and eventually saying he hated the place and 'certainly would not think of living there or of associating with the people he had met'. Pelly pressed Birchall to tell him what had happened after this, and Birchall replied simply that he had packed Benwell off to try his luck elsewhere, giving him the addresses of a few farmers and other people up country. Birchall said it was very likely that Benwell would wind up staying with Hellmuth, the lawyer who had become his friend on the *Britannic*, who had 'promised to make things pleasant' if Benwell ever came to visit.

Birchall was now forced to tell Pelly that, without consultation, Macdonald had leased the farm to a set of extremely dirty tenants who wouldn't be able to vacate the place for several days. In the light of this misfortune, Birchall proposed staying in Niagara for a short while. After everything Mrs Birchall had said, Pelly's idea of life at the farm had become so 'dismal' that he was glad at the prospect of a few days reprieve. Birchall mentioned that he had already called on several people he knew in Niagara, and added the good news that he had managed to pick up some dollars; but even with this information, Pelly felt that Birchall was 'not at all explicit as to his doings that day'. All the same, as the two young men retired to bed, Pelly was relieved that at least there did now seem to be some sort of a plan.

The short trip from Buffalo to Niagara on Tuesday 18 February was unstraightforward; but if both Birchalls had behaved a little oddly the day before, they now struck Pelly as being 'quite normal again'. After breakfast, he and Birchall collected all their luggage together, not forgetting Benwell's cases. When Pelly asked how Benwell was going to manage without his kit, Birchall reminded him that Benwell had sent two large bags directly to the Falls in bond. Birchall supposed that there would be enough kit in these bags to last Benwell until he sent for the rest of his things.

At around ten, Birchall and Pelly went to the railway station, where Birchall bought tickets to Suspension Bridge station, on the New York side. Pelly was surprised and disappointed by this, but Birchall said that he wasn't sure on which side of the border they would stay, and explained that he didn't wish to pass their luggage through customs too often. Once he and Pelly had arranged for two carriages to bring their bags down to the depot, Birchall had a quantity of mud cleaned off his boots – the same long field boots that he had worn in the country the day before.

After lunch at Suspension Bridge, Birchall suggested that he, Mrs Birchall and Pelly, all go to look at the Falls. As they strolled along the muddy streets by the railway tracks, sometimes forced to double back on themselves, Pelly became sure that Birchall did not know his way. When at last they made it out onto the upper suspension bridge, heavy mists spoiled the view. To Pelly's relief, however, they did cross over, and go on up the hill on the Canadian side. Mrs Birchall did not wish to walk too far, so they left her by the street car tracks in an old tram car that served as a waiting room. Pelly had imagined that after living in the vicinity on and off for eight years, Birchall would both know his way around, and be acquainted with everyone in Niagara, but when he asked Birchall who lived in various houses, Birchall seemed to know nobody.

In due course Mrs Birchall passed them in a street car. They had arranged that she should wait for them at the Imperial Hotel while they searched for somewhere to stay. Birchall had claimed they would find rooms easily, but it was a long time before they tracked down available lodgings in the residence of a Mr Baldwin. Pelly had 'pressed it considerably' that they spend at least their first night at the Imperial. He couldn't understand why, if it was only to be for a short while, they didn't put up at the hotel, rather than rough it in a boarding house. Birchall replied, implausibly, Pelly thought, that he wanted to cut a deal over a very nice black horse with the proprietor of the Imperial, an old acquaintance of his called Mr Bampfield, and that if they stayed at Bampfield's hotel it might compromise the business.

The next day Pelly and Birchall saw all the baggage through customs, including Benwell's, for which Birchall had the keys. Once this task was completed, they 'walked about', which included going to sort out their affairs at the post office. Birchall had told Pelly in England that he kept boxes 571 and 572 at the Falls. In consequence, all Pelly's letters from home had been addressed, and continued for some time to be addressed, to box 571. These boxes, however, actually belonged to someone else. Birchall swiftly explained that he liked to take these numbers wherever he went, to simplify his addresses for his friends, but as his usual numbers weren't available, he now took box 313. Either that evening or the next, Birchall asked Pelly for money to cover the costs incurred by his steamer and railway tickets, his lodgings along the way, and a few other expenses. Pelly gave him about twenty pounds, or a hundred dollars.

The day after, Thursday, Mr Bampfield suggested to them that they take a trip to the Star Theatre in Buffalo to see the English Gaiety Burlesque Company perform the operetta, *Faust up to Date*. Birchall had been forced to explain away to Pelly the fact that Bampfield was liable to call him Mr Somerset. This, he said, was because, when he had been a farm pupil himself, he had worked for a man called Somerset; indeed, it was Somerset's farm that Birchall had bought upon the old man's death. Birchall had been unable to prevent the idea forming about the place that he was Somerset's son; Mr

Bampfield making this mistake because old Somerset had habitually driven to the Imperial of an afternoon to get hopelessly drunk, and Birchall had had to come into town with a buggy in the evenings to fetch him home again. The mistake about Birchall's name had become so widespread that he found he sometimes even received letters addressed to him this way. Apart from Bampfield's stubbornness on this point, though, Birchall said he thought of him as a friend. Pelly privately wondered whether this curious information had any bearing on Birchall's refusal to stay at the Imperial.

Pelly's life with the Birchalls had proved sufficiently peculiar that the trip to see *Faust up to Date* felt to him very much like a happy interlude of escape, and this despite the fact that, their train home being mired in snow, they were forced to kick their heels at the railway station until well into the small hours. Nor was this adventure the only enjoyable aspect of their first days at the Falls. 'Burchell played the piano a bit,' Pelly later wrote, 'and in the evenings we had lots of singing and music (and hymns, of which Burchell knew *hundreds* by heart!).' Pelly also found that boarding-house life had its own fascinations, especially the startling detail that the housemaid whiled away her evenings in the drawing room along with everyone else. Both Birchalls took Pelly into their confidence a little, Birchall admitting that his family fortune was derived from a brewery in Liverpool, and Mrs Birchall letting out that her husband did not get on at all well with his mother. The couple repeatedly talked up the pleasures they were expecting to provide when good weather finally arrived. These were to include four-in-hand carriage drives, a trip to Manitoba to see Birchall's brother, and picnics at a nearby beauty spot called Pine Pond.

For a spell Mrs Birchall became distinctly nervous again, so that Pelly wondered if she was ill, but otherwise their

combined life soon settled into something of a routine.
Early mornings were spent browsing through the press, with
the foremost Toronto newspapers all available in Niagara.
Amongst the other stories of the day, these papers were carrying the occasional brief mention of an unidentified corpse
that had been found in the Blenheim township swamp near
Woodstock on Friday 21 February; but though Pelly noticed
the headlines, he read nothing more, and gleaned little about
the case beyond the fact that 'the unfortunate unknown', as
one paper called him, seemed to have been a young 'North
West American Indian'. After scanning the papers, Pelly and
Birchall often played billiards at a billiards parlour, and sometimes they then went to the Imperial to have their boots
cleaned. In the afternoons, more aimlessly still, they would
simply go 'walking around'. One day Birchall raised the idea
that they should perhaps continue to let out his farm house,
but keep on the land to provide a supply of horse fodder, or
that they should accept horse fodder from the tenants in lieu
of rent. They could then take a house and stables for themselves
in Niagara, where they could probably manage more business.
With this plan in mind, Birchall and Pelly added to their
unchallenging schedule a programme of looking locally at
houses and stables for hire.

While the Toronto press was not over-exercised about the
Blenheim swamp corpse, the local press in Woodstock provided a welter of copy on the case. One striking detail, on the
morning after the body had been found, was that the young
English lady, Miss Pickthall, had visited the undertaker's from
her home at Currie's Crossing, fearing the body would prove
to belong to her brother, Neville Pickthall, who had been
missing for over a week. When she saw the corpse, however,

The road leading into the Blenheim swamp.

she found that its identity was as much of a mystery to her as to anyone else.

Any attempt at a post mortem, or even at a proper investigation of the clothes, had been impossible on Friday 21 February, while the body, with its limbs bent this way and that, had still been 'frose solid and hard', as one of the men who had found the corpse would put it in evidence. Constable Watson, who had been given charge of the remains, later testified: 'I put the body near the stove and turned it round and round.' He started this process on the Friday night, but not until noon of the next day did it yield a complete thaw.

An unofficial press summary of the subsequent post mortem gave as the most interesting details, that there were two bruises on the victim's stomach, one of them the size of a man's hand, and that there were not one but two bullet holes in the victim's head. The obvious wound lay behind the left ear, but another had been found at the nape of the neck. Both shots had been aimed into the head in an upwards path at close range by someone using a revolver. The dead man had pin-head gold fillings in the middle of his two front teeth, and it was observed that his 'hands and ears were nibbled as if by the knawing of squirrels or mice'.

Despite a great deal of agreement in the analysis of the unfolding clues, both by the initial inquest witnesses, and by reporters, one crucial question was eliciting a less than clear-cut response. How long had the young man been dead? William Crosby, JP, submitted that the body must have been in the swamp 'previous to Monday last'. James Swarts, the undertaker, also felt that 'it seemed as if the body had been placed there before the sleet on Monday'. Joseph Elvidge, who with his brother had first discovered the body, said more vaguely that the slight covering of snow on the corpse had been 'about as much as would fall upon him during the snow storm of the last few days'. A local doctor called Welford, who had driven Miss Pickthall into Princeton, had stayed on out of curiosity to observe the post mortem. He reportedly believed that the body might have been in the swamp for as long as a week, though with the proviso that, as the freezing cold had prevented any decomposition, it would be very hard to be sure. At least the blood drops beneath the victim's head did indicate to Welford that, if the young man had been killed elsewhere, he must have been deposited in the swamp not long afterwards. Meanwhile, the two doctors who had officially conducted the post mortem reportedly believed that the dead man might have been killed as little as twenty-four hours before he was found. This more recent time of death was supported by the widely held view that the spruce, clean state

where the murder was committed

A hat marks the spot where the body was found.

of the corpse's bared 'linen' — a discreet term for a shirt or for underwear — indicated that the body could not have been exposed to the heavy rain that had fallen earlier in the week, before the very cold weather set in.

Given all these odd clues, the general sense in the press was that 'the more the mystery is looked into the more mysterious it becomes'. Dr McLay, the coroner, communicated through intermediaries with the Attorney-General of Ontario, Mr Mowat, and asked for a government detective to be sent to 'work up the case' immediately.

After several days at the Falls, Pelly noted to himself that Birchall had only openly conducted one piece of genuine business since their arrival, namely taking a box at the post office, besides the fact that he had drawn up a list in a Collins diary of horses that had been bought and sold to his account during the previous month. At the same time, Pelly observed that, contrary to Birchall's promises, there was no English Club in Niagara, though he decided it would be better not to mention this. Pelly had convinced himself that he was biding his time with regard to Birchall's mendacities:

I was becoming very suspicious of all he said and did and was waiting to see if he would not commit himself in some way and enable me to expose him for certain. My idea of his unsatisfactoriness had only been aroused by numerous small circumstances, each single one being too trivial to make a fuss about.

When Pelly did attempt to press Birchall on some opaque detail of his enterprises, he never got a straight answer. Nor, despite near daily requests, would Birchall take him to see the farm. There was always too little snow for sleighing, or too much mud to make a visit worthwhile, or Birchall was simply busy, or he had meant to take Pelly, but had forgotten until it was too late in the day. As they had on board the *Britannic*, Birchall and his wife continued to give inconsistent descriptions of their Canadian affairs, until 'by this time,' Pelly later wrote, 'I felt almost sure that there was no farm.'

On Tuesday 25 February, exactly a week after reaching Canada, he at long last worked up the courage to challenge Birchall outright. Perhaps Pelly was galvanized by the fact that this was his birthday, the day he turned twenty-five. They were taking a chilly walk together down the river road when Pelly said:

As far as I can see I think we shall work very well together once we get started, but at the same time I do not think you treated me straightly before we left England, for you gave me a very erroneous idea of what your business was and what the life was like. When I started I expected I was going out to a good business in full swing, but as it is, as far as I can see, there is no business at all and never has been any.

This denunciation seemed to make Birchall so angry that for a minute or two he couldn't speak. When at last he had gathered himself, he delivered the blunt reply: 'Well, you know you are at liberty to go or stay as you like.'

Strictly speaking, this may have been true, but Pelly was now nearly two hundred pounds out of pocket on the venture, almost the whole of his funds, and he had a great deal more in the way of *amour-propre* invested in their partnership. Though Pelly had gone to Canada bearing a small list of other contacts in case of need, he replied that he had no intention of quitting just now, but that he did wish they could 'begin something at once'.

This conciliatory response caused Birchall to change tack completely. He at last confessed that, as a result of his lengthy absence, his previous business had collapsed. He explained that he was even now expecting money to arrive from the Old Country to set him up again, and that as soon as this money came in he intended to start afresh. He expected to be hard at work within a week. Pelly quietly decided that another week was all he would give Birchall. If matters did not improve in that time, he would cut his losses, however great, and move on.

Pelly now asked about the large stock of horses that Birchall had claimed to possess. Birchall maintained that they were 'safely housed in Toronto', and added that he and Pelly would retrieve them as soon as the business was up and running.

Pelly also asked what news there was of Benwell, who had been gone for over a week, yet most of whose luggage was still piled up at Baldwin's. Birchall said he hadn't heard anything directly, and speculated that perhaps Benwell didn't know how to get in touch with them at the Falls, or even imagined they were all still in Buffalo. Upon this unlikely thought, Birchall had already, he said, wired to the Stafford House, and had heard back that very day that a letter and a telegram were waiting for him there. He and Pelly agreed that these must both be from Benwell. Birchall said that of course he would have to go to Buffalo to collect them, though Pelly countered that it surely made much more sense to instruct the clerk to open up the telegram and forward its contents.

They now came to some old stairs by the side of the road. Birchall told Pelly they ought to take a moment to go down because there was, at the bottom, a 'wonderful' view of the Falls. Pelly led the way down, Birchall following behind him. As they descended, the staircase proved rickety, even rotten. There was a thick mass of trees around them, and ice hung oppressively from the cliffs, trees and all about. At the base of the steps Pelly found there was no good view. He felt highly nervous, overcome by a 'curious sense of danger', but suddenly a stranger appeared from between the trees, and, with relief, Pelly turned back up the staircase at once, saying that he 'did not like the look of the place'. Up on the road again, without further comment, he and Birchall continued along their way.

Later that day Birchall told Pelly that he had followed the plan of wiring to the Stafford House for the contents of his telegram, adding that he had given the Imperial as his return address. The next evening, therefore, the two of them went up to the hotel to see about a reply. When they found that one hadn't yet arrived, they each drank a couple of glasses of lager beer to pass the time, and then walked to the banks of the Niagara beneath the cantilever bridge. Birchall stood at the very edge, 'pretending,' so Pelly thought, 'to admire the rapids'. He invited Pelly to join him; but once again Pelly found that he felt 'very nervous of him', and so he 'made an excuse not to go too near the edge'.

They returned to the Imperial to see if the telegram had come while they were out. There was nothing, so they now drank 'some sort of American drink' largely composed of whiskey. Birchall bought a few cigars, kept one out for himself to smoke straight away, and put the rest in his pocket. He decided to set about persuading Pelly to smoke one of the others, and when Pelly protested that he did not enjoy cigars, insisted that they were very mild. In the end Pelly felt forced to give in, and he smoked about a quarter, but, disliking the taste, he threw the rest of the cigar away.

Bampfield had invited them to a private dancing party that night, and under pressure from Birchall, Pelly had agreed to attend, though he thought the Bampfields 'were hardly the sort of people one cared to know'. Just as he sat down to tea at Baldwin's, however, he felt incredibly ill. Birchall, 'very much upset', immediately ran into town to get brandy, giving Pelly a stiff drink upon his return. Birchall had seemed 'unnecessarily anxious' for Pelly to go out that night, and seemed equally disappointed when he now decided he would stay in.

The next day the expected telegram still hadn't reached the Imperial. Birchall concluded that his only course was to go to Buffalo to find out what exactly was waiting for him there. Pelly suggested that he might himself take the opportunity to look up some distant relatives, the Clenches, at St Catherine's.

By the afternoon, however, a combination of still feeling unwell, and an inconvenient train schedule, led him to say that he had changed his mind. Birchall was again peculiarly displeased, and insisted that as they were likely to become extremely busy any day now, Pelly should not postpone an outing that might be impossible later. Birchall was, in fact, 'so strong in urging' Pelly to go, that he managed to make him change his mind again. Pelly went to St Catherine's only to find that the Clenches were out. He walked around the town, then made his way back to Niagara.

When Birchall returned from Buffalo, he said that he had been unable to retrieve his telegram and letter because the Stafford House clerk had sent both to the telegraph office so that their contents could be forwarded in detail to Niagara. Pelly found this exceedingly odd, not least as no forwarded messages had come through, but Birchall explained that it didn't particularly matter anyway. The clerk had remembered enough to be able to tell him that Benwell had asked for his heavy baggage to be sent down to the Fifth Avenue Hotel in New York. Apparently Birchall had been right that Benwell would prove hard to please, and he was already heading back towards England. Birchall told Pelly that he had wired to New York to confirm this arrangement, and that he would send on Benwell's luggage the next morning.

After tea Birchall announced that he had to go out to meet a man at the Imperial. Pelly, concerned that something either 'untoward' or 'odd' was going on, said that he would keep Birchall company. At this, Mrs Birchall asked Pelly to post a letter for her, and though Pelly and Birchall did set out from Baldwin's together, Birchall announced that he hadn't time to go via the post office, but would meet Pelly at the hotel. 'For some reason or other,' Pelly afterwards wrote, Birchall's manner came across as being 'rather strange'. Pelly started walking as quickly as possible to the post office, then actually broke into a run. He sent the letter, sped on, and finally intercepted Birchall on Front Street, just opposite the Grand Trunk Railway Station. Birchall appeared to be crumpling a piece of paper in his hand. Whatever this item was, he shoved it into his pocket and said to Pelly, in his own customary slang, 'I fixed up the party all right.' Pelly could not bring himself to ask who the party was, what had needed fixing, nor indeed what, in this instance, fixing had actually meant.

Throughout the nineteenth century it was thought a gratifying pastime to go and stare at unidentified corpses. Certainly the dead body from the Blenheim swamp attracted hundreds of visitors to Princeton. The local press reported that the 'diabolical' nature of the murder in question had sent a 'thrill of horror through the whole community'. After the post mortem, the naked remains had been placed on a stretcher upstairs at Swarts's. The body was covered with a white cloth, but the face was left open to view. Both a missing cigar maker and the missing overseer of a nearby lunatic asylum were thought by their friends to be possible candidates for the dead man, but no one who came actually recognized him. Several days passed, and still the press continued to describe the hotel bars of the area as being 'crowded all day and far into the night by horror-stricken country-folk discussing the tragedy'.

The inquest was resumed on Monday 24 February. The doctors who had carried out the post mortem now submitted an official written statement saying that they believed 'death was produced by injury to the brain caused by two pistol shots fired by some hand, as yet unknown, but other than the deceased's, either one of which was sufficient to produce death.' They remarked, furthermore, that this death had been instantaneous, that scorch or burn marks around the bullet holes indicated that the shots had been fired at close range, and that the wounds would have led to little loss of blood. Another witness, John Rabb, the nearest resident, at about half a mile away, to the spot where the corpse had been found, testified that he had heard unusual pistol shots in the swamp the previous Tuesday evening, 18 February.

Contradictory theories abounded in the press as to the identity of both the victim and any possible perpetrators, but there was general agreement that the dead man had been a stranger, that he had been disposed of by more than one person, that his body had been carried into the swamp from the road, and that 'the actors in the crime were well acquainted with the country', as 'a more forlorn or dreary spot could hardly be selected for the execution of such a deed'. Recently burnt cedar trees blocked the way to a small lake further inside the swamp, and it seemed highly plausible to many that the killers had originally planned to dispose of the body by sinking it in these obscure waters.

The parade of possible suspects that week was exclusively made up of people who were considered low-life types: drunks, pedlars, Indians and petty criminals; and the bruises found on the body were seized on by the press as evidence that a serious fight had taken place before the shooting. One paper tried to implicate a pair of 'hard seeds' who the previous Friday had attempted to rob the till at Dake's Hotel, Princeton, where the inquest was being held, and after that a private residence, reprobates who had gone on to try to pass counterfeit money in Gobles.

More serious candidates for the crime were then discovered in a pair of young men called Colwell and Baker. Baker, who was from the nearby town of Sarnia, had been up on robbery charges in Woodstock in the past, and when the inquest session resumed, the story emerged of how he and Colwell had gone on a spree the previous Wednesday night and Thursday morning. During the night they had woken up numerous people either to ask directions or simply out of 'pure cussedness'. The next morning they had begun drinking and splashing money around, including at Dake's Hotel, and were either wildly drunk or, as some thought, were feigning wild drunkenness. Once he knew he was suspected, Colwell, a local man, came forward. He was shown the corpse, but viewed it with composure and no sign of recognition. He was called to give evidence at a further inquest session on the night of Wednesday 26 February, but was not in the end required to speak.

Theories about the dead man were as muddled as the theories about those who had killed him. The victim was described in many reports as being obviously a 'Halfbreed', while several people who had viewed the body over the weekend thought that they recognized him as being a banjo player and tin-ware 'fakir', or jewellery seller, who passed through the area from time to time. The only name anyone could come up with for a known tin-goods pedlar in the region was Levi Isaac. Yet, as other reporters put it, 'Many circumstances point to the remains being that of a young Englishman, newly arrived.'

Messrs Westlake and Perry, photographers from Woodstock, were summoned to take pictures of the remains. The body was slightly raised for this purpose, and the dead man's clothes either draped over or tied on to him. One photograph showed him hatted, the other not. The newspapers printed engravings of these pictures, and put up copies of the

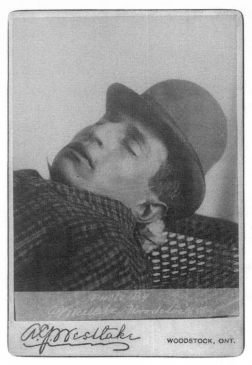

WOODSTOCK, ONT.

'The unfortunate unknown.'

photographs themselves in their office windows. In Woodstock these pictures were, of course, 'eagerly scrutinized', but as interest in the case grew, the Toronto *World* also claimed that a display in its windows in the big city was 'inspected by thousands'. This led to the corpse being independently identified by several Toronto mechanics as a moulder who had worked some months back in the 'dog shop' at the Gurney iron foundry in St Catherine's.

On Wednesday 26 February the body was again identified, this time as being that of Oscar Scarff, a visitor from British Columbia who had recently left the locality with six hundred

THE MURDERED MAN.

Description.—Height about 5 ft., 7 in., weight, about 150 lbs.; aquiline nose ; heavy lips ; dark complexion ; black heavy hair : low forehead. The body is that of a well built man—high chested, broad shoulders, and small feet.

IDENTIFIED.

He is Said to be Oscar Scarff

FROM BRITISH COLUMBIA

IDENTIFIED BY A SCAR ON HIS LEG.

He Had $600 on His Person When Last Seen.

The Princeton murder mystery is likely to be solved very soon. The body of the dead man has been identified as that of Oscar Scarff, of British Columbia.

Mrs. Miller who resides within four miles of the spot where the body was found, was in town to-day and related the following facts : Three or four weeks ago a young man from British Columbia arrived in the neighborhood on a visit to the Turnbulls. His name was Oscar Scarff and was a relative of Turnbull's wife. A few days ago he left to visit friends in either Petrolia or Sarnia and that was the last seen of him alive. Tuesday the Turnbulls drove to Princeton and recognized the body as that of the friend who had been stopping with them. A dark moustache which he had when he left had been shaved off. The body was positively identified by a scar on the leg.

The murdered man was engaged in the seal fishing business for several years and when he came here had $600 in his pocket.

The body having been identified, all that remains for the detectives to do is to ferret out the murderer, which it is thought will not be a very difficult task.

A false identification of the corpse.

dollars in his pocket; but when, the very next day, the Oscar Scarff identification was overturned, with a telegram from Petrolia confirming that he was alive, many reverted to the line that 'the deceased was an Englishman and was murdered for his money'. The only missing young Englishman from the area, Neville Pickthall, had been gone long enough now to rule out the possibility of his being on a mere jamboree; but once his sister had eliminated him from the list of possible murder victims, the oddity of his disappearance did not lead to him being proposed as a candidate for the killer. He was, instead, excoriated in a little article in the Woodstock *Sentinel-Review* for having deserted his wife of four months.

Once witness statements were becoming thin to the point of absurdity, the coroner, Dr McLay, adjourned the inquest hearings, to be resumed on 7 March. The thoroughly thawed corpse had been 'prepared to keep' so that it could be 'held for a reasonable time awaiting identification', but by the Thursday following its discovery, McLay also ordered that the young man at last be buried.

The ministers of the local Episcopalian church were absent, so the service had to be read by a churchwarden, F. Cheesewright. 'The remains were encased in no pauper's box,' wrote one reporter piously, 'but in a good casket decently and nicely mounted and the good people of Princeton turned out and gave him a Christian burial. The unknown man now sleeps his last sleep in the Princeton cemetery.' He was put in the 'pottersfield portion' of the graveyard, the area reserved for strangers.

Amid all the wild speculation in the press, one further small set of concrete details had emerged. On Saturday 22 February George and Joseph Elvidge had gone back into the swamp to hunt for extra evidence in the snow. What they had discovered supplied the very last particulars of the story to be threaded through local newspaper reporting in the days immediately afterwards. Joseph had found a cigar holder containing a stub of cigar, and gold-rimmed 'nose glasses' with short-sighted 'Peeble's' or pebble lenses. George, meanwhile, eight feet from where the body had been lying, found a cigar case with a name written inside. The two woodsmen gave these details at the inquest, but the little pile of possessions, and the name, meant nothing to anyone. Besides, as reporters noted, their relevance was unclear. The cigar case could have belonged to the victim, or to a perpetrator, or it might even have been 'placed there for the purposes of throwing the authorities off the trail'.

With this degree of uncertainty, the Toronto press did not relay news of the Elvidge finds in their columns for several days. The *Globe*, Toronto's biggest-selling daily, waited until Friday 28 February to describe the three items, and the *Mail*, its great rival, waited until the day after. Not until a week after the discovery of the body, therefore, was the widespread readership of these two papers given a chance to mull over the name that had been half buried in the snow. The case itself was of leather and contained two-cent cigars. The name stoutly inked inside it was 'F. C. Benwell'.

4. Big Difficulties

It was the doubt as to the reality of the whole thing that knocked me
over. I felt impotent, and in the dark, and distrustful.
   Bram Stoker, *Dracula*, 1897

On the morning of Friday 28 February, Birchall set off from
Baldwin's to see an express agent about sending Benwell's
bags on to New York. Pelly chose not to accompany him, and
instead sat around in the boarding-house smoking room. After
some time Birchall returned, rushing halfway up the stairs
before he remembered to throw Pelly down a letter that had
come for him from England. Birchall consulted his wife before
he then called down over the banisters to summon Pelly
upstairs. Out and about, Birchall had had a look at the morning
press. 'What do you think I have seen in the papers,' he said,
'about the man who was murdered up country? There has
been a cigar case found near him marked F. C. Benwell.' Pelly
still knew almost nothing of the details of the crime. He was
shocked, and replied, 'You don't mean it?'
   Birchall proposed that he and Pelly travel at once to see
whether they could 'find out anything about it', but Pelly,
desperately trying to digest what he had been told, asked
whether it didn't make more sense to telegraph the Fifth
Avenue Hotel first. It was there that Benwell had asked for
his luggage to be sent, 'and if we get an answer,' said Pelly
ingenuously, 'we shall know he is all right.' Birchall replied
that he didn't think this plan would do any good. His idea was

to go with Pelly straight away to Princeton where the body was being held: the nearest railway station, he said, would be at a small place called Paris. Pelly had gleaned just enough from the newspaper headlines to say that he thought Woodstock had been mentioned, but Birchall was sure that Paris was the nearest stop. When Pelly asked him if he had enough money to get them both there, Birchall was forced to admit that he hadn't. He proposed that they go first to the Imperial to ask Bampfield to cash a cheque.

As Pelly went to his room to get ready, he thought rapidly back over Benwell's movements, and for the first time, the circumstances of their travelling companion's disappearance struck him as really 'very curious'. It suddenly occurred to him that he was 'in a very difficult position indeed', and he became, as he later said, 'completely frightened'. He put four sovereigns in his pocket along with a clutch of spare revolver cartridges. The revolver itself he placed fully loaded in an outside pocket of his greatcoat, which he then carried over his arm. He didn't want Birchall to know that he had his gun with him; but nor, if it came to it, was he prepared to leave himself defenceless.

At the Imperial, Birchall went off to find Bampfield at the bar, while Pelly sat in the room opposite and scoured the newspapers. When Birchall came to retrieve Pelly it was with the news that Bampfield had refused to cash Birchall's cheque, though he had been prepared to lend him a few dollars. The two young men now consulted the railway timetable in the hotel hallway. It listed no suitable train to Paris before three fifteen. If they left that late, they would have to spend the night away. Pelly suggested that they return to the boarding house to tell Mrs Birchall how matters stood, but Birchall said they could inform her by wire once they had arrived. They walked over to one of the railway depots to check the timetable there, but had no better luck. Pelly did, however, notice on one timetable that there was a train to Princeton, the village he now knew to be close to the scene of the murder. Birchall, despite making remarks to the effect, 'I don't know the neighbourhood, nor have I ever been there,' still insisted that the station they needed to head for was Paris.

Given the train times, they now had several hours to pass before leaving. Birchall proposed that they cross the Niagara to the American side, to cash a cheque at his bank. They walked together over the Grand Trunk Railway suspension bridge, and Pelly was unnerved when, apropos, it seemed, of nothing in particular, Birchall volunteered that Benwell had his pistol. 'Oh, has he,' said Pelly. 'Did you give it to him?' Birchall replied, 'No, he took it.' A little later, equally abruptly, Birchall declared that if the dead man proved to be Benwell, they would no doubt find that it had been a case of suicide. He reminded Pelly of how

Benwell had once or twice during our intercourse expressed it as his opinion that life was hardly worth living, and that when he came to analyse the amount of entirely happy days he had spent they amounted to very little.

Pelly did remember Benwell talking like this, but hadn't for a moment credited these remarks with being genuinely morbid. Far from sympathizing, Pelly had actually assumed that Benwell spoke in this way 'merely from conceit as wishing to be considered quite too experienced and blasé'.

Once over the bridge, Birchall and Pelly caught the street car up to Birchall's bank. While they rode along, Pelly again brought up the question of telegraphing New York, sure that this would be the proper course of action. Either Benwell was there and alive, or, mystifyingly, the telegram about Benwell's luggage had been 'fictitious'. Birchall somehow succeeded in ducking the issue, and the two of them went into the bank where Birchall was able to raise twenty-odd dollars. Outside again, it had begun to pour with rain. Pelly put on his greatcoat but left it unbuttoned so that the revolver would not be too obvious. They huddled together on the steps of the bank, waiting for the return street car. During the ride back down to the bridge, Pelly, increasingly desperate, mentioned New York for a third time. He offered to go himself to look for Benwell there, if Birchall would pay. Pelly had concealed the exact amount of his own remaining supply of money, about twenty pounds at the most. He was afraid that if Birchall knew about this cash, he would leave him with absolutely nothing.

Birchall managed even now to leave open the matter of hunting for Benwell in New York. Pelly, meanwhile, 'practically insisted' that they at least take the opportunity to go back to the boarding house to let Mrs Birchall know of their plans, though his real wish was to try to snatch a private word with Baldwin. Birchall was displeased that Pelly was proving so unbiddable, and made it clear that he would prefer to remain on the American side until their departure; but he couldn't get round the fact that there was ample time for them to lunch with his wife before they were able to catch a train. When the street car reached the end of the track the rain was still pouring down. Birchall made one final attempt to stall proceedings, complaining that if they walked back over the bridge the drenching wet would spoil his overcoat. As he had another coat on beneath it, his objection seemed to Pelly ridiculous, and for once Pelly's wishes prevailed.

In 1890 the lower suspension bridge at Niagara Falls spanned

The two-tier lower suspension bridge at Niagara, circa *1889.*

the starting point of the seething whirlpool rapids. It had two levels. The upper deck carried the tracks of the Grand Trunk Railway, while the lower deck took pedestrians and carriage traffic. Earlier that morning, Pelly and Birchall had crossed by this under-bridge in reasonable weather. As they made their way back, however, they were buffeted by a hard, cold wind laden with rain. Pelly took a course straight down the middle of the bridge with Birchall walking to his left. After some minutes Birchall said what Pelly would remember as, 'Go over to the side, it is so cold here.' Pelly was seized by a fear that this was the moment he would die. It was 'a sort of revelation to me' he said later: 'I had instantly an instinct that he was going to push me over.' There was no one else in sight. The balustrade on the bridge was '*very* low', no more than eighteen inches. Pelly gripped his revolver, ready to fire. 'Gruffly' he told Birchall that he could walk to the right if he wished to be protected from the wind, but that Pelly himself did not mind the weather as his greatcoat had a large collar to it. Birchall drew away from him again, and Pelly stuck doggedly to his course, unsure whether or not Birchall had caught sight of the butt of his gun. The two of them completed their crossing in silence.

When they reached the boarding house, Birchall went immediately upstairs. Mrs Birchall left the dining table and followed him. Pelly, with relief, was able to ask Baldwin to step into the drawing room for a moment so that they might speak together alone. He told Baldwin it was possible that he might end up going to New York that night, but that whatever happened Baldwin was on no account to let anyone take his bags away unless they bore direct instructions from Pelly himself with one of his English visiting cards enclosed. Baldwin asked if there was anything wrong with 'the people upstairs'. Pelly replied, 'Oh, the woman's all right, but I don't altogether trust the man.'

After lunch, when the rest of the company at the boarding house had finished and left the room, Pelly asked Birchall yet again, 'What do you think about my going to New York?' While this appeared to him to be a logically sensible step, he also longed to get away, to have time to think alone. To his surprise, Birchall informed him that Mrs Birchall had decided to go on the trip to Paris. Birchall had therefore after all decided that Pelly should go to hunt for Benwell in New York. Pelly asked again for money for this journey, but Birchall said the best he could do was to give him a blank cheque for Maloney to cash if Pelly needed funds on arrival. They agreed that, as soon as they reached their separate destinations, each party would telegraph the other with the result of their inquiries.

That afternoon, Pelly went with the Birchalls to the railway station to see them off. He had slipped two more sovereigns into his pocket, and went into a bank to change some of his 'English gold into American paper'. When he got back he found the Birchalls were just boarding their train. Pelly and Birchall helped settle Mrs Birchall into a seat, then had a quiet word with each other while Pelly climbed down out of the car and Birchall balanced on the steps above him. 'If I were you,' said Pelly, 'I would not let Mrs Birchall see the papers, because I think it all sounds very bad.' Birchall agreed, and promised that, whether or not the corpse proved to be Benwell, he would try to keep Pelly's name out of the affair. He added that he regretted that these events might interfere with their business operations. Pelly thought this was nonsensical, and told Birchall not to consider him in the matter. If the dead man did turn out to be Benwell, he assumed they were all 'bound to get mixed up in it'.

Pelly himself left Niagara on the 5.09 service to New York. As he sped away, freed from immediate dread, he 'thought out the whole matter', and found that his suspicions 'began to weaken':

I felt that Burchell was probably, almost certainly a wrong'un, but most unlikely that he was a murderer. If he was a murderer it seemed to be quite impossible that his wife could be ignorant of it. Also he would surely, if guilty, have left Niagara in Canada, and at least have gone to the States where he could have quickly hidden his tracks.

The case as it stood made little sense to Pelly; besides which he did not even know yet whether the body was really Benwell's or not.

★

The man charged with solving the mystery of the Blenheim swamp corpse was Detective John Murray, chief of the small band of government detectives with a remit to cover the whole province of Ontario. The more notoriety the case attracted, the more public his success or failure in solving it would be. While Pelly and the Birchalls had been grappling with news of the named cigar case that Friday, Murray had been giving an interview to pressmen in Toronto. His present opinion of the case, he said, was that 'it was brutal murder perpetrated to accomplish robbery'. He added: 'My theory is that the man was shot in a dive for his money, and that then this effort was made to do away with the body.' He said he believed the victim to be twenty-three or –four, undoubtedly English, and a newcomer. Such items as a gold plate with three teeth in it and a wild cherry cigar holder indicated that he was 'in good circumstances', while the absence of money in his pockets showed that 'The motive of the crime was, no doubt, robbery.' It was clear that whoever was guilty of the murder must have been 'thoroughly familiar with the locality', and Murray agreed with the notion that the original plan had been to drown the corpse in the little lake deep in the swamp: 'Thither no doubt the murderers intended to convey the body, but they were probably unable to penetrate the thick scrub or undergrowth with their burden.'

Murray then revealed that he was pursuing Colwell and Baker, the men who had been on a spree in the area on the night of Wednesday 19 February: 'It is quite true that suspicion points to two men who were seen driving round the district in a buggy on the night the corpse is supposed to have been left in the wood,' he said. Murray told the reporters that he would be leaving straight after his interviews to search for hard evidence to this effect. 'These men have been questioned by

me,' he declared, 'but the account they give of their proceedings is not by any means satisfactory.'

This dry reference to Murray's own unsuccessful interrogation of two murder suspects had implications beyond
the immediately obvious. In a later memoir, describing both
the best and the most typical cases from across his career,
Murray would repeatedly note that in the absence of proof,
his habit was to rely upon being 'morally certain' of a person's
guilt. He tried to convey how this investigative technique
functioned:

To detect a liar is a great gift. It is a greater gift to detect the lie. I
have known instances where, by good fortune, I detected the liar
and then the lie, and learned the whole truth simply by listening to
the lie, and thereby judging the truth. There is no hard and fast rule
for this detection. The ability to do it rests with the man. It is largely
a matter of instinct.

Yet what if this instinct failed to lead to useable evidence?

Murray was not shy of revealing in his memoir that he had
had a relish for violence, though whether the fights noted in
his stories were offered up as the most spectacular instances,
or as commonplace, he did not disclose. In one example he
described running into Whitey Stokes, 'a burglar and all-round
bad man', late one night in a saloon. Stokes had pulled a gun
on Murray but only succeeded in shooting him between two
fingers, and the two of them had ended up pounding each
other horizontal:

A foot-rail ran along the front of the bar, several inches from the
floor. I managed to slide Stokes along the floor until I got his head
near this iron rail, and I jammed it under. He had been snapping

and snarling at me like a mad dog, trying to sink his teeth in me. Once I got his head under the rail I drew my own revolver, and used its butt so that Mr Whitey Stokes was not fit to be photographed for a month.

Such brutal outcomes are more the exception than the norm in Murray's anecdotes, and there is the obvious possibility that he exaggerated; yet, psychological violence, thinly suppressed, is present in almost all of the stories he chose to record.

Murray's speaking voice was described by his editor as having been

remarkable for its wide range, and particularly for its power to change from gentle, tender tones to ones so deep, so rough, so harsh, that at times the guilty, on hearing in it thunderous accusation, have burst into tears and confessed.

Murray himself used the suggestive phrase 'crowding' for a confession when he told the tale of how he had hounded a wailing widow at her husband's funeral into admitting that she had instigated his murder. On another occasion he had threatened to drown a recalcitrant thief, and on yet another, had led a cattle poisoner to believe he had consumed part of his own fatal mixture, in these ways extracting further confessions. Murray's first instinct with the Blenheim swamp murder case was that the two confirmed hard seeds, Colwell and Baker, were guilty; but whatever steps he took with them, they did not crack. Murray lost several days pursuing this lead in vain.

Pelly arrived in New York early on the morning of 1 March, and made his way to the Fifth Avenue Hotel on foot. When he got there he asked whether there was a telegram waiting for him from Birchall, but as yet there was nothing. He then tried to find out whether Benwell was a guest at the hotel, but not only was Benwell not 'stopping' there, it transpired that 'no one of that name had been registered there at all'. In a quandary, Pelly decided to take a room for himself, though he had no real idea whether he would need to stay.

He went upstairs to his room to wash and to gather his thoughts. The process by which his suspicions had weakened as he left Canada now began to reverse itself. He had travelled to New York to confirm that Benwell was alive. There was no immediate evidence that he was. Yet if Benwell and the dead man in Princeton were one and the same, how were the telegrams about his luggage to be explained? Pelly again trawled back through recent events. Two evenings before, running through the streets of Niagara, he'd caught Birchall shoving something crumpled into his pocket, saying, 'I fixed up the party all right.' After this, both Birchalls had given Pelly to understand that the forwarded telegram from Benwell had finally arrived in Niagara, but that they had thrown it away. Suppose by the phrase, 'fixing up the party', Birchall had actually been referring to a bogus wire, sent to himself, by himself, from Buffalo? If this were the case, it was possible not only that Birchall was involved in Benwell's murder, but that he was currently engaged in a process of planting false evidence to cover his tracks.

This was a shocking thought, but it didn't take an unusual leap of the imagination for Pelly to arrive at the idea. The telegraph system was already half a century old by the 1890s. London had received its first international news feed from Reuters in 1851, and the first sub-Atlantic telegraph cables had linked Britain and North America as early as 1866. Some

Victorians felt that this altered their world so profoundly that the human race seemed now to be, 'as it were, in a vast whispering gallery'. To others the picture was less ethereal, the telegraph wires, with their burden of intelligence, running under the pavements of big cities 'cheek by jowl' with gas pipes, water mains and sewers full of 'unmentionable mixtures, abominable to all'. Rudyard Kipling imagined with even greater horror how writhing submarine telegraph cables crossed 'great grey level plains of ooze', so that, from one continent to another, mankind disgustingly communicated 'o'er the waste of the ultimate slime'.

The telegraph system, however marvellous, was disturbing. As with steam-powered travel, previous and apparently natural limits to human concourse had been vastly extended by a new technology, and in a manner that provided novel opportunities not only for decent citizens, but for law breakers as well. The Victorians manufactured huge cipher books to allow for keeping the meanings of telegrams secret, but codes were a solution only for the well organized. Once a telegraph clerk or operator had transmitted the contents of a telegram, the handwritten original would be filed, not least against the possibility of later disputes about garbled or lost messages. If, as Pelly began to wonder, Birchall had had reason to send one or more fake wires to himself, then at least he would have had to consider the fact that copies might be kept by the telegraph company he used, whether he threw away the delivered messages or not.

Pelly spent that Saturday in New York in fruitless pursuit of information. First he went to see Maloney, Birchall's supposed agent, at the docks, to ask whether he had 'seen Benwell about lately'. Maloney said he hadn't, and privately thought, as he later told a reporter, that this news caused Pelly to become 'blue'. Not surprisingly, Maloney prevaricated about cashing, to any amount, the blank cheque that Birchall had supplied, saying that he knew Birchall only through having purchased railway tickets for him. Pelly next went to an exchange office to change two more of his 'English gold' sovereigns, then he revisited the business address at which he remembered Benwell to have delivered a packet of photographs to a friend. Pelly stared at the list of names in the entrance hall, but could not recognize any of them, and with his own detective work stalled, he came hopelessly away.

That same Saturday, the papers in Woodstock were able to report to their readers how the evening before 'a gentleman from Niagara Falls, whose name we could not ascertain' had arrived in Princeton claiming that the description of the dead man fitted that of 'a relative', who had come to Canada to look for a farm where he might 'settle down as an agriculturalist'. McLay, the coroner, sent word to Detective Murray instructing him to drop all other inquiries and come to interview the gentleman in question. McLay himself had asked that the gentleman go to Woodstock to look at the victim's clothes, but he had refused, pointing out that they might be newly bought.

It had been decided at once that the dead man would be disinterred for identification the next morning. At this news, one reporter expostulated: 'It is too bad that the corpse was so hurriedly put in the grave, for nearly every hour callers from a distance are here wishing to see the same.' Fortunately, the writer declared, 'the body is now to be taken from the grave for the purpose of preserving the head'. This casual assertion could have been true. Detective Murray would have at least two other murder victims decapitated in the 1890s to aid the process of identification. In the event, however, the Princeton corpse was spared a beheading.

The press went on to report the victim's exhumation as follows:

PRINCETON, March 1., 3 p. m.—The man found murdered here was positively identified to-day by Mr. J. Burchill of Niagara Falls, as F. C. Benwell, a young Englishman just out from the old country. He left him about three weeks ago for the purpose of looking up a suitable stock farm to purchase. Mr. Burchell had a letter from him three weeks ago dated London, Ont., and has heard nothing since from him. He has not the slightest doubt that he has been decoyed by some ruffians and murdered for the money in his possession.

During the hours that Pelly spent in New York, as he trailed after every imaginable clue, he returned twice to the Fifth Avenue Hotel to see whether a telegram from Birchall might not at last have arrived. There was nothing, and on one of these occasions, distressed and tired, and no longer with any good reason to remain in the city, Pelly sat down to write a letter to his brother-in-law, and close friend, Arthur Durrant:

Fifth Avenue Hotel
Madison Square, New York

March 1st 1890

My dear Arthur,

I have struck one of the biggest difficulties I ever was in. I will just give you the whole thing in detail.

You probably remember in one of my letters my mentioning a man called Benwell who came out with Burchell and was I found in Burchell's charge. We all four, Mr. and Mrs. B. and Benwell and I arrived at Buffalo on Sunday morning Feb. 16th. Early on Monday Burchell and Benwell went on alone to Niagara, ostensibly to prepare for our reception. This was I believe a plant of Burchell's. Benwell left all his kit with us and I have never seen him since. Burchell arrived at Buffalo <u>alone</u> that evening saying Benwell had gone to see some friends. We have heard nothing of him since. Burchell has told me however of the receipt of certain wires which he says come from Benwell, ending with one received the day before yesterday, i. e. Feb. 27th, asking for his kit to be sent to Fifth Avenue Hotel, N.Y.

During the last few days Mr. and Mrs. B's conduct has been so strange that our landlord and his wife and myself have been most curious to know if anything has happened, but we all kept our thoughts to ourselves till yesterday when the enclosed was in the daily paper. Burchell was most upset and wanted me to go with him at once to the scene of the murder to identify the body. I at once said, "Why don't you wire to 5th Avenue. If he answers we shall know he is safe". But he would not. Finally he said I was to go down to N.Y. and see if I could find out anything, and he and Mrs. B. went off to the place where the murder was.

Meantime his manner to me was so funny that I got my revolver and have carried it about with me since. When he had started I took the landlord into my confidence, to find out that he was as suspicious as myself. Fortunately he and his wife are charming and have been very kind indeed to me.

Well, I got here early today and find that Benwell has never been here. In fact, I think Burchell sent me off here to get rid of me. Luckily I have more money with me than I let him know of and I return to Niagara tonight.

I do not think Burchell is mixed up <u>actually</u> in the affair, but

I do think he knows more about Benwell's movements than he pretends. He, among other things, told me that Benwell had taken his (Burchell's) revolver with him, which I fear may be in order to prepare me for hearing that the pistol used in the murder was Burchell's. I don't want father bothered unless necessary, so I write to you. Probably my next letter home will clear up matters and then you can shew him this. If nothing should be heard of me, my landlord's name is Baldwin and his address is P.O. Niagara Falls, Ontario. He is entirely reliable.

I am going to break with Burchell <u>at once</u> if any one of my suspicions seem true. I fear this is a horrid scrawl, but I have been in the train all night and I feel quite in a state of nervousness. I have already during the last three days proved Burchell to be one of the most shifty lying brutes unhung. Almost all he told me in England is only partly true, although on the other hand nothing is quite false. I have a real friend in Baldwin, only I felt as if I must unburden to someone.

If I break with Burchell I shall probably go for advice to Mr. Bland at Hamilton, and then very likely go and finish my year out here with Beecher, the man I saw at Hastings. He is at any rate a gentleman. My only fear is that I have seen the last of both the Burchells and my money. However, I shall have a good try for the latter anyway.

But for all this I am fairly happy and find the Burchells very pleasant people. Shan't I feel a fool if all this proves to be only imagination.

How are you all at home? If Queen sees this letter from me you must use your discretion about letting her hear its contents.

Your very loving brother,

Douglas R. Pelly

If you like you can send this on to Godfrey.

Pelly was 'more than ever puzzled as to what was best to do,' but at least he did still have enough money in his dwindling secret supply to be able, that evening, to catch the Erie Flyer back to the Falls.

With the day at an end, Pelly found that his suspicions took 'the very worst form'. It now seemed highly likely to him that when Birchall had returned to Buffalo from Niagara the previous Monday night, the dollars with which he had been so pleased to have provided himself had actually been stolen from Benwell. Meanwhile, the argument that Pelly had earlier used to exonerate Birchall — that if he were involved in a capital crime he would surely have fled to the States — was replaced by another, more potent reflection. Pelly could no longer understand how Birchall had been 'fool enough' to make his endless double-dealing so obvious, unless he had always intended to kill both Benwell and Pelly 'immediately on our arrival in Canada and before we could find out all the lies he and his wife had told'.

As Pelly journeyed on through the night, there were two outcomes in particular that he dreaded. First, he might arrive at the Falls to discover that the Birchalls had permanently disappeared, taking his money with them. Worse than this, as his remark to Arthur Durrant implied — 'If nothing should be heard of me' — was the chance that he would return to Niagara only to be killed himself. Pelly completely failed, however, to anticipate a third dire possibility, and what actually happened. At seven thirty on the morning of Sunday 2 March, after a sleepless, thirteen-hour train journey, he stepped down out of his compartment on to the station platform at the Falls to find that he himself was wanted on suspicion of murder.

★

Several policemen had been posted to wait at the station in the hope that Pelly would return, though they were under orders merely to shadow him if he did. As he walked away towards Baldwin's boarding house, one of the constables, who knew him a little, fell in with him and 'expressed great surprise' that he had come back. It was this constable who, in defiance of orders, let Pelly know the bewildering new difficulty he faced. He could hardly believe what he was being told. He walked in at the boarding-house door to find another constable posted there on duty in the hallway, and Baldwin and yet a further constable, McMicken, at last confirmed for him that Birchall had identified the Princeton corpse as being Benwell's. Baldwin told Pelly that the police had turned up at the house in the middle of the night, and that Birchall and his wife were themselves under grave suspicion; but he also admitted that he understood Pelly was very soon to be arrested.

Pelly sat down and fortified himself with breakfast. Just as he finished, Mrs Birchall lent over the banisters and requested him to come upstairs. Pelly did as she asked, to find that she was 'in a dreadful state of terror and nervousness, walking up and down the room'. Birchall, also 'frantic with nerves', was still in bed, where he remained. Pelly was the first to speak. Awkwardly he said, 'What a terrible affair this is.' Mrs Birchall, panicking, replied, 'Do you know who the man downstairs is?' When Pelly lied and pretended that the constable was simply a friend of Baldwin's, Mrs Birchall started to pour out to him how the arrival of someone in the night had frightened her and her husband. Pelly, unable to bear this, and wondering why an innocent person should mind such a thing, backed out of the conversation on the excuse that he had got hold of some English newspapers and wanted to go away and look at them.

Once Pelly was downstairs again, Baldwin suggested that he go voluntarily and at once to see the police magistrate, Mr Hill. This sounded like a sensible plan, and so the two of them slipped out of the back of the house together, making sure that the Birchalls wouldn't see them. On the way to the magistrate's house they were stopped by the chief of the Niagara police force, Thomas Young. Baldwin explained what they were doing, and Young allowed them to continue. At Mr Hill's, Pelly found himself being asked to describe his movements during the whole of the time he had spent with the Birchalls. He didn't realize that Hill had open in front of him Pelly's diary, which the police had taken from his room at Baldwin's during the night. The account he gave of himself so completely accorded with what he had written that Hill was persuaded of his innocence. He became 'extremely kind', told Pelly not to worry, and proceeded to cancel his arrest warrant. It had been issued at Detective Murray's request, Hill said, because Birchall had told Murray in Princeton 'that his party had included a young man named Pelly, who had skipped off to the States as soon as he had seen the papers with the account of the finding of the cigar case with Benwell's name on it'.

Hill told Pelly and Baldwin to return to the boarding house, saying that something would happen soon; and, indeed, shortly after they got back, Birchall was forced from his bed and arrested. Young later described how when he 'announced his errand', Birchall had said, 'All right,' as he might have said, 'How d'ye do,' after which he 'calmly, leisurely got up and completed his toilet. He did not utter another word, nor even ask the officer why he had been pounced upon.' There was a warrant out for Mrs Birchall also, but she, by this point, was 'in such a state of prostration and so evidently unable to move', that the decision was taken to leave her under guard in her room. Birchall said goodbye to his wife and was 'at once taken off to the police cells'. He just had time in the boarding house hallway to ask Pelly to wire Mr Hellmuth, the lawyer who had befriended Benwell on the *Britannic*, to ask for advice. Despite having been informed that Birchall had tried to frame him for murder, Pelly promised to do as asked, and telegraphed without delay.

Mrs Birchall remained 'very much upset' all that day, and dismayed Pelly by turning to him for support. She now admitted to him that there was no farm and never had been. She also admitted, seemingly unaware that he already knew, that during their previous visit to Canada, she and Birchall had passed under the name of Somerset, though 'only for business purposes and in an honourable manner'. She asked if she should tell the detectives about this. Pelly replied stiffly that he 'thought it better by all means to tell them everything that could throw any light on her or her husband's movements'. Mrs Birchall, agitated, asked Pelly whether he really thought, 'Or if anyone thought that her husband was mixed up in this affair.' Pelly replied that Birchall's many deceptions were 'a great pity', as they made people 'very much disinclined to believe anything he said', but as to Birchall really being 'mixed up' in Benwell's killing, 'of course' he said, he 'did not think anything of the sort'.

Just as Mrs Birchall began to incline towards the truth, Pelly felt himself compelled to deceive her. His surface civility masked the fact that he was now wondering whether, far from the woman being 'all right', as he had previously said to Baldwin, she might not herself be complicit in a murder. One of Pelly's earlier lines of thought, that had seemed to go in Birchall's favour, had been that 'if he was a murderer it seemed to be quite impossible that his wife could be ignorant of it'. Were Birchall to prove guilty, however, this same argument, if valid, would make Mrs Birchall guilty too.

While Pelly was out sending Birchall's appeal to Mr Hellmuth, he also wired his own father: 'BURCHELL IMPRISONED CHARGE MURDER DON'T WORRY SEE NEWSPAPERS DOUGLAS.' By 'don't worry', Pelly no doubt meant to reassure his father that he himself was safe. After his earlier, genial leave-taking from the magistrate, Mr Hill, he presumably felt confident of being on the right side of the law, whatever events might follow; but if he believed this, he was mistaken. The next evening, infuriated by the way events had been handled, Detective Murray showed up at Baldwin's boarding house in person, with two policemen, handcuffs, pistols, and a fresh warrant for Pelly's arrest. Argument proved useless. Pelly was transferred under close guard to the American Hotel, where Murray put him through a demoralizing interrogation. It wasn't until the small hours that the detective called a halt to proceedings, and Pelly, 'almost too tired to be angry', spent that night as a prisoner in an attic room of the hotel.

5. A Swell, Sharper and Deadbeat

A subject presenting such very strong lights and shadows necessarily produces a powerful and Rembrandt-like effect on the public mind.
 Thomas Hood, *Hood's Own*, 1859

On Monday 3 March the Woodstock press astonished its readers with news that the man who had positively identified the Princeton corpse, 'Mr. J. Burchill of Niagara Falls', was the same person the whole town had known only a few months previously as Lord Somerset. He and his supposed wife had arrived in November 1888, and 'after cutting a pretty wide swathe', had departed again very suddenly on 15 May 1889, 'leaving several creditors behind them'. Lord Somerset was especially remembered for his flaming waistcoats, his love of horses, and his 'enormous' champagne bills. 'He wore the finest of toothpick shoes of patent leather. He was groomed to the queen's taste. He was an exquisite in every way,' wrote one paper. Another, wise after the event, and freakishly pompous, commented that although nobody had really believed that he was a 'lordling', still 'it could be seen that he had evidently been brought up in luxury, as he knew intimately the ways of such gentry as those he pretended to be one of.' His wife, meanwhile, if they were really married, which struck commentators as doubtful, had 'looked like a lady of culture and lived like a woman of the world'. The papers soon speculated that Birchall had refused to go to Woodstock to identify the dead man's clothes from a justified fear that, had he done so, he would at once have been recognized by the townspeople.

Given his two identities, great confusion now arose in the press as to what Birchall should properly be called. One paper hedged its bets to ludicrous effect when it discussed 'Mr Birchall or Burchell,' 'Mr Birchall, Burchell or Somerset,' and 'this Mr Birchall or Lord Somerset,' who might or might not really be 'Mr Somerset,' or 'the son of Lord Somerset'. The possibility was even floated, under the subheading, 'History of Somerset. Alias Burchell', that 'his name was Burchell (Birchall) and that Somerset was his father's title, or his own', putatively allowing both 'Burchell (Birchall)' and 'Somerset' to apply.

Whether or not it had been he himself, in 1888, who had instigated his own elevation to the peerage, once the title had come into play in Woodstock, Birchall had not discouraged its use. Somerset was actually the name borne by the younger children of the Duke of Beaufort, and was also the family name of the duke's second cousin, Baron Raglan, grandson of the Baron Raglan who had presided over the disastrous charge of the Light Brigade in the Crimean war. Between them, these two men had enough uncles, cousins, brothers and sons for one more well-born Somerset male to be easily invented; and while the bald designation 'Lord Somerset', used by Birchall, strictly applied to no one, it must have sounded plausible enough, most probably summoning up in the ordinary mind the younger sons of the Duke of Beaufort, his massive Badminton estate, and the family's boundless passion for horses.

The Duke of Beaufort during this period was notoriously the president of the Four-in-hand Club, the super-exclusive pinnacle of a sport that involved racing carriages at high speed using four horses. Recreational four-in-hand driving, an expensive and dangerous hobby, had emerged in England at the point that commercial stage-coach travel was destroyed by the railways. Outside the rules of the club, amateur and unregulated four-in-hand driving had soon become a mania amongst wild young men, Birchall, in time, becoming one of them. He had boasted to Pelly on the journey to New York that while in Canada 'he constantly drove four-in-hand', and no doubt on his first visit, posing as an aristocratic Somerset, Birchall had relished the chance to ally himself with this element in the Duke of Beaufort's reputation.

After Birchall's arrest, reporters soon interviewed his old Niagara contact, Bampfield, at the Imperial Hotel. Bampfield divulged to them that the Somersets had stayed at his hotel in 1889, and that he had recognized them straight away upon their recent return to the Falls with Pelly. Birchall had been forced to explain to Bampfield why Pelly knew him by a name other than Somerset, and had told him that he was now masquerading as 'Burchell' out of shame, 'on account of his good family connections and his coming on this trip trading in horses'.

Once it became clear that of Birchall's two names, Somerset was the false one, reporters concluded that 'in connection with his career here as a swell, sharper and deadbeat, his previous record is important. The fact that his whole career here was a lie will be very much against him at the present time.' This left open an important question. Ignoring the matter of how he had chosen his alias, why, in 1888, had Birchall wanted an alias at all? Piece by piece an explanation began to emerge. The press discovered that in the bankruptcy columns of the London *Times* for 12 January 1889, listed shamefully amongst butchers, builders and publicans, was

'Reginald Birchall, late of Lechlade, Gloucester, present address unknown.' Someone in Woodstock, meanwhile, had preserved a solicitor's letter sent to Canada on 6 June 1889, and addressed to 'Mr. Reginald Birchall, c/o Messrs. Somerset & Co.' This letter would have arrived some days after the abrupt departure of Lord and Lady Somerset on 15 May. In it, Birchall was tersely informed that a trustee had been appointed for him, and 'We only think it right to let you know that you have rendered yourself liable under the Criminal Law, and that he has the power to have you arrested and brought back to England.' Some of Birchall's creditors were noted with amounts of up to fifty pounds by their names. In order to avoid criminal proceedings, the solicitor added, 'We are glad to consider any reasonable proposal.' From this evidence it appeared likely that Birchall had fled to Canada under a false name the previous autumn to avoid financial disaster at home.

After identifying Benwell's corpse in Princeton, 'Mr. J. Burch-ill of Niagara Falls' had given a statement to the press. His comments had been poorly thought out, and would prove to contradict key details of an interview he had later the same day with Detective Murray. To the press Birchall revealed that Benwell was twenty-four, well connected and 'of temperate habits'. He also claimed that they had parted company 'at the Grand Trunk railway depot, Niagara Falls', with Benwell saying that he was 'going to London prospecting'. Birchall told reporters that 'it was through no inducement from me that Benwell came to this country', and added that he had received a letter from Benwell the previous Wednesday, from London, Ontario, containing the ticket that would release the young man's two baggage chests from bond. Birchall had finished on a rousing note:

There seems to be a deep mystery enshrouding the death of poor Benwell in a foreign land, and no doubt the detectives will ferret the whole affair out and expose one of the most cruel murders that has taken place in Ontario for some years.

Far from Birchall trying to keep Pelly's name back, as he had promised to do when they parted company in Niagara, he now invoked him as another member of their party, saying, 'When Pelley returns from New York we will consider what we will do with the remains.'

The Monday newspapers carried many other threads of the story as it had unfolded over the weekend. Crucially, others besides the Birchalls and Pelly had been galvanized by seeing the name 'Benwell' in the press. Mr Tuthill, agent at the Canadian Express Company's Falls office, had recognized that the name matched one painted on two wooden chests lying unclaimed in the office's bonded compartment. Mr Flynn, who was a customs agent, had tipped off the police chief, Mr Young, and inquiries soon pointed to the English party at Baldwin's. The young men there, Baldwin attested, had also been startled to see the name in the paper, since when they had all left town, Pelly in one direction and the Birchalls in another. Young had wired Detective Murray to come at once, and had then himself made straight for Buffalo to inquire into the previous movements of these characters. When news reached him in Buffalo that the Birchalls had returned to Niagara, he had hastened back, giving instructions that constant surveillance be maintained over Baldwin's boarding house, and that a watch be set at the Niagara railway depot for all incoming trains from New York.

Another reader had been startled to notice the name 'Benwell' in the papers that weekend. Isidore Hellmuth, the barrister who had befriended Benwell on the *Britannic*, had hurried to his local *Free Press* newspaper offices in London, Ontario, and had asked to see a photograph of the corpse. At once he had recognized the young man with whom he had become acquainted a mere two weeks before. News of Birchall's Sunday arrest was not yet in print, but wires with this information were already circulating amongst newspaper offices. A *Free Press* representative asked Hellmuth whether he thought Birchall could possibly be guilty of the crime. Though, as one paper put it, 'everyone who has crossed the Atlantic knows how many sharpers and scoundrels are to be found on the Atlantic steamships', the idea that Birchall might be an assassin was more than Hellmuth could credit. Birchall, Benwell and Pelly had struck him, he said, as being upon 'the most familiar terms'. Furthermore, 'A murderer does not generally identify the victim of his fiendishness, and I can't think that Mr Burchell was a party to the tragedy.'

While Birchall's arrest attracted tremendous attention, Pelly's, which took place on the Monday evening, did not. He would later describe his first brush with Detective Murray in unusually forceful terms: 'I was furious. He was gruff and rude. I pointed out that the Magistrate had satisfied himself of my innocence. I insisted that if he put the "darbies" on my wrists I would make him bitterly regret it.' Murray was doubtless most unimpressed. After one of the policemen present had smoothed matters over a little, Murray seems to have decided on the expediency of letting his suspect believe that he had gained his point. Pelly, his anger somewhat quelled, agreed to go to the American Hotel for questioning. Of all this, reporters gleaned only that Murray had arrived at the Falls and had had 'a long closeted conversation' with the second young Englishman; but while Pelly's later description of their encounter is not explicit, it is evident that as the hours went by he found his position to be far less secure than he had been led to imagine, and it dawned on him, to his impotent fury, that the detective did after all still 'strongly' believe him to be 'mixed up in the matter'.

Only in the small hours did Murray finally call a halt to proceedings. He told Pelly that he had booked a room for him right there in the hotel, took him upstairs, and, as Pelly later recorded, 'saying "I hope you will be comfortable" slammed the door and locked me in'. Whatever game Murray had been playing, Pelly now knew that he most certainly was under arrest. Though he would wake up the next morning to find himself called upon to act as a prosecution witness, and would, in this guise, be publicly paraded as Birchall's victim, 'for the next forty-eight hours,' Pelly would write, 'I was virtually a prisoner and never allowed to move without a policeman to guard me. It was,' he adds, with defiant understatement, 'a most uncomfortable position to be in.' His haughty dislike of Murray as a result of this clash was undisguised: 'He was a lower-class American and gave me the impression of being more like one of the criminal classes than a detective.' Murray himself later tried to strike the entire episode from the record, telling reporters that 'a minute's conversation' had convinced him Pelly was innocent, and that he had immediately let him go free.

Despite the fact that an inquest into Benwell's murder was currently under way in Princeton, the Niagara police magistrate, Mr Hill, had decided to hold his own parallel 'magisterial enquiry' into the crime; and so on Tuesday 4 March, the press in Niagara prepared its readers for the day's court proceedings with portraits of the two men who would most importantly feature. A degree of exaggeration made for gratifying contrasts:

'Burchell is dark-complexioned, with a black moustache, sharp features' and 'front teeth badly decayed' wrote one reporter, while 'Mr. Pelley' is 'of slight build, with a fair moustache. He is well educated and has a refined manner.' Pelly was reckoned to be 'a young man about 22 years old', while Birchall, who had sauntered about the Falls in a loose overcoat 'which reached down to his heels', and whose 'tired expression around the eyes' bore witness to a suspiciously 'jovial disposition', seemed, reporters ventured, to be 'about 30'. In fact, Pelly had just turned twenty-five, while Birchall was a few weeks short of turning twenty-four.

As a background to his first court appearance, Birchall faced extreme prejudice in the press, not all of which originated with the reporters themselves. On the advice of both the magistrate and the police, Pelly had refused to provide any information to newspaper men. This had given Detective Murray full freedom to exploit the available evidence to suit his own purposes. In the middle of the night of 3 March, therefore, after he had locked Pelly up in the American Hotel, Murray had held a press conference. Reporters composed hasty news telegrams, writing that Murray, from information he had received at the Falls, had not 'the slightest doubt' but that Birchall was the murderer of Benwell. He considered the affair, 'one of the deepest and most diabolical schemes to entice young wealthy men away from England to murder them in this country for the money they may bring with them'. Not only had Benwell been done away with under this scheme, but 'young Pelley' had 'escaped very lucky', as 'Burchell evidently intended to kill him on two or three occasions.' Murray can only have been delighted the next day to discover that his comments were printed in the evening papers as a prelude to preliminary accounts of the hearing.

The 'greatest excitement' had 'prevailed on the streets' the whole of Monday, with crowds of people standing around the police-court doors hoping that the case would 'come up for a hearing' at once; but Birchall was not actually brought before the police magistrate, Mr Hill, until eleven o'clock on the Tuesday morning. One reporter noted that 'There was a complete jam of people seeking admission to the Court room, and when the doors were thrown open the room filled to the doors within a minute's time.' Birchall 'looked pale and appeared nervous'. In response to initial questioning he claimed to be twenty-five and said he had been born in Church, Lancashire. His father was dead. He himself was married and had 'no occupation', but he had had a college education, he said, and belonged to the Church of England. On the charge of having 'wilfully and feloniously' murdered Fred. C. Benwell on or about 17 February 1890, in or around Princeton, Ontario, he 'replied in a hurried voice, "Not guilty."'

The first witness called was Detective Murray. All his important evidence had 'already been published in all the papers', but he did give the court an account of his interview with Birchall in Paris three days earlier. This had been 'fishy' for many reasons, Murray said, but two were specially important. First, Birchall had falsely claimed that on his previous visit to North America, he and his wife had come as tourists, and had never been further west than the Falls. Second, Mrs Birchall had provided her husband with a false alibi for 17 February, confirming that they had both gone with Benwell to Niagara that morning, and had both parted with him there. The press noted that Birchall objected to a couple of 'unimportant' points of detail in Murray's evidence, without recording what these objections were. Mr Hellmuth, who had supposedly agreed to represent Birchall, was nowhere to be seen.

At noon Pelly stepped into the witness box, where, apart from a break for lunch, he remained until six thirty in the evening. Though listeners took him to be describing his experiences in 'almost painfully exact detail', he seems to have exercised a great deal of self-censorship. According to press accounts, he said nothing incriminating about Mrs Birchall's complicity in deceiving him over Birchall's Canadian affairs, but confined himself to the comment that while in Buffalo on 17 February, 'Mrs. Burchell during the day looked into store windows and remarked that they would purchase some wall paper for the house at the Falls.' He also referred to only one incident where he felt Birchall had come close to an attempt at murdering him in the Niagara waters, saying simply: 'He said, Let us go down here. We went part of the way down, and met a man coming up. Not liking the appearance of the place, I suggested we follow the man up, and we did.' Pelly also said next to nothing about his dead travelling companion, beyond, 'I did not take to Benwell.' It is clear that, as the principal witness in a murder case, Pelly felt he must be painstakingly fair.

By six thirty that evening he was exhausted, and the magistrate took pity on him. One more witness would quickly be dealt with, said Hill, and then he would adjourn the case until Pelly took the stand again at ten o'clock the next morning. The new witness was 'Wm. Macdonald from Woodstock'. Macdonald was a farmer, and the local representative of Ford & Rathbone, the farm pupillage agency that had sent Birchall out, as Somerset, on his first visit to Canada. Macdonald stated that during Birchall's stay in Woodstock, he had driven 'fast livery horses around the town, and finally left the town owing debts and was a regular dead–beat and swindler'. Hill asked Birchall if he had any questions for the witness. Birchall asked Macdonald why he called him a swindler. The imprecise reply, as given in the press, was: 'MacDonald said he had his fingers burnt when he was at Woodstock, and that should be sufficient reason.'

Murray had primed the press to expect that Pelly would 'plainly show' that Birchall had extorted money, that 'the whole thing was made palatable by the introduction of a woman claiming to be Burchell's wife', and that 'inducements' had been offered to Pelly 'whereby he could easily be shoved into the angry rapids of the Niagara River below'. During the lunch adjournment, Murray again spoke to the reporters, expounding his theory of a 'villainous conspiracy', and promis-ing 'strong evidence' yet to come. Pelly's restrained court statement must therefore have exasperated the detective. At any rate, immediately after the inquiry closed for the day, he gave yet another briefing. It was now that Murray chose to issue a highly damaging and deceitful statement, in what was perhaps the single most important move in his campaign to see Birchall hang. On the basis of the initial inquest evidence in Princeton, Murray had publicly described Wednesday 19 February as 'the night the corpse is supposed to have been left in the wood'. Yet when he came to interrogate Pelly, Murray found that, if his story was true, then the young man provided a cast-iron alibi for Birchall on 19 February, and all the other days on which the murder might have happened, apart from Monday 17 February, the day Benwell had actually disappeared from view. There was no hard evidence that this really was the day the murder had occurred; nevertheless, as waiting reporters now discovered: 'Detective Murray says there is not the slightest doubt but that Benwell was murdered

during Monday, February 17th.' This bald assertion did exactly
what Murray hoped it would do, starting off a process by
which almost all press commentators would come to accept
the timing of the crime as a given. Murray must have calculated
that it was going to seem deeply incriminating if he could
prove Birchall to have been in the rough vicinity of the
Blenheim swamp on the very day the killing was already
agreed to have taken place.

While Murray was evidently displeased with Pelly's court
testimony, reporters wrote favourably that the witness had
come over as a 'thoroughly honest young Englishman'.
Despite Pelly's extreme tiredness, however, and his importance to the prosecution, Murray required him that night, as
Pelly later wrote, 'to be present at the searching of Burchell's
kit, papers, etc. till 1:30 a. m. when I was again locked into
my room'. At least this would be his last night as a prisoner.

Birchall, unlike Pelly, appeared to be unruffled by the
day's events, sitting 'right through the whole ordeal with an
expression perfectly calm and serenely composed'. The gravity
of his circumstances, however, could hardly have been over-
stated. Despite appearances, Hellmuth had arrived in Niagara
early the day before, but his aid seems to have been minimal.
Birchall had refused to be interrogated by Murray in the police
cells, 'as a lawyer had by some means gained admission', Murray
revealed, 'and told him to keep his mouth shut and say nothing'.
If so, this would seem to have been the only legal advice Birchall
received going into the inquiry, 'Mr. Hill refusing to allow' the
right of 'I. F. Hellmuth of London, Ont., to interview the
suspect'. Hellmuth had then inexplicably failed to appear in
court, so that Birchall was left to manage by himself the
cross-examination of hostile witnesses. Press summaries of the
day's proceedings were bleak for the prisoner:

Everyone should be held innocent until he is proven guilty, and no doubt the court will hold this when Somerset is put on his trial. But it is not too much to say that at present it looks as if the rope were tightening very hard around a murderer's neck.

If the odds looked bad, Birchall nevertheless kept his nerve so successfully that one reporter wrote of him: 'He seems to be the most collected and the most cool individual connected with the whole affair.'

When the doors opened for the second day of the inquiry, 'about three times as many as the room would hold were on hand'. Those who failed to get in were apparently 'satisfied to stand outside in the cold and listen to the meagre news that their friends would bring out as the examination went on'. Pelly was weary and deeply demoralized. When he wrote up his experiences of that day, he acknowledged that after another three hours in the witness box he had been 'almost in tears with utter fatigue and nervousness'. He cannot have been allowed to read up the favourable overnight press reports, as he still felt that his story was hopelessly unconvincing:

my evidence seemed to me to become more and more formal and to contain little or nothing which could be corroborated and I began to wonder if the case against Burchell would be dismissed.

Once more up in the box, Pelly confirmed his lengthy statement of the previous day, and then added details of events still left unaccounted for; that Birchall had stated that Benwell had taken his revolver; that Birchall had claimed to have horses stabled in Toronto; that the missing Englishman, Pickthall, had apparently been in their hotel in New York, and so on.

Besides giving information on these strange and suspicious details, Pelly found himself being questioned about two matters in particular: Birchall's familiarity with the area in which the murder had taken place, and Mrs Birchall's share in her husband's crimes. On the prisoner's knowledge of rural Ontario, Pelly was able to say that Birchall had joked about the little town of Drumbo being 'the most awful place in America', had known that Paris railway station was close to the murder site, and had talked up the 'delightful' social pleasures of picnicking at Pine Pond, mentioning this place both on board the steamer to New York and afterwards in Canada. Pine Pond was the small lake where Birchall had said they could 'drive out four-in-hand when summer came around', supposedly convenient to the Falls, though in truth it lay near to where Benwell's corpse had been found. This new detail suggested to reporters that Birchall had had the murder area in mind long before the crime was committed. Indeed, as most of them mistook Pine Pond for being the very lake where Benwell's killer was thought to have intended to dispose of the corpse, they interpreted Pelly's testimony as all but conclusive evidence of Birchall's guilt.

Pelly was also drawn out on the matter of Mrs Birchall's complicity, and now mentioned that she had 'volunteered' to him, after Birchall's arrest, that 'she could not understand why her husband had worked the farm fraud'. On her return from Paris, she had also said that Birchall had told her that Benwell had been found 'in a seedy worn-out suit as if he had been killed by a tramp and stripped'. She had tended to confirm the impression given in this lie, Pelly noted, by remarking to him that the whole area 'was infested with tramps', and by saying that she knew a lady there who had had to use a gun to save her own life because the place was so dangerous.

Murray was now called back to the witness box to give an account of his search of Birchall's luggage. He had found the keys to Benwell's bags and the receipt for Benwell's two cases left in bond. He presented letters he had found from Pelly to Birchall, including their quasi-legal agreement, and business letters to Birchall from both Benwell and Benwell's father. Murray also confirmed that he had found a certificate that proved Mrs Birchall to be genuinely married to the prisoner. Murray now added that in Paris, Birchall had described Benwell as a man 'given to wine and bragging about his money', another set of details about the victim that Pelly had denied.

After Murray, the Niagara police chief, Mr Young, was asked to give an account of Birchall's arrest. He described finding a gold pen marked 'Conny, N.Y., 1869' in Birchall's luggage, plus a pair of folding scissors in Mrs Birchall's bags. Conny was Benwell's nickname, his middle name being Cornwallis, and the scissors, with a slight nick in them, were said in the press to be just such a pair as might have been used to snip the name tags out of Benwell's clothing.

The evidence against Birchall seemed to dry up at this point. There was even a note of sympathy in the press for a prisoner who had had 'no able attorney to fight for him', and whose own questioning of witnesses, where he attempted it at all, had appeared to be irrelevant. Murray asked that the inquiry be postponed for eight days while he gathered more witnesses, and Hill agreed to this. He remanded Birchall to the county jail at Welland, his case to be resumed on Wednesday 12 March.

Throughout the hearing so far, Florence Birchall had been sequestered at Baldwin's boarding house under constant police guard. It seems to have been true, as one reporter wrote, that 'although she appeared to feel the position of her husband

*The same picture as rendered by a
newspaper engraver.*

Florence Birchall

very keenly she took her own arrest with perfect coolness and
reserve'. As the days passed by, however, it was rumoured that
she was often to be found 'crying bitterly', even 'at times
reaching hysterics'.

Late in the afternoon of Wednesday 5 March, she was
brought before Mr Hill to be arraigned. Reporters who had
earlier wavered over whether to cast her as Birchall's innocent
victim or his immoral consort, unhesitatingly found in her
favour. Here was

a fair-haired little creature, her blue eyes red from recent tears, with an air of refinement from the top of her pretty little head to the sole of her dainty feet, and the soft voice and charming manner of speech characteristic of the English well-bred woman.

The charge read out against her was that she did, 'on or about the 17th February, at Niagara Falls, aid and abet one J. R. Burchell to murder and kill Benwell', and also that after the murder she 'received and did comfort said Burchell contrary to statutes'. Mrs Birchall pleaded 'Not guilty'. The marriage certificate that had removed a slur on her moral character, now proved also to be an important element in her defence. There was a common law presumption at the time that a wife was not responsible for most acts that would otherwise be criminal if she committed them in the presence of her husband. On these grounds, Hill judged that it would not be illegal for Mrs Birchall to have been an accessory after the fact to a murder committed by Birchall. He later conceded to a reporter that she must have been aware of Birchall's swindles, but he believed that 'as his wife, she was bound to shield him in every way of course'. Hill's strict adherence to this doctrine of presumed coercion was not justified by Canadian statutes, which stated straightforwardly that 'every accessory after the fact to murder' was liable to punishment. Nevertheless popular opinion was in Hill's favour, one commentator asking, 'Is it not the nature of woman to cling even to the beast who kicks and maltreats her?' In this spirit Hill confidently declared that the second half of the charge against Mrs Birchall was void, and that all evidence should be restricted to showing how she might have aided and abetted her husband in the murder before it was committed. Even Hill agreed that if she had conspired in advance, this would be a crime.

Detective Murray was only able to provide evidence to the court that concerned Mrs Birchall's actions after Benwell's death. Pelly, meanwhile, required to expand on her capacity to deceive, gave such details as the fact that in Buffalo she had discussed needing to re-paper the farmhouse, telling him how monotonous she found life on the farm. Yet even if this demonstrated that Mrs Birchall had colluded in her husband's 'gigantic' scheme of fraud, as one paper called it, Pelly, too, fell far short of proving that she had had any advance know-ledge that he planned a murder.

Just as Pelly's evidence petered out, Hellmuth appeared in court. Hill interrupted proceedings to describe for him the case so far, after which Murray asked that Mrs Birchall be remanded in jail for a week along with her husband. Hellmuth's first act in the entire inquiry was to reply, on Mrs Birchall's behalf, that as he could see 'no evidence connecting Mrs. Burchell with the crime', she should at the very least be allowed to remain at Mr Baldwin's, 'of course, under police surveillance'. Hill fell right into this trap, agreeing with Hellmuth that 'So far there was practically no evidence connecting Mrs. Burchell with the murder'. In that case, said Hellmuth, abruptly shifting ground, surely Mrs Birchall should never have been arrested in the first place?

Hill's position was suddenly very awkward. To accommo-date Murray, he decided upon a delay, and declared that Mrs Birchall should be brought up the next morning for a further remand. As a sop to Hellmuth, Hill indicated that he would be prepared to accept bail if any were offered, saying that Mrs Birchall might spend at least one further night at Baldwin's. This decision was 'loudly applauded by the crowd present'. The 'fair-haired little creature' had appealed to the sentimen-tality of her immediate audience, amongst whom the belief was 'steadily gaining ground that she was innocent of all connection with the murder'.

Murray, conversely, had hit his first real stumbling block. For fear that Hellmuth might actually get his client discharged, the detective communicated late in the night with the Attorney-General's department in Toronto, and hastily organized that a new arrest warrant for Mrs Birchall be issued in Woodstock, the police area in which the murder had taken place. As a result of these machinations, at four o'clock in the chilly morning of Thursday 6 March, Mr Wills, the Woodstock chief of police, started out for Niagara, paperwork in pocket, ready to rearrest Florence Birchall the instant anyone might set her free.

In court the next morning Murray stood up to request a further remand for Mrs Birchall while Hill waited for a wire from the Attorney-General ruling on her case. Murray also told Hill that he had secured some witnesses, railwaymen, who would offer new evidence against Birchall. Hill decided to reconvene the court in the afternoon, and to bring Birchall back from prison, 'as life was uncertain and these important witnesses might not be available next week'.

Court resumed at one o'clock, with Birchall arraigned first. Only one of Murray's promised witnesses was brought forward. George Hay, a railway brakesman, testified that he had seen Birchall on the platform of Eastwood railway station, about six miles west of Princeton, on the afternoon of Monday 17 February. Birchall, dressed in a checked coat and a 'black curly cap', with muddy shoes and rolled-up trousers, was the only passenger to board the train at Eastwood, getting into the smoking car. Hay said he had discussed with Birchall the fact that his ticket was for Hamilton only, though the train went further, and was scheduled to pass through the Falls at ten past seven. When they arrived at Hamilton, Birchall had jumped off and bought a second ticket to complete his ride to the Falls. Hay said he already 'knew the prisoner by sight'. He had seen him once in 1888, in Woodstock, where Hay then lived. 'Curiosity', said Hay, had drawn his attention at the time to the man talked of as Lord Somerset. He had also recognized Birchall exactly two weeks previously, in the middle of the night, travelling with Pelly, whom Hay pointed out across the court room, and 'a lady', on the nine minutes past two train from Suspension Bridge over to the Canadian side. This had been the night that the Birchalls and Pelly had gone to see *Faust up to Date* at the Star Theatre in Buffalo. Hay's evidence was compelling.

An astrakhan cap, taken from the prisoner's trunk, was produced, which Hay said he recognized. Suddenly the tension in court was broken. 'The placing of the cap on the prisoner's head brought out some laughter, and the prisoner's face was covered with a broad smile.' Hill later told a reporter that Birchall's 'assurance' over the cap was 'something astonishing,' and added, 'I am inclined to believe the fellow's head is turned.' After the court settled down again, Hay mentioned that he had already identified Birchall that morning 'in the lock-up'. Hellmuth now at last spoke on Birchall's behalf, asking how this identification had been conducted. Hay replied that Detective Murray and the Niagara police chief, Mr Young, had asked him whether he thought he could recognize the man from his train. 'We went to the lock-up and I did recognize the prisoner as the same man.' Hay agreed that Birchall had not been removed from his cell for this procedure. There was nothing more to be said. Hill remanded Birchall to the county jail for seven days and Young removed the prisoner from the court.

Mrs Birchall was now ushered in to replace him. Her 'petite and pretty figure', noted one reporter, was hidden by a dark green Newmarket coat, 'lined with old gold silk topped with a coachman's beaver collar, a feathered hat, with a lace veil concealing her blue eyes from the gaze of the spectators'. The Attorney-General's telegram had arrived. When she was 'nicely seated' Hill said to her, 'Mrs. Burchell, I have brought you down to court to notify you, that on request from the Crown, you will be remanded to gaol for seven days.' Mrs Birchall 'looked wistfully at the Magistrate', and Hellmuth leapt to his feet to address Hill in an 'imploring way'. There was still no evidence against his client. Surely, said Hellmuth, as the presiding magistrate, Hill was duty bound to allow bail. Hill confessed, what was already clear, that he personally agreed with Hellmuth; but he was compelled to inform him: 'The responsibility has been removed from me. The Attorney-General has stepped in.' Hellmuth argued that this was an 'absurdity', but Hill repeated simply that he 'could not help himself'. Hellmuth 'raved and Mrs. Burchell wept', until Hellmuth finally put it to Hill that Mrs Birchall be allowed to spend one further night at Baldwin's, as ever under surveillance, while he repaired to Toronto to argue for bail with the Attorney-General himself. This was a canny compromise, and Hill capitulated. Excitement 'ran high' in the court room as the spectators noisily applauded. Murray, temporarily outsmarted, slipped away to make straight for Toronto himself.

A reporter waiting in the big city recorded that at twenty past eight that evening, 'Government Detective John Murray and a well-dressed young man stepped off the cars' at the railway depot. The well-dressed young man was 'none other than Douglass R. Pelley, who considers himself one of the luckiest young Englishmen in the land of the living today'. Pelly and Murray repaired to the Hotel Metropole, where the 'suave' desk clerk and the 'loungers' in the lobby were all 'electrified' by the identities of the new guests. The two of them had supper there, and then went for a preliminary meeting with the Deputy Attorney-General. After this, they returned to the hotel to receive 'a small army of reporters'.

A Toronto *Mail* representative asked:

'Did you suspect anything, Mr. Pelly, on account of the equivocation of Burchell?'

'No, but I see it in a different light now.'

'Do you think he was in league with any other person?'

'I think there is no doubt that Burchell was in league with a man in England who was to send out young men of means to this country.'

Pelly may only have suspected complicity in the Cheltenham agent, Mr Mellersh, with whom he himself had first communicated, but Murray's view of the case was considerably more sinister. He was unable to let the matter rest, and broke in on Pelly's interview to say:

'I have no doubt that there is a gang of these fellows at work in this business. I believe that many men have been induced to come out here, and have been murdered and nothing has ever been heard of them.'

Murray issued a second corrective to a statement of Pelly's, in another of their interviews that night. Pelly, asked about Mrs Birchall's part in her husband's crimes, made it clear that he had no doubt whatever that the woman knew perfectly well that he was a confidence man of no mean order; that he lived by fleecing strangers, and young Englishmen in particular.

When pressed, however, Pelly 'shuddered' to think that Mrs Birchall, 'with her cultured and ladylike ways', could possibly have known of her husband's 'intention to murder Benwell'. Again Murray intervened. He by no means shared 'these fine sentiments,' he said, but was 'convinced of the woman's knowledge of the whole crime'.

If the two men disagreed about the extent of Mrs Birchall's involvement, they were nevertheless both efficiently promoting the belief not merely that Birchall was guilty of Benwell's murder, but that the murder had been premeditated – that a 'whole' plan had existed which encompassed the killing. Yet there was still no hard evidence of Birchall's guilt, and there was absolutely none, even if he did commit the crime, to show that he had nurtured a prior 'intention to murder'. Murray, however, keenly fostered exactly this supposition:

Some of the victims may have been amongst the scores of unrecognized humanity fished from the turbid Niagara and buried in Lewiston's lonely cemetery, or they may have been lured to what will henceforth be known as the 'Swamp of Death,' and shot down from behind, as was poor Benwell. It is certain that he was killed in broad daylight between 11 and 3 o'clock of Monday, Feb 17, and that the deed was perpetrated by Burchell, alone and unaided, with no eyewitness to the deed but that of Omnipotence and perchance a stray hawk or owl perched in one of the cedar boughs above.

Murray failed to explain his insistence here on Birchall's solitary guilt, after his apparent certainty in previous interviews that Birchall had had a gang behind him; but the desire, indeed the passion of the detective to secure a guilty verdict for the man already captured, was obvious. This particularly ghastly speech was delivered to a reporter for the Woodstock *Sentinel-Review*. Murray must have understood that his words would be spread across the pages of the primary newspaper from amongst whose ordinary male readership Birchall's trial jury would ultimately be drawn.

Many stories had started to pepper the press about young English gentlemen who had gone out to Canada only to disappear without trace, and Murray's faith in his own claims about a gang running a 'diabolical scheme' would seem to be confirmed by the efforts he now went to to keep Pelly safe. Despite the ending of Pelly's 'kind of open arrest', he was not freed from the 'constant company of a police man'. His experience of custody quietly shifted from a type of imprisonment to an exercise in protection. He was informed that the authorities believed Birchall had many friends who might attempt to cause him to act in such a way as to discredit his own evidence. As a result it was considered 'important' to 'deter unsuitable people' from even approaching him. Pelly later wrote that he had also been aware of rumours 'that there was a gang of men who had sworn to do me in before Burchell was tried'. Murray knew as much as anyone about organized criminal violence in Ontario. When he had at last satisfied himself that Pelly was in no way implicated in Birchall's crimes, he felt it imperative to provide him with a twenty-four-hour guard. The principal witness in an increasingly notable murder case needed to be kept alive.

6. Terrible Domestic Calamity

He bought *The Times* newspaper, and looked instinctively at the second column, with a morbid interest in the advertisements of people missing – sons, brothers and husbands who had left their homes, never to return or be heard of more.

    Mary Elizabeth Braddon, *Lady Audley's Secret*, 1862

In 1883 Reuters agents and correspondents around the world received a circular from headquarters that was to become famous within the company, listing all the kinds of disasters on which they would henceforth be required to report. These included 'shipwrecks attended with loss of life' and 'duels between, and suicides of persons of note', as well as 'murders of a sensational or atrocious character'. The London *Times*, with its own sprinkling of foreign correspondents, had made great efforts to resist Reuters in the early years of the service; but annual spending on telegraphy, and especially on its most expensive form via the submarine cable network, took up a worrying portion of a serious newspaper's budget. After a while even *The Times*, not without resentment, was forced to subscribe to Reuters in order to have any hope of leading its rivals in its standards of international coverage. The conflict between newspapers and the wire services was what led papers to start billing stories, where possible, as having been written by their 'own correspondent'. It was as a result of the relationship, however uneasy, between Reuters and *The Times*, that on 4 March 1890 the Birchall case took its first step towards

The Battery and The Boiler.

by R.M.Ballantyne.

R. M. Ballantyne imagines hazards in the laying of submarine cables.

genuine transatlantic notoriety. Amongst a set of seven 'Foreign and Colonial News' telegrams, there appeared, on page five of *The Times*, an item with the headline, 'Murder of an Englishman in Canada'.

The next day a second Reuters telegram about the case drew attention to what the British audience was likely to find most disturbing in the whole story: 'A statement made in connection with the murder of Mr. Benwell tends to show that a plot was concocted in England to lure young men to Canada and there murder them for their money.' In short, information was being uncovered about a confoundingly heinous business operation.

As this news reverberated through the British press, the Pelly family received various offers of help, including an anxiously florid note from a Mr Cuthbertson, written on heavily illustrated, out-of-date company notepaper:

Dominion Organ & Piano Company
Bowmanville
Ont.

Mar. 22 188–

30 Norfolk Street
London

Rev. Pelly. M. A.

Rev and Dear Sir,

You will no doubt be surprised, (tho I trust not annoyed) at receiving this from me, an entire stranger. I desired to congratulate you on the escape of your son from the clutches of a fiend, whose rascality seems to be unbounded. Being a resident of Woodstock for four years past, I am thoroughly conversant with the antics of Birchall while in Woodstock. I have been in England but three weeks but return the week after next to Woodstock. If I can be of any use to you or your family, my services at [*sic*] entirely at your disposal.

Again congratulating you all

Believe me Sir

Very Respectfully Yours,

S. F. Cuthbertson

30 Norfolk Street

London

The family had already been reassured by an intervention from a rather more elevated sphere:

42 Eaton Terrace
London
S. W.

March 7th, 1890

Dear Mr Pelly,

I was much concerned to see in the press telegrams that your son had been a victim of Burchell, and sincerely glad that he escaped, though very narrowly, from his companion's fate. I have telegraphed to Lord Stanley of Preston, the Governor General, that Mr Douglas Pelly is a man of high character, thoroughly trustworthy, and deserving of every consideration, and I have no doubt that he will receive the fullest sympathy in Canada, and that any assistance which he may need will readily be given to him. I trust that his evidence will be instrumental in bringing the murderer to justice.

If there is anything further that I can do for you or for him in the matter, be kind enough to let me know.

Yours very truly,

Robert G. W. Herbert

Pelly's father circulated this letter amongst friends and relatives, scribbling in at the end: 'This is from Sir Robt Herbert, Under Secy of State for the Colonies. Is it not splendid. Douglas will be watched over by the very highest in Canada. I knew Sir Robt. & asked him to help us.' A few days later, the Canadian press reported that a letter from Sir Robert Herbert had been forwarded to Mr Mowat, the Attorney-General for Ontario.

Others wrote to Pelly's parents revealing curious details of Birchall's past. One particularly interesting correspondent was a provincial actor called Charles Emery:

8 Francis Cottages
Lower Edmonton N

8. 3. 90

R. P. Pelly, Esq,

Sir,

Permit me to thank you for your courtesy.

I have not now the slightest doubt about the person I know being the accused; being in the theatrical profession, to which he formerly belonged for a short period, I was promised most lucrative engagement's in America & Canada, where, he informed me, he was holding the post of Manager to one of the first class of proprietors; I advertized a house for sale, intending with the proceeds to try my fortune in America, and even wrote to the tenant of the house that I was going abroad in the spring, but other business fortunately prevented my carrying out the idea.

I shared apartments with Burchell at some of the towns we visited while touring and learned many of his private matters, therefore should necessity arise I could give some important clues to his antecedents—swindling lodgings—theatre proprietor &c; on one occasion he and another adventurer (now in London, & whom I firmly believe to be in Co with him in some of these affairs) threatened me with loaded sticks in a small room & made me sign a document in their favour, but at that time I did not think this Burchell was so bad as the other—afterwards the other party decamped and Burchell, protesting himself a much injured party, took over the entire management & lesseeship of the theatre then under their management—then came Burchell's exodus, leaving billposters, landlord & others unsatisfied; so you perceive, Sir, altho' young in years, he was scarcely so in crime.

I think I informed you that I had forwarded a photo to Toronto & I have also sent a short note to Scotland Yard. Apologising for troubling you, I remain, Sir, Yrs respectfully
          Chas P. Emery

In Emery's sentence about loaded sticks – sticks weighted with lead – the word 'threatened' was a correction inked over the top of 'assailed'. If the incident in question really took place, and was violent enough for 'assailed' to be the first word to come to Emery's mind, and if he knew Birchall to be a crook, then it is some sort of testament to Birchall's powers of persuasion that Emery was still prepared to consider surrendering his house and position in England to go abroad with such a man.

Another illuminating letter arrived from a businessman called N. F. Robarts:

City Liberal Club
Walbrook, E. C.

7th March 1890

Dear Mrs. Pelly,

I just learn what is so extraordinary that I think you will like to know. The J. Burchell who took your son out to Canada, was until quite lately in the employ of Mayall & Co. Ld. Photographers Bond St with which business I am connected.

I knew the man quite well & we dismissed him only a few weeks ago, principally because we found him lying.

He represented to us when engaged that he married the daughter of the goods Manager of the L. N. W. R. at whose house he lived. He had very good testimonials when he came to us about six mos ago. He must have met your son almost immediately he left us. I should much like to know how you became first connected with him.

He is a well educated University man (Oxford I think) & we considered that he was rather coming down to do the work he did for us getting actors &c to come to be photographed – it never struck me even last night when I saw the name in the paper – but I heard from Mayall's about it this morning.

Yours very sincerely
N. F. Robarts

Mayall & Co. was a long-established and famous business. Mayall himself, amongst all London's portrait photographers, had come to the fore in 1860, when he asked for permission to take a set of relatively informal *carte-de-visite* images of Queen Victoria and her family. She thought him 'the oddest man I ever saw', but agreed, and the subsequent royal pictures not only sold in their hundreds of thousands, but were credited with launching in Britain what would soon be a hugely popular new photographic format. In a less exalted context Birchall's job with the company, in 1889, required him to persuade theatre stars that the publicity arising from the sale of their photographs was viable recompense for the bother of sitting for them. It was not customary at the time for the subject in such a transaction to be paid.

Robarts wrote again to the Pellys a few days later, when he had informed himself a little better about Mayall's erstwhile employee:

Rosebrae
Woodford, Essex

11th Mch 1890

Dear Mrs. Pelly,

I was much interested in your letter. I find Birchall left the business on about 31st Dec—I thought it had been rather later. I should like to see his photograph if your correspondent has one. I have made enquiry & find he would never be photographed when at Mayall's. If you can get me the ones you refer to to see (if they are of him) I will return them at once.

I find after he left in Dec.r he was staying at Morley's hotel & a man I know dined there with him & an American "Colonel."

The two talked of going to America & wanted the other man to go with them. It might be interesting to find out who this associate was—perhaps it could be learned at Morley's Hotel—my friend did not remember the name. I see the papers say it is not known if he had associates—but I dare say you know more than appears in the papers.

I see also that he could not be found in London last year— now if he was at Mr Stevenson's & with us under his own name I should have thought his creditors could have easily found him.

Curiously too I have a friend who was in Canada last year, who stayed with a Mr Currie who had a private Secy named Somerset who swindled him & whom the Canadian police wanted for other things.

My friend expects this is the same man—but no doubt if this is so the Canadian police know all about it. Naturally I am very curious to see all that is proved & shall watch the papers with interest. I can't help thinking there is some insanity in the matter—he was such a quiet looking young fellow. I hope you have good news from Douglas—it will be a heavy strain on him.

Yours sincerely,

N. F. Robarts

The Mayall job may have been 'rather coming down' for Birchall, but as well as supplying him with a modest income, it must have represented an enjoyable challenge to his verbal gifts, while keeping him parasitically connected to the theatre, to which he was evidently very drawn. Eventually Birchall's lies got him sacked, but as this happened after he had opened his Canadian negotiations, it seems likely that he no longer cared to be retained anyway. In all this, Robarts wondered why Birchall's creditors had not caught up with him, but Robarts himself had silently corrected his spelling of Birchall's name between his two letters, and Birchall seems to have adopted the false version, Burchell, when he came back from Canada in 1889, precisely in order to protect himself from being hunted down. Though to those who knew the correct spelling he could have explained away the new one as a naturally occurring error, he had a ready justification when later challenged on this point. The two spellings were used in different branches of his family, he said, and he himself had adopted both, 'So that in case anything was willed to him in either name he would have no legal difficulty in securing it.'

Robarts's second letter gave evidence of Birchall having tried out his emigration swindle on yet another young man that January, even mentioning the colonel, whom Pelly had also met. The inverted commas that Robarts applied to this man's rank almost certainly reflected a widespread understanding at the time that the American civil war had led to a plethora of men sporting over-inflated military credentials. However, though Robarts had independent knowledge that Birchall was a dubious character, and suspected his American associate, his suggestion that there might be 'some insanity in the matter' reflected a reasonable puzzlement at the entire story. It certainly struck some observers that if Birchall really was guilty of Benwell's murder, then the crime was out of all proportion to any discoverable motive for committing it.

The various letters sent to the Pellys tended to open with congratulations, so that for a correspondence inspired by a murder, they have an oddly celebratory air. Florence Birchall's family, by contrast, and especially her father, David Stevenson, were placed in a grim position by unfolding news of the case.

Stevenson was known as 'one of the most esteemed railway men in England'. His career had started in 1837, the year he turned sixteen, and also the year that Queen Victoria, barely older, had come to the throne. After a rackety, Dickensian childhood, with not one but two substitute fathers quite the equals for wickedness of Mr Murdstone, Stevenson had found employment as first clerk to the first manager of the London and Birmingham Railway. He would in time rise through the ranks to a position of great prominence as manager of the vast quantities of goods traffic that ran, at this period, through Camden Station in north London.

In a letter to a close friend Stevenson once tried to give a sense of how overwhelming this job actually was. As ever, he said, goods were 'rolling in upon us unrelentingly', to be 'tumbled out' of the trains, then to 'pour through our sheds', where they would be sorted out on to horse-drawn wagons. The different products mentioned are striking in variety: anchors, beer, blankets from Witney, bobbins, bonnets, bottles and blacking bottles; butter, buttons, cables, cannon balls, Scottish canvas and Worcestershire carpets; American clocks and British clogs, clothing for soldiers and corn 'tons on tons'; 'thousands of tons' of cotton goods from the 'clicking, snorting factories of Lancashire'; crates from Staffordshire, and Sheffield cutlery 'from Birmingham, in bewildering quantities'; fish, flax, flour, furniture, glue, grease, grates and grindstones; guano, gum, gun-barrels, gutta percha, hides for tanning 'and no end of other stuff to tan them'; hops packed up in 'tightly stuffed pockets', stag horns, ice, ironstone and iron bedsteads; Nottingham lace and Scottish linen, and 'hundreds of tons' of meat and potatoes; nine thousand head of animals weekly, sent to Camden 'to feed the cockneys'; plus six hundred thousand tons of coal 'to light the fires to cook the grub';

needles 'in awfully heavy little packages', oil, perfume, pianos and pitch; pumice-stone and reaping hooks, and Coventry ribbons and Coventry watches; salt provisions, biscuits, wines and spirits for voyages in 'astounding' quantities; raw silk to go up to Macclesfield, manufactured silk coming back down again; sugar and tea and elephant tusks, and wax, thread and leather for the bootmakers of Northampton; toys for the wives of manufacturers, beeswax, twine, and woollen bales from Yorkshire; plus the terrors of the occasional live tiger or bear, and the bother of the occasional unclaimed corpse.

In 1887 Stevenson began writing an account of his working life, which he called *Fifty Years on the London and North Western Railway*. He described how he regularly saw members of his own workforce run down, crushed, mangled, minced and strewn about the tracks, squashed, decapitated, burnt, and in other ways maimed or killed through an endless series of accidents involving the trains. These disasters prompted some of the frequent religious reflections to dot his writing. In one single-paragraph essay he described the profound relief to him of his weekly day of rest. On a Sunday, he wrote, 'there is time to be oneself', and to 'quiet the poor torn and weary spirit', when

the gas of the world, which has puffed up thoughtless impulses, and carried us high away into the clouds of danger and temptation, is turned off for the day, and we walk on *terra firma*. The sins of the week descend also with our balloon and lie in their deformity around us. We gaze and deplore and resolve; and, remembering former deplorings and resolutions, pray for better strength.

Chastened meditations of this nature give an idea of how hard it must have been for Stevenson to contemplate the possibility, inescapably laid before him, that he might in some way have helped to smooth his son-in-law's criminal path.

It was beyond question that Birchall had successfully exploited Stevenson's name in order to borrow respectability. Mr Robarts's letter concerning Birchall's employment at Mayall's confirms this, as would Pelly's father, who told a reporter that he had not altogether liked Birchall's appearance when he visited Saffron Walden, but, 'Burchell at length overcame the doubts of the Rev. Mr. Pelly and convinced him that he was bona fide by talking of father-in-law David Stephenson.' Pelly himself later directly blamed the old railwayman, saying that it would appear he had been 'very wrong in not giving us even a slight hint that we were dealing with an unsatisfactory man'. This was a difficult charge to answer.

There could be no defence in saying that Stevenson had been unaware of his son-in-law's duplicitous side. Almost the moment news of Benwell's murder reached England, a reporter tracked Stevenson down, only to be treated to the old man's rattled outpourings. The Canadian press picked up this interview and reproduced it verbatim under headlines such as, 'A Father's Sorrow', 'Her Father Opposed the Union', and, 'The Old Gentleman Heart-Broken by the Revelations Concerning his Rascally Son-in-law – He was Opposed to his Daughter's Marriage, but is Confident of her Innocence'. Stevenson explained that he had been against Florence's marriage because

I looked upon Burchell as an unprincipled fellow, but of manners so amiable that it was difficult to believe that he could commit such a terrible crime as murder. Still of that kind of people the worst may always be expected. It was with extreme reluctance that I agreed to my daughter going to Canada, where Burchell pretended to have made arrangements to settle on a farm.

Soon after Stevenson gave another interview on the subject in which he was induced to be more specific, now describing what had essentially been an elopement. His daughter and Reginald Birchall, known as 'Rex', had met at a party and 'instantly became attached'. Though Birchall had 'seemed a thorough gentleman and had plenty of money', Stevenson had been disturbed when after only three months the young man had asked for permission to marry immediately, giving as his reason the fact that he had urgent business to see to on his estates in Canada. Stevenson had refused to give consent, feeling that this was 'too sudden to be proper'. He may well also have had qualms about the fact that Birchall was only twenty-two, if Stevenson even knew this, while his daughter was rising thirty. Though Birchall had furnished him with a letter of recommendation from an eminent Oxford churchman, Stevenson wanted more time to look into his previous career. Florence was unhappy at the delay, but all talk of a wedding ceased, and Stevenson assumed that the love-struck pair were biding their time until he was ready. One day, Stevenson told the reporter,

I was surprised to hear my daughter had been married secretly the day before. Two of my daughters were present at the ceremony, which was by special license. The couple never came to see me but went direct to Canada. I received letters from each of them while they were there.

He added that they had eventually come back again, whereupon he had forgiven them. Birchall and Florence Stevenson had married on 19 November 1888, in Croydon, south east London. In order to have travelled all the way to Woodstock before the year was out, as they did, they must have left for

Canada almost immediately after the ceremony. It follows that Birchall's switch of name to Somerset, and therefore Florence's too, was a necessity planned in advance of their wedding.

As he told the story of his daughter's marriage, Stevenson 'spoke in broken accents', and struck the reporter as being 'overwhelmed'.

My only desire now is to succour my daughter, my favourite child, beloved by everybody for her sweet, loving disposition. She cabled me today for money in her dire distress, and I sent her £40 and hope she will return at once, but fear she will be detained to give evidence.

Stevenson was clearly unaware, as he spoke, of the exact seriousness of his daughter's position. A Canadian newspaper editor was simultaneously reflecting that 'One of two things is certain. Either Mrs. Burchell is very innocent or she is very guilty.' Her father, trusting to her innocence, seemed to have had no idea that concerted efforts were under way within parts of the Canadian legal system to have his child tried on a capital charge.

In early 1890, aged sixty-nine, with a large, feckless family to support, Stevenson was still labouring for the L. N. W. R. One year later his editor would add a depressing little end-note to the railway memoir, saying that the old man's career had finished when 'a terrible domestic calamity befell Mr Stevenson'. This calamity had a swift impact on his working life. Shortly after his press interview Stevenson must have grasped more completely the nature of his daughter's plight and within a fortnight he had packed up his travel bags and was journeying to the New World.

★

When the Benwell family first read about the murder in a newspaper report, there was at least room for hope that the story would turn out to be a mistake. Colonel Benwell sent a cablegram to the authorities in Niagara, immediately reprinted in the press, in which he anxiously asked 'if it was true his son had been murdered'. Canadian newspapers were also able to report that Colonel Benwell had taken a close hand in organizing his son's affairs, Detective Murray allowing them to print much of the correspondence between the Benwells and Birchall that he had found in Birchall's kit. These letters showed how similar to Pelly's the Benwell family's experiences had been, as they attempted to come to a settled understanding with Birchall. As early as 10 December 1889 Colonel Benwell had written: 'I will be glad to have the earliest intimation when you have quite fixed the exact date of departure.' This intervention did not yield results. Three and a half weeks later, on 3 January, Benwell himself wrote, in tones of civil annoyance, a letter that acquires a chilling secondary meaning in retrospect: 'I must say I should like to know as soon as possible, if not the exact date of my departure, at least as near as possible, that I may know what time I have at my disposal.'

On 4 March Murray informed Canadian reporters that he had, the day before, 'sent a cablegram to Cheltenham, Eng., to the father of the murdered man, to come here at once'. If so, this cablegram never arrived. On 7 March Colonel Benwell sat down and wrote Pelly's father an agitated, poorly punctuated letter, in thick black borders. After starting with formalities directed to Pelly's maternal aunt, and after noting an intent to be restrained, by the end Colonel Benwell had said much more than he meant to:

Iseultdene
Cheltenham

March 7.th 1890

My dear Sir,

Thank you for your letter of the 4th inst. which I got yesterday and please thank Lady Snagge for hers which I received this morning, I hope to write to herself later on, meantime no doubt she will see this letter as she appears to be staying with or near you. I cannot bring myself to enter very fully into details but you will no doubt obtain them from the papers during the next few days as I have gone through the painful ordeal of being interviewed by two or three Newspaper Correspondents to whom I thought it advisable to give a correct version of the whole sad tale from beginning to end as far as I knew—for the present it is sufficient for me simply to say that I took every precaution against fraud, but it never entered my head to guard my son against murder.

Having written so much I may as well go on further and tell you that my son was taken aback at Liverpool on finding your son appearing on the scene thinking that Burchell was playing a fast and loose game by having two strings to his bow in the matter of the partnership, and he called upon Burchell for an explanation and he wrote to me from Queenstown to say that all was perfectly satisfactorily explained Burchell having told him that Pelly was a friend of his travelling for his health and was going to stay with him, Pelly being the son of a Clergyman and was an Underwriter at Lloyds, drawing a large salary—

On last Tuesday night I received a letter from Burchell undated from Niagara Falls but the envelope bore the Niagara

Falls postmark of Feb. 20th stating that they had a pleasant trip, my son was well & in good spirits and pleased with everything, so much so that he thought it best to <u>complete</u> the Partnership at once without waiting for <u>my stipulated trial</u> of <u>three months</u>—that the Deed of Partnership was duly executed and requesting the money to be sent at once—here then was the clear "motive" for the murder for I never believed until I saw Burchell's arrest that he could have had a hand in it for the sake of the paltry sum of money in my son's possession & his clothes, jewellery &c—this letter is positive proof of Burchell's guilt and I sent it with the fullest particulars of all I know to the Secretary of State for the Colonies on the night I received that letter—

I am glad to find that your mind has been relieved as regards your son's safety from his telegraphing to you that he "was all right"—

I will be very thankful for any news you may receive from him for I have heard nothing except through the newspapers, though I telegraphed to Burchell on Monday asking if it was true that my son was murdered and I telegraphed again on Tuesday to the Chief of Police at Niagara Falls when I saw that Burchell had been arrested requesting them to communicate with me as to my son's murder but nothing has so far turned up—

From what I gather from the papers, my son must have been murdered on the 17.th inst. and was actually dead when Burchell wrote that letter—in which he also said that my dear boy was writing by the same mail—

In fact I never heard from him after he left New York on the 15th Feby.

Yours very truly,

<u>F. W. Benwell</u>

There was, as this letter highlighted, a crucial difference between the arrangements Birchall had struck with his two victims. Benwell had wished to see over Birchall's businesses before giving him any money. Pelly, by contrast, had accepted Birchall's word as a gentleman, and had written out a cheque in advance. Pelly was derided in the Canadian press for showing this much trust. Under the heading 'The Gullibility of Englishmen', one reporter declared that he had fallen for a ridiculously improbable lie if he believed that there was any farm near Niagara, 'heated by steam and lighted by gas, and with barns illuminated by electricity'. Pelly's supposedly legal agreement with Birchall inspired another acid commentator to note that the terms were absurdly favourable to the pupil, adding that it was to be hoped Pelly would go back home again as soon as possible, there to be 'taken care of by his friends'. Yet, as matters fell out, Pelly's gullibility seemed to have helped preserve him from danger. When they all left England, it had been Benwell who set the challenge of still needing to be milked.

A month after his first letter to Pelly's father, Colonel Benwell sent another:

Iseultdene
Cheltenham

April 7.th 1890

Dear Mr. Pelly,

I hope you have not thought me remiss & unmindful in not thanking you before now for sending me the copies of your son's letters, "Nos. 3 & 4," but my mind & pen have been so much engaged—

I have to thank you now for another which I received yesterday & which I forwarded on to Mrs. Pelly, Hollington, as you requested, by last evening's post.

I can fully understand what a trying time your son is having, but he has had what I can only look upon as a most providential escape of being another victim, for there can be no doubt had a favourable opportunity offered he would have been murdered also, not only for the money he had already parted with but there were ~~so many~~ several other obvious reasons for Burchell wishing to put him out of the way which he would not have scrupled to have done—

With those who knew our beloved boy he was a favourite & was much liked—generous & kind hearted to a degree, frank & open, & to strangers usually polite; I can now however understand how it was that your son did not take to him on the voyage, but at first it surprised me greatly why they did not compare notes & so at least have found the Villain out in time to ~~spend~~ save his life—even now it seems strange to me that neither appears to have suspected anything <u>very</u> wrong.

The evidence seems amply conclusive & to justify the expectation that justice will be met but that will be but poor satisfaction to us and no consolation at all—and I hope I may be spared the painful ordeal of appearing as a witness at the trial & the inconvenience of a trip to Canada especially as I have many family ties & engagements at home & besides which my health has not been of the best for some time past.

My wife joins me in kind regards to you & Mrs. Pelly,

Yours very sincerely,

F. W. Benwell

Colonel Benwell could not suppress a faint hint of hostility in this letter, not least in the judiciously corrected but still legible comment that there were 'so many other obvious reasons' besides money why Birchall might have wished to murder Pelly too.

In the days after news of the killing reached England, Revd Raymond Pelly, David Stevenson and Colonel Benwell all felt compelled to speak to the newspapers. In Colonel Benwell's first letter to Pelly's father he actually opened by referring him to his newspaper interviews for information, so painful a task was it for him to face writing to the man whose son had survived. In their press interviews all three men contradicted details they had read in previous press articles. They understood the unreliability of the medium, but seem nevertheless to have felt that it was an important means by which stories could be put straight again. Colonel Benwell, in particular, wished to stop a rogue theory invoking *crime passionnel*, saying, 'I wish you would also deny the insinuation of my son's improper relations with Mrs. Burchell. He met her only once before he went to America. That was in her father's house in Norwood.' Beyond simple corrections, however, there was a more complicated aspect to their various attempts at managing how the story was told. In each case, the prevailing sense is that they hoped to influence how the tale would later be pinned down, thousands of miles away, in a series of crammed court rooms in Canada.

At the same time that the Pelly, Stevenson and Benwell families were being approached, reporters in England naturally attempted to discover all they could of Birchall's background. Few of those who might have spoken authoritatively about him were immediately willing to do so, but as the weeks passed by, a fairly consistent set of anecdotes began to appear in the press. It was established that Birchall had originally

Birchall as a student.

grown up in Church Kirk, near Accrington in Lancashire, where his father had been rector. Revd Joseph Birchall had died in 1878, and since then his son had had a 'most romantic career'.

Birchall's time at Lincoln College, Oxford, where he had gone up in the spring of 1886, had been 'unduly brief'. He was remembered as having been an excellent pianist and a member of the Lincoln football team, but also for having frequently been 'mad drunk'. He had set up an illegal club called the Black and Tans, whose members had driven carriages around the countryside at great speeds 'in defiance of all rules and regulations'. Though Birchall had been an excellent horseman, he was said to have killed a horse 'while driving home from Eynsham against time'. He had also been notorious for his prize bulldog, Bill, whom he kept to scare away those tradesmen foolish enough to come to his rooms to make him settle his debts. Bill, apparently a 'savage brute', had once, 'when in company with his master, worried and killed a pig, for which the owner claimed £5 damages'.

Even in the accounts of Birchall's detractors, it is clear that he got by at Oxford largely on immense charm. He had been known there, above all, for his 'absolutely unlimited and totally unrestrained propensity for lying', telling 'fictions of the most vain and purposeless character. He lied because it was a pleasure to him to lie.' Yet he was attractively 'daring and self-possessed', and, coupled with a keen intellect, had had 'a sort of wild anarchic generosity'. It was said that wherever he went the number of friends he had made had been 'perfectly astonishing'. Birchall had appealed to many people in Oxford, through oddities ranging from his desire to start up a circus to his preference for leaving buildings by their windows. By the time he was asked to leave, he had made himself known throughout the city.

When Dr Merry, the rector of Lincoln College, finally allowed himself to be interviewed about Birchall, he declared, remarkably, that the young man's downfall had been the more lamentable because he had been 'a brilliant young fellow'. Merry implied that Lincoln had allowed Birchall to pursue his abominable career at Oxford much longer than might be expected, because the college had hoped he would eventually settle to work, and expected much from him if he did. It had taken nearly two years for them to accept that he had gone 'irretrievably to the dogs'. In essence, Birchall's greatest

Birchall's name removed from the Lincoln College Order Book.

difficulty had been that he had joined the fast set at Oxford without having adequate means to keep up. One acquaintance recalled that, after being sent down, Birchall had made a habit of entering into expensive schemes or negotiations, only to pull out at the last moment. 'These actions, apparently, had no purpose except to feed his vanity and give an impression of wealth and influence.' Another corroborated this, describing how Birchall had once, purely for fun, begun the process of buying a brewery, though he had had almost no money to his name. After Oxford, Birchall had worked for a time as a theatre manager in Burton-on-Trent, where he was remembered as having been a 'showy and plausible' character, handling 'any unpleasant incident with a sort of reckless bonhomie'.

Beyond these details there were many rumours about Birchall's previous liaisons with women. There was supposed to have been a jilted bride in Pembrokeshire who had died of a broken heart and had been buried in her wedding dress. It was also suggested that Birchall had once been engaged to a young actress named Carrie Terry, who had 'died through choking by a piece of rabbit bone'. In addition to these stories, Birchall's kit, when examined in Niagara, had proved to contain many letters dating from his time as an agent for Mayall's photographic company, seemingly kept by him because they demonstrated that he had had fleeting contact with famous actresses, such as Sarah Bernhardt and Ellen Terry, with whom he had negotiated for their pictures.

His financial circumstances proved particularly difficult for reporters to untangle, though one article claimed that in 1888 he had sold out his patrimony to his sister Maud. This was a process whereby one person would make over part or all of a future inheritance to another in return for an agreed sum less than the worth of the inheritance, but payable immediately. The figures quoted by the press suggested that Birchall had received three thousand seven hundred and fifty pounds for an inheritance of four thousand, due to come to him in May of 1891; and this story seemed to be validated by reports that before he left for Canada the first time he had paid off at least some of his creditors in Oxford. Along with the letters from actresses, in Birchall's kit Detective Murray had found what he described to pressmen as a bogus bank book, supposedly issued by the Paris Banking Company in 1888, and declaring Birchall's credit at the end of that year to be four thousand pounds. This was just the sort of item, Murray explained, that confidence men carried to mislead their dupes. Birchall's address within it had been given as 'R. Burchell, Esq., Buscut Rectory, Lechlade'.

Buscot Rectory was located some two miles up the river Thames from William Morris's retreat at Kelmscott, and was the home of Revd Oswald Birchall, Birchall's half-brother, described in the press as his 'former guardian'. A diligent reporter was eventually able to establish that when Birchall's father died, a 'very slight and inadequate provision was made for his widow', while 'the great bulk of the funds and property was to be divided between the two sons'. In Birchall's case this money had been 'strictly tied up' until he was twenty-five. At the point that his father died, therefore, both Birchall and his mother were left relatively impoverished. Birchall became a member of Oswald's household at Buscot, where he would go for school holidays, no longer sharing a home with his mother.

Revd Oswald Birchall was a quarter of a century older than Reginald, and had a wife ten years older still. He had been rector at Buscot for many years, and was a cohort of William Morris's in the work of preserving ancient buildings. Morris's daughter May later remembered Oswald Birchall as having been an inspiring and saintly man, extremely poor and frugal, yet willing to share anything he could with those still poorer than himself. He was also a militant socialist, defying the local gentry in order to allow Morris to deliver anti-government addresses to the Buscot field-labourers. Oswald Birchall wrote letters over several years to a socialist journal in which he argued against trade competition, accumulated capital and 'extortioner' middlemen, and in favour of social education, total land nationalization, worker co-operatives and graduated income tax. In perhaps his most radical statement, he contemptuously described the prevailing political system in England as 'the Divine Rights of Property', and pointed out that Jesus Christ had been an advocate of 'voluntary communism'. It would be hard to dream up a half-brother for Reginald Birchall more different from the Revd Oswald Birchall.

Oswald had a 'long iron-grey beard, and gentle, kindly

eyes'. When he was finally persuaded by a reporter to speak, he described with great affection how Birchall had been 'a wild, harum-scarum lad', mischievous, but with no harm in him: 'His nature was bright and cheerful. He was a frank, impetuous, kind-hearted boy, and, I think I may say, a universal favourite with those acquainted with him.' He had first got into real trouble running up huge debts at Oxford, to extricate himself from which he had employed, Oswald admitted, 'very questionable – in fact, absolutely dishonest means'. Even then, however, Birchall's charm and 'profligate liberality' had ensured that he remained 'very generally liked'. Oswald was clearly deeply pained as he added: 'Between dishonesty and murder there is a vast interval.' Though he did not wish to impugn the Canadian legal system, for anyone who knew his half-brother at all well, he said, it was simply 'impossible to believe that he could be guilty of so foul a crime as that which he is declared to have committed'.

7. A Wreath of Mildew

'Do you – do you bury anyone to-day?' he said, eagerly.
'No, no! Who should we bury, sir?' returned the sexton.
'Aye, who indeed! I say with you, who indeed?'
'It is a holiday with us, good sir,' returned the sexton mildly.
    Charles Dickens, *The Old Curiosity Shop*, 1841

Dr McLay, the Woodstock coroner, had opened Benwell's inquest in Princeton on the day the body was found, but had suspended it on 26 February, for lack of pertinent evidence, to be resumed on Friday 7 March. In the days in between, the murder continued to create 'a most profound sensation' in the part of the country where it had been committed. On 7 March large crowds gathered at Woodstock railway station in the hope that the Birchalls would pass through. Princeton, too, was 'worked into a paroxysm of excitement'. Extra constables were sent over from Woodstock, but even so, 'a howling mob of excited farmers stood around the station waiting for the train to come up', while 'the space in front of the little town hall, where the inquest was to be held', became 'literally black with human beings'.

These crowds couldn't know of the backstage legal machinations that had been taking place. The previous evening Murray had rushed with Pelly to Toronto to oppose Hellmuth's direct appeal to the Attorney-General for Mrs Birchall's liberty on bail, though the matter was actually dealt with by the Deputy Attorney-General, Mr Cartwright. After much

A crowd starts to gather for the Princeton inquest, 7 March 1890.

thought overnight his only concession to Hellmuth was to telegraph Hill to agree that Mrs Birchall could remain at Baldwin's guest house rather than being thrown into jail. Cartwright then telegraphed Dr McLay in Woodstock to say that if he wished to demand the presence of both Birchalls at the inquest, he was free to do so. As it was now only hours before the scheduled resumption of the inquest, and as Murray and Pelly had been delayed in Toronto, Cartwright further asked that the inquest be held over until the next day, Saturday.

His telegram was handed to Dr McLay, and the county Crown attorney, Mr Ball, just as they were leaving Woodstock for Princeton, and the two men decided irritatedly to ignore Cartwright's request for a postponement. At the town hall in Princeton, as one pressman put it, they found that 'some gigantic intellect' had 'conceived the idea of keeping the doors closed to all except officials, witnesses and reporters until they were accommodated'. Those privileged to go in first were therefore 'compelled to squeeze through several rods of human beings packed as closely as sardines in a box'. Another newspaperman provided a feeling account of this process. By two o'clock, he wrote, 'A crowd of about 500 men blocked the entrance to the hall, clamouring for admittance. I never saw such an excited crowd in my life. It took the coroner and Constable Wills nearly half an hour to fight their way to the door and open it.' He continued:

After narrowly escaping being one of the principals in several free fights I got into the hall. Four constables with clubs beat the frantic crowd back from the door until the coroner, pressmen, jury, and lawyers had been admitted. In one end of the hall on a raised platform or stage with some scenery for a background, the jury, Crown Attorney, reporters, and witnesses took their place. The coroner then asked the constables to admit the crowd, and with a yell in the people rushed pell-mell. The hall has standing room for about 300, and in a moment it was filled and overflowing. The stage windows, stove, and even supports for the scenery were utilized as standing places. The fair sex was not unrepresented by any means, and still the crowd clamoured for admittance at the door-way.

Every reporter felt drawn to comment on the interest shown in the case by women: 'Even a couple of women,' wrote one, 'were seen perched up so high that their heads almost touched the ceiling.'

With such witnesses as were present, evidence could be heard only on the train rides taken by Birchall and Benwell on 17 February, and on sightings along small parts of the route they had taken on foot, both young men going towards the swamp, and Birchall coming away again alone. Annoyingly, however, with Birchall himself absent, witnesses could not be asked to identify him. The press wrote: 'It is no longer a secret that there is a hitch somewhere. Coroner McLay was certainly handicapped because the prisoners were not sent on.' The immediate suspicion arose that Hill, jealous of handing over the Birchalls while the inquiry in Niagara was not yet finished, had refused to part with them.

McLay was plainly angered, even 'disgusted', by the non-appearance of the Birchalls, and was still 'quite ruffled' when he telegraphed Cartwright that evening 'instructing that officer to send up Detective Murray and Mr. Pelley to Princeton to-morrow to identify the body'. As Birchall was now a suspect in the case, his identification of the corpse had become invalid, leaving officials with 'no evidence under oath on this point'. McLay was worried that the body 'would not keep', and reinforced his demand by stating that 'if Mr. Murray and Pelley did not come he would issue a warrant for their arrest. "That will bring them," remarked the gentleman.'

On 3 March, with uncharacteristic levity, the Toronto *Globe* had printed the headline: 'The Victim Came to Buy a Farm and Got Six Feet of Soil'. While in a grisly way this statement was true, it was not that the victim rested in his little patch in peace. Benwell's remains had first been buried on 27 February. Two days later they had been dug up again to be identified by Birchall. They were then exhumed a third time for the Princeton inquest witnesses assembled on Friday 7 March. John Grigg, the sexton, who charged two dollars a go to 'raise' the body, would do exceptionally well out of this single corpse. The next day he had to raise it again.

Pelly arrived at the cemetery in Princeton early in the morning. The Toronto *Mail* provided its readers with a detailed account of the scene:

The sun is shining very brightly and melting dark patches in the thin mantle of snow that covers the earth. Quite a crowd has assembled round the grave, waiting for the arrival of Mr. Pelly. The coffin has been raised, and lies on trestles alongside the grave, the lid unscrewed, and the pale, calm features exposed. If Birchall is

the murderer what an effort was required on his part while identifying the body to assume an air of calm indifference. When Pelly
walked up to the grave he bent over the coffin, visibly affected.
'That is Benwell, poor fellow,' he said. The people stood around
awed and silent. For a moment he stood looking at his dead
companion on that fatal trip to America, and then turned away.

Perhaps not surprisingly, Pelly himself later remembered the
event in comparatively exaggerated terms:

The most horrible job I had was the identification of Benwell's
body which was again exhumed for the purpose. Notwithstanding
the great cold (it was fifteen degrees below zero) there was a crowd
of some five hundred people at the Princeton cemetery. I was hating
the affair, with the natural reluctance of what was to be my first
view of a corpse, and also in expectation of a particularly nasty one
as Benwell had been buried for nearly three weeks. However the
cold weather had prevented much change in Benwell's face and he
was easily recognizable, though he presented a somewhat comical
appearance as he was dressed, according to local custom, in sort of
evening clothes! I shall never forget the kindness of the Woodstock
Chief of Police who must have realised what I was feeling. At any
rate he took my arm and led me to the grave side and did all he
could to make the beastly job as easy as possible.

The *Mail*'s claim that Birchall had assumed an air of calm
indifference when put through the same ordeal was inaccurate.
Unlike Pelly, he had 'filled up, according to the expression of
the bystanders, and remarked, "That's the man."' No one
at the time had seemed to doubt that Birchall's tears were
genuine.

   Pelly, having identified Benwell, now moved on to the

inquest. At the close of the previous night's proceedings, McLay had 'humorously' informed 'the jostling, perspiring audience that the morrow promised to be fine, and that they had better work on their farms, since the inquest would be conducted with closed doors'. Most people took him at his word, and 'the seething, restless crowd' did not reappear. Like Murray, Pelly largely repeated his Niagara testimony. Birchall had told him that 'two men named Peacock' lived on his farm, and that Macdonald owned an adjoining farm. Reporters noted Pelly's comment that 'we called Benwell the colonel', and that Benwell had been 'very fastidious'. Beyond this, both Murray and Pelly attempted to bring out ever more strongly facts 'of particular importance as throwing light on Mrs Birchall's share in the case', Pelly emphasizing that she had been present when Birchall arranged with Benwell to go on 17 February to see the farm. Despite this, the jurors were 'slow' to decide on the degree of her guilt, besides being worried about the propriety of bringing in any verdict at all in the absence of the prisoners. After a couple of hours of debate they came to a decision that was rendered as follows:

The jurors of our Sovereign Lady the Queen, empanelled by Dr. McLay on the 21st day of February, 1890, to enquire into the cause of the death of the young man found dead in the bush near Princeton, commonly called Hersee's Swamp, lot 22. con. 2, Blenheim, whose name now appears to be Frederick Cornelius Benwell, do on their oath present that the said Frederick Cornelius Benwell came to his death by two pistol shots fired into his head from behind, one at or near the nape of the neck and another a little behind and above the left ear, either of which was sufficient to cause death, and your jurors have reason to believe, and do believe, that

the said shots were fired by the hand of Reginald Birchall, alias
Somerset, with deliberate purpose and wilfully and feloniously to
commit murder, on or about the 17th day of February, 1890, and
we are of the opinion that Carolina Birchall, wife of Reginald
Birchall, was accessory after the fact.

Dr. McLay, Coroner
Robt. Rutherford, Foreman

Unlike the magistrate's court in Niagara, the coroner's court
in Princeton had accepted that a married woman who was an
accessory after the fact to a murder committed by her husband,
was guilty of a crime.

Mr Swarts, the undertaker, assured a reporter on 10 March
that Benwell's body had been embalmed sufficiently 'to
keep for a considerable length of time, besides being disem-
bowelled'. This boast was put to the test a week later, when a
mantle or cloak-maker called Miss Lockhart came forward as
a new witness to Birchall and Benwell's 17 February train ride
together. At this disinterment, a local reporter noted that
Benwell's skin was now 'slightly discoloured', with 'his eyes
sunken a little', and a distinct 'wreath of mildew on his
forehead'. Nevertheless, Miss Lockhart 'at once recognized
the deceased'.

In parallel with daily reports on legal proceedings in the
Birchall case, a highly charged debate now took place in the
columns of Ontario's newspapers concerning the legitimacy
or otherwise of the farm pupillage system. Hardly anyone set
out to defend the actual practice of farm pupillage. Instead,
the debate focused on the question of who was most responsible for the fact that the system didn't work. The general
verdict was that 'the blame rests entirely upon the shoulders

of the agencies in England', though some in Canada did accept that there was local culpability as well. The Mayor of Woodstock, for example, was prepared to admit that he understood that the pupils were 'not only wheedled out of their money by the agents, but worked and starved to death by some of the farmers', while Dr McLay had declared during the inquest that the pupil system, which had been common in that section of the country for at least fifteen years, was 'dishonest' and 'pernicious'.

Why, though – if this was really true – should a farmer wish to starve a hand almost to death? The main reason to take on a pupil was for the bonus paid up front. If his labour proved unsatisfactory, it was then a simple matter to torment him until he defaulted on his contract.

Viewed from this perspective, the phrase 'Pupil Farming', as used in one press headline, took on a sinister second sense, suggesting the deliberate cropping of a type of young man who could be expected to turn a profit of fifty dollars odd, with a spell of free labour thrown in, before being made to disappear. Once Benwell's murder had exposed the risks of signing up as a farm pupil, it seemed in Canada as though the 'nefarious traffic' in young English gentlemen might grind to a halt.

As this debate continued, many Canadian commentators were affronted by the idea that their honest tillers of the soil were being presented to the world as a gang of murderers, and repeatedly asserted, regardless of normal standards of proof, that it was 'a fortunate circumstance that no Canadian is mixed up in the Benwell tragedy'. These writers blamed the failure of the farm pupillage system most roundly on the pupils themselves. In England, they explained, 'a gentleman is still looked upon as one who does not require to work. How foreign all this is to our ideas everyone knows.' The pupils were intrinsically weak specimens, were inept by upbringing, and could not be expected to succeed.

This debate naturally drew in farm pupils and former farm pupils as well, several of whom wrote to the papers or were interviewed. One who came forward had been sent out by Ford & Co., the company that succeeded Ford, Rathbone & Co., which had originally taken on Birchall as a pupil. This young man had been placed by Macdonald on a farm where he had been required to pick stones in the fields all day long. After his health broke down he had managed to shift to a job in a rattan factory. Another former pupil, working in the same factory, said that of five 'poor pupil farmers' whom he knew, three now worked in Canadian banks. Perhaps the most interesting of these accounts was provided by a young man called Arthur Johns, described as a nephew of the Irish peer Lord Lurgan, and now prospering as a fruit grower in Delamere, California. Johns explained that he had gone a couple of years previously to Canada, aged nineteen, travelling under the aegis of a farm pupil agency out of 'enthusiasm for the free, adventurous life of America'. He admitted that 'Buffalo Bill was then in London and somehow I mixed him up with my dreams of life in Ontario', seeing only 'the sentimental side of the life'. Johns had handed over about a thousand dollars in cash to the agency. He had met two other farm pupils at Liverpool, and had travelled with them to New York on first-class tickets, 'but on a 10-day boat', so that the expense to the agency would have been no more than fifty dollars. When they reached Niagara, they had been taken to a farm by wagon. The very first night the farmer had 'got mad' when Johns asked for a glass of ale with supper. The pupils went to bed unsatisfied, only to be roused again at four in the morning to start work in the fields. They had set about this with a will, but had become so sore, with swollen hands and feet, that they had been unable to work further for a couple of days. They now found out that the farmer had sacked his hired hand in their favour, yet the three new boys, paying to work, were temporarily incapable of discharging their duty. The farmer became increasingly brutal.

We had to sleep in a wretched garret where it was frightfully cold and they wouldn't give us a light to read or write by at night. We used to lie in bed and talk over our hard lot and the homes we had left behind, wondering should we ever see them again, and often we cried ourselves to sleep.

The food, said Johns, 'was wretched, and we began to lose flesh rapidly'. The farmer 'took a delight in taking it out of us, as he said, and humiliating us in every possible way'. They had found they were 'tied by an iron-bound agreement', and were told stories of other pupils who had attempted to flee from similar arrangements, only to be captured and returned to a state of virtual slavery. The young men planned that as soon as one of them should receive an adequate remittance from home, they would split it three ways and attempt to escape together. One night, however, Johns had found that his sufferings, from 'excessively laborious work and insufficient food', had become more than he could bear. He bid his companions a tearful farewell, escaped over a roof top, and fled on foot, under cover of darkness, to Niagara. From there he managed to get to New York on a freight train, and had had just enough money to buy a steerage ticket on a steamer back to Liverpool. His change had been exactly twenty-five cents, which he had spent on a brandy and soda. Besides his

lost fee to the farm pupil agency, he had left behind kit –
clothes, hats, shoes, gloves, fowling-pieces, a new saddle,
trunks and bags – worth more than a thousand dollars; and
but for the solicitousness of a groom who lay next to him in
steerage on the journey across the Atlantic, he felt he should
have died. His two companions had both also subsequently
escaped the farm, although one of them, Albert Luttrell, had
died on the steamer as he made the voyage home.

No Canadian writers seemed to disbelieve such accounts,
but many were completely unmoved by them. Not only could
the pupils be blamed for being too weak to cope with Canadian
farm life, their prior failure to thrive at home also rendered
them suspect. If they had been found to be useless in the Old
Country, why should anyone want them abroad? Birchall,
viewed from this perspective, had been a total failure, spending
only one day on a farm. He had come out as a pupil with
money in hand, and remittances from home to follow, had
been disinclined to work, and had instead squandered his
resources on 'making a reputation'.

Birchall's history as a farm pupil could have been fixed in
these terms: he had been one of the lowest types, who ended
up doing nothing but lounging around the hotels. In the
final day's evidence at Benwell's inquest, however, Detective
Murray cannily revealed to the court that Birchall's previous
experience in Canada had not been so straightforward. Under
the guise of having Pelly confirm Birchall's handwriting,
Murray submitted a copy, made by Birchall, and kept in his
trunk, of a letter that he had sent to England the year before.
Once Pelly had identified the writing, which he did without
hesitation, this letter was available to be transcribed by the
press and printed for all to see:

Box 572
Woodstock
Ont.
Canada

Dear Sirs,—Thank you for the bonus of $125, which came safely to hand. I duly sent receipt by Mr. Macdonald. I cabled you last Thursday, 24th, to send me £30, which I suppose you would get all right. I am at present looking round and staying in rooms and only pay $8 a week, board included. The people in the town have been very friendly to me, and we have been out a good deal. The English people out here don't appear to be at all successful. Mr. T. Levy I found slept in a pretty dirty stable without any apparent source of existence, and this week he has been committed to gaol for vagrancy by the mayor. He is almost without clothes, and was turned off one farm on account of his dirty habits. Mr. Charles V. Childe disappeared, or "skipped out" as they call it here, last week, owing some $1,300. He removed most of his goods by night before writs, etc., were issued against him, and the remains of his stock were sold by the bailiff yesterday. Mr. Overwey tells me he has done nothing, and on enquiry I find that when he did work the farmers said they were too poor to pay anything, or avoided payment. He left last week for the North West. It appears that S. O. Burgess was a most dishonest man. The people here do not like the system of the pupil farmer business at all. One of the clergymen here came to see me the other day about it, saying that young fellows must be discouraged from coming here: he is getting up representations about it. I told him that you gave very full representations before coming out, but I presume he judged by the few instances I quote. Levy ought to be seen to at once. My governor will be here

in a day or two. He has been making a stay in New York with
friends. Mr. Pickthorn also is doing nothing except potter
about the Commercial hotel, a favourite resort. Mr. Radley
has been terribly drunk off and on for over four weeks; we
have had to turn him out of this house, where he boarded.
He gets terribly abusive and noisy. He does nothing, but gets
$7 a week from his people.

With kind regards, believe me yours ever,

F. A. Somerset

Messers. Ford, Rathbun & Co.,

21 Finsbury Pavement, London S. C., England

From the reference to 'last Thursday, 24th', it can be deduced
that this letter was written in January 1889. Apart from the
desolation amongst his compatriots that Birchall so cheerfully
described, it was conspicuous to those who read these words
that he had been operating to some extent as an agent for
Ford, Rathbone & Co. The letter did not reveal exactly what
Birchall's understanding with them was, nor did it identify his
mysterious 'governor', but once these paragraphs were in
circulation, Birchall stood revealed as not merely one of that
class of pupils who got packed off to the colony to escape their
own dissipation at home, but as one who, from the very
beginning of his connection with Ontario, had been complicit
in the exploitation of his peers.

Even with an inquest verdict on the books, the Niagara police
magistrate, Mr Hill, insisted that his inquiry be resumed on
Wednesday 12 March. Rain fell 'incessantly' in 'torrents'
that day, so that the whole of Niagara looked 'gloomy and
foreboding', yet reporters on the spot described how 'from
early this morning until long after dark hundreds of men and

women of all ages and degrees tramped the muddy streets'. Visitors came from the American side of the river also, and 'the Court room was packed with people as early as nine o'clock'. Many others waited at the train station for Birchall to arrive. He was expected to reach Niagara from Welland jail at eleven, but did not arrive until five in the afternoon. Most spectators remained where they were 'in the drizzling rain and in the mud'. Hours later it seemed as though 'at least a thousand people were in the depot when the train steamed in', and, stepping to the doorway of the car, 'when the prisoner looked over the multitude of faces staring at him a broad smile covered his face'.

Pressmen described Birchall in great detail that day: 'The "darbies" were fastened over a dainty pair of tan-coloured kid gloves;' he wore an English box coat of dark blue; 'his head was covered with a black Christie stiff' – a bowler hat – while 'his shoes were pointed to a degree; his black moustache was artistically turned up at the corners', and 'the balance of his dress consisted of a pair of dark checked tweed trousers, flannel shirt a la summer tourist and a neat scarf'. In short, he was 'faultlessly dressed', and he stepped off the train 'as lightly as if he were a school boy starting on a holiday trip'.

While Birchall was moved quickly to a cell underneath the court house, the crowd made 'a general rush' to a court room designed to hold perhaps one twentieth their number. In no time an estimated total of three hundred people had squeezed in, and the interior was soon darkened by crowds peering through the windows from outside. Hill was sufficiently worried by the potential for injury, to remove proceedings to the larger 'town hall room', or concert and theatre venue, upstairs. Within five minutes this new space was packed with spectators. Hill immediately issued them with the warning that unless they kept quiet he would send them all away. This 'brought the scrambling, edging, noisy crowd to a standstill', and 'they behaved fairly well from this out'. The space on the stage was reserved for the press, all legal personages, the witnesses by turns, and, one after the other, the Birchalls.

As Hill reopened his inquiry at twenty to six that evening, he knew that once again he had an adversary in Detective Murray. Apparently daring Hill to frustrate him, Murray had said in advance to reporters, 'I do not know what the proceedings will be at Niagara Falls. I expect the prisoners will simply be handed over to me without further comment.' However, though there can have been little doubt in anyone's mind that Birchall would soon be removed to Woodstock's jail, Florence Birchall's prospects were still distressingly uncertain. Mr Ball, the Crown attorney in Woodstock, had declared that, as a result of the inquest, 'while the evidence against her is not strong yet, she will be held for trial'. On the other side of the argument, Hellmuth had indicated some days earlier that the defence would at all costs attempt to spare Mrs Birchall the indignity of a spell in jail.

Mrs Birchall was called up first. She walked into the hall leaning heavily on the arm of Chief of Police Young, and appeared to be 'almost broken down'. Though Hill had already quieted the spectators with his threats, now 'a hush fell upon the crowd as she made her way to the platform'. Once again she was wearing her Newmarket, the 'bottle-green rainy-day garment of very fashionable cut', and once again her face was so thickly veiled that nothing of it could be seen but a glimpse of her chin. As she sat on the stage next to her counsel, Mr Ivey, who was Hellmuth's partner, she was mute, still, and effectively almost invisible.

Ivey's opening move was a brief argument to the effect that

Mr Hill might not technically be competent to 'adjudicate the woman's case'. Hill took great pleasure in his reply, which he addressed to Mrs Birchall:

I find that the information charges you with being an accessory in the town of Niagara Falls, before the murder of F. C. Benwell, to your husband Birchall, who is now held on that charge. This would seem to raise the question whether or not the whole case, as far as the information is concerned, should be heard in this county. If such was the case it would be my duty to discharge you, as sufficient evidence to commit you on this charge has not been brought before me. (Applause.) If, however, the information charged you with being an accessory before the fact in the County of Oxford, it would be my duty to remand you for further evidence to Oxford.

As the information on the charge was specific to Niagara, Hill continued bluntly that he saw 'no reason why I should not try the case. Bring on your witnesses. Mr. Murray, have you any testimony to offer?' Detective Murray was the only figure representing the prosecution. He replied, 'None whatever your Honour.' Crown policy, as executed by Murray, was to prove to be one of barely polite non-compliance, emphasized by *sotto voce* 'kicks' at the magistrate, audible to the newspaper-men sitting around the detective on the stage. Murray quietly noted, 'I do not agree with those proceedings at all. They are not in accordance with my instructions.'

Mr Ivey altered his stance immediately, saying that he now 'had not the slightest doubt of Magistrate Hill's jurisdiction'. Instead, he 'asked for the absolute discharge of his client at once, as there was no evidence whatever or grounds to hold her upon'. For the second time Hill asked Murray, 'What do you say?' For the second time Murray answered that he had 'nothing to say whatever at present Your Honour'. He was, as reporters now knew, 'in possession of warrants issued at the insistence of Coroner McLay for the arrest of Mr. and Mrs. Burchell', and must have believed that if he sat out the inquiry doing nothing, he could catch his prey afterwards. If so, he was quite wrong. Hill announced that it was his duty to discharge Mrs Birchall (applause), but added, despite this 'duty', that he would nevertheless remand her for eight days more 'to the same custody' as previously, at Baldwin's. 'I think it will be better,' he said, without legal explanation. At the cost of confining her to her boarding house, Hill had neatly scuppered Murray's ability to re-arrest her, while giving Mrs Birchall's defence a further eight days in which to try to work out how to bring about her release on bail.

The two prisoners passed each other wordlessly as Birchall arrived to take his wife's place on stage. Murray continued to try to sabotage the inquiry, whispering: 'These proceedings are foreign to anything I ever saw in my life.' Yet even the drama of Murray's asides was no competition for the interest reporters took in Birchall's quiet but almost facetious disdain. Birchall, wrote one, 'faced the audience like an end-man in a minstrel show; never once did he look in another direction'. This was not merely to say that Birchall played up to the theatricality of the event, but that he made a joke out of it. Minstrel shows were highly formalized in the late nineteenth century. The end men, got up in black face, and wearing ludicrously exaggerated check suits and bow ties, performed gags and tricks between the songs.

Various new witnesses were called by the prosecution to attest to Birchall's movements on 17 February, but he displayed 'the most thorough contempt or unconcern' for what they said. Then Ivey stood to speak, attempting to ensure that it 'be borne in mind' that at the inquest 'only such testimony was submitted as would tend to strengthen the case presumed by the detectives against Birchall'. Even given this objection, Ivey did not now submit any evidence for the defence, and so Hill was free to announce to Birchall:

'I have concluded to commit you to the Woodstock Jail to stand your trial for the charge of murder. I do not know when the trial will take place but you can govern yourself accordingly. Have you anything to say?'

Burchell looked at his counsel, Mr. Ivey, who motioned him to say nothing.

Then he replied: 'I have nothing to say—'

The Magistrate: 'Then you are fully committed for trial.'

The prisoner: 'At this particular time,' Burchell added after a whisper from his counsel.

Murray now walked over to Birchall to take charge of him. Birchall complemented the detective on his 'handsome gold-headed umbrella stick', and asked him where he had got it, then the two of them 'shook hands and walked downstairs'. The hearing had lasted until eight o'clock in the evening – too late to take Birchall to Woodstock until the next day. He was returned under 'strong guard' to a cell beneath the court house.

That night, for the first time, two reporters were allowed to interview Birchall. The press had been 'after him like flies in June', he said, but until now he had not been allowed to speak to anyone. Mr J. A. Currie of the Toronto *Mail* observed him as he worried over a burst paper parcel of clothes and a consequently missing sock. The prisoner also seemed concerned about obtaining money so that he could buy hotel food once he was installed in the jail at Woodstock. After these practicalities, Birchall turned his attention back to Currie.

He started by declaring that he did not wish to speak about Benwell's death: 'I know you will not put words into my mouth,' he added politely, but, 'my dear boy, it would hardly be right to say anything.' Instead, he was very anxious to correct a falsehood presently being aired in the press. A former farm pupil called Young had gone to the local papers a few days before to say that he had recognized Lord Somerset the previous year. They had attended school together when they were both about ten. Somerset was in truth the son of a humble livery stable keeper, and was 'quite a coward among the boys'. Young would later admit that he had been entirely mistaken in this identification. With all the ignominious accusations cast at Birchall after his arrest, it is hard to understand why this particular one annoyed him to such a degree, unless it was that it seemed to impair his standing as a gentleman in a way that even being called a murderer did not. When Currie was leaving to file his copy at the telegraph office, he must have made a gesture of sympathy. 'Good night, old man,' said Birchall,

there is no use being down-hearted you know. One minute a man is on the top of the heap, and the public idolize him; the next they will trample him under their feet and not give him the slightest show. But it's the way of the world. Good night.

In this comment, Birchall gave no sign of recognizing that fame and approval did not necessarily go together.

In speaking to the second reporter, Mr Long of the Toronto *Empire*, Birchall attacked the press for the prejudice displayed in its reporting on the case, and newspaper readers, in turn, for being swayed by such reporting:

if I am to stand trial in this country with the public feeling there appears to be against me at present, regardless of what defence I may offer, my case is cooked even before I am placed on the spit.

He must be supposed to have taken a dim view of the impartiality of Canadian juries, as he also said:

Why do I take the matter so coolly? Just *Because I Am Innocent* and when the time comes I shall be able to prove beyond doubt by tangible evidence that it would have been impossible for me to have committed the crime with which I am charged.

Birchall declared that the detectives had made a terrible error, and added warningly, 'God knows the real murderer will avail himself of their blunder and put land and sea between him and the scene of the tragedy.'

Murray and Birchall slipped quietly out of the lock-up together first thing the next morning. Birchall's clothes looked 'seedy' after a bad night, but once again he wore his kid gloves, both to ward against the cold and to stop the handcuffs chafing his wrists. Wills, the police chief from Woodstock, was at the railway station waiting to accompany them, as were Currie and Long. Once they were all settled on the train, Birchall joked with the two reporters saying that as there had been no mattress in his cell, he had had to sleep 'upon the soft side of a board'. When he suggested that his lot would be improved by a proper breakfast, Murray took the hint, and soon Birchall was provided with a tray bearing 'a large beefsteak, three fried eggs, a pot of coffee, several slices of toast and a piece of corn

Posing in the Swamp of Death, 13 March 1890. From left to right: *Unknown, Murray, Mr Currie, Mr Rabb.*

bread'. The prisoner 'proceeded to sail into the food', with the remark, 'O, I say, you are a jolly fellow, Murray.' Word travelled up the line by telegraph, and in Hamilton an 'immense crowd gathered round the car and swarmed into it' to gawp at Birchall. As usual, 'that gentleman appeared in no way disconcerted'.

Nor did he falter when he reached Woodstock. 'While matters may look black for me just now, you may bet I have strong evidence to prove my innocence,' he said again. Looking over the crowd of people at the railway station, he smiled at those whom he had known on his previous visit, before being hurried to a waiting cab. The hundred and fifty or so people who had gathered for his arrival remained in eerie silence.

Birchall was taken straight to the 'common gaol of Wood-stock'. There had recently been an official report on the jail, and the findings were not impressive:

a large number of prisoners have been committed to the gaol for no crime except poverty, old age or other misfortune and being unable to provide for themselves are confined in the gaol with criminals and insane persons.

Neighbouring counties had complained that the vagrants of Oxford County, or 'vags' as the press called them, would 'drift over' to their poor houses because of the lack of a county poor house in Oxford; and just two weeks before Birchall arrived, Mr Cameron, Woodstock's prison governor, informed a reporter that of about fifty inmates in the jail, 'only three are actual criminals'. If this was an unsuitable arrangement, it was also highly unsuitable that reasonably healthy indigents and criminals were incarcerated at close quarters with others who were plainly dying of tuberculosis.

When Birchall reached the prison, he jumped 'nimbly from the cab, and walked boldly in as if in a hurry'. He was met by Turnkey Forbes, whom he already knew, and who said, 'I'm sorry to see you here.' Birchall smilingly shook hands with Mr Cameron and the others 'as if he were greeting his warmest friends', and he was then officially registered. He was described as white and English, with the occupation of 'gentleman'. His 'social condition and habits' were listed as 'married and intemperate'. The charge was murder, date of committal, March 13, and so on. When asked if he was married, Birchall had replied, 'Yep!' However, the question, 'temperate or intemperate?' he had not at first understood. When it was reinterpreted as, did he take 'a nip' occasionally, Birchall had admitted that he did. He looked over the prison register and asked if the Ford & Rathbone farm pupil, Levy, remained inside. He was told that Levy had been released.

Reporters, jailers and police officials all trooped up with Birchall to see him to his cell in the west wing of the prison. There he was provided with a single dish, served to him without cutlery, containing 'some potatoes, a piece of bread and some scraps of meat'. Given what he had already eaten that day, he could afford to neglect this meal, but he made a strong point of asking Murray to intercede on his behalf with the prison authorities, to enable him to buy in hotel food, and avoid this 'gaol bill of fare'. He bade the reporters 'a hearty good-bye', then also said farewell to Murray. 'I'll do anything I can for you outside of this case,' said the detective. 'Thank you, thank you,' replied Birchall. 'Of course,' added Murray, 'you understand my business.' Birchall replied, 'Of course. That's all right, thank you.' With this civilized warning in the air, it was at last time to leave Birchall to himself.

8. Outrivalling the Detective Tales of Fiction

To anyone who has any practical acquaintance with the proceedings of detectives and with the transactions which they try to detect, this detective worship appears one of the silliest superstitions that ever were concocted by ingenious writers.

James Fitzjames Stephen, 'Detectives in Fiction and in Real Life', 1864

Murray had become the first permanent full-time police detective in the province of Ontario in 1875. Only in 1884 had a second government detective been appointed to cover the entire province, and not until 1892 would there be a third. However, these men were supported by a network of local police constables, and there was, in addition, a small band of provincial constables with a remit to work across the whole of Ontario. Thomas Young, chief of the Niagara police, was one of these, with his sensitive position on the frontier. While the job was difficult enough with such limited numbers, Murray was often tempted to give the press the impression that he had achieved his better results unaided, and he followed the same pattern in the book he later wrote, brashly entitled, *Memoirs of a Great Detective*. In this work Murray described his two favourite novels as being *The Count of Monte Cristo* and *Gulliver's Travels*, novels about figures who are forced to struggle against extraordinary viciousness and absurdity in the societies in which they find themselves. Furthermore, Dantès, the hero of *Monte Cristo*, is a self-appointed agent of justice

John Wilson Murray

allowed to indulge in acts of pathologically luxurious and frightful revenge for a crime committed against himself. It seems fair to conclude that a romanticized picture of the hero as a solitary and fearless force for justice was appealing to Murray.

In the memoir he would explain how 'the best detective' is a man 'who instinctively detects the truth, lost though it may be in a maze of lies. By instinct he is a detective. He is born to it; his business is his natural bent.' What Murray vaunted here was not the patient unravelling of clues, but an instant ability to penetrate deceit. This mystification of his trade reinforces the impression, given in numerous newspaper interviews in the first days of the Benwell investigation, that he had made up his mind about Birchall's guilt long before he could possibly have formed a fair judgement as to whether or not there was adequate evidence to support this verdict. Indeed, as early as the small hours of the night of 3 March, Murray had told a reporter in Niagara that he had 'not the slightest doubt but that Burchell is the murderer of Benwell'. The uneasy conjecture follows that Murray's subsequent investigation was aimed not at putting his detective instinct to the test, but at demonstrating at all costs that it was correct.

To achieve his ends, Murray made aggressive and unsubtle use of the press; and though the Canadian papers naturally allowed him to speak from their pages, there was a tension underlying the arrangement. Murray's pronouncements on his supposed progress were a form of news, but the men who reported on him were simultaneously his rivals in a race to uncover evidence about Birchall's crimes. On 13 March the Toronto *Mail* noted that Murray had been 'working night and day on the case' where 'many a man would have gone under with the strain long ago', but it was pressmen, the newspapers declared, who had given the detective 'many of the most important clues'. This claim was true. Frequently, important witness testimony had been elicited by reporters, had appeared in print, and was being analysed by the public in this form, days before it was delivered on oath in a court room.

Murray might simply have been grateful for the assistance; but he was not a man who liked to share his laurels, and he seems to have felt from the start of the case that he had ground to recover. He had not discovered the single most important clue, Benwell's named cigar case. He had interviewed Birchall in Paris, but had then let him go. He could not claim the distinction of having arrested Birchall, nor, though repeatedly speaking of a well-organized and vicious Birchall gang, did Murray succeed, as the days passed by, in providing the names of any other of its members. None of these deficiencies was particularly discreditable, but Murray appears to have found it galling to have had to repeat on record, several times over, an account of the murder inquiry where the bulk of his contribution consisted either in chasing red herrings, or in following up the discoveries of others.

The first hint of outside criticism of the investigation was directed not at Murray but at Watson, the local constable in Princeton who had first taken charge of the case. 'Considerable feeling' had been worked up against him for his failure to arrest Birchall on the day he visited Princeton to identify the corpse:

Watson says he suspected Birchall, and on the way to Paris as much as told him he had half a notion to arrest him. Burchell said, folding his arms, 'If you have the slightest suspicion that I had any complicity in the murder, Mr. Watson, arrest me right now.' This bluff completely satisfied Watson.

As Murray had interviewed both the Birchalls the next day, he perhaps felt that the sting of this criticism extended to him too. In one paper he claimed that at this first meeting with Birchall, his 'suspicions were at once aroused that he knew too much'. In another paper Murray pitched this line even more vividly. When, in the hotel room in Paris, he had shown Birchall Benwell's name inside the cigar case, Birchall had 'staggered' and 'his wife became excited'. As a result, Murray said, before he had allowed them to leave, 'I was sure in my own mind that they were guilty.' He explained letting them go by saying that he had wished to leave Birchall free to make mistakes. After the inquest Murray was reported to have said that he regretted 'that Burchell's arrest was so hastily affected [*sic*] by Chief Young. He thinks that had the young man been thrown off his guard and placed simply under surveillance, he would have incriminated himself by his conversation.' This point was repeated elsewhere: 'the arrest was made, Detective Murray says, sooner than he would have advised'.

This explanation does not tally with remarks Murray made in a separate interview about Mrs Birchall. When embroiled in his initial fight to have her jailed, he told a reporter that he was sure she was deeply implicated in her husband's crimes, and believed that 'the woman' had had ample time after her husband's arrest to 'plant' the money taken from the murdered Benwell. Murray continued that this was why he had 'so strenuously opposed the admitting of Mrs. Burchell to bail'. If so, it would imply that Murray had no faith in the efficacy of the very surveillance techniques he elsewhere claimed he would have liked to have employed against Birchall. Taking the two interviews together, the main aim behind Murray's explanations seems simply to be to shift blame away from himself.

The printing of these unfortunate contradictions should perhaps have served as a warning to him, but Murray continued throughout March to feed untested progress reports to the press. He revealed that he intended to take the pair of nicked scissors found amongst Mrs Birchall's effects to match them to the cuts made in Benwell's clothing. He mentioned that he was having a civil engineer, Mr W. Davis, make an exact plan of the locality around Eastwood railway station and the swamp, to prove that Birchall would have been able to commit the murder in the time between the train rides that he apparently took on 17 February. On 19 March, with unusual mystery, Murray divulged that he had some evidence that he was 'not yet able to make use of', but that for the time being he was off to Buffalo to get hold of the originals of the telegrams Birchall was thought to have sent to himself. Murray then revealed that he was considering travelling to New York with Pelly 'to see if we can hunt up that broker', in an attempt to find out how much money Birchall had taken out of Canada the year before. After the Buffalo trip, Murray spoke yet again to reporters, letting out to them that while he had now made 'some important discoveries' which it would be 'inopportune' to reveal, he was prepared to declare, on his own authority, that a telegram Birchall had received instructing him to send Benwell's baggage to New York had indeed been sent by Birchall himself.

When the Benwell case broke in England, an enterprising reporter, working there for the New York *Herald*, had gone to Scotland Yard to find out whether the English police force was concerned by news stories about the Anglo-Canadian farm pupillage scandals. He was given short shrift. Mac-Naughten, head of the Criminal Investigation Department, and at the time closely involved in trying to solve the Jack the Ripper murders, denied that Scotland Yard was in any way concerned by the problem. He explained that a killing on Canadian soil, no matter by or of whom, was a subject solely for Canadian justice; and with regard specifically to the Benwell case, he added, 'the officer who is to leave London tonight for Canada is purely mythical. He does not exist.' Despite what MacNaughten had said, Murray told Canadian reporters that the English police were busy facilitating his inquiries, and in his Buffalo interview even confided that he himself might be 'compelled to continue the investigation in England'. He claimed: 'I am working on both ends of the case now. There may be some surprising developments.'

Murray seems to have been much absorbed by a misplaced need to fill a gap in Birchall's history, presumably generated by Birchall's claiming to be two years older than he really was. At the same time, the area of information Murray most openly pursued, and publicly discussed, was largely determined by the belief that Birchall was a pivotal member of a large criminal gang. A month after Benwell's corpse had been discovered,

Murray was asked whether he still believed that Birchall had lured others besides Benwell to their death. 'I have not the slightest doubt of it,' he replied. 'Only yesterday I received some very important evidence on this point.' The evidence was a letter from a New York businessman called Alderson about two English farm pupils, Augustus Rawlings and Frank Begbie, both of whom had completely disappeared, one of them last heard of at Niagara Falls. 'I know that Burchell has been out to this country several times,' said Murray, although, in fact, Birchall had been out only once, 'and I have little doubt that he is one of a gang of conspirators, who were in league to first rob and then murder their victims.' Two days later Murray gave the same details from Alderson's letter to another reporter. The detective said he was 'working on these cases', and expected, when the 'proper' time came, to have 'some startling revelations to make'.

Murray's confidence in this line of investigation was so great that before long he decided to allow the press to publish a copy of Alderson's letter. Alderson was himself then inter- viewed by a reporter for the New York *Evening Post*. Between Alderson's letter to Murray, and his account in conversation, it emerged that Rawlings, of Maud Villa, Camberwell, London, whom Alderson had not known particularly well, had gone out to Canada through Ford, Rathbone & Co., had written home when he reached Niagara Falls promising more news soon, and had never been heard of since. His mother, in consequence, had died 'of a broken heart'. Begbie, by contrast, had been a close friend of Alderson's son. After failing to get into the army, Begbie had been so cut up that he had decided to leave home. He had been placed by Ford, Rathbone & Co. on an impoverished farm in Canada's 'primaeval forest', where he had stayed for a long spell hoping to get back the three hundred pounds he had naively invested in the business. In the end, however, he had lost heart, had surrendered his money, had left for another, unknown farm, and had never been heard of since.

When Murray spoke to the press about Begbie and Rawlings and 'surprising developments' to come, he did not yet know that Rawlings had disappeared a full eight years before. This completely ruled out foul play on Birchall's part, who would have been a schoolboy of fifteen at the time. Begbie, too, was soon off the list of Birchall's likely victims. On 9 April Robert H. Lawder wrote to the Toronto *Mail* in reply to Alderson's assertions, saying that he himself had been a fellow pupil with Begbie on the farm in the 'primaeval forest'. Conditions, he wrote, had been far better than Alderson suggested. Begbie had indeed left to try to make a go of it on a farm of his own, but he had failed at this, and had joined the mounted police instead. He soon deserted after getting drunk in Winnipeg, and had fled to the States, where he was now settled and married. Far from having been pitched head first into a Niagara whirlpool by a Birchall gang member, Begbie had vanished from Canada to avoid arrest. Murray's keen wish to cast Rawlings and Begbie as Birchall's victims had proved incautiously premature.

Where Murray was more successful, with press assistance, was in tracking down witnesses to the train journeys taken by Birchall and Benwell, and then by Birchall alone, on 17 February. As a result, despite any set-backs, the detective was soon happy to announce that he had 'one of the strongest cases of circumstantial evidence I ever had in my life'. While it may have been strong, however, it remained far from complete. It was true that Birchall had had the opportunity to commit Benwell's murder on 17 February, either very close to or actually at the place where the body was subsequently found; but there was still no hard evidence that he was the killer, nor indeed that Benwell's killing had taken place in the short space of time that Birchall had been free to do it. Besides establishing opportunity, therefore, and with time of death debatable, Murray needed to find a motive, and to show in the process whether or not the murder had been premeditated. The question also remained as to whether or not Birchall had had accomplices in his supposed crime.

Most commentators, including Murray, at first appeared to believe that the murder had been a secondary necessity arising out of a primary desire to steal Benwell's cash and valuables. As late as 27 March the *Sentinel-Review* reported that the detective was waiting anxiously for a letter from Colonel Benwell that was 'likely to shed some light as to the amount of money the murdered man had in his possession'. Colonel Benwell, interviewed by a reporter in England, had contributed the suspicious detail that before his son set sail, Birchall had advised him 'not to have his things marked, telling him that they would pass the custom authorities easier, but Colonel Benwell insisted on his son having them marked'. The press valued Benwell's baggage and kit at what they considered the extraordinary sum of around a thousand dollars, though as far as Colonel Benwell was concerned, a desire to misappropriate his son's cash and effects did not explain the crime if it was committed by anyone above the class of a desperate backwoodsman.

What did clinch the matter in Colonel Benwell's mind, giving, as he had written privately to Pelly's father, 'positive proof' of Birchall's guilt, was the letter that Birchall had sent him from Niagara, undated, but postmarked 20 February, and later transcribed by the press as follows:

Please address Messrs. Birchall & Benwell, P. O. Box 313, Niagara Falls, Ontario, Canada.

My Dear Sir,—We arrived safely here after a very pleasant journey, the sea being rather rough than otherwise. We came up by sleeping car from New York, and had a very pleasant trip indeed. Your son has inspected all my books and all my business arrangements, and I introduced him to people who know me well. He suggested taking other advice, so I, of course, was perfectly willing, and he consulted a barrister in London, Ontario, concerning the business, with satisfactory results; and he has decided to join me, as he has found all that he wished to be satisfactory. I think we shall make very good business together. The books show a very good profit for last year. I think the best way is to place the money in our joint names in the bank to the credit of our reserve fund. We shall take the additional piece of land that I mentioned to you, as we shall now require it for produce. The best way to send money out is by banker's draft. Drafts for us should be drawn on the Bank of Montreal, New York. They have a branch in London, and I think the London and Westminster also do business for them. Letters of this kind should be insured and registered. We are holding a large sale early in March, and your son was somewhat anxious to share in the proceeds of the sale, which I am quite willing that he should do, and so we have signed our deed of partnership, and shall, I am sure, never regret doing so. Your son is, I think, writing you by this post. Kindly excuse bad writing on my part, but I am rather in a hurry to catch the mail. My letters are generally written by typewriter, as they are so much more legible and clear of any doubt as to words. We are having paper printed properly, and this will be ready in a few days.

I think you will be pleased that your son has found things satisfactory, and I quite agree that he did much the best thing in coming out to see the business first. I shall send you weekly particulars of all business done, so that you can see for yourself how things go on. This will be satisfactory to you, I think.

Of course, with regard to the money, any bank in New York would do for a draft. We have opened a business account in our joint names at the American Bank here.

Your son will, doubtless, explain his views in his letter.

With kindest regards,

Believe me, dear sir,

Sincerely yours,

J. R. Birchall

There is no question but that this letter was part of an attempt to deceive Colonel Benwell into making a five hundred pound investment in a non-existent farm business. Beyond this, Colonel Benwell assumed, when reading these glib paragraphs, not only that his son was dead on the day the letter was posted, but that Birchall knew it, having committed the crime himself. In this light, Birchall's certainty that a second letter, from Benwell, would shortly arrive in Cheltenham, coupled with reference to the future use of a typewriter for correspondence, seemed decisively incriminating.

Typewriters had first been manufactured in the early nineteenth century as aids for the blind, and it took some decades for their potential to be more generally recognized. Early examples of the machines were extremely laborious to use, sometimes with vast numbers of keys. It was only in 1883, when the shift key was invented, that touch typing became possible; and the commercial benefit of typewriters was finally made clear after a much-publicized speed competition in America, when a blindfold typist beat, by a huge margin, a rival typist who was allowed to look at his fingers. From 1890 onwards the market for the machines escalated hugely.

Besides being speedy and clear, typewriters allowed people to produce letters anonymously, and to send them much more easily under false signatures. Not only criminals but crime writers saw great potential in this new mode of fraud. In 1891, for example, as Conan Doyle cast around for twenty-four ideas for a series of short stories to engage his new creation, Sherlock Holmes, the third plot that he cooked up hinged on the duplicitous use of typed letters. Colonel Benwell had no hesitation in concluding that Birchall had had criminal intent along these lines, and when this interpretation was put side by side with Pelly's story of Birchall challenging his two charges, in Buffalo, to a game of replicating one another's signatures, the case against Birchall seemed beyond all doubting. If Colonel Benwell thought the attractions of his son's kit didn't explain the murder, he believed that an attempt to steal five hundred pounds certainly might.

Even if Colonel Benwell was right that Birchall's letter supplied a clear and adequate motive for assassinating a blameless young man, questions still remained for Murray to answer. In particular, given that the detective had 'not the slightest doubt' that Birchall had a gang of secret confederates, who were its members, and what part in his crimes were they supposed to play? If Birchall was happy to escort his victims across the Atlantic himself, to take them off alone and shoot them down in swamps, or shovel them into the swirling Niagara rapids, if he was happy to manufacture fake letters, telegrams and bank books by himself, what help did he need from anyone else, besides perhaps his wife?

The idea that Birchall was a fiendish spider in the middle of an extended criminal web had gained force from an array of disparate details. It was said in the press, for example, that he had been in possession of a suspiciously large sum of money when he quit Canada in 1889; though in fact many farm pupils, often referred to as 'remittance men', lived on money sent out by their families, and it would not have been so very odd if Birchall had left Canada bearing a last injection of cash from home. The press had also made much of the fact that on his first visit Birchall had made many references to a person of unknown identity, his 'governor'. When Murray examined Birchall's kit after his arrest, information had leaked out that:

In the correspondence from Mr. Stevenson, that gentleman refers to an income allowed by an adopted father which is dependent upon caprice. Whether there is a person who befriended him in England is a question so far unknown. In Woodstock he was constantly speaking of his governor and about remittances from his governor.

This might, of course, suggest that Birchall's 'governor', far from being a shady associate, was actually a convenient fiction: an imaginary figure who could be blamed for erratic fluctuations in Birchall's income. In response to details of the murder case, a London reporter had managed to interview Mr Ford, one of the agents who had originally sent Birchall to Canada. This interview, to the extent that it could be deemed trustworthy, both helped to explain Birchall's previous finances, and confirmed his willingness to create phantom patrons:

LONDON, March 18.—A reporter has had an interview with Ford, formerly member of the firm Ford, Rathburn & Co., of Finsbury Pavement, now Ford & Co., that made a business of sending young Englishmen to Canada. Ford said that he dissolved the partnership in 1888, soon after he concluded his negotiations with Burchell, whom he knew only as Somerset.

'He came to our office,' continued Ford, 'and deposited £500 sterling. We sent him to a farmer in Canada, but he turned out to be lazy and restless, and was transferred from one farm to another. During the negotiations Burchell forged his father's signature and gave a wrong address.'

Ford referred the reporter for further details to Rathbone, who is now manager of the International Investment Trust, but that gentleman was unwilling to give any additional information, and both of the late partners appeared nervous and anxious to conceal the particulars regarding their connection with the alleged murderer.

By entrusting his funds to Ford & Rathbone in 1888, and in hiding behind forged names and false addresses, Birchall seemed to have been using the agents as a bank that would be usefully beyond the reach of his creditors. If he really did have a 'governor' of some kind, the man's identity was never discovered.

A single large influx of money, and a possibly fictitious governor, did not add up either to a crime, or to a murderous gang; but there were other leads from Birchall's past for Detective Murray to pursue. In January of 1890, as Benwell and Pelly had negotiated their deals over buying into Birchall's Ontario businesses, Birchall had had no farm; but numbers of the people whom he had mentioned in describing his Canadian business interests were undoubtedly real, and were really farmers, principally Pickthall, the young Englishman who had now disappeared, two men called Peacock, and Mr Macdonald. Birchall had described Pickthall as a close friend and English gentleman farmer who owned a neighbouring property. In inquest evidence Pelly had detailed how both the Birchalls had told him that Pickthall 'had a farm adjoining theirs, and that in the harvest they used to help each other'. Pelly had also mentioned Birchall's claim that in his own absence, his farm 'was looked after by two hired men, Peacock, and his overseer, who was a Scotchman named Macdonald'. It would emerge in the press that Pickthall's manager, genuinely called Peacock, had a brother who 'also formerly lived there'. Pelly had further explained that: 'I understood privately from Mr. Birchall that he was to leave Benwell at McDonald's. McDonald, he said, had a farm adjoining his.'

The William Macdonald in question, a 'retired farmer' who had lived in Woodstock for 'several years', was the local farm pupil agent for Ford, Rathbone and Co., later Ford & Co. He claimed to a reporter, in the days after the murder, that he habitually used 'a great many of the best farmers in this section' for pupillage; but one of the pupils he had placed, a young man called Graham, told the same reporter that Macdonald had put him on a farm so impoverished that he had had to live in a room five feet by seven, with a floor that was often under an inch of water. Graham had regularly been bullied and his health had rapidly declined. After having been laid up for two weeks with inflammation of the lungs, the farmer had attempted to bill him twenty dollars for wasted time, simultaneously threatening him with vagrancy charges and a period in jail. Graham had sensibly cut his losses and quit. In the winter of 1888 Macdonald had placed Birchall on a comparably dismal farm, but Birchall had lasted there only a day, after which, as locals recalled, Macdonald had become one of Birchall's drinking partners.

From these details alone, Macdonald might be dismissed as nothing more sinister than a small-time farmer on the make. The case of the absent Neville Hunter Pickthall, known to his friends as 'Pick', was more complicated. Pickthall's history was extensively raked over by the Ontario press in February and March of 1890 after he abruptly disappeared. He had first come to the Woodstock section 'some two or three years' previously, had then joined the Mounted Police, only to reappear in Woodstock at just the time the Somersets first arrived in town. Local informants told reporters that the two young Englishmen had drunk 'wine together and were boon companions. Pickthall was rather reckless'. Some time that winter he had bought a farm about six miles south of Woodstock. Roughly a year later, about four months before he disappeared, Pickthall had married the daughter of Revd R. W. Johnstone, rector of Port Rowan; and Pickthall's young wife, who was thought to be wealthy, was whispered to be propping up his farm.

At first all that seemed certain about Pickthall's 1890 flight was that he had raised a thousand-dollar mortgage on his property on 10 February, and had left the same day, saying to his wife, 'I am going to double this money before I come back.' He told the lender that he would need to borrow the sum for two weeks only, adding that the return on this money 'was coming from England'. Pickthall's disappearance was variously blamed in Woodstock on temporary insanity, on some fateful brush with money counterfeiters, 'the green goods men', or on woman trouble, though his friends vehemently disputed the last theory, saying that he had an 'aversion' to the female sex. Press inquiries, meanwhile, showed that on

11 February Pickthall had registered at the Metropolitan Hotel as 'H. H. Jackson, New York', without being assigned a room. On 13 February he had re-registered at the hotel, signing in as 'H. Jackson, Buffalo', and taking room 265. The next day the Birchall party had arrived, and Pickthall had settled his bill, though he had remained at the hotel until 17 February. There was no further evidence of his whereabouts until 28 February, when a telegram reached Woodstock that Pickthall had sent from Tucson, Arizona, where he proved again to be registered under his alias, H. H. Jackson.

With the necessary resources to pursue a sensational story, an editor at the New York *World* sent a reporter to hunt H. H. Jackson down. On 13 March this strategy paid off, yielding the *World* a notable scoop. Pickthall, cornered at last, gave as his story that he had abandoned Woodstock because he had lost heavily in speculation and feared suits against him. He had hoped to make up his losses in California, he said, and had left New York for the West on 14 February. In Deming, New Mexico, he had lost all his money and baggage, as well as his ticket, and he had reached Tucson only on the 27th. He had remained there ever since, stranded for lack of funds, and sheltering from any creditors under his false name. As he gave out this tale, Pickthall clearly did not realize that it was public knowledge that he had remained at the Metropolitan Hotel in New York three days longer than he was claiming.

Back in Woodstock, amongst Pickthall's friends, who believed his financial affairs to be at least passable, his explanation for his behaviour 'but made the mystery more mysterious'. They were yet more astonished when in the third week of March, negotiating from Arizona, Pickthall deeded over to his wife all his property and land. The continuing confusion in his story led metropolitan reporters to claim that the local

Woodstock newsmen were on their guard: 'There is something in the Pickthall mystery that cannot be got at,' wrote
one in frustration. If so, at least one local paper, the *Sentinel-
Review*, was prepared to print a pair of paragraphs that
undoubtedly made the cloud over Pickthall seem darker. First,
without naming names, the paper reported that a 'reliable
source' had proffered the information that a few weeks before
disappearing, Pickthall had asked a local farmer

if he would take a young Englishman as a farm pupil, explaining
that he was in this business in connection with some parties in
England. Now Pickthall was never known to have any connection
with such a business, and he was asked how he carried it on, so that
nothing was heard of it. He replied that he communicated with
England by cipher telegram. He also spoke about having rented
two hundred acres of land near his own place.

The next day the following addendum appeared in the paper:
'We find today that Pickthall, not very long before his departure, talked to other parties than the farmer alluded to yesterday
in reference to his being engaged in the farm pupil business.
The purport of his conversation was about the same to all.'

By this stage in its reporting the press had latched on
to another extremely disreputable young Englishman from
Birchall's past. In late 1888 Pickthall had had a friend in tow
called Dudley, who had been 'railroaded' out to Canada, and
who was 'dashing and handsome like Burchell', with 'plenty
of guineas in his pocket'. He had been a 'queer card'.

He used to work out on Mr. Pickthall's farm and ape the manners
of a cowboy with a big bowie knife and a revolver stuck in his belt.
Many queer stories are told of the wild life he and Pickthall used to

'*Frederick A. Somerset*' *photographed with Dudley.*

lead while they were keeping 'batch' on the farm. Quite a few think it is just possible that Pickthall has gone to join his old chum.

'Keeping batch', in the slang of the time, meant keeping house as bachelors. By the spring of 1890, Dudley, like Pickthall and Birchall, was in real trouble. Within days of Birchall's arrest the Woodstock press revealed that Dudley, too, was now in prison, in a lock-up in Detroit. Owing thirty-five dollars, he had stolen eighty, plus an overcoat and a pair of overshoes, from an establishment where he was rooming in that city.

Birchall had not appeared at the inquest in Princeton, but he had actually come face to face with Macdonald as one of the first witnesses called against him at the magisterial inquiry in Niagara. The press felt it had been 'an evident shock to the prisoner when he saw his former friend in court', with Birchall going so far as lightly to question Macdonald when the old farmer denounced him on oath. Some days after this exchange in court, the Toronto *Globe* reported details of Birchall's small talk on the subject with one of his guards. In the train on the way to Welland jail, Birchall had continued merry:

Macdonald, the man whom he had palmed off to Benwell and Pelly as his manager in Woodstock, and who had called him a 'dead beat' to his face in Court, he referred to as a 'rum 'un.' Then he prattled away about the gullibility of the people in Ontario. He treated the whole thing as a huge joke, and laughed at the performance.

From the way this story is written it seems that it was not just Birchall's good humour that was sinister to the reporter, but the fact that he had not responded appropriately to the insult Macdonald offered him in court. What true gentleman could laugh this off? When, the day after this paragraph went into print, Birchall was finally able to talk directly to the press, he felt compelled to adjust the record: 'He seemed to feel very sore at Mr. Wm. McDonald for calling him a deadbeat in his evidence.' From his cell in Woodstock, Birchall was later reported to have inquired 'very anxiously' as to Dudley's whereabouts, as well as being 'intensely interested in the Pickthall mystery', but at the same time he took a joky and wholly uninformative approach to the subject: 'It would be a capital dig on the detectives and the reporters,' he apparently said, 'if someone took some clothes resembling Pickthall's and laid them beside a stream of water.' Birchall gave little clue as to the precise importance to him of these men.

It would have been reasonable for a detective leading Benwell's murder investigation to wonder whether public statements made about Birchall by characters as dubious and possibly desperate as Pickthall and Macdonald could be taken on trust as reliable indicators of how loose their relations with him really were, but it remains that whatever inquiries Murray made into Birchall's known Canadian associates, these inquiries came to nothing. Murray never openly discussed investigating Macdonald at all. His first response to the Pickthall story, meanwhile, was confidently to declare that the absent farmer must be another victim who had 'met his fate at the hand of Birchall'. After Murray was wrong-footed on this point by H. H. Jackson's Tucson interview, he let one paper know that he had been investigating this new aspect of the case 'all day', stoutly 'endeavouring to probe the Pickthall mystery' to 'ascertain if there was any connection' with Birchall. If his probing did take place, then whatever it yielded the conclusions reached were not based on talking to the man himself. Pickthall crept back to Woodstock the following month, but Murray left him alone.

On 24 March, less than a month after beginning his investigation, Murray received a stinging dose of censure when his professional methods were attacked by the opposition leader in the Ontario Legislature. Mr Meredith objected to the fact that Murray, as a government officer, had given extensive interviews to the newspapers about the case of a man who was being held 'under the most serious charge probably which the law knows'. It was not in the public interest that 'what the detective was doing should be known', and 'it was most unfair that the prisoner should have his case prejudiced by the statements made by Detective Murray'. This was 'most improper conduct', said Meredith, and he urged the Attorney-General, Mr Mowat, to put a stop to it. Murray worked directly for Mowat, who, although he now 'paid a high compliment to the detective', was 'understood to agree with Mr Meredith'. Mowat promised to look into the matter. Not only was this dramatic rebuke reported across the Canadian press, but Murray's 'extraordinary conduct', so 'greatly calculated to prejudice people against Birchall', was also front-page news the very next day in the British edition of the New York *Herald*. After this, the detective became a little more discreet.

While the contemporary press record of Murray's investigation is very patchy, and in respects unreliable, there is another skewed record to set beside it for comparison. In his memoir Murray would write a lengthy chapter entitled 'Reginald Birchall: Occupation, Murderer'. Pelly later noted of this account that it was 'grossly inaccurate', but if the changes that Murray made to the story served to conceal how his results were really achieved, they also betray areas of weakness in the case that continued to haunt him.

Murray's retrospective account of what became his most famous case would not merely obscure but falsify many details of the story. His pronouncements about the necessary timing of the murder, for example, have no analytical force: he provides two different dates for the discovery of the corpse, never states that the body was frozen when found, and fails to mention the date when Benwell actually disappeared. Meanwhile, sheer vanity and desire for dramatics gives rise to many shameless improvements, as when Murray talks up his own investigative brilliance and adds in quantities of blood when, in fact, almost none had been found: 'I saw the crimson stain where the head had been. I crawled on hands and knees over the surrounding ground, and I found a crimson trail.' He also maintains that he was the person to find the first vital clue, which he describes as a 'cigar-holder with an amber mouth-piece marked "F. W. B."' The reason Murray teasingly uses only initials here, it transpires, is that he will go on to claim to have cracked the mystery of the dead man's identity by far less arbitrary means than this clue. He notes his own decision to circulate a photograph of the corpse, and spuriously has Pelly describe how this was the key to the case: 'I saw the awful picture of the dead man in the paper. I took it to Birchall. "That looks like Benwell, I said."'

Murray time and again alters the facts for purposes of self-aggrandizement, and in order to add colour to his narrative; but in a subtle fashion, these changes also serve to draw attention to those strands in the story that he must have felt did not add up. One question to linger in his mind was clearly that of why Birchall, if guilty, did not skip over the frontier to the States and disappear when the net around him began to close, as he could well have done, and as Pelly, in New York, certainly feared he might. Murray raises the matter briefly in his description of his initial interview with Birchall in Paris: 'The man was lying, I was sure of it. Yet, if he knew aught of the crime, why should he come to Canada at least a week after the deed was done, and identify the body?' Murray chooses to dispose of this problem by an easy departure from the truth. Though in reality it was Birchall who initiated the trip to Princeton, Murray makes Pelly claim that it was he who 'compelled' the visit after seeing a photograph of the corpse: 'I told Birchall it was Benwell, and that he ought to go and identify the body and make sure.' Even if this had really been what happened, Birchall could still have skipped to the States, but Murray presents Pelly's fictitious act as though it fully explains Birchall's failure to flee.

In another telling change, Murray introduces a much better reason than Pelly was able to provide for why Birchall, if he was an unhesitating and callous murderer, did not go through with a plan to eliminate the person who would become the biggest threat to his own life, and 'shove Pelly into the rapids at the Falls to be pounded to pieces'. Supposedly in Pelly's voice, Murray writes:

We started to walk back to Canada across the lower suspension bridge. It was storming and blowing. When out near the centre of the bridge, Birchall walked over to the edge and looked down at the roaring rapids. 'Come, see the view; it is superb,' said Birchall, beckoning me close to the edge. I drew back. He grew white and walked on. I lagged behind, out of his reach. 'Come, walk with me,' he said, halting. 'Your great coat will keep off the rain.' I shook my head. He repeated the invitation. I declined. He stopped, turned squarely and looked back. Then he advanced a step towards me. I stepped back and was about to run over the bridge when two men came walking across and Birchall turned and walked on to Canada.

Murray adds complacently that 'Fate' chose to 'put the two strange men on the lower suspension bridge the night Pelly was to be hurled into the rapids'. This is all very well, but it wasn't night time and it wasn't 'Fate'. If Birchall did wish to push Pelly off the bridge into the Falls, it was not the presence of witnesses that stopped him.

Murray's account seems almost to make a habit of bringing up unassimilable aspects of the Birchall case, without alerting his readers to the fact that this is what they are. The most bizarre example of this phenomenon is his decision to print, almost without explanation, the following letter, presumably a copy found in Birchall's kit, which Murray apparently kept secret until he wrote his memoir:

Midland Grand Hotel
London
England

My Dear Mac,

You must have been surprised to find me gone. I went down to New York for the wife's health and while there got a cable the governor was suddenly taken ill. I rushed off, caught the first steamer over, and got here just too late, the poor chap died. So I have been anyhow for some time. I am coming out to Woodstock shortly, I hope, as soon as I settle up all my governor's affairs. I owe you something I know. Please let me know, and tell Scott, the grocer, to make out his bill, and anyone else if I owe anybody anything. I was in too much of a hurry to see after them. I have several men to send out to you in August. Tell me all news and how you are. Many thanks for all your kindness.

Fredk A. Somerset

All Murray says about this highly suggestive letter is, 'Lord Somerset did not return to Woodstock promptly.' He allows Pelly to mention Macdonald in passing, but does not indicate to his readers that Macdonald was a farm pupil agent, nor that he must surely have been the 'Mac' who was the recipient of this letter. Murray describes Macdonald only as an irritated creditor of Birchall's. Pickthall also appears in Murray's version, though merely as 'the farmer Pickthall of Wood-stock' who had met the Birchalls in New York on 14 February 'by merest accident'. In as much as Murray's account acknowledges that farm pupillage played a part in the case at all, he writes that Birchall 'was familiar with the emigration business, through his father-in-law's knowledge of it'. Murray raises the names of Pickthall and Macdonald, and gestures weakly to the problematical farm pupillage business, but cannot bring himself to pursue either thread. Instead he disclaims any suggestion that he pursued a gang theory:

Some folks declared the murder of Benwell was but a part of a plot of wholesale killing of rich young men of England by an organised band of red-handed villains, who enticed their victims to Canada. This I never have believed. Birchall had no male confederates, and he acted singlehanded.

Such an excessive example of revisionism calls into question whether there were not perhaps other truths that Murray buried completely. His story is presented as a rambling reminiscence, though his account of interrogating Pelly in Niagara is plagiarized, in some segments verbatim, from Pelly's court testimony, and various grossly inaccurate details of Birchall's past, passed off by Murray as inside information from Scotland Yard, can be traced to errors in what would by then have been aged press cuttings. Still, Murray's memoirs weren't published until 1904, two years before he died, and over a decade after the events of the Birchall case. As he cobbled together his narrative, he presumably relied upon people's memories being short.

If Murray harboured doubts about the Birchall case, it is clear that the colour he added to his account was partly a response to the pressure exerted on all real detectives at this time by the icy mental strength and infeasible scientific abilities of their fictional counterparts. Murray was not shy in the memoir of admitting to the rough and ready violence, hard drinking and law bending that went with his work, but in his account of the Birchall case he also added in the suspense, gratuitous gore and cleverness of fiction. Genuine detectives, writing from the 1840s onwards, had produced, in the main, a remorselessly crude literature, which described everything from the beating up of suspects and their forced confessions, through to grisly sentences based on trumped-up charges. Men with experience of the job wrote in this low-brow, gritty manner because nineteenth-century detection was almost always a dirty business, and they were describing how their work was actually done. By the end of the century, however, these men faced pressure from an awkward set of rivals, the bands of imaginary and idealized detectives who wafted in ever-increasing numbers through the pages of popular litera-ture. An introductory tribute in Murray's memoir, claiming that his career was 'a record of events outrivalling the detective tales of fiction', touched on a relationship with fabricated stories that was far less honourable than this confident assertion implied.

At the very start of the Niagara inquiry, a pressman reported that 'the impression here may be summarised in the remark of an onlooker at the court to the detective: ' "If you haven't got a murderer you've got a d—d scoundrel." ' In the ensuing days this verdict would come to seem positively charitable. Birchall's press image swiftly deteriorated from that of a mere scoundrel into that of a scheming killer predisposed to inhuman displays of light-heartedness. For a newspaper wishing to exploit a first-rate story it was natural to promote a devilish picture of the debonair young swindler, but serious investigation of the total known circumstances surrounding Benwell's death should have continued to leave ample margin for this being a case where an ill-planned fraud had led to an unplanned killing by person or persons unknown.

From late March onwards, however, Murray quietly gave up all talk of Birchall's gang of dastardly conspirators. Perhaps it came to seem a nuisance that the logic of the gang theory militated against the argument that Benwell's death was a ghastly premeditated murder unquestionably committed by Birchall himself. Perhaps, too, Murray was conscious that if alternative identities for the murderer were to include members of the community of local farmers, Canada's international reputation would suffer. One thing, at any rate, is certain: his investigation into Benwell's murder ossified after about a month. On 17 March the Toronto *Mail* reported that the detective was about to start work on the 'Cayuga mystery', and though he continued sporadically to follow up the Benwell case, it does seem that Murray only sought evidence to confirm the story that he had already fixed in his mind. He knew that the eyes of the world were upon him. He had an outstanding villain – a suave, upper-class English swindler – safely behind bars. What more did he need? He talked up Birchall in the press as 'the coolest and most wonderful man he ever saw', and left it at that.

9. Installed for the Summer in a Villa by the Sea

And herein he ranged with that very numerous class of impostors, who are quite as determined to keep up appearances to themselves, as to their neighbours.

Charles Dickens, *Our Mutual Friend*, 1865

Once Birchall had been formally incarcerated in Woodstock jail his demeanour interested almost all who encountered him. The governor, Mr Cameron, with more than fifteen years of prison experience, confessed to being amazed by his new inmate: 'He is an enigma. The gravity of his situation and his apparent peril do not seem to affect him in the slightest degree.' More surprisingly still, Cameron found that 'this appearance of nonchalance is not assumed by any means but natural. There is no question but he has plenty of sand in him.' In a different interview, the governor commented cheerfully: 'He has adapted himself to his surroundings as if he were installed for the summer in a villa by the sea.'

Murray, who did not wish anyone to interpret Birchall's *sang froid* as a mark of innocence, swiftly entered this debate as a knowing detractor. 'I have in my time come in contact with a great many murderers,' he told the Woodstock *Evening Standard*, 'and in the large majority of the cases where the murder was of a cold-blooded character the murderer always appeared cool and collected under arrest.' Taking the question the other way round, he added: 'I consider that I am a man of considerable nerve, but if I, being innocent, were charged

THE WEST CORRIDOR WITH BIRCHALL'S CELL AT EXTREMITY, MARKED A.

THE GAOL LOOKING NORTH.
(The Cook Execution took place just East of the Main Entrance)

BIRCHALL'S DAY CELL.   BIRCHALL'S NIGHT CELL.

Newspaper illustrations of Birchall's jail quarters.

with murder, I am sure that my nerves would weaken.' For some time the press kept up a game of daily reports on Birchall's frame of mind, but Canada's newspaper readers were eventually informed, in one way or another, that 'the general idea is that he will not break down'.

These accounts of Birchall were all second hand. Only priests, lawyers and prison officials now had automatic access to him, and he therefore 'spent a very seclusive time' as a prisoner. He was, however, allowed most of the post sent to him, which included copies of American humorous weeklies, as well as religious works sent anonymously by individuals with feminine handwriting. Mr Bampfield, of the Imperial Hotel in Niagara, sent him a box of cigars; and Woodstock's sheriff, Mr Perry, did decide that he should be allowed to buy in the best meals that Woodstock could supply. With this much traffic, there was considerable paranoia in the jail about security, so on 23 March a special guard, Mr Entwhistle, was appointed to sleep outside Birchall's cell, and to keep constant watch over him while he was awake.

The local Woodstock pressmen jeered on their pages at the 'city reporters' who, without the requisite contacts in the town, were 'compelled to work their marvellous imaginations to supply material'. Readers were warned that any 'alleged interviews with Burchell originated solely in the fertile brains of the reporters'. The most notable example of such an invention came in an article under the headline 'Face to Face with His Wife'.

Burchell told his wife that he had about $300 left, and said she could have part of it if she desired. He also told her that she could have a divorce from him if she wished it.

'I will make no trouble about it,' he said (and here he showed the first emotion since his arrest). 'You can separate from me if you wish to.'

The poor wife sobbed and said that she would not desert him, and sank down exhausted as he was led away.

Birchall was said to have been highly annoyed when he read this story.

Because he had not been present at the inquest in Princeton, many important witnesses had yet to identify the man they claimed to have seen four weeks earlier on 17 February. In the days immediately following Birchall's arrival in Woodstock, therefore, numbers of witnesses were brought to the jail. When Murray was asked by a newspaperman to describe the identification process, he stated simply that 'the witnesses are brought in separately and asked to pick out Burchell from among all the prisoners in custody'. This may have been the truth, but it was not the whole truth. As it was organized, 'The prisoners who were not in solitary confinement were assembled in the dining hall. The witnesses were then taken separately and asked to point out the man they saw.' After this procedure failed, these witnesses were 'taken upstairs to the cells' to try again. Once they had been shown to 'the corridors and asked to find Birchall', apparently in every case where the identification was important, 'the witnesses succeeded'.

The prisoners assembled in the dining hall would have been the majority of the inmates, all the vagrants and lunatics dressed in their prison uniforms, lacking only those who were too old and sick to move. The two prisoners in the jail on criminal charges, however, Birchall, and a man accused of being a horse thief, were restricted to their cells, and, as unconvicted prisoners, wore their own clothes. Leaving aside these con-spicuous differences, a witness who was an attentive reader of the press would have had little trouble finding Birchall's cell unaided once given the run of the corridors: its location had been minutely described in various papers a day or two earlier, 'up the winding stairs' and along 'the western corridor'.

The prisoner's cell is at the west end of the west wing of the gaol. It is well lighted but does not command an extensive prospect. About the only furniture in it is a small table, on which lay a couple of books, one of them a Bible. Burchell will sleep in another cell opening into the corridor which leads to the first one.

One paper had even noted that his night accommodation was in 'cell No. 12'. There were also numerous pictures of Birchall, engravings or 'cuts' taken from photographs, being reproduced in the press. Even if these cuts were often of 'very poor' quality, the original photographs themselves were widely on display as well. In a letter to the Toronto *Mail* that carried an unusual appeal for fair play in the Birchall case, a correspondent wrote: 'I always thought that under the old flag a man was not held to be guilty until he had been tried and condemned,' but in Birchall's case, 'His photograph is all over the city labelled "the murderer".' With all this information in play, a false or deluded witness could very easily have picked out the man Murray intended.

Birchall's lawyer, Mr Hellmuth, had been acutely aware of the iniquities in the identification system that was used in Niagara, and told one newspaper afterwards that 'at the approaching trial the method of identification of the witnesses for the Crown will be strongly objected to. It is said that, instead of being required to identify Birchall among a number of persons, the witnesses were confronted with him alone in his cell.' The procedure in Woodstock was also so flawed

Reginald Birchall

that it could in theory have been argued that not a single identification was legitimate. In practice, however, any hope of destroying the impact of Murray's work must have seemed slim.

If Birchall was jolly as a king in jail, his wife, so far as pressmen could determine, was 'greatly harassed at her unpleasant position', and slept and ate 'but little'. She was still under guard at Baldwin's guest house, and until 19 March, also inhabited a strange legal limbo, courtesy of the Niagara police magistrate, Mr Hill. At last, on the morning of the 19th, before a packed

The same picture as rendered by a newspaper engraver.

court, his inquiry into her possibly criminal behaviour came to a close. A second magistrate sat along with Hill, and the prosecution was now reinforced by a county Crown attorney, not that Detective Murray, also present, wasn't 'as keen and wide-awake as ever'. Mrs Birchall, accompanied by Hellmuth, arrived deeply veiled as usual. 'She was dressed in exquisite taste,' noted a reporter, 'but appeared to be very nervous in her manner.' The prosecution team had no new evidence to offer against her, and Hill was therefore soon free to sum up the case. Consistent with his beliefs about marital coercion, he maintained that she could not be prosecuted as an accessory to Benwell's murder after the fact, and he found no evidence that she had been an accessory before the fact either.

As a *coup de grâce*, Hill now pointed out what he must at some point have seized on as a highly favourable freak of timing. All the evidence, he said, indicated that the murder had been committed on 17 February. As Mrs Birchall 'did not arrive in this country until February 18th, if she is guilty of

being an accessory before the murder her crime must have
been committed in New York State'. In his view this meant
that while Mrs Birchall was potentially 'amenable' to American
law, she could face no charge in Canada. He let her go, amid
the 'rapturous' applause of the crowd. Rarely can a day spent
wandering around looking at wallpaper samples have done so
much for a person as Mrs Birchall's tedious time-wasting in
Buffalo on 17 March now seemed to have done for her; but
this argument should have left Hellmuth, at least, in a quandary. Hill's finding that Mrs Birchall was outside the grasp of
Canadian law assumed her husband's guilt, and only held good
if the belief that Benwell had been murdered on 17 February
was correct. It would be imperative for Birchall's defence to
argue that Benwell might or even must have been murdered
after this date. Hellmuth did not press the point.

In Toronto Hill's interventions on Mrs Birchall's behalf
were considered deeply 'irregular'. There was much speculation in the press as to how the authorities would 'extricate
themselves from the muddle'. Hill, it was felt, should have
deferred to Coroner McLay in Princeton, remanding the
prisoners without taking evidence. A bizarre consequence of
this rivalry over jurisdiction was that, on 20 March, Mrs
Birchall travelled with Hellmuth to face a judge in Woodstock
on a charge that, only the day before, the Niagara court had
declared not to exist.

When she arrived in Woodstock Mrs Birchall was thought
by those who remembered her from 1889 to have 'failed perceptibly'. Besides the local judge, she faced Mr Finkle, Pickthall's
solicitor, in the person of a magistrate. All concerned admitted
that there was no strong evidence against her yet, but it was
charged that, knowing him to be guilty of murder, she 'the said
Reginald Birchall did feloniously receive, harbor and main-

tain'. With the continuing weakness of the case against her, and the public mood so strongly in her favour, her release on bail was virtually a foregone conclusion, and she was rapidly 'liberated on her own recognizances to appear before the court when called upon', with bail set at a thousand dollars.

Now, at last, a meeting really did take place between the two Birchalls, in the presence of the Inspector of Prisons, Dr O'Reilly. The various accounts of this event that leaked out to the press tended to agree. Far from Mrs Birchall falling on the floor, the atmosphere between husband and wife was very formal, and 'there was scarcely a trace of emotion on the part of either one. Birchall held out his hand with a mere "how do you do?" Mrs. Birchall took it and submitted to a kiss and that part of the meeting was over.' She did not stay for more than about a quarter of an hour, and throughout the visit seemed 'sad but unruffled; gloomy but firm'.

Three days later, Mrs Birchall's father, accompanied by her sister, Mrs West-Jones, finally reached New York. As they stepped down on to the docks, they were mobbed by reporters. 'When asked what he would do towards the defence of his son-in-law, Mr Stevenson said that he came to the country solely to look after the interests of his daughter.' If she would not come back with him, he said, he would see that her affairs were well looked after. He insisted that she knew no more about Birchall's business 'than did either Benwell or Pelly'. He hoped to take her home again as soon as possible. Evidently at this juncture, he remained unaware of her legal position.

Pelly would recall his interactions with the Stevenson family members, then and thereafter, as uncomfortable. While he wrote that Mrs West-Jones 'I thoroughly disliked, though she was very polite to me', he also had increasingly troubled recollections of Stevenson himself, let alone of Mrs Birchall:

I learned that poor old Stevenson had had a very hard life and been quite taken in by his children who all seem to have been rather a curious lot. He admitted to me that when he gave me a good testimonial for Burchell he knew that he was 'rather wild,' but thought that for his daughter's sake he was justified in commending the arrangements between us, as they would give his son-in-law another chance to reform and generally 'make good.' He had no idea that his daughter could have any idea of Burchell's misdeeds. He said to me 'My favourite daughter is quite incapable of the least deceit.' Nor did he know what I had by this time discovered, that Mrs. Burchell was much too fond of the bottle, and was occasionally very drunk.

It is not surprising that Pelly's feelings about Stevenson and his daughters ranged from doubt to considerable dislike, but he and they did maintain a level of civility that now enabled them to spend over a fortnight together in the same boarding house.

Pelly was still considered by the authorities to be at risk. 'Wherever he goes he is guarded by an officer. The department fears that Burchell may have confederates who will attempt to remove Mr. Pelly, and for a time at least he will have police protection.' The government also paid him a witness retainer of ten pounds a month, a sum he considered adequate but scarcely luxurious.

He had one extremely serious task to perform for the authorities, which he completed on 29 April. He had been asked, while the details were still fresh in his mind, to prepare a full account of his dealings with Birchall for the use of the Crown prosecutor. It seems that he must have used a transcript of his existing court evidence as a primer, not least because he frequently interjected bracketed comments into his narrative, as though the main account needed to be slightly revised or amplified. These comments tended to emphasize the deceit of the Birchalls: 'He also told me that he had left enough money with her to pay our bills at the hotel in case he did not return (Lie),' or 'He then told me that he had telephoned me from the Falls at about midday (Lie),' or 'I knew that she had been deceiving me as much as her husband. (She can lie superbly).' However, Pelly did not stop at a simple record of facts and falsehoods. He also made some effort to solve the case. In one unusual example of leniency, he mentioned how the story of his own illness after smoking a cigar pressed upon him by Birchall, had caused many people to suspect that it had been poisoned: 'I don't think so.' Elsewhere, however, he wandered off into pure speculation, for example saying about an item of clothing that Birchall might have worn on 17 February: 'Is it possible that Burchell destroyed the vest on account of blood stains?'

This chronicle for the Crown prosecutor only survives because Pelly dropped a copy of it wholesale into a memoir of his life that he wrote for his family in 1933. The memoir begins: 'I have been worried into this by those I love best in the world. I know I cannot write, so if all that follows is stilted and dull, I am not responsible.' Included in the long document that follows is a second version of Pelly's Canadian adventure, written, as he explains, 'chiefly from memory, aided by a number of letters'. He did not re-read the Crown prosecutor's account in order to compose this family history, and was justly afraid that in his later rendering of the story 'some of the details and the sequence of events' would be 'a little inaccurate'. As almost all his letters from Canada were eventually lost, however, the memoir functions as a slightly distorting filter through which to catch a glimpse of how Pelly wrote to his family about the events of the murder case at the time it actually happened.

Pelly was right to claim that he was not particularly accomplished as a writer, though in his later version he did leaven his narrative with descriptive passages, about storms in the Atlantic, for example, or mud and mist in New York, or the impact on him of the Niagara Falls. He had found himself marooned in Niagara just as the spring ice harvest was taking place. By mid March of 1890 the press was dotted with tales of teams of men and horses having to be rescued from freezing waters after their own cropping of the ice caused it to break under the wagons. Pelly became entranced by the power of the Falls in different weathers. On some days the land around Niagara trembled, and the roar could be heard for miles; and when the spring thaw finally arrived, vast ice-floes were released which he watched, fascinated, as they dropped thunderously over the edge of the precipice into the churning waters below.

For all this enthusiasm, there is a bluff Englishness that hovers over Pelly's way of presenting himself to his readers in both of his accounts; and some of the tension generated in his writing derives from his unwillingness to express much of what he really felt about the extraordinary crisis into which he had been catapulted. As with Murray, though, Pelly's faulty memory, or indeed revisionism, gives a fine pointer towards the areas of real difficulty for him in the story as he lived through it. His exaggerated recollections of identifying Benwell's corpse provides one example. The remembered nightmare of giving evidence at the initial inquiry, and his inaccurate sense that no one believed him, provides another. However, the most striking incompatibility between the 1890

Crown prosecutor's account and Pelly's much later memoir
lies in his portrayal of the Birchalls. In the Crown prosecutor's
account, Pelly sought, almost distastefully, to sink them both.
He had no apparent doubts that Birchall was guilty of the
murder, and wished to ensure that Mrs Birchall would also
face retribution in court. He went beyond calling her a liar,
and detailed how

at the time of the murder I had a much better opinion of Mrs.
Burchell than I have now, as I know from personal experience that
she is very much too fond of drink of all sorts than she ought to be,
and on one occasion at least I have myself seen her in a state of
intoxication.

It is surprising after this to find in Pelly's memoir that he
describes both the Birchalls as charming, and Birchall in particular as having been 'a rather good-looking man and a most
amusing companion', whom 'no one could help liking'. Yet
this discrepancy can be explained. Pelly must have started by
finding Birchall much more genial than it was politic, in the
immediate aftermath of Benwell's murder, to admit. By 1933,
however, Pelly appears to have been governed most strongly
by a wish to justify ever being fooled by Birchall in the first
place. From this perspective, emphasizing Birchall's attractions
makes perfect sense. Pelly's letters to his parents concerning
the Benwell case do not survive, but his letter from New York
to his brother-in-law, Arthur Durrant, gives another clue as
to why the discrepancy between memoir and Crown prosecutor's account is quite so pronounced. Pelly wrote to
Durrant that he strongly suspected Birchall of being in some
way mixed up in a murder, and yet, 'But for all this I am fairly
happy and find the Burchells very pleasant people.' Pelly

Frederick Cornwallis Benwell, alive.

added, 'I don't want father bothered unless necessary.' Revd Raymond Pelly later told a reporter that at the outset his son had found Birchall's behaviour to be 'perfectly straightfor-ward'. Taken together, Pelly's desperate ambivalence about Birchall, and his desire to protect his parents from bad news, suggest that any letters written home before Birchall's arrest would have painted the brightest picture possible. If, in order to write his memoir, Pelly refreshed his memory by consulting the letters he wrote to his parents, they may well have misled him, almost half a century later, as to the original complexity of his feelings.

While Pelly's memoir implies that he enjoyed the company of both the Birchalls far more than the Crown prosecutor's account would indicate, it is a sorry fact that at all points in both versions he would maintain the justice of his dislike of Benwell. Pelly was particularly affronted that Benwell had 'put on a lot of side', and tried to 'patronize' him. Beyond this, Pelly seems to have made a more or less conscious leap of understanding about his 'disagreeable' and 'sallow' travelling companion, that Benwell was what Pelly would loosely call a 'half caste'. It was later confirmed to him that Benwell's mother was 'Eurasian', the illegitimate child of a British officer in India and his Indian paramour. Benwell, therefore, resolving an apparent contradiction that the men who discovered his corpse could not comprehend, was both a young English gentleman, and someone who 'had Indian blood in his veins'. Pelly comments in the memoir, 'When I learned all this history Benwell's dark complexion was explained.' Whether or not Pelly fully understood his own way of expressing himself in these lines, he unpleasantly implies that the explanation for Benwell's 'sallow' skin was also the explanation of his dark nature. Pelly's account for the Crown prosecutor was less forthcoming, but reverted in its closing paragraph to a further rehearsal of how the Birchalls had managed deliberately to stir up dislike between him and Benwell. The last sentence read: 'I have no doubt that if the Burchells had not done this Benwell and I would have discovered Burchell's falseness long before our arrival in New York.' Pelly, perhaps motivated by a degree of guilt, tried here to have it both ways: Benwell was frankly dislikable, yet Pelly's dislike for him had been induced through the evil machinations of the Birchalls. This last sentence is particularly revealing in its disclaimer about Birchall's 'falseness'. Pelly and Benwell did discover Birchall's duplicity during the voyage. The astonishing fact is that he was able to persuade both of them to ignore it.

Apart from writing up his experiences for the Crown, Pelly had no formal employment while he lingered in Niagara. His evenings were spent at dances or card parties, or on trips to the theatre, though it is clear that any time he chose to appear in a public place he suffered for it. During a show at the theatre in Buffalo, for example, he was dismayed when 'during the entre-actes the whole audience stood up and stared at me'. If he went on regular trains, 'cues [*sic*] of people' would pass by his seat, and crowds would gather at the stations. He was also 'worried to death by reporters' from all across Canada and the States. Wherever he happened to stay he found there were always 'numberless visitors' of all kinds, including 'the inevi-table stream of prostitutes'. He was also 'bombarded with letters' that proposed anything from clandestine assignations to marriage. One of these letters, that he seems to have memorized, came from a servant girl on a farm, and said: 'I am always interested in romances in real life. You are my romance. I offer you my trusting little heart.' Pelly was not tempted by this deluge of overtures. His police protectors were constantly on hand to remind him of his vulnerability to strangers, telling him that 'anyone who tried to make my acquaintance might be an emissary of Burchell'.

If the stream of prostitutes was inevitable, so too was a desire in various other business quarters to exploit Pelly's notoriety. He was offered sums of up to fifteen dollars for his photograph: 'Fortunately I had none to sell.' He was also approached by 'theatre and music hall directors, and theatrical agents', and was offered 'quite a high salary to stand for over an hour or two a day in a "dime museum"'. Dime museums at this time seem to have been in a state of mild crisis. As well as displaying living human exhibits – the snake charmers, glass eaters, stone breakers and broken-backed men, or the natural 'monstrosities' like albinos, bearded ladies and the enormously fat – it had become necessary for the showmen running each of the hundreds of these little museums across North America to keep a stock of dummy freaks. A reporter in November 1890, who visited a freak maker on New York's East Side, found that this market was urgently 'calling for something new'. The museums were glutted with dummy mermaids, demon children and elephant fish, supposedly embalmed, dried, or mummified. The freak maker could do an alligator boy for thirty dollars, double-bodied babies for forty dollars, or the fifteen-foot sea serpent, 'Africanus Horidus', for fifty dollars; but he, too, longed for some weird discovery to provoke a demand for hundreds of copies of an entirely novel oddity. It is no wonder that the beleaguered small-time showmen who were clients of the freak makers wished to snap up Pelly for the edification of their ghoulish public; and if these museum curators could not persuade the young Englishman to pose as himself, the obvious alternative was wax.

Pelly soon discovered that dime museums all over Canada were displaying figures of himself, Benwell and Birchall. At one point he amused himself by going into a cheap waxworks establishment 'and asking the curator to show me which was Pelly, which he did, assuring me that it was a wonderful likeness'. No one in the place, he realized delightedly, had the faintest idea that they were in company with the original. The curator of this particular museum had doubtless followed normal practice in recycling a limited stock of wax figures to fit the requirements of the stories of the day. In the East End of London at this time the proprietor of one waxwork museum had infuriated the authorities by splashing one after another of his female figures with red paint, and adding each to a repulsive display whenever Jack the Ripper claimed a new victim.

Mrs Birchall left Baldwin's guest house on 10 April, three weeks before Pelly. Presumably it was a relief to him when he no longer had to get up from scribbling condemnatory remarks about her in the Crown prosecutor's account, only to meet her at the lunch table. She had been making occasional visits from Niagara to Woodstock to see Birchall in prison, accompanied by her sister, Mrs West-Jones, but intended now to move to Woodstock properly. On 16 April Stevenson compelled himself to visit his son-in-law for the first time since reaching Canada. A local paper confided to its readers that this meeting was 'not very enthusiastic'. The two men 'shook hands with cold formality and discussed some general matters in a very general way'. Stevenson then left the prison quickly, and the press reported that he would be returning to England within a week. He must have felt that there was nothing more he could do to ease his daughter's miserable lot. She and her sister planned to accompany him to New York, and then to return for an interval of forlorn waiting in rooms at the Commercial Hotel, where Birchall had once got drunk with his pals, a few streets away from the jail.

In Murray's memoir, the detective casually mentions that Pelly 'had desired to go home after the preliminary hearing, but the Government decided he should remain, and he stayed with me until after the trial'. This was completely untrue. Pelly hadn't the money to visit England, nor did he stay with Murray. He started out at Baldwin's, but soon found that trying to survive on his witness allowance left him 'very hard up', and felt that he 'could not stand the prospect of months of this sort of life'. One avenue of hope was provided by T. C. Patteson, director of the General Post Office in Toronto. Almost every smart young man from the Old Country who spent any time around Woodstock at this period seemed to be introduced to 'T. C.', whose farm at Eastwood was 'the rendezvous of all English visitors in the section'. Patteson's standing in the expatriate English community was such that

after Benwell's murder he had been forced to deny through
the press that he had ever been fooled into entertaining the
louche Lord Somerset. Pelly must have imagined that he
would be received with considerable sympathy after a telegram
arrived from Patteson one day that said, 'I see you are in
difficulties, you had better come and see me.' Pelly went to
Toronto and introduced himself to Patteson in his rooms at
the GPO:

After a few minutes of silence, he suddenly said, 'Well, you are a
damned young fool!' He then proceeded to say what he thought of
the general run of young Englishmen coming out to Canada and of
me in particular, and then ended by saying, 'Well now, what can I
do to help you? I will do anything in my power to help a fellow
countryman.'

Though Patteson at first came up with suggestions of dreaded
office work, after some weeks he managed to strike a chord
with the idea that Pelly might go West to try out as a railway surveyor. This, at last, was a proposal that 'thoroughly
appealed' to him. Patteson wrote to the Canadian Prime
Minister, Sir John Macdonald, and the machinery of influence
began to crank into gear.

On 25 March, the sexton at Princeton, Mr Grigg, had
exhumed Benwell's body for the fifth time. With the ice
harvest well under way, and temperatures starting to rise, the
wreath of mildew on the corpse must have been much more
pronounced. Pathetically, though, 'through some misunder-
standing, no one was present to identify it'. Benwell's remains
were packed back into his stranger's grave in the 'Pottersfield
portion' of the cemetery, while his kit and luggage, the excess
of expensive accoutrements that he had brought out for his

new life, rested for safe keeping in Woodstock jail. A request from Colonel Benwell for a proper plot for his son, and the promise of a reward for any trouble, only reached Princeton in late April. The sexton's final bill, covering in all six 'raisings' and seven burials, indicates that one of Canada's worst-treated prospective farmers at last acquired his own little lot, and final resting place, on the 25th of that month.

A week later, on 3 May, Pelly quit Niagara to head for a life of 'chronic dirt', grass stew and exhaustion in the construction camps along the route of the new Regina, Long Lake and Saskatchewan Railway. His decision to disappear into the wilds, in conjunction with Murray's quiet abandonment of any hunt for other members of Birchall's gang, brought to a natural close Pelly's round-the-clock police protection. He left Baldwin's 'prepared to do anything'. He was armed with a pass to Regina, courtesy of Canada's Prime Minister, and a letter of recommendation addressed to Hugh D. Lumsden, Chief Railway Engineer of the Canadian Government. He also carried with him a copy of Lord Wolseley's 1869 *Soldiers' Pocket-book*, which would prove extremely useful. Pelly was finally about to get a taste of the tough outdoors life that he had wanted all along.

A day or two after his departure from frontier civilization, a correspondent for the Toronto *Mail* was granted the right to make an inspection of the prison at Woodstock. Whether or not this was a ruse to catch sight of its most famous inmate, an article appeared in the paper shortly thereafter under the title 'How the Little Man Comports Himself in Woodstock Jail'. This scoop provided a rare first-hand glimpse by a press-man of Birchall during the dog days of his incarceration. In the jail yard, the reporter asked to have Birchall identified, and was amazed when he turned out to be 'a shabby-looking little man', in outsized boots, a faded waistcoat and no collar. The pallor induced by cell conditions made a striking contrast with Birchall's 'raven hair and black moustache', the second of which Birchall 'constantly caressed' – but this was no longer the 'dashing figure' of the photographs. When the reporter politely expressed to Birchall 'the hope that his trial would free him of the charge now hanging blackly over his head', Birchall replied, 'You bet it will.' His trial was scheduled for September. He would have four more months to wait to find out if he was right.

10. A Little Deluge of Literary Slops

'I felt attracted towards this most foul and fiendish assassination. The paper stated that the throat had been cut and the body ripped open, several parts having been taken away entirely.'

Dr N. T. Oliver, *The Whitechapel Mystery*, 1889

From April onwards there was an extended lull in the investigation of Birchall's crimes, but newspaper editors compensated for the shortage of hard news by writing about the way that Birchall's story was generating distorted variants. Commentators went so far as to declare that inaccurate reporting in 'unscrupulous journals' had dragged the case down to the level of the worst literature available, the Toronto *Globe* noting loftily:

Full scope seems to have been accorded writers and correspondents to exercise their imagination in concocting all sorts of absurd yarns and theories, of the approved dime novel type, imputing to Burchell all the crimes that people can fancy he might possibly have found time to commit.

Amongst those papers to purvey 'absurd yarns', the New York *Herald* was conspicuous for its brazen improvements to the story. It had been a *Herald* writer, for example, on 6 March 1890, who had promulgated the idea that Mrs Birchall's role in her husband's schemes had been that of a calculating sexual decoy. 'If the victim was not pliable, it is claimed that Mrs.

Burchell, who is a very pretty woman, used her influence to induce the young man to emigrate to America, and she generally succeeded.' The article went on: 'Pelly thinks it was Burchell's intention to kill him first and then Benwell, but when Pelly left for New York, Burchell decided on Benwell's doom, despite his wife's supplications.' This claim completely garbled the facts, not least considering that the only reason Pelly left Niagara for New York was to try to discover where the already missing Benwell was. Undaunted, the *Herald* continued: 'Pelly said he overheard Burchell and his pseudo wife talking loudly and angrily concerning Benwell, and from what words were dropped he learned of relations between Benwell and Mrs. Burchell.' By the time this tale came to be reprinted as part of a Saturday round-up of news, another *Herald* writer had decided to dress it up a little further. Pelly, the story now read,

had heard Burchell and his wife talking in angry tones about Benwell, and from what he heard imagined that Benwell and Mrs. Burchell were on very intimate terms, and that Mrs. Burchell was opposed to the killing of her lover by her husband.

Colonel Benwell felt driven by this article to deny on record that his son had been involved in any such impropriety, and Pelly also commented to the press that there had been a 'terrible sensation' over an interview in which he had been represented as saying things he had 'never intended or dreamt of saying'.

This particular *Herald* story, while untrue, had been written in the style of a cold report of the facts. Elsewhere on the paper's pages, writers were given licence not merely to add dime-novel plot details to the Birchall story, but to write in dime-novel prose as well. A reporter telegraphing from

Toronto with the latest news on Benwell's inquest was allowed to begin:

They are weaving strange figures, the busy shuttles of the law, in this latest and greatest of murder mysteries. It is tapestry—Gobelin, I might say goblin, tapestry—and starting from the web and woof in colours that are dark as midnight and lurid as hell itself I see the form of a gallows tree, with mayhap more than a single branch taking shape.

'Mayhap more than a single branch' was revealed a few sentences later to be the speculation that Mrs Birchall would swing for Benwell's murder alongside her husband.

The *Herald* sank to these ploys because it was engaged in cut-throat rivalry with other American newspapers. The New York *World*, for example, the paper that had tracked down the elusive H. H. Jackson in Tucson, Arizona, produced another notably unrestrained early summary of the case. The opening confirms that one of the main fascinations of the case for its contemporaries was the idea of a well-bred gentleman dispassionately killing for money:

Here is the story of a quiet murder. Not one of those brutal killings where, inflamed by red passion, one man leaps upon the other and crushes the soul out of his body. Not that kind of murder. That is animal like, a dog might kill a dog that way. Now and then a man goaded to desperation, set fire by jealousy or hate or drink, kills his enemy so. But this murder is not such. It is distinctly human, appallingly quiet, horribly manlike.

The author was confident that 'the place had been selected, the manner of killing mapped out, and the only thing that remained was to take the animal to the grounds and complete the work begun so long ago. There was no ill feeling on either side.' When Birchall and Benwell had reached the designated spot, Benwell had been killed for 'his clothes and a little besides'. The question of Mrs Birchall's guilt was left open in this account, though perhaps it is telling that her blue eyes seemed to display 'the unconscious innocence of babyhood'.

The *World*'s version of the story provides a clear example of the sinister influence of fiction on the way the case struck its original audience. After Birchall had been described snipping the name tags out of Benwell's clothing, with devilish, pre-planned cleverness, the reader was to be brought up short by the archaism: 'But hold!' Unconsciously, it seemed, the murderer had allowed his victim's marked cigar case to slip to the ground at the scene of the crime:

Curious fatality! We read of it in our hours given over to fiction and say that the exigencies of the author drive him to have some such clue for the discovery of the murderer. But here in real life we find the thing repeated in the most flagrant manner—and that, too, in the hands of the murderer careful and painstaking to a fault.

The inescapable conclusion for the author of these lines was that Fate had intended Birchall to be caught. How untidy it would be, how dramatically wasteful, if come his trial in September, he were somehow to escape a guilty verdict.

With many offerings like these to consider, the Woodstock *Sentinel-Review* soon noted that Birchall was inspiring 'a little deluge of literary "slops"', slops in which 'a great show of descriptive writing in the highly florid, penny dreadful style' was matched by 'much moralising and simulated indignity at the enormity of the crime and its awful consequences'. This criticism was offered by the paper to shore up its defence of its own motives in reproducing such material, the explanation being that it was quoting extensive passages of slops purely as an educative 'matter of curiosity'. The hypocrisy of newspapers both denouncing and exploiting a public appetite for gore did not pass unnoticed. In September of 1890, for example, under the headline 'Newspapers as Bugaboos', the *Globe* reported on a 'recent meeting of the American Social Science Association'. Dr F. W. Russell had read a paper in which he declared 'that the newspaper accounts of the details of crime produced moral and mental deterioration, monomania and even criminal acts'. In a perfect example of 'simulated indignity', the *Globe* responded that 'the fact is that the wildest and most exaggerated accounts of these occurrences circulate when the newspaper man is not at hand to investigate the facts'. This is exactly what a newspaper would be expected to say, but the Birchall case makes it plain that the wildest and most exaggerated accounts of crimes were just as likely to circulate when newspaper men were paid to slouch off to the telegraph office and make them up.

On 8 April Birchall's lawyer, Mr Hellmuth, went to court to prevent a Toronto journal, the *Fireside Weekly*, publishing what it advertised as a forthcoming 'thrilling serial story' called *Who Killed Benwell? or, The Mystery of the Blenheim Swamp*. Though Hellmuth eventually won the case, on grounds of libel, he halted only one prejudicial story about his client amongst the countless others that were already circulating. These unstoppable libels no doubt tainted the public's grasp of the truths of the case in exactly the way that Hellmuth feared. *Who Killed Benwell?*, if it was ever subsequently published, is now lost to view, as is a separate rendering of the tale that was called *Birchall; or, the Life and Adventures of a Graceless*

Scoundrel; and presumably there were yet other versions that have now vanished so completely that not even their titles remain. However, the grade of literary slops with which publishers deluged the public at this time can after all be measured, as at least one dime novel about the murder has survived.

Not long after Birchall's incarceration in Woodstock jail, a jobbing writer in Chicago called John Arthur Fraser started to work on a 'pulp' based on the case. Fraser had only recently begun to make his mark in this field. In 1888 and 1889, using the pseudonym 'Hawkshaw the Detective', he had had three dime novels brought out by the Eagle Publishing Company: *Escaped from Sing Sing*; *Blinky Morgan, the Detectives' Foe*; and *The Story of a Dark Crime; or, Shadowed from Europe*. It was probably his fourth title, however, about a current, real case, though the book had come out anonymously, that sprang to the publishing mind when Benwell's murder hit the news stands: *The Cronin Mystery. A complete history of the murder, and the quarrel in the brotherhood. Written by an ex-member.* Needless to say, Fraser was not an ex-member of the Irish Republican Clan-Na-Gael brotherhood, nor, indeed, was he a detective. His pseudonym had been taken from Tom Taylor's hugely popular 1863 play *The Ticket-of-Leave Man*, about a detective called Hawkshaw, known as 'the Nailer'.

In March 1890 with the aftermath of the Cronin case still echoing through press reports, and with Birchall's name beginning to filter in, Fraser must have been awaiting developments in yet another running crime story, which he was writing up for a book that would be published as *Kemmler; or, The Fatal Chair*. William Kemmler had committed murder on 29 March 1889, and had been sentenced a few weeks later and

*A Hawkshaw title with typically irrelevant
cover picture.*

sent to Auburn prison, New York. There he found himself
set to become the first person ever to be executed using the
electric chair. In October 1889 lawyers had mounted an appeal
against the sentence on the grounds that this would be a 'cruel
and unusual punishment' and therefore unconstitutional; but
by mid March of 1890 there had been a new ruling that the
chair must be used. While the appeals process continued
across the summer, the authorities found they had the greatest
difficulty procuring a mechanism for the execution, let alone
the power source itself. Neither of the rivals for the domestic

trade in electricity, George Westinghouse and Thomas Edison, was the slightest bit keen either to supply a generator for this purpose, or to have their product endorsed as the best for killing human beings.

Books of the grade that Fraser was knocking out in this period were published between soft covers and printed on cheap, rapidly disintegrating paper made of acid wood pulp, hence 'pulp' fiction. The term extended itself to imply that the prose content of a 'pulp' was of no more value than the paper on which it was printed; and though pulp publishers did deal in pirated editions of some of the greatest works of literature, books written specifically for this market were mostly of a standard where blood on the ground is 'carmine dew', and 'carmine dew' is all over the place. Many authors in the pulp business used multiple pseudonyms, and successful fictional characters were often dished out to more than one writer. It was a confusing and ephemeral scene.

The books weren't designed to last, and most haven't, but even so a handful of copies do survive of Hawkshaw the Detective's *The Swamp of Death; or, The Benwell Murder*. Odd details in this work indicate that Fraser must have sat down in the early summer of 1890 and steeped himself in newspaper articles on the Birchall case, from England, America and Canada. How much effort he put into the next stage of the process, the actual writing, is unclear, but he apparently cranked out the first three quarters of his novel in a matter of weeks, adding to such facts as amused him an absurdly convoluted explanation for the crime.

Right through the nineteenth century there was a market for books hastily produced in this way, to exploit recent, sickening murders; and Fraser's effort in this instance was to be typical: a mishmash of facts, summaries and of real documents, copied out of press reports, all carried on a surging tide of invention. As Fraser began, he must have decided to make *The Swamp of Death* as crazed as the craziest works in this vein. Certainly he added more twists to the original story than it could bear. He set a time bomb ticking on page twenty, for example, with the invented heroine of a side-story, Miss Emma Clifford, being made to reveal that despite her surname, the name of her real, deceased father, was Benwell. Sad to say, in all the complexities of the novel's surplus plot, this was a bomb that Fraser would never remember to detonate. He also decided on having not one but two characters called Dudley, for no discoverable reason, one in Oxford and the other in Canada, though as Fraser had them show a 'strong resemblance' to each other, most readers would presumably have expected a dramatic mix-up. If this was a wasted opportunity, Fraser did derive mileage from the almost perfect resemblance he created between Rex Birchall and a character called Reggie Somerset, the only difference between Somerset and Birchall being Birchall's rotten teeth. The social world of Oxford, meanwhile, was one in which terrible debts were run up, so that the weaker chaps could live in dread of the day when they would 'go to everlasting smash'. Philip Dudley in Oxford – not to be confused with Pickthall's friend, the thief in a lock-up in Detroit – was conceived as an extremely good-looking but impoverished cad, and the main figure of evil in the book. Like Rex Birchall, he would act as a farm pupil agent, helping to dispatch to Canada the university's ever-increasing number of scapegraces and failures; but the crux of the plot was to revolve round the fact that while Philip Dudley had long been in love with Reggie Somerset's sister Marion, she, after a chance meeting on a London omnibus, would fall in love with Benwell.

Fraser took the basic facts of the real Benwell murder case, distorted them using the complications described above, and achieved a result that allowed him to add in five largely woeful love affairs, a ruthless seduction compounded by a faked marriage, cruel card sharps, a ghastly cancer operation, an attack of brain fever, inheritance disputes, two definite murders, two presumed murders, one presumed suicide in the Niagara Falls, and the execution, after frivolities, of a horse. He was also unable to resist making the suggestion that Birchall was wont to lark about pretending to be Jack the Ripper. This wild hotchpotch in the novel's contents would be marked by startling fluctuations in its style. At his worst, Fraser was a poor writer even by the standards of late nineteenth-century pulp output:

The waning moon was shining down with subdued radiance, a soft, chastened light like the memory of past joys, and fell with the tenderest touch, through a delicate tracery of leaf and vine, upon the young couple who sauntered along the paths of Sir Godfrey Arnold's garden.

It is typical that a few pages after this fantasized courtship scene, the reader was to be confronted by transcripts of the tedious letters that Benwell and his father genuinely wrote to Birchall about railway and steamer timetables.

After a hundred pages of narrative disorder, Fraser managed somehow to hook together enough of the mad strands of his plot to be able to propel Rex Birchall and Marion Somerset's lover, Benwell, into an Ontario swamp. Press accounts for March 1890 had agreed that a fire some months before Benwell's murder had brought down many of the trees in the area, making the swamp's interior virtually impassable, though the New York *Herald* had preferred the idea that the 'dismal quagmire' was 'a cemetery of trees that had died, as trees sometimes do, of cold'. Fraser clearly digested a large portion of these stories before he set about killing Benwell himself. He described the area as a 'gruesome spot', and a place 'in which one stepping unwarily might sink and struggle for hours without being able to escape from it'. His two young men venture in a certain distance before Birchall stands aside to let Benwell go first:

The path, if path it could be termed, was blocked with trees felled and half burned, and Benwell was stepping across one that lay in his way, when a pistol shot rang sharply out, and he fell from his slight elevation, crashing down across the stump of a tree, DEAD.

Not one thought of life, death or the hereafter, could have passed through his mind, not a thought of home or loved ones visited him—he died instantly, shot through the brain by a *cowardly assassin, who sneaked up behind.*

The second bullet is administered in this version simply 'to make assurance doubly sure', and in this manner Benwell becomes 'an inanimate thing, that just a moment before had been a living, breathing soul'.

Anyone prepared to apply their critical faculties to Fraser's writing will observe that Benwell's *cowardly assassin* is not named in these sentences. In all the novel's plot before it reaches Birchall's trial, there are only two points at which Fraser retrospectively added in a detail that he could only have known once the real trial had taken place. Otherwise, every item that he drew from documentary material was there in the press reports for March and April. It follows that Fraser must have devised the first three quarters of *The Swamp of Death* as a stupendous exercise in bet-hedging, of which the murder scene is the zenith. He needed to write as much of his novel as possible ahead of the trial in order to be able to publish the book as soon as possible after it; but what if Birchall should emerge from court not guilty?

As Fraser worked out his plot for *The Swamp of Death* over the summer of 1890, he was simultaneously waiting to be able to give a speedy finish to his book about the electric chair. Appeals and writs in the Kemmler case had continued throughout the summer, but he was finally 'electricized' in Auburn prison on 6 August 1890. An official report into the execution subsequently noted that 'for obvious reasons the only means of determining the question of death was by ocular demonstrations'. After seventeen seconds the electricity was turned off, but Kemmler's continuing pulse, and the froth that he emitted – 'slimy ooze' in Fraser's version caused officials to lose their nerve and they electrocuted him again. Despite eyewitness accounts of his death that invested it 'with an air of repulsion, brutality and horror', the authorities declared that the chair had been entirely successful in its main purpose, and thus the strong recommendation was made that a central electric execution 'plant' be constructed.

However distracted Fraser was by the hideous details of Kemmler's death in August, he had already worked out his most important piece of insurance against the narrative crisis that would result in his other book if Birchall should walk free from court the month after. This was to make his Dudley doppelgänger a vicious wretch and probable multiple murderer with an insanely jealous loathing for Benwell. Once Fraser had got this much on paper, it seems fair to assume that he must have sat back and prayed that no big revelations would come out at the trial in September.

★

As the summer of 1890 slipped by, many newspapermen invented details for articles about Birchall that made his story seem to conform to the standards of pulp plotting. Part of the reason the case was increasingly described as being 'like a romance taken from the pages of an impossible fiction' was that so much fiction was laid óver it. This probably contributed to a second strain of press comment where editorialists remarked that the Birchall drama was proving to be 'more interesting than the last chapter of the most thrilling fiction ever written', or in other words, that it actually exceeded the dime-novel genre. However, when the Toronto *Mail* turned to a local detective, Reburn, for his ideas on the case, he responded cautiously: 'To say that a conspiracy may be in existence to deliberately decoy and kill human beings for the sake of robbery is often laughed at in dime novels, but may have a foundation in fact.' The implication behind this remark was fair enough: for a real story to seem as bad as a pulp novel was as much as anyone could reasonably desire.

11. The Curtain Rung Up at Last

The public has read from day to day of the murderer's complete self-possession, of his constant coolness, of his profound composure, of his perfect equanimity. Some describers have gone so far as to represent him, occasionally rather amused than otherwise by the proceedings.

Charles Dickens, 'The Demeanour of Murderers', 1856

As Woodstock prepared, in the third week of September, for the opening of Birchall's trial, the little town took on a carnival atmosphere. One of the local papers billed the centre 'like a circus', and painted an advertisement for its forthcoming trial reports, along a thirty-foot fence, 'in gorgeous red and yellow'. A cigar-store owner placed a pine stump in the window of his shop claiming it was 'the one against which the murdered man lay while in his death agonies', and hotel prices trebled as people flocked in from both the backwoods and the cities. Reporters wrote that 'the murder trial has simply blotted out all other subjects of conversation'.

Woodstock's worthies, conscious of unparalleled scrutiny, regretted only that the town lacked a proper court house. They had pulled down the old one the previous winter, and the new one was not yet completed. During this period most of Ontario's court rooms were 'ramshackle', with the worst so 'abominable' that judges were beginning to refuse to sit in them; but Woodstock's laudable decision to start again from scratch meant that in 1890 the only suitable venue for a trial

THE BENWELL TRAGEDY !

A LARGE AND VALUABLE OIL PAINTING

Of the scene of the above tragedy painted and sketched on the spot by Prof. Lennox

Is Now on Exhibition in our Show Window.

DICK BRO.S'   NEW MONSTER CLOTHING HOUSE.

444 Dundas street, Opposite Caister House, Woodstock.

Local exploitation of the trial.

was the town hall. The *Sentinel-Review* admitted that this building was 'far from a credit to the town', bearing 'the scars of many winters and more variety troupes'.

In their latter phases, both Benwell's inquest and the magisterial inquiry in Niagara had taken place in halls usually used as theatres. Now, by accident of circumstance, Birchall's murder trial would follow suit. When reporters saw inside Woodstock's temporary court house, they noted with glee that pieces of scenery and other 'paraphernalia' were still visible at the side of the stage. Furthermore, 'the scenes depicted upon the wings' were 'strangely like the pictures taken of the "Swamp of Death"'. The headline writers set to ebulliently, one of them writing: 'The Curtain Rung Up at Last—on the Drama in Woodstock's Temple of Thespis'. No play or opera, it was claimed, could conceivably approach the 'drama in real life' about to be performed upon the boards of this shabby rural theatre.

The judge in the case, Hugh MacMahon, who had had

years of experience as a criminal lawyer, was forced to preside from the stage, and, with the court officials, to use the area behind the wing curtains as a retiring room. His workload began on Thursday 17 September. There were only four criminal cases listed on the docket: Benwell's murder, two rapes, and an instance of cattle poisoning. The rapes and the poisoning, not to mention six lesser cases on the civil docket, caused 'but the slightest ripple of excitement'. MacMahon dispensed with them all in two days.

While he ran through these other trials, the legal teams in the Birchall case made their final preparations. The immense publicity given to the story had led several lawyers to make overtures to Birchall in jail, including James Archibald Macdonald, nephew of the Canadian Prime Minister, who had gone so far as to attend part of the Niagara inquiry. The Chicago *Tribune*, meanwhile, had offered to provide Birchall with a lawyer at the paper's expense; but despite these approaches, for a long time Birchall had retained only Mr Hellmuth, along with two local Woodstock lawyers, Mr Finkle and Mr McKay. In addition, on advice, Birchall had employed a detective, who bore the pantomime name of Charles Bluett. Bluett's primary job was to gather evidence for the defence, though in the weeks leading up to the trial he found himself distracted by the need to 'ventilate', or expose, various fakes, most notably a con set up by two men called Leslie who attempted, through the press, to sell Birchall a false alibi. Bluett did not work entirely alone. Under the heading 'A Woman Detective', one paper noted that he was receiving considerable assistance from his wife, though its exact nature was never made clear. As with Mrs Birchall, Mrs Bluett seemed to register in the case as, more or less willingly, an accessory of her husband's:

Mrs. Bluett, the detective's wife, has been in Woodstock during the past five weeks, and for a time was looked upon with suspicion by the Crown officers. She was 'shadowed' for several days, and was greatly annoyed by the persistent efforts of an individual who was anxious to ascertain her name and business. Mrs. Bluett is a plump young Englishwoman of neat appearance, and it is said that she has been of great help to her husband.

The practice amongst nineteenth-century detectives and police officers of employing their wives to aid them in sensitive areas of their work appears to have been widespread, suggesting that a considerable number of Victorian women operated as detectives in all but name. The general lack of publicity given to their work may reflect its disreputable nature. Another unusual contemporary reference to 'women detectives', used in the hunt for Jack the Ripper, reveals that they were 'the very class of women' he favoured as victims. These decoys would 'nightly prowl through the squalid thorough fares of Whitechapel, shadowed not far away by members of the regular force'. Whatever the relative contributions, regular or irregular, of the Bluetts, Mr Bluett was said in the end to have amassed seven hundred pages of foolscap notes for the defence.

Birchall had hoped to be able to bring out legal help from England, but he failed to raise enough money for this, and did not retain senior counsel until early August, five months after his arrest. The man in question, George Tate Blackstock, was thirty-four and a rising legal star, a criminal lawyer from Toronto characterized by his use of invective. Even despite this late start, other commitments meant that Blackstock was unable to give his full attention to Birchall's case until seven days before the trial began.

His opponents were undoubtedly formidable. Woodstock's county Crown attorney, Mr Ball, might have been expected to lead the prosecution in a local murder case, but although he did much of the preparation, in early July the Attorney-General, Mr Mowat, had selected Britton Bath Osler to lead. Mowat also sent his deputy, Mr Cartwright, to be his special representative at the trial. B. B. Osler, by this stage in his triumphant career, had 'come to be looked upon as one of the cleverest manipulators of the evidence in the whole Province'. He was particularly renowned for having been part of the prosecution team that had managed – by means fair and foul – to secure the conviction and ultimately the hanging of the French–Indian Métis leader, Louis Riel, after Riel led an armed rebellion against the Canadian government in 1885. While Osler was a dominating presence, he was also known for the fact that his manner was 'always gentlemanly in court'. In this respect he contrasted powerfully with Blackstock. The press looked forward to a gripping clash of styles.

The town hall may have been old and battered, but during the weekend before Birchall's trial began it was smartly wired for outside communication. The Great North Western Telegraph Company ran lines to the press tables, and provided a dozen operators, so that court reports could be sent to national and international newspaper offices 'hot from the pencils of the reporters'. Startlingly, though, the hall was also rigged up with suspended telephone transmitters. Four feet above the judge's seat, hanging from the ceiling, there was a 'telephonic transmitter, from which ran half a dozen wires connecting with the residences of some prominent townspeople'. In addition, the owner of a Woodstock hotel, the Thompson House, ran further telephone wires into his establishment, sixteen to a general parlour and four to a 'private room for

Woodstock town hall, on the right, circa 1890.

ladies', so that 'every word' said in court could be 'leaked into the ears of the listeners in the hotel'. These telephone 'tubes' were advertised at twenty-five cents an hour. A live broadcast of the trial was being offered for profit.

While these preparations were being made, Murray corralled a huge number of witnesses in Woodstock. He, Osler and the Niagara police chief, Thomas Young, then set about interrogating them and putting their evidence together. In March Murray had informed the press that he was finding the witness statements to 'agree to a nicety'. It was now time to make certain this remained true. The press noted that the Crown's 'systematic' preparation would ensure that, marvellously, court reports 'from day to day' would 'read like chapters of a book'.

On the morning of Monday 22 September Birchall's trial finally began. This was the only day on which the crowds were held back and relative calm prevailed inside the court-room. There were about six hundred seats for the use of the public in the hall and gallery, but over two thousand tickets had been issued; and with many more people guaranteed to be attempting to attend, it must have been clear from the start that there was a danger the trial would become the focus of mobbing and disorder. The 'long array of counsel' sat at two tables in front of the judge, with Detective Murray at the Crown table and Detective Bluett sitting with the defence. Crushed round five other tables down the side of the hall sat thirty odd reporters, one of whom described the assembled pressmen as 'a bright, brainy, galaxy of young men'. Up on stage behind the judge, meanwhile, sat a handful of Wood-stock's most prominent ladies, as well as wives and daughters of the Toronto lawyers who were working on the case. In addition, sixty or more potential jurors arrived, as did some seventy Crown witnesses, plus a few townsfolk and clergymen who were specially allowed in. The aisles were covered with matting and the floor between the seats with shavings in the hope that this would prevent footfalls 'disturbing the judicial serenity of the court room'.

When Birchall arrived it was instantly clear that seven months in a small-town lock-up, surrounded by lunatics and beggars, had done nothing to inhibit his élan. He was wearing a black, faux-chinchilla coat, and 'from his Christy stiff hat to his pointed, highly polished shoes', struck onlookers as 'the picture of nattiness'. As he entered the court, brought in by Police Chief Thomas Young, he 'walked down the aisle sprightly', and seemed charmed to be the focus of attention. A New York *Sun* reporter was disconcerted, writing: 'Perhaps

Birchall pleads not guilty, 22 September 1890.

no man charged with murder was ever before in such an apparently easy frame of mind as Birchall appears to be.' The prisoner, he added, had had a 'smile upon his face that would honor a bridegroom'.

The prisoner's dock had been salvaged from the old court house. The metropolitan press dismissed it as looking 'much like a dry goods box', but no doubt what actually mattered to them was the fact that when Birchall sat down, only the very top of his head could be seen. It took two days for officials to lower the rail.

Birchall was arraigned at once, and 'in a steady voice' pleaded not guilty. It was then necessary to select a jury. As each potential juror entered the witness box, Birchall was made to stand up and face him. The defence had first right of refusal, though no questioning was allowed. In all, twenty-three men were dismissed, eighteen by the defence, possibly because they lived near the swamp where Benwell had been found, and five by the Crown. Any selected juryman was required actually to look at Birchall, and, 'In every instance', reporters agreed, 'the glance of the juror fell before the bold glance of the prisoner.' It had been expected that finding an acceptable jury might take a very long time. Instead, the whole process was completed in under an hour. A Toronto paper described the twelve good men and true as intelligent and, 'it is believed, unprejudiced'. This hint of equivocation was nothing to what an American reporter was prepared to say after he had canvassed opinion amongst the people milling around outside:

The crowd was composed not only of townspeople, but there were many farmers present, and they seemed to take a great deal more interest in the trial than anybody else. That this interest is felt to be against the prisoner is shown by the general impression that if the jury is composed of farmers, Birchall's doom is sealed.

As it transpired, this prediction would be put to the test. Of the twelve jurors, eleven were farmers; and while the last, the foreman, George Christopher, was listed merely as a 'gentleman', he was at least a retired farmer. Their anticipated ground for prejudice was reflected in the local newspaper sentiment that

the belief that both the murderer and murdered were strangers to the place will not help the place any. It will be mathematically proven that a murder was committed there and in consequence the decent farmers of that neighborhood will have the statistics pointing their fingers at them as criminals of the worst class.

Beyond such defensive attitudes, it is notable that at least seven of the jurors – John McKay, James McKay, A. S. McKay, A.

McCann, D. McLean, Donald Murray and Robert Murray –
were ethnically Scots. Woodstock and the surrounding area
had originally been settled by upper-class English half-pay
officers, but the English had not thrived there for thirty or
forty years. They had left traces behind them in their failed
histories, grandiose mansions and the preservation of their
surnames, or towns of origin, in the names of local villages
and streets; but since the demise of this unsuccessful body of
the English, Woodstock's corporation had been run, long and
proudly, 'in a canny Scotch way'. A criminal who happened
to be a dissolute English gentleman was likely to inspire yet
further instinctive mistrust in those decent local farmers who
were Scots.

As Osler rose to open the Crown's case 'a solemn stillness per-
vaded the court'. He warned the jury to 'put away' all im-
pressions they might have derived from the press. Birchall, he
reminded them, was innocent until proven guilty: 'Your oath
is to pass upon him according to the evidence – nothing else.'
This point dispensed with, 'in deadly array' Osler 'marshalled
forth his facts.'

He contended that the case was one of murder; that
Benwell, a young Englishman aged twenty-four, had been
killed roughly where he had been found, in the Blenheim
swamp, on 21 February of that year, and that, taking weather
conditions into account, the state of the body indicated he
had been dead since the 17th. He talked about Birchall's
duplicitous, swindling past, and brought out the fact that on
the prisoner's first trip to Canada he had visited Pine Pond, a
picnic spot in the northern part of the same swamp. He also
explained that Birchall had hunted there, and so was very well
acquainted with the area. He discussed Birchall's deceitful

farm pupillage agreements with Pelly and Benwell, and noted that on the voyage from Liverpool, Birchall had signed the ship's register using the name 'Bushell' for himself, and 'Petty' for Pelly. He then informed the court that several witnesses, some of whom had previously known Birchall as Somerset, would testify that on 17 February they had seen him and Benwell travelling, by train and on foot, all the way from Niagara to the Blenheim swamp via Eastwood railway station. Other witnesses would confirm that they had seen Birchall later that day, returning alone from the swamp to Eastwood station. Osler explained that the times of the various train journeys involved meant that Birchall would have had ample opportunity to commit Benwell's murder. He also pointed out that, although Birchall had told Pelly he would communicate with him at around two o'clock that day, the telegram he eventually sent, to say that their party must remain in Buffalo another night, was wired in the evening from Suspension Bridge, Niagara, under the name Bushell or Bastell, minutes after the train Birchall apparently took from Eastwood had arrived at that station. He claimed that Birchall told Pelly the next day that Benwell had taken his revolver, and he also discussed Birchall's suspicious possession of Benwell's baggage keys, of a nicked pair of scissors that matched the cuts in Benwell's clothing, and so on.

These details had been extensively reported in the press already, but Osler's next move was surprising. Though it had long been common knowledge that Birchall had sent a letter to Colonel Benwell after 17 February suggesting that Benwell wanted immediately to invest five hundred pounds in Birchall's businesses, and that Benwell would be writing to confirm this, the precise wording of the letter had not so far been made public. It was highly improper for Osler to read out a document not yet admitted in evidence, but neither Blackstock nor the judge objected as the Crown lawyer caused 'a sensation' by doing just that. Osler observed that although the letter was undated, it had Birchall's Niagara post office box, number 313, as a return address. Birchall had not taken this box until 19 February, and the letter was post marked 20 February. Osler contended that this proved that there were only two days on which it could have been written. As the references in the letter to Birchall's farms and to his business accounts were 'all imagination', Osler drew the inference that Birchall had intended to counterfeit a letter from Benwell to his father: 'It was not likely the money would be sent without a letter from the son.' Osler then recalled Pelly's account of Birchall and Benwell copying each other's signatures, and asserted that altogether 'the position on this letter throws a very heavy burden of disproval on the prisoner at the bar'. He now outlined Birchall's various attempts to throw off suspicion once details of Benwell's cigar case had been given in the national press. He also remarked that Benwell's gold pen had been found in Birchall's possession on his arrest.

With these points noted, Osler returned to the matter of the corpse and the swamp. He put forward the theory that Birchall had known of a trail going beyond where the body was found that led to a feature called Mud Lake, and had intended to dispose of Benwell's body by sinking it there. He proposed that Benwell had been killed somewhere very close to the spot where his body was discovered, and that dents found on the underside of the corpse indicated that rigor mortis had set in after the body had been placed across the array of raised saplings. He described how Benwell's clothes had been hurriedly pulled open for the name tags to be cut out, and how various of the young man's possessions and bits of torn clothing had been found around where he lay. Benwell's left foot had been frozen hard into the sodden ground below the body, and as his left arm had been propped up by branches, its waterproof sleeve had filled with slush, rain or snow, which had also frozen solid. Osler had obtained detailed records of the weather conditions across the days between 17 and 21 February to account for the precise state of the corpse. As to the injuries Benwell had sustained, the post-mortem findings were that either of the bullet wounds in his head would have killed him, while the bruising in his groin area could be accounted for by the impact of his fall to the ground once he had been shot. Otherwise, Benwell seemed to have been fit and healthy at the point of death. Last of all in this summary of evidence, Osler revealed that witnesses who had been hunting in the swamp on 17 February would swear to having heard two unusual shots fired nearby, in close succession, during the middle of the day, in exactly the span of time during which the Crown believed that Birchall had murdered his companion.

This opening statement took Osler over two hours. A reporter wrote that the lawyer's manner betrayed 'a studious absence of any attempt at dramatic display or theatrical gesture', but that the impression he made was 'masterly'. The first witness Osler called was William Macdonald, requiring him to explain that, as a farm pupil agent, he had placed Birchall on the farm of a man called Wilcox late in 1888. Birchall had remained there one night only, had stayed with Macdonald afterwards for two and a half weeks, and had then lived in apartments in Woodstock for some months 'entered upon no particular business'. This innocuous start to the prosecution evidence gave way at once to a grinding cross-examination by the defence.

Under a barrage of questions from Blackstock, Macdonald denied that local farmers bribed him to recommend their farms for pupillage. He denied that his presence in Niagara just in time to denounce Birchall at the original magisterial inquiry had been anything other than a coincidence:

the reason he went there was to see a man named Dudley, who was over at the Falls on the American side. Dudley had run away from Detroit. He robbed a man up there, and witness went up there thinking to have him arrested.

Blackstock did not linger over the peculiarity of the fact that if this explanation was true, then Dudley and Macdonald, each of them old friends of Birchall's, had both been headed for Niagara just as Birchall arrived there. Instead, Blackstock pressed Macdonald on his relationship with Birchall in 1888 and 1889. Macdonald denied that they had ever had any unpleasantness in the past, but was immediately forced to concede that he had remonstrated with Birchall after finding out about the letter Birchall had written to Ford & Rathbone, which effectively accused him of swindling various pupils. 'When caught and asked by Blackstock why he hadn't told the truth the first time,' wrote one reporter, Macdonald 'said he didn't know the defence knew so much about him.' By painful degrees, Blackstock now elicited from Macdonald that he had initially placed Dudley on Pickthall's farm – Pickthall who was yet another former friend of Birchall's – and that he had received the full amount of money from Ford & Rathbone for a successful one month's trial even though Dudley had left the farm before the month was up. Macdonald was also 'made to admit' that he might, 'while drinking, which happened frequently', have proposed to Birchall that they start a farm pupil business together. Osler now re-examined Macdonald to establish that Dudley himself had been the recipient of the money falsely obtained from Ford & Rathbone, not Macdonald or Pickthall, but this was hardly much of an improvement to the story. Osler must have been extremely displeased by the shifty revelations of his first witness. Pelly, effectively the chief witness for the prosecution, would surely stand up better.

As Pelly's name was called, sympathetic pressmen saw that he had 'nerved himself for an unpleasant ordeal'. The less sympathetic view was that he looked 'as if his six months of ease and travel at the expense of the Government thoroughly agreed with him'. This dig was unfair. Pelly's summer had been dominated by filth and slog as he lived the life of a railway surveyor in the prairies between Regina and Saskatoon. He had worked for a dollar and a half a day plus 'grub', which usually consisted of a stew made from hard tack, sow belly and anything the prairie offered that was green and didn't look poisonous. These suspect rations were washed down by a mixture of whiskey from the boss's flask and fetid water out of old buffalo wallows. Not surprisingly, the men suffered endless stomach upsets. They were plagued by flies during the day and by wolves at night. In a letter home, Pelly described the man above him in the chain of command as 'a first-class type of the worst sort of blaspheming, dirty, tobacco chewing, Anglo-American cad', but apart from hating this man's 'beast-liness', he had thrived on hard outdoor labour. Pelly had by no means been living in ease, but it was true that his summer had agreed with him.

There was a 'ripple of excitement' through the court as he entered the witness box. Blackstock immediately attempted, but failed, to block as immaterial Pelly's testimony about how

Pelly gives evidence,
22 September 1890.

Birchall had swindled him. Even so, though his evidence would take up the whole of the rest of the day and would spill over well into the next, Pelly gave only the same, restrained account of events to which he had sworn previously. As before, Pelly appeared anxious, even over-anxious, not to say anything unnecessarily incriminating about Birchall, despite feeling certain of his guilt. He contradicted Osler's opening claim that Birchall had brought up the subject of his missing revolver on 18 February, placing this remark not one but twelve days after Benwell's disappearance; but apart from this, Pelly performed for the prosecution much as anyone might have expected. One reporter wrote, perhaps correctly, that Osler 'wished the jury to look upon Pelly as the ghost of Benwell, which had come from the grave to confront and confound his murderer'.

The press expected Blackstock to give Pelly 'a hard time of it' in cross-examination, but this process lasted little more than fifteen minutes. Blackstock's main aim seemed to be to draw out positive evidence on his client's behalf. He rattled Pelly somewhat over the question of whether or not Birchall had been responsible for Pelly's own dislike of Benwell. Pelly would admit only that, 'in a mild sort of way', he had rather avoided his travelling companion. He did, however, freely agree with Blackstock that Birchall had shown no special anxiety about Benwell's luggage, beyond what might be considered 'reasonable care', the implication being that this was not the behaviour of a man intent on comprehensive theft. Pelly also established categorically for Blackstock that it had been Birchall who had drawn attention to Benwell's name in the newspapers, and who had initiated the idea of going to Princeton to identify the corpse. Again, this was not obviously the behaviour of a guilty murderer, although the press had anticipated this point with the argument that 'instead of being presumptive proof of innocence', it only demonstrated 'the super human nerve of the man'. Pelly confirmed that Benwell was 'short, thick-set and of dark complexion', a point that would be useful in contradicting identification evidence, but denied that he had ever gathered from Birchall that either Macdonald or the Peacock brothers were actually involved in the farm pupillage business.

When on day two, Tuesday, Pelly had finished his testimony, there was another ripple of excitement in court as Charles Benwell, Benwell's younger brother, entered the witness box. He had been called by the Crown because his father, Colonel Benwell, was too ill to attend the trial. Two days earlier Charles Benwell had been to visit his brother's grave where he 'gave vent to his emotion in tears'. Pelly later recalled how he had then been to see him, to offer any help in his power:

To my astonishment he received me with the greatest coolness and was barely polite. I then learnt that the Benwells all considered that I could have saved their son and held me largely responsible for his death. A friend of Mrs. Benwell told my parents that her (Mrs. Benwell's) daily prayer was that I might come to a violent death.

In court, though Charles Benwell sat within six feet of Birchall, he was never once seen to look in the prisoner's direction. Under sober questioning from Osler he described how, in the five years since leaving school, his older brother had spent time with tutors in Switzerland, had intended to go into the army but then decided against it, had farmed in New Zealand for a year and a half, and had spent considerable time in England afterwards more or less at leisure, rowing, playing football and so on. He was asked to identify various crucial small articles, including a dental plate, that had belonged to his brother. He told the court that the waterproof coat Benwell had been wearing when shot had previously been worn by their father, and there was 'moisture in his eyes' as he was shown the 'Conny' gold pencil. Otherwise he stated that his brother had been in good health when he left England for Canada, and when asked about his brother's disposition, remarked that he was 'always cheerful'. Blackstock established that Benwell would freely lend his gold pencil to his brother, but otherwise made little use of the witness.

   The reporters at the press tables were keen to understand what the main defence argument would actually be, and as time went on, it seemed more and more likely to them that Blackstock had found himself in a position where he would be compelled to construct his case largely out of shortfalls in the prosecution. If, as these pressmen suspected, Blackstock had no strong defence witnesses up his sleeve, able or prepared to testify positively to his client's innocence, the destructive force of the cross-examination of the Crown witnesses would prove crucial. Blackstock had shown with Macdonald that he was prepared to go on the attack. He was known for being a 'caustic questioner' with 'a habit of repeating sarcastically every answer given by the witness that does not please him', and this characteristic would now come to the fore. Once Charles Benwell's testimony was finished, Blackstock's anger started to permeate proceedings.

For the rest of Tuesday, Osler called a series of less important witnesses. A provincial land surveyor, William M. Davis, vouched for the map he had produced of the location of the crime, giving the distances and plausible timings involved in Birchall's alleged walk to and from the swamp. Blackstock had to badger Davis before he would admit that the walking times he had given had been measured in July, when the roads were hard, rather than muddily sodden and obstructed as they had been in February; and also that a line on his map showing a broad trail leading to Mud Lake had been added in under instruction, 'in furtherance of some theory in connection with the tragedy'. After conspicuous hesitation Davis admitted to a seething Blackstock, 'Yes, I suppose it was.' He also agreed, though only when Blackstock reminded him that Birchall's life was at stake, that it would have been impossible for a single man to have carried a corpse any distance through the swamp.

The Elvidge brothers, Constable Watson, Swarts the undertaker, Grigg the sexton, and others, all gave evidence about the discovery of Benwell's body, footprints in the snow, the state of the corpse when found, measures taken to thaw it out for the post mortem, and Birchall's reactions and claims when he came to Princeton to identify it. Under cross-examination, Swarts was insolently unhelpful, and received an 'awful tossing' from Blackstock over the fact that he had embroidered stories about the unknown corpse being an Indian tinker. Though Blackstock chipped away at the credibility of many of these witnesses, however, as Tuesday's evidence drew to a close, the logic behind his questions remained opaque to people in the court room. One reporter wrote that it would require 'a good deal of guess-work' for anyone 'to attempt an under-standing or description of what the defence were driving at'. It was consequently very hard to tell which side had the advantage.

There had been one other piece of legal business transacted that day. Mrs Birchall had not attended court on the Monday, but on Tuesday she and her sister, Mrs West-Jones, did arrive. They had been offensively written up in the Woodstock press as two women who dressed 'rather clamorously, and are quite giddy in their walk and conversation'. If true, there was no giddiness now. Although, oddly, Mrs Birchall's name seems not to have appeared on the criminal docket, the lingering case against her as some sort of an accessory to her husband's crime had to be addressed as a matter of form. At the same time, it was clear that 'the Crown had no intention of prosecuting'. When the moment came for a formal decision, therefore, 'No Bill' was found against her: she was finally free. To the disappointment of reporters she did not return again that week to attend her husband's trial, but kept to her hotel room, suffering, it was said, from abject nervous prostration.

On day one, the court had initially been filled with unsorted jurors and witnesses. Once the case properly began, most of them were asked to leave the hall, and departed in a 'mighty host'. For some reason their empty seats were not given up that afternoon to the spectators waiting outside. The *Sentinel-*

Review was annoyed. The ticketless masses, including, of course, 'well-to-do farmers', had every right to come in: 'This is a democratic country. Just open the door of the Queen's court room please!' Infuriating as this had been, day one was the last time there would be any vacant spaces at the Birchall trial. From Tuesday onwards, spectators filled every seat and took almost every inch of standing room. Ticket enforcement was lax, and there was excitement 'at fever heat' as the crowds tried to push their way in. The fact that only one entrance was used for all comers meant that even the judge got pushed about. When, at one point, 'his Lordship had his judicial robes rumpled by the mass of common people,' he finally 'grew very wrathful'. He chastised the town's elderly constables for their failure to keep order, and from then on these benighted old men struggled 'like madmen to subdue the raging curiosity of the natives'. Nothing, however, prevented the fact that day after day the court was 'packed to suffocation'.

On day three, Wednesday 24 September, the local doctors who had carried out the post mortem on Benwell were called. Dr Taylor told Osler that the corpse had appeared to have been in the swamp for a period ranging from four to seven days, though Dr Welford, who had attended the post mortem on a whim, put the figure at only one and a half to two days. They agreed that the two bullet wounds ruled out suicide and that death had been instantaneous, whichever of the bullets – 'about 32 calibre' – was responsible. Dr Taylor, meanwhile, theorized that the indentations in the underside of the body had been made by the saplings upon which it had lain before the onset of rigor mortis. It was therefore important to establish, with regard to how far away Benwell might have been killed, how speedily rigor mortis was likely to have come on.

Both doctors believed that two to three hours was normal for this process. They also both believed that the bruises in Benwell's groin area must have been sustained at about the moment of death, as he fell over. There had been a considerable amount of fluid and a handful of split peas in his stomach. A third doctor, called Staples, who had helped to carry out the post mortem, corroborated Dr Taylor's testimony.

When Blackstock cross-examined Dr Taylor he made him agree that details he had just given were notably more extensive than those he had supplied in his inquest evidence. Blackstock added:

I observe that my learned friend, Mr. Osler, was examining you from a statement you had given to somebody? A.—Perhaps so. Q.—It is so isn't it? A.—Yes.

Taylor admitted that he had declined to give Hellmuth, for the defence, an explanation of even the original post-mortem notes, let alone allowing him to see this new, expanded statement. When Blackstock asked angrily whether, in the quasi-judicial position that the doctor held, his behaviour towards the defence could possibly be considered fair, Taylor refused to answer. Lawyer and witness moved on to discuss barking on the knuckles of one of Benwell's hands, Taylor agreeing that it had looked as though this had been caused by some form of violence other than a fall at the moment of death. Blackstock was even more exercised over new and contradictory details concerning a wound to Benwell's scalp: an area of tissue had been broken or bruised on the inside, adding to the possibility that there had been some kind of brawl.

In cross-examination, the second official medic, Dr Staples, had to fight to maintain his composure. He was especially weakened when Blackstock made him admit that he had originally believed Benwell to have been killed not more than two or three days before he was found. He now said that this view had been formed from looking not at the body, but at the clothes, and that he had not examined them closely anyway. Like Dr Taylor, he admitted that he had obstructed Hellmuth's attempt to get clarification on details of the post mortem. Osler quickly re-examined Taylor on this point to establish that their reluctance to facilitate members of the defence team had been the consequence of Osler's own advice in the matter.

Dr Welford, the third medical witness, was much more forthcoming with Blackstock than the other two. He had made the trip to Princeton with Miss Pickthall when she feared the dead man might be her missing brother, and had examined the body out of simple interest. He expanded on his previous testimony to add that the corpse had had what looked like about twenty-four hours' worth of beard growth. Blackstock then raised the fact that there had reportedly been a mark on Benwell's underdrawers, as though the body had hit a charred stump, and also that there had been what was possibly a corresponding abrasion on the leg. Welford agreed that this was so, Blackstock's point being that it reinforced the theory that the corpse had been carried through the burnt area of the swamp. Blackstock also elicited from Welford that Benwell, though small, had appeared sufficiently muscular and fit to be perfectly capable of taking on someone his own size in a fight.

Further witnesses were called by the prosecution and quickly dealt with. John A. Orchard confirmed that no one called Somerset or Birchall had ever owned a farm near Niagara. It transpired in cross-examination that one of

Blackstock's defence points was going to be that only a most
peculiar murderer would pass through Niagara with his intended victim, only to commit the deed elsewhere. For once
a Crown witness was positively pleased to oblige the defence,
Orchard agreeing 'that his long years of experience in and
around the falls had convinced him that there are great facilities
there for murder, suicide, etc.'

Osler now called post office and telegraph personnel who
identified letters and telegrams sent by Birchall after
17 February. A bank teller from the Bank of Niagara also
gave evidence that Birchall had opened an account there on
24 February, depositing $152. Then an expert witness, Professor
Woolverton, stepped into the box as the man in charge of
the observatory at Woodstock College, a 'chief station' of the
Dominion Meteorological Department. He explained to the
court that his institution logged six weather records a day, as
well as noting down readings from various self-registering
instruments. In theory this information would be vital to the
case. According to his notes, Monday 17 February had been
overcast, temperatures had fallen below freezing and there had
been about half an inch of rainfall during the night, 'a pretty
heavy storm'. On Tuesday 18 February there had been little
rainfall with temperatures again partly dipping below freezing.
On Wednesday 19 February there had been gusty winds and
temperatures had fallen well below freezing, but there had
been no recorded precipitation. On Thursday 20 February
there had been snowfall, from five a. m., to a depth of two
inches, with steady winds and temperatures again falling well
below freezing. Finally, on Friday 21 February there had
been one inch of snowfall, again steady winds, and again
temperatures had fallen below freezing. With difficulty Blackstock got from Woolverton what he clearly considered an

important admission regarding this evidence: that the fact
that no precipitation had been recorded by the Woodstock
Observatory on Wednesday 19 February did not necessarily
mean there had been none. The professor grudgingly allowed
that 'a very small quantity' might have fallen without having
registered on the instruments.

Wednesday's evidence, on day three of the trial, ended in
a slight hotchpotch of testimony, with witnesses speaking of
having seen Birchall in the general vicinity of the swamp in
1889. George Hersee, in particular, who lived near Pine Pond,
described Birchall riding out there four-in-hand in the spring
of 1889 to go 'sporting', and described their discussions about
the area generally, including Mud Lake. He was another
witness who proved extremely reluctant to help the defence,
but he did in the end admit to Blackstock that, contrary to
what he had just sworn, he had no specific knowledge of
Birchall actually hunting in the swamp. Blackstock asked
whether it wasn't the case that Hersee had once offered the
prisoner a commission of one hundred dollars if he could sell
off a farm of Hersee's to one of his English friends. The Hersee
family owned many lots in the area, including the very lot
where Benwell's body had been found. Hersee was bullish as
he agreed that Blackstock's assertion, potentially linking him
into a farm pupillage racket with the prisoner, was true.

Though he had given extensive evidence in the previous
hearings, Detective Murray had remained in court on day one
of the trial when it was cleared of witnesses, indicating that
the Crown did not intend to call him. The press was disappointed by this, one reporter writing that many people had
been 'tickling their fancy' with the idea of how, 'if this sleuth
hound was cooped up in the box, Mr Blackstock would give
him a combing down that would be worth a long journey to

see'. It was generally suspected that enough doubts had been raised about Murray's conduct that the Crown preferred to sacrifice his testimony rather than risk offering him up for cross-examination. Though Blackstock could have called the detective himself, he would then have been bound to accept whatever version of events Murray chose to give: rules of evidence would have prevented him throwing doubt on one of his own witnesses, let alone on calling him a liar. Blackstock was therefore reduced to making repeated swipes at Murray through the cross-examination of other witnesses. He pushed many of them to say whether or not they had been interviewed by Murray, and if so, quite how, repeatedly implying that the detective had coached them both to expand and to polish their stories; but one of the most damaging facts against Murray that Blackstock established in this incidental fashion emerged on the Wednesday, when the Niagara police chief, Mr Young, conceded that after Birchall's arrest Murray had attempted to interrogate the prisoner both highly abusively and without cautioning him first. Osler tried to intervene to curb Blackstock, but without success.

On Thursday Osler called a long series of witnesses, each of whom claimed to remember having seen Birchall and Benwell on 17 February on the trains between Niagara and Eastwood or walking on roads into the swamp together. Further witnesses said that they had seen two sets of tracks appear in the snow some time during the middle of the day, across a field that would be a natural short cut on this route into the swamp. In cross-examination, Blackstock was no less aggressive with these witnesses than he had been with others, showing over and again that they had misdescribed the young Englishmen's clothes, their heights, their colouring and so on. Furthermore, he was able to demonstrate that, even if individually plausible, the times these witnesses gave for their sightings were mutually contradictory. He also threw doubt on the ability of many of them to date their sightings accurately in the first place. Faced with confused evidence, even from two worthy, middle-aged ladies, Miss Lockhart and Miss Choate, who claimed to have seen Birchall and Benwell on the train to Eastwood, Blackstock was liable to bully the witnesses 'terribly'. This may have made a good spectacle, but many of the witnesses were neither professional experts nor tough backwoodsmen, and there was every danger that Blackstock's treatment of them would be offensive to local sentiment. He carried on regardless.

Three witnesses told Osler that in the middle of the day on 17 February they had heard two gun shots in quick succession in the swamp, possibly from a rifle; but these men were inconsistent about exactly when and where the shots had been fired, and how many minutes had passed between them. Blackstock attacked them with special ferocity, showing that, over time, their memories had changed, causing the shots to be fired in ever more rapid succession. He seemed to wish to suggest that whoever killed Benwell would have had no reason to fire a second shot several minutes after the first one if, as suggested by the post-mortem report, either of the bullet wounds in question would have been instantly fatal.

The two most important witnesses to events on 17 February were a retired miller, Alfred Hayward, and his granddaughter, a young servant girl called Alice Smith. Their testimony was crucial because both had been on friendly terms with Birchall, as Somerset, the previous year. Alfred Hayward told Osler that he had seen Birchall and Benwell going away from Eastwood train station towards the swamp at just past midday.

Birchall, he said, had shied a snowball at a cat. Hayward had recognized the once-prominent figure of Lord Somerset and had also registered that the clothes both young men were wearing that day were distinctly English. He had been particularly struck by Benwell's waterproof, caped overcoat. Blackstock had prepared for this witness. First he demonstrated that in original testimony, Hayward had not identified either of the young men. Then he revealed that he himself had sent four men, including the lawyer, Mr Hellmuth, to see Hayward at his mill one month previously. Hellmuth had spoken to Hayward for half an hour, but in court Hayward was unable to recognize him. Nor could he remember what any of the men had been wearing that day, though three of them had deliberately sported caped coats similar to the one Benwell had been wearing. Blackstock now asked Hayward to identify a man in the gallery of the court at a distance of about seventy-five feet. Hayward's eyesight was so atrocious that he was unable to recognize this man, Thomas Midgely, though they had been friends for years. The distance at which Hayward claimed to have recognized Birchall, not having seen him for many months, was two to three times as great. This assault on the old man's testimony caused 'a great sensation'. The Toronto *Evening News* reported that during the lunch adjournment that day there was much talk that any prospective guilty verdict had been 'shattered'.

When Alice Smith entered the witness box after lunch, she explained to Osler that she had been acquainted with Birchall, as well as his friend Dudley, on Birchall's previous visit to Canada. She was asked by Osler to identify Birchall in the court room, and 'recognized the prisoner as the man, which caused great excitement, the prisoner first flushing crimson then turning white'. Not only had she and several others seen him at Eastwood station on 17 February waiting to catch the 3.38 Hamilton train, but she had spoken to Birchall at some length while he stood around on the platform. He had come up to her and said, 'How do you do?' She had then asked him if he was Somerset or Dudley, at which Birchall had chaffed her for not being sure. They had chatted for some minutes about her grandfather, and about where Birchall was going. Five other people had been on the platform at the time. Miss Smith recalled, as did various other witnesses, that Birchall had been wearing muddy boots and rolled-up trousers. Her own present circumstances were that, with one other girl, she was living in as a domestic at the home of Mr Zybach, a photographer at Niagara Falls.

Whatever advantage Blackstock had seized in his cross-examination of Hayward, it was blown to the winds by his handling of Miss Smith. She was seventeen years old, and so beautiful that one paper described her as 'artistically well-nigh perfect', which no doubt added to her aura as a star witness. Blackstock clearly felt that he must cast doubt on her evidence at all costs. He required her to explain to the court that Zybach's wife had recently left him, and to admit that she had spoken to various newspapers about her evidence. Blackstock accused her of having a saucy tongue and of having improved her memory over the months, her present testimony being more detailed than that given in earlier statements. He then produced a flood of questions to try to get her to confess that she had, in the past, spent time alone with Dudley. It was inconceivable that she should have been unable to remember at Eastwood whether Birchall was Somerset or Dudley, not only because the two men were physically completely different, but because, Blackstock implied, Alice Smith had earlier had some sort of improper relationship with Dudley. At this

MacMahon, the judge, grew 'restive', and asked Blackstock to halt, provoking a quickly suppressed burst of applause from the audience. Blackstock protested that he was trying to establish the degree of Alice Smith's credibility as a witness. MacMahon reluctantly allowed him to continue, but Blackstock got little further with her before again being asked to stop. This time Blackstock's 'exhibition of bad temper and harshness' called forth a 'stinging rebuke from His Lordship'. Osler promptly re-examined Miss Smith to bring out the fact that she roomed with the second servant girl at Zybach's, that Mrs Zybach was the guilty party in the breakdown of the Zybach marriage, and that Miss Smith was herself engaged to a night policeman in Niagara called Blount. The Toronto *Mail* was doubtless correct in writing that 'it is the general impression that the cross-examination of Miss Smith touching her private character was a mistake'. Not only had Blackstock not succeeded in casting any real doubt on the truth of her statement about 17 February, but women in the court were said to have wept in sympathy at her ordeal. When she left the building 'about twenty ladies rushed up to her and began kissing and petting her'. It was almost entirely the fault of the defence that Alice Smith suddenly became 'the heroine of the hour'.

After this riveting scene, the brakeman, Hay, who had been on the Hamilton train, swore that Birchall had travelled all the way to Hamilton from Eastwood, had bought an onward ticket there and had then proceeded to Niagara; while a news-agent who worked the route described selling Birchall oranges, cigars and a copy of Mark Twain's *A Tramp Abroad*, saying further that he had sat down and chatted with Birchall over a cigar. The very last Crown witness produced counterfoils to show that he had sold only two train tickets from

Niagara to Eastwood between three o'clock on Saturday 15 February and three o'clock on Monday 17 February. There had been no other tickets sold to Eastwood in the two days previous to this, nor for a week after.

It was now lunchtime on Friday. The prosecution case had taken up four and a half days. If Blackstock had made gains in cross-examination, reporters nevertheless had it on good authority that 'the crown officers are not weakening in their opinion of the prisoner's guilt by reason of the breaking down of a few old women in the witness box'. Taken at face value, Osler's argument seemed to establish that Birchall had had ample opportunity to murder Benwell in the Blenheim swamp in the middle of the day on 17 February, with additional evidence to show that he had been seen going very close to where the body was subsequently found. Gun shots had been heard, and he was then seen leaving again. Any question as to the viability of Birchall's motive was taken to be superfluous in the light of his 19 or 20 February letter to Colonel Benwell. One Crown lawyer remarked to a reporter: 'There is murder in that document if ever there was in anything in the shape of writing.' As far as the prosecution was concerned, nothing more needed to be said on the subject.

12. An Exhibition of Weakness

Too late to know for certain whether injuries received before or after death; one excellent surgical opinion said, before; other excellent surgical opinion said, after.

Charles Dickens, *Our Mutual Friend*, 1865

Popular fascination at the drama inside Woodstock's little theatre strengthened with each passing day. The town's officials, expecting large crowds to be marooned outside the court room, 'liberally sprinkled with sawdust' the pavements round the town hall. This did not dampen the sound of voices 'clamouring for admission', and hour after hour 'the grounds around the courtroom were packed for blocks by people eager to hear anything new'. Reporters wrote that hundreds of spectators 'covered the roofs of the houses and filled all the windows commanding a view through the windows of the Town hall'. Those at a distance did not hesitate to use opera glasses. Even on a day when there was fine rain and a biting east wind, people were undeterred: 'Umbrellas glistened so thickly as to seem like a continuous awning.' The court adjourned every evening just as the town's shops and factories closed, swelling the crowd further. As individuals strained to catch a glimpse of Birchall leaving each night, 'every visible object seemed strung with humanity'.

Inside the court room, however, the nature of the audience perceptibly altered over time. On Monday a handful of prominent women had sat on the stage behind and to the left of the

Britton Bath Osler

George Tate Blackstock

judge, but otherwise only men had attended. On Tuesday, day two, the number of women on stage had swelled to seventeen. The *Sentinel-Review* noted that it was distinctly 'not usual in this country for ladies to form part of the audience in court rooms', but any sense amongst Woodstock's less exalted womenfolk that attendance was 'infra dig', was swept aside by the example of their betters. On day two, therefore, ordinary women took possession of the gallery, and on day three overflowed into the main body of the hall. The system of issuing tickets, already criticized in the press as 'an utter disgrace' that rendered the trial 'a sort of "special attraction for the morbid"', was partly undone by the fact that 'maids and matrons' were given precedence at the door, until, by the Thursday, women were estimated to outnumber men inside the court by three to one. At the same time, more and more telephone transmitters had been added, at the legal tables and near the witness box, until, according to one reporter, the court room became a really 'strange sight', with wires strung 'all over it'. Parts of the trial were listened to live as far away as Toronto. One paper did weakly condemn this provision as 'a lax form', but it does not appear to have occurred to officials to ask whether any of the witnesses might illegally be listening in as a means of cross-checking their evidence.

As the trial progressed the New York *Herald* informed its English readership that

with the regularity of the swing of a pendulum the report is circulated each morning that Birchall is breaking down. With the same regularity Birchall smashes the report. His air is even debonair. He stands the scrutiny of 500 pairs of eyes as coolly as if he were deaf and blind.

He was also debonair at the close of the day, when he would lean out of the dock to remove all the newspapers he could reach from the press tables, before being

brought briskly (almost on a run) down the steps by stalwart Tom Young and a couple of officers, bundled into Cabman Stewart's covered hack and whirled away to jail at almost breakneck speed.

Despite the incredible crush at the entrance to the town hall, the one person for whom a path was always made was the prisoner, 'such', noted the *Globe*, 'is the unconscious irony of the mob'. The fact that Birchall would grin at the crowd as he was hurried past 'was received by the congregated hundreds with amazement'. His calm led to speculation that he was 'a man born without a moral nature' and someone 'utterly without feeling', though this claim was belied by a tiny, nightly drama where Mrs Birchall, entrenched in the Commercial Hotel, would watch 'eagerly at her window for her husband's return to jail', Birchall waving to her as his carriage rushed by.

However he behaved on the streets, Birchall's coolness in court was something he ceased to be able to sustain. During the first couple of days, his poise had been faultless, so that, rather than seeming to concentrate on proceedings, he had spent much of his time in the dock sketching the witnesses as they appeared before him. By the third day, however, reporters observed a change. The prisoner no longer sketched now, but 'riveted his eyes on the witnesses'. He 'frequently sent memoranda over to his lawyers', and 'at times his pale face became overcast with anxiety'.

As the successive Crown witnesses were called, Birchall, like everyone else, must have been assessing Blackstock's attempts to unsettle them. The *Globe* wrote that Blackstock had done 'good work in his cross-examination'. The *Evening News* went much further, arguing that 'had the crown not been able to prove the swindling its case could easily have been broken, for with the exception of Miss Smith's testimony the identification evidence has been badly shattered'. Other papers, however, had been completely unimpressed; and it seems improbable that Blackstock himself felt sanguine. At least the preparation of positive defence evidence had 'gone forward rapidly'. The defence team was at last in a position to try to 'best meet' the case against them, now they actually knew what it was.

Reporters were still left guessing at the likely defence strategy. From the conduct of Blackstock's cross-examinations, it seemed highly improbable that Birchall had an alibi for 17 February. If Blackstock was really going to be unable to break down evidence of Birchall being 'in the vicinity', the jury would need to be persuaded that while he had perhaps travelled with Benwell to Eastwood, they had separated there by agreement, Benwell being murdered some very few hours or days afterwards by others unknown. The Crown itself appeared to have assumed this was going to be the defence argument, Osler having defended 'as thoroughly as possible the idea that Benwell was really shot in the swamp'.

The defence was set to begin early in the afternoon of Friday 26 September. 'Interest in the progress of the case' had 'sensibly deepened' that morning with the knowledge that the prosecution evidence was almost complete, and there was a 'breathless hush' as Blackstock finally rose to his feet. His opening salvo was to declare to the court that, with the Crown evidence all in, there was 'a very grave question of the sufficiency of the case'. He felt satisfied, he said, that the Crown had failed to produce adequate grounds for a conviction, and he implied that it was a matter of decorum that he bothered to answer its case at all. Unlike Osler, who had begun the prosecution with a detailed review of the arguments he was about to produce, Blackstock went straight to the examination of his first witness, announcing that he would weigh up the evidence when all the testimony was in.

He first called an elderly German, John Rabb, who lived near to the road opposite the entry point to the part of the swamp where Benwell's body had been found. Rabb described how, from his house, he had heard two shots fired in the swamp in quick succession on the evening of Tuesday 18 February, and had seen two men walk out of the swamp afterwards, taking a westerly direction. His evidence as to the sound of the gun shots was corroborated by an elderly female neighbour, though in cross-examination Osler went some way towards throwing doubt on her ability to date the events she described. The next witness, John Friedenburg, was the brother of one of the Crown witnesses who had claimed to

have heard gun shots in the swamp on 17 February. Friedenburg's evidence was that he, too, had been in the area that
day, and had given two unknown young men a lift on his cart
when he was drawing logs to a mill. Categorically neither man
had been Birchall. In cross-examination Osler showed that
Friedenburg had originally stated that both these young men
had had moustaches, whereas now he claimed both were clean
shaven. Blackstock, past master himself at showing up such
errors of memory, tried doggedly to reassure Friedenburg:
'Don't let anybody get you excited or beat you out of what is
the truth.'

Next, Blackstock called several of those who had testified
at the inquest to details about the inebriated spree taken by
Colwell and Baker, the first suspects in the case, on the night
of Wednesday 19 February. He asked them in particular to
confirm that Colwell had been wearing rubber overshoes.
Blackstock ran into sullen obstruction when one of these
witnesses defended Colwell as perfectly respectable apart from
his sporadic drunkenness. Blackstock asked the man if he was
aware that Colwell had once been up on a robbery charge.
'I didn't know that he did it, though,' the witness replied.

Another point Blackstock sought to establish, using various
witnesses, concerned the question of whether or not there
was any long-standing trail that went into the swamp as far as
Mud Lake and led past the point where Benwell's body had
been found. Contrary to what the prosecution had established,
many ancient residents of the area were quite certain that no
such route existed. Blackstock then questioned Samuel Stroud,
who had acted as a member of the coroner's jury at Benwell's
inquest. Stroud testified that the tracks in the snow around
the corpse had seemed to belong to two men. He and other
jurors had gone to examine the swamp as a matter of duty:

We first tied our horses and walked along the side of the road to see if anybody had entered the swamp. We came to a place that looked as if some person had got out of a rig and walked into the swamp. The tracks appeared to just have been made by moccasins or felt boots of rather large size.

Stroud did not believe Benwell's boots could have created either set of tracks, and felt it would have been impossible for a man to carry a corpse into the swamp alone. Osler cross-examined Stroud as to why he had not brought this evidence forward at the inquest. He also asked why, if the footprint evidence was in Birchall's favour, Stroud had signed the original verdict against him. Stroud replied simply that, after sitting through the inquest, 'I was satisfied that there was enough evidence against the prisoner.' Joseph Martin, another member of the coroner's jury, swore that the two sets of tracks in question appeared to have been made before the hard frosts had set in. The earlier prints had gone through the soft under-snow, while the later ones hadn't. Osler asked Martin if he had been visited by Detective Bluett, a question he had asked previous witnesses. At this Blackstock suddenly snapped, though he himself had repeatedly used the tactic of throwing doubt on the probity of Detective Murray. Blackstock re-examined Martin, causing him to reveal that he was a property owner. 'I ask you this,' said Blackstock trenchantly, 'to show that you are not likely to be susceptible to the influence of bribery from Mr. Bluett, for that seems to be what my learned friend suggests.' Osler objected at once, saying, 'I made no such imputation.' The judge was not amused.

Blackstock now called several of those inquest witnesses who had wrongly identified Benwell's corpse as belonging to an itinerant tinker or Indian fakir. He had previously drawn attention to this same error during his cross-examination of Crown witnesses. On the matter of false identifications, however, there was much more surprising new evidence from Frederick Millman, a Woodstock grocer, and thus a well-known local figure, who swore with complete confidence that he had seen Birchall in Woodstock on 17 February, recognizing him as Lord Somerset.

There were a few other witnesses who simply corroborated points already brought out in the defence testimony. Once they were dispatched, late on Friday afternoon, Blackstock asked MacMahon for an early adjournment as he had no more 'short witnesses' left. The next day was Saturday, the day MacMahon had originally intended to end the trial. While he considered this request, Blackstock also pleaded to be told whether, if he failed to plough through his remaining witnesses fast enough to leave time on Saturday afternoon for the closing arguments, it would be possible to carry the case over to the following Monday. He spoke of the enormous pressure he and the rest of the defence team had been under every evening that week assessing the Crown's evidence and devising ways to meet it; and although he explained that he would deeply regret having to delay the judge or inconvenience the jury, he said that it would be an immense 'relief' to have the Sunday in hand. MacMahon calmly agreed that if it must be so, it must be so.

Blackstock had produced a large part of his case in a single afternoon. The Toronto *World* was scathing: 'The defence, in the shape of evidence, was simply a fiasco.' Meanwhile the *Mail* felt that Blackstock had actually detracted from the case he had built in cross-examination: 'When several witnesses had been examined the outlook seemed if anything darker.' The New York *Sun* thought the evidence on false identifications, instead of helping Birchall, 'only seemed to adjust more neatly the noose around the murderer's neck'. What most disturbed reporters, however, was how the defence had actually selected those whom it called. The Crown, on its side, had initially called about one hundred and twenty witnesses for the trial. When Murray had had them all gathered in Woodstock before the case began, Osler had dismissed numbers of them as un-suitable or too unreliable. Bizarrely, these failed prosecution witnesses then formed a primary pool out of which Blackstock selected witnesses for the defence. The *Mail* thought these Crown rejects 'did more harm to the case than good', and characterized the plan of the defence as not only 'discon-nected', but 'a search in the dark'. The *World*, too, found that 'as an exhibition of weakness in the line of defence nothing was probably ever heard like it in a court of justice'.

On the Saturday morning the first of Blackstock's 'long' witnesses was a Woodstock doctor called Mearns. He ex-plained to the court that he had derived his specialist know-ledge from many years of practice in Petrolea, where he had become experienced in the effects of all kinds of machine accidents on the men working the oil springs. Mearns started by disputing Crown evidence concerning rigor mortis. He thought the average time until onset was five to six hours rather than two to three, and that in a case of sudden death in a healthy young man in cold conditions it would take even longer. In Benwell's circumstances he put the probable timing at eight to twelve hours. Mearns also strongly disputed that Benwell was likely to have received the described bruises to his groin area from a fall in death. Their bluish-green colour indicated to him that they must have been received one to two days earlier. Osler's cross-examination of this witness was well prepared and extensive. He tried to make Mearns concede that it was the colour on the margins of bruises that indicated their age, not their general colour, and read out highly technical works on the subject that seemed to contradict Mearns's testimony. Osler then proposed that the best way to judge a disputed bruise would be to see it. Mearns was not intimidated by this, and conceded nothing. Osler now switched to the issue of congestion or swelling in a wound. He suggested that the lack of any swelling in these bruises indicated they had been caused roughly at the time of death. This, too, according to Mearns, was a matter of dispute, and depended on the precise conditions prevailing when an injury was inflicted. When the judge, MacMahon, suddenly pitched in to query the point again, Mearns replied bitingly that he did not believe, from the quality of the post-mortem notes, that the doctors who had produced them had looked carefully enough to determine whether there had been a degree of swelling or not.

Mearns's evidence was largely corroborated by Dr J. H. Richardson, professor of anatomy at Toronto University. He calculated that Benwell's rigor mortis would probably have set in after eight to ten hours. He thought it 'exceedingly improbable' that the groin bruises were received through falling in death, and thought from descriptions that they must have been inflicted about twenty-four hours previously. A bruise sustained in the moment of death would have remained purple, he insisted. He also disputed the idea that there would necessarily be inflammation to a wound arising from a violent blow. To an unusually sarcastic remark from Osler, Richardson replied coolly, 'I have seen hundreds and hundreds of such cases.' Osler 'tried hard to shake this witness but failed completely'.

Local defence counsel, the solicitor Samuel McKay, was

now called to confirm details of the trap that he and colleagues had set up for Alfred Hayward when they visited the old miller in mid-August wearing caped coats like Benwell's. McKay also gave evidence that one of the Crown's witnesses, who had sworn to the sound of two quick gun shots in the swamp on 17 February, had previously told him that these shots were four or five minutes apart.

The next witness, Norman McQueen, was the eminently respectable son of a judge. He stood in the witness box and swore that he, too, like the grocer, had seen Birchall in Woodstock at about noon on 17 February. Questioning showed that he had impeccable means by which not merely to date, but to give the time of this event. Osler tried to shake him, but McQueen stuck rigorously to his story. Blackstock had McQueen explain that he had 'never much cared for' Birchall: he had no motive whatsoever for protecting him. This evidence created an instant 'furore'.

Saturday's final witness was Howard J. Duncan, a Woodstock barrister, who testified that he had been on a train coming into town overnight between 20 and 21 February, the day the body was found. As the train passed between London and Woodstock in the small hours, he said, there had been a heavy snowfall in progress. When Duncan stepped from the witness box, Blackstock announced that he had one or two further small witnesses whom he could not call before Monday morning, but that he had now presented the majority of the defence case.

From the Thursday MacMahon had extended the hours the court sat in order to try to get the case finished. He was extremely unhappy at Blackstock's wish to leave witnesses pending, and warned: 'This case must go to the jury on Monday night.' MacMahon then addressed the jury themselves, regretting 'exceedingly' that they would have to be held over an extra day. He was also deeply annoyed on his own account that he would have to postpone cases he was scheduled to hear elsewhere. Once again, however, he announced that if this was necessary for justice, so be it.

Panic ensued as people found that they were unable to leave the court room because of pressure from the crowd outside trying to get in. Birchall had 'maintained his nonchalant appearance' during proceedings that day, appearing to take 'very little interest'. Afterwards, though, 'just as he reached the hack that was waiting for him a murmur arose, and then half-suppressed cries of "Lynch the——" were distinctly heard.' Nevertheless, 'no active demonstration was made'.

The Toronto *Evening News* was inspired to run a long string of headlines: 'The End is Near – Birchall's Defence Nearly All In – A Witness Throws a Bombshell – Belief That the Prisoner Will Go Free – Monday Night May See the End of It.' The paper reported that on the basis of McQueen's evidence, betting on the streets, a practice the paper condemned as 'utterly abhorrent', was now three to one that the jury would disagree, a result that would provoke an automatic retrial. The New York *Sun*, however, read the case completely differently, informing its readers that there was little doubt Birchall would be found guilty: the defence had plainly failed, and 'the general impression is that they should have started out on the insanity theory'.

As Blackstock left court he knew that he had one day only in which to write a speech to save Birchall's life. While he worked frantically at this task, others would take that Sunday at their ease. 'The jury,' noted one paper, 'closely guarded by a posse of police, were out for a walk today.' At the same time, hundreds went to visit Benwell's grave, 'upon which some kind hand had strewn flowers and ferns', and thousands went to the swamp. The previous Sunday the number of such tourists had been estimated at two thousand. On Sunday 28 September even this astounding figure rose. Amongst them were MacMahon and his wife. For the last half mile the road to the swamp was 'so completely blocked by turnouts' that it could only be reached on foot. People took away souvenirs 'of every possible description'. Though the 'relic hunters' came to see how Benwell had died, between them they had 'cleared the thickly studded swamp of vegetation and felled tamarak trees' until the area presented 'a clearing of about sixty feet square'. There were stakes in the ground to show where the body had been discovered, and on the trees left standing the crowds of visitors had 'carved and written their names and addresses over every place where an autograph would stick'. Even so, it remained a dismal spot, and Mud Lake continued to be very difficult to reach: 'Farmers, city clerks, merchants, and even a good number of women in silks and satins, jostled each other over the fallen logs, trees and gnarled roots in their struggle for a glimpse.'

Reports on Birchall's condition that weekend varied, some being blatant inventions; but the Toronto *Evening News* provided an oddly touching portrait of him as sighted in the jail yard, sitting quietly on a bench. 'His feet were drawn close up under him with the heels on the same board on which he sat, and he was nursing his knees. His hat was tipped down over his eyes and his face was calm and rather thoughtful.' Another paper wrote that the strain which had 'been noticeable in Birchall the past few days' had developed into an 'anxiety painful to witness'.

13. Having Murder in Your Heart

Judge and jury gave the verdict forth which had the looming gallows
in the rear . . .

Elizabeth Gaskell, *Mary Barton*, 1848

Monday 29 September, the final day of Birchall's trial, dawned
'warm and beautiful'. People began to congregate outside the
town hall from six o'clock in the morning, their number
including 'many prominent lawyers from all parts of Ontario'.
Mrs Birchall felt driven to attend, and she and her sister,
wearing 'dark-blue velvet poke bonnets', added to the fascination felt by the crowd. Woodstock's constables feared to
open the town-hall doors, yelling out of the windows that
they would arrest members of the crowd if they did not
disperse. This threat was completely ineffective.

'The crush to get into the hall' was 'something awful, far
surpassing any previous day'. Constables 'caught citizens by
the collars and threw them bodily off the steps. They rapped
people with their batons indiscriminately.' It was noticeable
'that the gallantry of the men had run down to zero', so
that the predominance of women inside was finally ended.
MacMahon, for his part, concluded that proceedings had
reached the point where it would be undignified for the
phalanx of favoured ladies to continue to occupy the stage.
These women, therefore, were at last compelled to 'seek
seats in the body of the court room'. Not only local, but

international interest had been unflagging throughout the trial. Word circulated that the London *Times*, at 'enormous' expense, had ordered the closing addresses to be cabled to England in full.

Birchall remained composed as Blackstock quickly dispensed with his last few witnesses. Only one of them was really significant. A telegraph boy from Niagara testified to having delivered a telegram to Birchall on 25 February. This had been sent by the Stafford House hotel in Buffalo in response to an inquiry from Birchall about possible messages from Benwell that might be waiting for him there. The Stafford House telegram had informed Birchall that there was indeed a telegram waiting for him. Where, asked Blackstock, was this original telegram that the Stafford House had received in Birchall's name? Who had sent it, and what did it say? He left in the air the suggestion that the Crown had not pursued this enigma because the existence of this mysterious telegram suggested that Birchall had had an ally.

Blackstock's final piece of evidence was the register of the Metropolitan Hotel, New York, which he produced as an example of Birchall spelling the names of all members of his travelling party correctly. With these preliminaries out of the way, it was time for him to deliver his final speech. All that had so far been inexplicit in his conduct of the defence must now be made completely clear if there was to be any chance of his winning the case. 'The court room was as peaceful as death,' though the silence that prevailed was so deep that all through 'the clicking of the telegraph instruments which were spreading the speech broadcast sounded loud and clear'. Mrs Birchall, behind a thin veil, looked 'colourless' to the point of seeming ill. She kept her eyes upon the jury throughout Blackstock's address, while beside her, her sister, Mrs

West-Jones, sat with a bottle of smelling salts, breathing them in 'almost continually'.

Blackstock began on a note almost of despair:

If in rising to address you I find myself almost exhausted before I begin, if I find myself filled with dismay and terror, it is not because of the evidence given from the box, it is because I stand charged with the responsibility of defending a man pilloried for a crime of which he is innocent.

He told the jury that the case was an extraordinarily difficult one, and that it would require them to use not only their best 'fidelity', but 'every power of analysis' with which they were familiar, in order to reach a just conclusion. They were, he said, 'participating in the gravest and most responsible and most awful function which civilisation presents to a human being'. He observed that numerous people were opposed to the death penalty, and that many civilized countries had abolished it. He then explained that while, under Canadian law, a prisoner charged with murder was not deemed competent to speak as a witness under oath on his own behalf, much of the circumstantial testimony in the case could only effectively be refuted by Birchall himself. He further claimed that a great deal of the Crown evidence had been 'sprung' upon the defence, giving them no opportunity even to attempt to counter it. This was plainly true. Birchall's letter to Colonel Benwell, for example, was not shown to the defence until a day before the trial began; and Osler himself, during his opening statement, noted that he was running through prospective Crown evidence 'somewhat fully', as a gesture to the defence. Until that point, Blackstock had only been able to guess at the case he would have to answer.

'I wish that I could even here stop naming these difficulties,' he said, but there were more. Some arose out of financial embarrassment. The defence had had no funds to bring witnesses from far and wide, let alone from England, and their work had been 'crippled' as a result. The lawyers themselves had laboured 'almost without reward' rather than abandon Birchall, but 'I wonder,' said Blackstock, 'what farmer in the county of Oxford would stand a defence against the preparation of the Crown.' This was an unusually direct appeal on his part to the very constituency of people he had most reason to fear. The papers that morning had placed the cost of the trial to the authorities at just under $10,000, while Birchall's defence had been funded out of assorted small contributions from family and friends, as well as donations from the Duke of Norfolk, and a secretary of the former Empress Eugénie. As for the witnesses whom the Crown had paid so lavishly, Blackstock maintained that while Osler had been unable to demonstrate that any of the defence witnesses were frankly dishonest, large numbers of the prosecution witnesses manifestly had been.

Blackstock also spoke with deep contempt of the press. He did appreciate its value, he said, arguing that all the 'honest' detective work in the case had been done by reporters; but if there were to be a guilty verdict, it could only be explained by the influence of months of biased newspaper reporting. A guilty verdict would arise, he said, not through a balanced assessment of the evidence presented in court, but 'because the dragnet of the newspapers has been abroad through the slimy sloughs of innuendo, of whisper, of interested malice and imagination'. He asked each juror to 'sink the plummet line of your intelligence' to avoid a triumph of mob law as mediated by the press.

Blackstock was now faced with the need to accommodate

Birchall's own dishonesty within his argument. As regards the prisoner's business arrangements with Benwell, the lawyer confessed that he was 'wholly unable' to point out 'an explanation of the course observed by the prisoner that is consistent with his innocence'. Yet Birchall was not on trial for dishonesty: 'I am, therefore, not careful to defend him on these points,' said Blackstock, 'first, because I should be at a loss to do so; secondly, because it is not the charge made in the indictment.'

He moved quickly on. 'I feel that it would be an insult to your intelligence to say that the great body of witnesses would swear deliberately to what is false,' he said, but all the same, the frailty of human memory had been abundantly proved. Blackstock gave several new instances of how this might have told against his client. As a sample re-reading of events, he said that when Birchall had told various people in Princeton he had received a letter from London containing Benwell's baggage receipts, these people had assumed, or had later come to believe they remembered, that he had meant something more than merely an envelope bearing the receipts themselves. Blackstock continued, 'You must understand that in a criminal case there is no such thing as an admission. I have no right to admit anything.' If an actual letter had come, he could not say so, though if an actual letter *had* come, he continued, then Crown officers had stolen it from Birchall's luggage to put him in a false position.

It is hard to believe that Blackstock's decision to argue this point two ways did not make a bad impression on the jury. He followed the same procedure in addressing the evidence of Millman and MacQueen, the two men who claimed to have seen Birchall in Woodstock on 17 February. Blackstock insisted that it remained an open question whether or not they should be treated as providing Birchall with an alibi. 'I don't care which way you take it,' he said. Either their testimony cleared Birchall, or it showed how respectable witnesses were ready to swear falsely on the basis of mistaken identity. By either interpretation, said Blackstock, the Crown's case was diminished. His own, however, was surely also weakened by the common understanding that Birchall really hadn't been in Woodstock that day: local reporters had identified Birchall's double as an over-dressed man called Nesbitt. A third question that Blackstock intended to play two ways was that of whether or not Birchall had been in Eastwood on 17 February. The defence could not admit that he had been, but even supposing he had, 'What then?'

Blackstock left this question hanging as he went on to claim that Murray's had failed to produce key pieces of evidence of Birchall's supposed journey to Eastwood, such as punched railway tickets, because the actual evidence 'would not be in favour of the Crown'. The idea that Murray had not seen these tickets was nonsense: 'You might as well make us believe that the moon is made of green cheese.' Blackstock then anticipated the question, why did the defence itself not call witnesses to such evidence to bolster its own case? His answer was grim. Most potential witnesses would not comply:

They go into the Crown office and tell Murray, and the Crown counsel would go there; but when we ask for the statement that they are going to make they tell us that we will hear them when they go into the witness box.

In the face of such hostility, he implied, the defence had not dared to risk the consequences of placing unexamined witnesses on their oath.

Blackstock dealt with the fact that many of the original accounts of the two men whom witnesses had seen on 17 February did not fit descriptions of Birchall and Benwell. Yet once these witnesses had identified Birchall in jail, and once Murray had told them 'a million of times, in all probability' what Birchall was thought to have worn that day, their descriptions had begun to converge. While Blackstock conceded that discrepancies of this kind will always occur, it was also true that people 'talk until they come to believe it'. The jury's greatest challenge would therefore be 'to be on their guard against false testimony that is honestly false'.

When discussing once again the iniquities of the prison identifications of Birchall, and of how Murray had 'sneaked off with the witnesses' without independent verification of the legitimacy of the proceedings, Blackstock became wrathful, describing Murray as a 'human hellhound', and adding, 'I am ashamed that a man of such unfairness should be a detective officer of the Crown'. Any detective's statements, he said, were 'very likely to be false or very highly colored' and it was plain how well the phrase applied, 'Set a thief to catch a thief.' During this 'tirade' reporters noticed that 'Detective Murray sat at one end of the lawyer's table with a copy of a paper before his face. Every eye was turned upon him but he was not ambitious of notice.'

Blackstock now took considerable time to review examples of men executed when circumstantial evidence had led to false conclusions, as well as noting stories where dreadful consequences had arisen from cases of mistaken identity. He explained that the reason he had questioned witnesses over the false identifications of Benwell's corpse was to confirm that such mistakes were easily made. Blackstock then repeated the claim that, for the defence, it was 'immaterial' whether the jury believed Birchall had genuinely been seen at Eastwood on 17 February or not, but he did attack those who claimed that they had seen him in and around the swamp, showing their stories to be inconsistent as to descriptions, timings and routes taken.

Blackstock was particularly scornful of the evidence of the three young men who claimed to have heard gun shots in the swamp on 17 February. Not only had this testimony clearly been altered to fit the Crown's theory, he said, but it was also the case that if these men were to be believed, then Birchall had apparently killed Benwell within earshot of the firing of their own guns, and of the barking of their dog. Blackstock accused the three men of having completely invented their evidence in order to get the Crown to pay the fare home from Nevada of one of them who had been working down there, so that he could come back and enjoy the 'jamboree' of the trial.

Blackstock now posed a long series of what he hoped would prove unanswerable questions. With regard to the Crown's medical witnesses, he especially damned Dr Staples, who had changed his mind as to the number of days Benwell had been dead in order to include 17 February, and whose expert opinion on bruises was clearly flawed. The best evidence suggested that the bruises to Benwell's groin predated his murder. If he had been killed on 17 February, however, then how could these bruises have been inflicted beforehand without Pelly having known about it? What, too, of the wounds to Benwell's head, knuckles and ear? If he had been in a fight with Birchall on 17 February, how was it that Birchall hadn't had a scratch on him? Concerning another post-mortem detail, why, asked Blackstock, would Benwell not have eaten a decent breakfast on 17 February, or did the

Crown really mean to suggest, from the few split peas in his stomach, that he had had pea soup that morning?

The record of weather conditions suggested to Blackstock that the amount of frozen slush in Benwell's sleeve was consistent with him having been in the swamp since some time before the rainfall on Tuesday 18 February, or even in time for the snowfalls of the day after. It was not proof that he had been there before the rain that fell during Monday's storm; and if Benwell's body had really been exposed to the earlier rains, how did the Crown account for so much starch having remained in his bared and crisp shirt front? How was it, furthermore, that Benwell's boots had been completely clean, while Birchall's had been caked with mud? Even the Monday rains could not have washed them free of all dirt, especially as one had been frozen into the ice. Crown witnesses had sworn that it had grown muddy in the afternoon of 17 February, after the two young men had gone into the swamp, but in time for Birchall's boots to become caked on the way out again. Blackstock declared that this was an 'absurd' adjustment of the facts.

His questions continued. If Birchall had carried Benwell some way through the swamp alone, as the Crown seemed to argue, though Blackstock noted that no witness had thought this possible, was it really likely that there would have been no blood at all on his clothes? Again, why would he have chosen a relatively public part of the swamp for the murder when his putative route took him past much more obscure areas of swampland? How, indeed, had he persuaded Benwell to go beyond their original destination of Niagara in the first place; and if the murder really had been planned, why not commit it at the Falls? Niagara wasn't just a 'fashionable resort' for terminating human life, but, unlike Eastwood, was a place where Birchall would not have been 'courting observation from those who knew him'.

The Crown's evidence of a trail to Mud Lake struck Blackstock as completely false, and Stroud and Martin's testimony about footprints all went to show that Benwell's body had been placed in the swamp by two men wearing soft overshoes. Why had the Crown not called any witnesses to dispute this evidence? If the two sets of tracks had been made before Monday's storm, why had the rain not washed them out again? If they were made after the storm, and Benwell had been killed on the Monday, surely whoever had made the tracks would have found his body? Meanwhile, why had the Crown not called Colwell and Baker, the original suspects, to prove beyond doubt that they could be eliminated from suspicion? If Birchall's gun was smaller than Pelly's, as Pelly had testified, then it was smaller than a .32 calibre revolver, so where had Birchall got the larger gun with which, by the evidence of the bullets, the murder was committed? Furthermore, if guilty, why had Birchall not destroyed Benwell's baggage checks and got rid of his keys and his gold pencil before being arrested? Birchall's possession of these items demonstrated 'no evil intention that in any way he should be ashamed of.' Finally, if Birchall was supposed to have sent to himself the telegram that claimed to be from the Stafford House hotel to say that Benwell wanted his luggage in New York, though this 'would not prove murder in any way', why did the Crown not produce someone from the Stafford House staff to give evidence that they themselves had not sent it?

Blackstock's great run of lingering questions demonstrates in part how hampered he was by the crude forensic standards of the day. Both the recording of information about the murder and the analysis of these records were desperately flawed and ambiguous. The amount of ice melted out of Benwell's sleeve could have given a strong clue as to how much rain or snowfall had filled it. Blackstock had evidently had reason to believe that Constable Watson or Detective Murray poured boiling water into the sleeve to speed up the thaw, though neither would admit it, and the quantity of water poured out again was never accurately measured anyway. The amount of post-mortem beard growth on Benwell was never analysed. There were questions about gunpowder marks on his coat collar that were never properly explained, nor was the suspected discrepancy between the bullets used to kill Benwell and the type of Birchall's gun ever satisfactorily disproved. No one made experiments with a starched shirt front to find out how much precipitation in freezing temperatures the starching process could withstand. There was no demonstration in court that the nicked scissors in Birchall's possession really would have produced the type of cuts found on Benwell's clothing. Evidence arising from the footsteps left around Benwell's body was hopelessly contested; and the evidence of the wounds and bruises to the corpse was not fully conclusive either, though Osler's obsessive attention to this subject suggests that he perceived it to be a weak point in the Crown case. Blackstock clearly, and with 'terror', realized that in the absence of reliable analysis, the jurors would be free to choose whatever interpretation of these key details they preferred.

Undoubtedly one of the most important of Blackstock's questions was simply: what on earth was Birchall's motive in killing Benwell supposed to have been? Osler did not 'pretend that this man was murdered for the dollars that were on him', and so the case was deemed by the Crown to turn on Birchall's letter to Colonel Benwell. This letter did contain 'some things that appear to be utterly untrue', but, startlingly, Blackstock argued that it actually pointed 'absolutely to the prisoner's innocence'. He read out Birchall's remark about Benwell: 'And I introduced him to people who know me well.' Here the lawyer made the fascinating comment:

He may have introduced him to somebody, and that somebody unfortunately may have been guilty of foul play. I am not going to theorise about that. It is impossible for me to prove to you that it is true.

At last, if fleetingly, one of the simplest counter-explanations for what might have happened on 17 February was brought into view. Perhaps Birchall had had a fellow blackguard in the backwoods who had committed the deed some time after Birchall and Benwell parted company that day. Blackstock did not dwell on this possibility, but selected another quotation from the letter: 'I think the best way is to place the money in our joint names in the bank to the credit of our reserve fund.' By such a system, Blackstock argued, the money could not be removed again from a bank without Benwell's signature.

On the matter of typewriting, and the Crown's claim that Birchall had intended to counterfeit a letter from Benwell to his father, Blackstock again disingenuously slipped in a theoretical explanation of his client's innocence:

Now, remember that Birchall undoubtedly expected Benwell to turn up. I could have understood my friend if he had raised a theory that Birchall intended to compel Benwell to send such a letter, shutting him up somewhere and keeping him there until the money came from England, and then compelling him to endorse the draft, and after getting the money letting him go. I could believe something in such a theory. But if Benwell were dead the prisoner's only reliance on getting the money would be gone.

This was not a pretty defence, but Blackstock, unable to admit anything, did at least offer it for the jury's consideration. He continued, 'If the Crown had produced a typewritten letter signed by him there would be something to go upon, for Birchall says in effect, "Don't send the money until you hear from your son."' Blackstock pointed out that no such typed document had ever emerged, even though Birchall had had over a week before Benwell's name got into the national press to fake this essential item. If a letter had been part of Birchall's plan, why had he not created it? Blackstock once again indulged in brief speculation, this time producing an even less damaging theory than the previous one as to his client's original intentions:

I have no doubt that in all probability Birchall's idea was that when Benwell came back to Niagara Falls he would be able to coax him into writing to his father for money. He might intend to say to him, 'You are out here now. I did not treat you squarely, it is true, but you had better get the money and let us go into a farm or horse business, or something of the kind.'

It seemed 'very likely' to Blackstock that Birchall was 'getting these young men out to this country, intending, when he got out, with their capital to start a business in which he was to share'. This was a plausible argument, but one that Blackstock apparently dared not pursue. He could have proposed, with force, that Birchall was likely to have believed that he would be able to acquire the money he wanted through duplicity alone: Birchall had, after all, got away with some amazingly casual deceptions already, and had brilliantly manipulated Pelly; but Blackstock had opened his address by instructing the jurymen to eliminate from their minds all question of Birchall's known character as a swindler: 'If you let that enter in the smallest degree into your judgement of this case you will be doing what is contrary to the oath you have taken.' With this stricture, Blackstock had put out of bounds possibly the best available line of defence.

This difficulty also prevented him answering the Crown's argument that the use of the name Bastell or Bushall on his telegram from Niagara indicated that Birchall had wished to cover up an act of murder. Birchall's fondness for false names long predated Benwell's death, or even a conceivable plan for such a murder, and seems to have been a compulsive trait. The Woodstock court itself had recognized that no one knew whether the Crown should be indicting someone called John Reginald Birchall or simply Reginald Birchall, opting in error for the longer name. Birchall had also pointlessly lied about his age at the magisterial inquiry in Niagara. Blackstock had manoeuvred himself out of being able to exploit the prisoner's senseless deceitfulness as an indicator of his innocence, and so was left to make the claim simply that the prisoner's behaviour in bringing Pelly's attention to the story about the corpse in Princeton, and to the named cigar case in particular, his initiating a visit to identify the corpse, and the fact that he then actually gave the correct identification, did not suggest a man guilty of murder.

As Blackstock wound his way towards a conclusion, he said to the jury, in a mixture of flattery and attempted coercion:

I believe if you once come to the conclusion that this is a case in which you can lay aside all feeling and all extraneous judgement, you have reached a very large way along the road to acquittal. I know every man on the jury will struggle to be honest and decide the case according to the evidence. Of course you will, and, gentlemen, the day will come when you will be glad that you did. Depend upon it, the day will come when the mystery which surrounds the case will be cleared up. Depend upon it, the time is coming when every transaction in connection with this will be made clear. Depend upon it, the time is coming when perhaps the confession of the one who is guilty of this crime will put it beyond peradventure. Then, indeed, it will be that you will be glad that you have acted only upon the evidence, and have laid aside any passion.

At the very end of this speech Blackstock turned his 'elastic imagination' to Mrs Birchall, and in what one reporter felt was a 'marvellously unique and energetic turn of eloquence' brought up the 'love that burned' in her soul for her husband, she who, by contrast with the threatened noose, 'clung like a beautiful garland around his neck'. How would the jury feel, Blackstock asked, if they sent this woman's husband to the gallows, only to discover afterwards that he was innocent? Mrs Birchall would 'cry out to them in pathetic tones for the deliverance of her husband, but it would be too late'. The woman in question shook with sobs. Tears poured down her sister's cheeks also. Every other woman in the court seemed to be crying, and 'scores of young and old men in the audience were seen to use their handkerchiefs'. In the words of the *Globe*, Blackstock's 'bright rays' also 'fell upon the most sacred chords of the prisoner's nature, causing them to reverberate through his whole system'. Birchall was observed to lose his 'statue-like' form. He first 'looked blankly out of the window above the heads of the jury', but 'a second later his lip trembled and his eyes filled with tears'.

Blackstock's address closed somewhat as it had begun. He had, to the best of his ability, done his duty towards his client, but 'I should be guilty of an unutterable affectation,' he said, 'if I did not admit how this case has weighed upon me; how often during the last week I have felt oppressed by the enormous responsibility of it.' Amongst other things, Blackstock had evidently grown afraid that his aggressive manner with many witnesses might have prejudiced his client's case. One of his last pleas to the jury was that 'If this witness was unduly pressed, if that witness was not fairly treated, if this or that remark ought not to have been made, visit the consequence not upon the client, but upon the advocate.' Despite these qualms about his own manner, in his final address Blackstock kept to the mode of speaking that fitted him best. His tone had ranged from 'caustic invective' to an eloquence that 'played upon the very heart-strings of his listeners', creating an effect that was 'thrilling indeed'. Many papers speculated that he had been left in a position of terrible weakness by Birchall's continually changing his story and altering his instructions, but one sympathetic reporter did write that under Blackstock's skilful treatment 'Many points which had seemed to bear fatally against the prisoner took on a new aspect and seemed explained in the most natural manner.'

It was three o'clock when Blackstock finished. His 'deep bass voice' had 'rolled through the court' for five and a quarter hours. The judge, Mr MacMahon, granted twenty minutes for lunch, to be taken without the court rising. Many spectators remained where they were and went hungry rather than lose their seats, while those who could sent out to the local hotels for food to be brought in to them. Mrs Birchall stood up and looked for the first time into the eyes of her husband. 'The scene was most pathetic.' The two of them did not speak.

Then, with her sister, she walked from the court. One reporter later claimed that the two women were 'received by the crowds outside with hoots and yells and coarse expressions, and were followed some distance along the street'. They did not return.

Osler began to speak at half past three, and 'it was a cold, hard statement of his case'. As was his normal practice, he placed himself 'directly opposite the 12 good men's line and talked all through those long hours to the jury and the jury alone'. He frequently directed the jurors to look at Birchall, 'apparently endeavouring to detect some sign of guilt upon the face of the prisoner', but this – as the Toronto *Mail* reported in a subheading – was 'Futile in Every Instance'.

Osler started by reassuring the jury that if they came to a verdict later disproved, the responsibility for the error would lie not with them, but with the witnesses. After making this point, his answer to Blackstock involved a good measure of not answering him at all. There were some defence points that he addressed directly, but many of Blackstock's arguments he simply ignored, instead reiterating the accusations that he had made already. Benwell, said Osler, 'came here to take part in an established business. He did not want to work on a farm. The moment he found he had been deceived he would have communicated with his father.' Osler felt that Birchall's letter to Colonel Benwell was designed to prepare him for his son's becoming a 'careless correspondent'. Only by killing Benwell and forging a letter in his name could Birchall possibly have hoped to extract any money from England. Birchall wished this money to be sent in the firm's name, 'and any member of the firm could draw the money', said Osler with blunt certainty. Birchall's remark to Pelly, on 25 February, that he expected money from England soon, was a reference 'no doubt' to Colonel Benwell's expected draft. Osler did not square up this claim against Blackstock's point that Birchall had *not* actually counterfeited a letter so as to receive the money within the time promised to Pelly, but as Osler believed Birchall had planned to secure funds through assassination, he saw no reason to suppose that the prisoner would have shown compunction about faking Benwell's signature for the bank:

Look at this letter, look at the prisoner's scheme, and you can see but one awful word—murder. If you can suggest any other method by which the prisoner was to get hold of Benwell's money, then give the prisoner the benefit of the suggestion. But you cannot, and the prisoner's counsel did not.

This was untrue. Blackstock had, if briefly, raised more than one alternative theory, and in a back-handed acknowledgement of the possibility that Birchall might have had an unknown collaborator, Osler now said that, while Benwell's body had been found near where his glasses and lit cigar had fallen, and while Birchall alone had murdered him, nevertheless, Birchall was

equally liable if he got another man to do it. He was probably unaided, but he is equally liable if he had help. You may find that two men carried the body, and yet you may find the prisoner guilty.

Naturally Osler did not go so far as to entertain the idea that this putative assistant might have been solely guilty of an unplanned killing, or that Birchall might therefore have penned his letter to Colonel Benwell not yet knowing his son was dead.

   Osler now argued that the torn pieces of clothing and other

possessions found scattered around the corpse, and especially the presence of Benwell's glasses and his cigar holder containing a stub of cigar, made it completely implausible that the young man had been murdered somewhere else and brought into the swamp. 'We are asked to believe he was shot elsewhere and the cigar-holder and stub dropped from his dead lips,' said Osler contemptuously. Only the Crown's explanation held: there was 'no other conclusion, no other theory'. Osler now produced a new argument which some reporters felt 'beautifully exploded' one of Blackstock's implied lines of defence. Though Blackstock had wished to implicate Colwell and Baker, the spree in which these two reprobates had indulged had been so intoxicated, said Osler, that it was inconceivable that after murdering Benwell they would have thought of cutting the name tags out of his clothing.

Regarding the peas in Benwell's stomach, Osler reminded the jury that when Birchall had returned to Buffalo in the evening of 17 February, he had told Pelly that Benwell had been sulky all morning and had refused to eat anything. As for the quantity of ice in Benwell's waterproof sleeve, the opening to this sleeve was so tight at the wrist that only Monday night's storm could have infiltrated sufficient rain through the gap to account for the 'vast amount' of ice found within. Having made this claim, Osler seemed to contradict it at once by saying that the rain must have frozen as it fell, both to account for the ice crust over the slight amount of blood found beneath Benwell's head, and to explain how the starch had remained in his shirt. All the same, Osler concluded that this evidence was irrefutably in favour of the Crown's argument: it was a 'record of the date written in nature'. He went on to make short shrift of the footprints around the corpse. There was no reason why Birchall might not have made both the sets of disputed tracks, in and out of the swamp. Perhaps he had killed Benwell, left the body, walked out of the swamp, remembered he needed to cut out the name tags, and gone back in again.

Osler provided further speculative explanations. Whoever had killed Benwell, he said, knew that his face would not be recognized by anyone in Canada, and that it would be necessary only to remove his name tags in order to render his identity a total mystery should he be discovered. Osler also claimed that Birchall's subterfuge in mis-signing his Niagara Falls telegram could 'only be explained on the ground that there was some crime to conceal'. The crime, by implication here, was the crime of having murdered Benwell, but this did not answer a question of Blackstock's, namely why, if Birchall had voluntarily made himself known to Alice Smith at Eastwood Station, he thought he would gain anything from later disguising his name on an apparently unimportant telegram.

Osler reserved one of his strongest attacks for the idea that Benwell had been beaten up in advance of his murder. He dismissed the expert evidence on bruises provided by the defence, saying of the local doctors who had conducted the post mortem: 'Are you not almost compelled to believe the witnesses who saw these wounds rather than those who give their opinion without seeing them?' It was ridiculous anyway to imagine

that 24 hours before death he was attacked, that he liked the company of his assailants so well that he remained with them 24 hours, and then went with them to the swamp, where he was shot like a bullock. Oh! pitiful defence if there cannot be a better theory than that, and there is none other. Oh, the man who shot poor Benwell gave him no warning, but is a cowardly assassin who sneaked upon him from behind and foully shot him down.

Osler ignored what Blackstock had implied, that in an account of the crime in which a beating took place in advance of the murder, there had to have been compulsion involved in what happened afterwards. It would not have been ridiculous to imagine that Benwell had proved an unexpectedly awkward customer, had been beaten up in consequence, had been incarcerated for twenty-four hours while his assailants decided what to do next, and then, nothing better having suggested itself, had been taken into the swamp at gun point and killed.

Osler continued to disparage the defence case without fully answering it. He was scathing about Blackstock's analysis of the unreliability of the Crown witnesses:

You are asked by the defence to say that these crown witnesses have entered into a conspiracy to slay this man through the law; that for mere notoriety these reputable men and women come here to swear this man to the gallows although they know their story is untrue.

This was not a fair interpretation of what Blackstock had said, but Osler was unabashed. He even defended Alfred Hayward, whose poor eyesight had been exposed before all the court. 'What interest had Alfred Hayward in the matter, except to do his duty as a citizen and to tell what he knew?' asked Osler. 'It is very close to having murder in your heart when you tell a story that puts a man's life in danger, and that is what the prisoner's counsel charges old Alfred Hayward with.' By putting his argument this way, Osler seemed to be asking the jury to choose which man they were more inclined to brand an instinctive killer, Hayward or Birchall. For the jury there was presumably no competition between the two.

Osler's most flagrant misrepresentation of Blackstock's case came in his own defence of Detective Murray. He denied that

Blackstock had called Murray a hell-hound out of genuine outrage at Murray's investigative techniques. Instead, this 'abuse' was simply a reflection of the 'terrible resentment, anger, and dismay of the prisoner, who finds himself hunted down and brought to justice'. This was clearly untrue. Blackstock was obviously deeply frustrated by Murray's conduct, seeing it as improper at best, illegal at worst, and potentially a fatal barrier to justice. Osler made the insouciant counter-accusation that it had been 'nothing gentlemanly' to attack Murray when the detective was not a witness and therefore could not defend himself. Blackstock must have been particularly incensed by this line of argument.

As he drew towards the end of his address, Osler was not content to gamble on having persuasively held together the links in the Crown's chain of evidence against Birchall. Quite the reverse. He did ask the jury: 'Will you take the romantic view of circumstantial evidence that we get as the turning point in modern fiction, or will you take the practical view and believe the evidence of the witnesses you have heard?' After this, however, Osler dramatically aborted all question of worrying about consistency amongst the witnesses: 'If the prisoner could be identified as being at any point between the Falls and Eastwood that day,' he argued, then

the Crown had substantiated its case. If the jury could believe the evidence of one of the witnesses who had sworn to seeing him on the way, there was no need to accept the testimony of the others.

'One spot,' said Osler 'covers the whole journey.' The jury could choose a single witness and ignore all the others. They would even be justified in forming a guilty verdict, he stated, without 'one particle' of any 'testimony as to the identification on the journey'. In an amazing move, Osler declared that 'the Crown has already proved the presence of the prisoner by the finding of the body in the swamp'.

Osler grindingly continued to play fast and loose with the understood means by which a jury is supposed to reach its verdict when he placed on the shoulders of the accused the burden of proving his own innocence. It 'rested with the prisoner to show where he was on that fatal 17th of February, but he has not shown where he was,' he said. 'Think of that long blank on the 17th February which the prisoner could fill in, but he dare not, although his life is now trembling in the balance.' In 'all that frontier country' he could not bring 'one man to say where he was on that day'. Although the law permitted Birchall to make an unsworn statement from the dock, Osler observed, with no opportunity for the Crown to cross-examine him, he preferred to remain silent and to 'seek to discredit the evidence of the crown' consequent upon the fact that the witnesses were 'a little disagreed'. Osler's 'eyes and face took on a most tragic appearance' wrote one reporter,

and turning from the jury for a moment he looked straight at Birchall, and pointing with his finger said in tones of thundering eloquence, 'There locked up in the breast of that man is The Whole Terrible Secret. Why, why, why, I say, does he not speak?'

For all the claims about Osler's gentlemanly calm, he ended on a histrionic challenge that drew everyone in: 'To a certain extent we are to try if society is powerless to protect itself against foul murder.'

'There was a general movement in court as Mr. Osler sat down,' the press reported, 'as if people had been released from a spell and sought to learn of their surroundings.' He had spoken for just over four hours, and had 'seemed like an old warrior who was about entering a battle which he had already won, like a race horse who looked with contempt on his fellow competitors'. Observers disagreed about the relative force of the defence and Crown speeches, but concurred in writing that Osler had 'ascended to the very pinnacle of his inimitable and ingenious eloquence in dealing with the nefariousness of the prisoner'.

It was twenty to eight in the evening. As the 'shades of night had gathered', the gas had been lit in the court room. MacMahon, increasingly anxious not to lose another day to the Birchall case, made no allowances for people's hunger, but decided to launch at once into his summing-up. Within the town hall there was a profound silence, but this was in peculiar contrast to the menacing yells of the mob beyond the doors:

Outside in the square there was a dense crowd and they howled and yelled themselves hoarse in revenge for not being admitted to the already crowded room. Their unseemly disturbance did not in the least appear to disturb the judicial serenity of Mr Justice MacMahon at his court, for it was while his Lordship was speaking that the throng outside yelled their loudest.

MacMahon's bias was all-pervasive and glaring. He 'spoke to the jury as a teacher would to a class of pupils', and instructed them 'as if it was a foregone conclusion' that 'the strong arm of the law had descended upon the right person'. He did make a very few points in favour of the defence. He criticized Murray, for example, saying that 'the method adopted when the witnesses were taken to the jail here was no proper mode of identification', so that the results were 'hardly to be counted'. Nevertheless, most of MacMahon's understanding was in line with Osler's view of the case. He mentioned failures and contradictions in the testimony of Crown witnesses to Birchall's movements on 17 February, but added: 'If you believe the evidence of all these you must come to the conclusion that he is guilty.' He agreed with Osler regarding Birchall's instructions to Colonel Benwell over how to send a draft: 'If a draft was sent to a bank either member of the firm could draw the money. The prisoner could draw the money. I tell you that as a matter of law.' He also interpreted the evidence as leading to the definitive conclusion that 'The murder must have been committed before the sleet storm on Monday night, because the crust of snow had to be scraped away to reveal the bloodstains underneath.' He felt that the condition of Benwell's body showed, 'if it showed anything', that it had been bruised when dragged to where it was deposited. He interpreted the defence theory as being that Benwell had been murdered simply for plunder, and felt that the removal of the name tags suggested otherwise. Meanwhile, Birchall's lies about how he came to be holding articles of Benwell's property provided, MacMahon said, 'a very cogent argument that they came into his possession in an improper manner'. Furthermore, regarding telegrams, if the jury 'believed the one to Birchall at Niagara Falls signed "Stafford" was sent by himself to himself it was a grave piece of evidence against him, for it was sent the day prior to his learning of the finding of the cigar case with the name "F. C. Benwell" on it'. MacMahon asserted that if Birchall had gone into the swamp with Benwell, then 'Birchall is accountable.' Like Osler, he only raised the possibility that Birchall might not himself have killed Benwell in order to declare that if someone else had done the deed, then Birchall was still responsible for it.

Shortly before ten o'clock, a little over two hours after he

The jury photographed against a single panel of a genteel studio backdrop.

had begun, MacMahon brought all public argument in the Birchall trial to a close. He pronounced that there was no point in commenting further upon the evidence, but submitted to the jury that 'the links in the chain of testimony were strong'.

With tears in his eyes, his Lordship impressively reminded the jury of the great duty which devolved upon them. The Government of the country provided the punishment; it was for the jury to pronounce upon the guilt of the prisoner.

MacMahon gave them 'until 11.30 to agree upon a verdict'. No one knew if they would comply, but they were under

TWO FINE PHOTOS.

The publishers of THE SENTINEL-REVIEW have had two excellent photographs made by WESTLAKE. They are

THE JURY	CELEBRITIES
ON THE	OF THE
BIRCHALL TRIAL.	BIRCHALL TRIAL.

These photographs have been copyrighted and can be obtained only from us. Size 10x14 inches, just right for framing.

The price of these Photos is 50 cents each.

HOW TO GET THEM FREE.

Any person may get either of the photos free on the following conditions :

1. By paying in advance $2.00, for THE EVENING SENTINEL-REVIEW, that is, all arrears and six months from date of payment.

2. By paying his own Weekly subscription in advance up to January, 1892, and securing for us one new yearly subscriber for THE WEEKLY SENTINEL-REVIEW. This new subscription also to be paid up to January, 1892, in advance. By new subscribers we mean anyone not at the present time [Nov, 1890] getting the paper regularly. Only the person who gets the new subscriber gets the photograph. The Weekly will be sent to all new subscribers until January, 1892, for $1.00—14 months.

3. By paying for The Weekly Sentinel-Review until January, 1893, in advance.

Pay your Daily subscription in advance or get a new Weekly subscriber for The Sentinel Review.

☞Photos may be seen at Sentinel-Review Office.

Address:—

PATTULLO & CO.,
The Sentinel-Review,
Woodstock.

This offer is only good to subscribers until November 15th.

A circulation gambit by the Woodstock Sentinel-Review.

instruction to deliberate for no longer than an hour and a half.

Though Birchall was deemed to have stood up well under Osler's 'withering' address, he 'appeared tired and worn out', and was quickly removed to the jail, 'it being expected that there would be a long struggle in the jury room'. Next, the entire crowd in the court room was 'bundled out into the chilly atmosphere with very little ceremony'. This was accomplished 'only after a good deal of difficulty, many ladies showing a remarkable reluctance to leaving'. The pressmen, too, were indignant at being made to vacate the town hall. In the end, however, it was completely emptied. As the spectators joined the unseemly masses outside, some fifteen hundred people found themselves loitering in the cold of the night–time square.

One person on tenterhooks about the verdict that night was Pelly. After months of marking time, he was desperate to return to his family in England, but he knew that if the jury failed to agree, this would trigger a retrial. He would be forced to remain, and would have to go through the entire procedure all over again. He had, however, received permission from the Crown to leave the country immediately should Birchall be found guilty. By this stage Pelly himself was far from convinced about what the outcome was going to be, telling a reporter that he 'rather expected' a disagreement.

Perhaps he had been more certain of a guilty verdict before he heard all the evidence. At any rate, when the trial began on Monday 22 September, it had been understood that it would be all over by the weekend, so Pelly had booked a passage from New York to Liverpool for the Wednesday of the following week. He had little financial leeway to alter his ticket, and had become increasingly worried as the trial wore on longer than expected. When it ran over on to Monday

29 September, he discovered that the last train to pass through Woodstock that would get him to New York in time left that very night.

This train was due to pull up at the station at around midnight. As time drifted by, Pelly said a provisional goodbye to all his friends. He had his 'kit at hand', and only needed to know the verdict. The jury retired and the minutes continued to pass. Finally, Pelly left the scene and 'drove to the railway depot'. It had struck him that, thanks to the wiring of the court room, he did not need to be on hand in the market square to discover whether or not his liberty was assured. Over at the station, he could ask the railway clerk to 'have his phone connected with the Town Hall'. The clerk could listen in to the trial for him, and give him the result.

As midnight drew close, Pelly waited by the tracks in the cold and darkness for either the sound of the train, or the cry of the clerk.

Only three or four minutes before the train was due he said, 'The jury have come into the court.' Then after a long pause, 'The judge is in court.' Another pause, and I heard the train approaching! Then, 'The jury are being asked for their verdict.' The train headlight lit up the station and I could hear the brakes grinding. It was for me an intense moment. As the train stopped the Clerk shouted 'Guilty.'

From the chill of the lonely platform, Pelly leapt aboard his train – released from his hideous adventure, and free, at last, to go home.

14. More Stimulants

' "No, your Majesty, I think we won't hang him. I think we'll send him to penal servitude for life;—if your Majesty pleases." That is so easy, and would be so pleasant.'

Anthony Trollope, *John Caldigate*, 1879

As Pelly sped away in the night, he was weirdly cocooned from the closing moments of the trial that had weighed on him for so long. MacMahon had asked for the verdict to be reached by eleven thirty, so at twenty-five past the hour the doors to the town hall had been reopened. The crowd had 'poured into the court room in wild confusion' as one reporter noted, 'until the hall was packed to the doors. But the vast audience was as still as death for several minutes awaiting the arrival of the prisoner.' For once there were virtually no women. After the court had been cleared at ten o'clock, Woodstock's ladies must have felt that it would be improper to linger on the streets indefinitely at night. At the peak of their attendance at the trial, their number had been estimated at about four hundred. Newspapers now ranged in their count from one woman present, through two, to a maximum of half a dozen.

Promptly at half past eleven, MacMahon arrived. The jurors indicated that they had complied with his wishes in reaching a verdict, so he sent for the prisoner to be brought to the court. Birchall arrived at a quarter to twelve. When MacMahon sent for an almanac, reporters assumed that he was selecting a date for the hanging. Most papers agreed that as Birchall entered the court room, he 'looked cool and collected, but his face was ghastly in its whiteness', and that he 'gave no evidence of any fear save in a deep pallor and the restlessness of his eyes'. Several reports noted that when he walked up the aisle, 'the rattle of the chain fell discordantly on the silence of the court', while the constable charged with removing his handcuffs 'fumbled and bungled' for what seemed like several minutes. When at last the handcuffs were off, and Birchall was closed into the dock, 'a dead silence ensued'. Now 'every face in the hall had on a look of intense anxiety'.

The clerk of the court asked: 'Gentlemen of the jury, have you agreed upon a verdict?' Eleven jurors looked towards their foreman. 'We find the prisoner, Birchall, guilty,' said Mr Christopher. According to the press, 'not by the twitching of a muscle did the prisoner betray the awful gloom which must have settled down upon his heart as he heard the words. He kept his eyes fixed upon the floor, and never flinched.'

Blackstock had collapsed at his hotel and was not present. Hellmuth stood in his place and asked MacMahon to poll the jury for individual confirmation of the verdict. 'As the judge asked the questions his voice faltered,' wrote a reporter. 'How say you?' inquired MacMahon. 'Is John Reginald Birchall guilty of the offence charged?' Each juror rose in turn to condemn him.

Hellmuth now made a last desperate effort at delay, arguing that the case should be reserved because letters from the Cheltenham agent, Mr Mellersh, had never been proved. Without them, Hellmuth asserted, there would be a critical break in the Crown's chain of evidence. MacMahon replied that this gave no grounds for a stay in proceedings, and at this Osler 'moved for sentence'. MacMahon told Birchall to stand up, and asked, 'What have you to say, John Reginald Birchall, that sentence should not be passed upon you for the felony you have committed?' Birchall replied in a steady voice, 'Simply that I am not guilty of the crime, my Lord.'

As he protested his innocence, 'The audience looked on with something almost akin to paralysis.' The silence, deep as it already was, 'became oppressive beyond measure'. MacMahon had never before pronounced a death sentence. 'With some- what of a tremor in his voice,' he addressed Birchall directly, remarking, 'I can only say I fully concur in the verdict which has been returned by the jury on the indictment against you,' and 'almost everyone' who had listened to the trial, he declared, had come to the same 'inevitable' conclusion. 'Without any compunction,' Birchall had 'conceived and premeditated and carried out the murder', in order to reap a 'miserable reward'. MacMahon continued:

I can hold out to you no hope whatever of any commutation of the sentence I am about to pronounce. There is, I may say to you, but a short time in which you may be permitted to live, and I earnestly implore you to take advantage of every hour that remains to make your peace by supplicating the Throne of Heavenly Grace for for- giveness for offences committed by you in the flesh. The sentence of the court upon you, John Reginald Birchall, is that you be taken hence to the place whence you came, and that there within the walls of the prison between the hours of 8 o'clock in the morning and 6 in the afternoon on Friday, Nov. 14 next, you be hanged by the neck until you are dead, and may the Lord have mercy on your soul.

As Birchall sat down again, 'his legs and hands were uncontrol- lable and twitching nervously', while on his face there was a 'dazed, haunted look'.

Birchall's guard, John Entwhistle, 'took the sentence very hard'. His 'whole system shook with intense feeling' during the judge's charge, and he now 'leaned for support against the dock and bowing his head on his hands wept bitterly. Great sobs shook his frame and tears flowed freely.' Birchall, by contrast, swiftly recovered, commenting lightly to reporters that 'there's only a few years difference between the life of one man and that of another, and it does not make much difference, anyhow.' He was once again handcuffed or, in the quaint phrase of the time, 'heavily ironed', and was hurried away to the jail where he could now expect to die.

A Toronto reporter was afterwards disgusted as he reflected on the attitude of the jury:

The close of the Birchall trial was marked by one of the greatest travesties which ever cast a stain on the annals of Canadian jurisprudence. Twenty minutes prior to the appearance of the prisoner in court, and more than that time before the announcement of the verdict was made to his Lordship Judge MacMahon and the court, the decision had been written out in the form of a cable for England. When the jury came out it was noticed that several of that body wore a self-satisfied grin. One of them whispered to a reporter that they had found a verdict of guilty, and long before the foreman began to tell his Lordship that the jury had reached a verdict, the news was waiting on paper far over the sea, with only a blank left for the date of execution.

The day after the trial ended, one juryman told a reporter that their decision had been reached 'in seven minutes at the first ballot'. Another juror calculated that it had taken them a mere four minutes. Either way, it emerged that the verdict simply had not been deliberated at all. The one question that the twelve men had heatedly debated was that of how long they should appear to have taken, some of them being afraid that it would not 'look well' if they were too prompt. The vote had eventually come out at ten to two that they should return their verdict some time on the Monday night, rather than pretending to argue until the following morning.

The Toronto *World* managed to acquire the most detailed insight into the attitudes of particular jury members:

Foreman George Christopher is a cousin of Miss Choate, whose evidence as to identity was criticized so severely by Mr. Blackstock, and the manner in which the defence alluded to her testimony did not have the effect of strengthening the justice of its cause in Mr Christopher's mind. The two members of the clan Murray on the jury also became more set in their views owing to what they considered the uncalled-for reference to the government detective, whom Mr. Blackstock characterized as 'the crown in this case.'

It may seem extraordinary that the suggestion that Murray had rigged the trial could be taken to reflect upon all men of the same name, but these shabby revelations show how even those who had prophesied prejudice in Birchall's jury had underestimated the number of grounds upon which prejudice might apply.

Despite disquieting articles of this kind, in many quarters the verdict was received with relief. Numerous Canadian commentators had written, in advance, sentiments to the effect that

the trial is of no mere domestic interest, but in all its phases will be watched by the world at large, and it must be proved that the majesty of the law is as sacred and well guarded in the backwoods of Canada as in any assize town of Great Britain.

In this spirit, the *Sentinel-Review* afterwards declared that it had been universally felt that any other verdict 'would have been such a failure as to create a bad impression abroad'. The *Presbyterian Review* claimed even more strongly that 'a failure of justice in this case would have been nothing short of a national calamity'. As the ensuing days would show, however, many people believed that a drastic failure of justice in Wood-stock's makeshift court room was the very definition of what had just taken place.

After his conviction all observers reported that Birchall swiftly recovered his cool, and 'treated the verdict as philosophically as he would a horse race'. When he found himself lodged back in jail, however, he did want desperately to talk. Two prison officials kept him company, and only at around four o'clock in the morning had he unwound enough to be able to sleep. Even then, one of his guards remained resolutely awake. The prisoner had been sentenced to hang. From now on, he would have a death watch.

There was also a general agreement in the press that after walking out of the trial, Mrs Birchall had returned to the Commercial Hotel and cast herself across her bed, lying there the whole night in an opiated stupor. When, upon waking the next morning, she had been told by her 'fond and inspiring sister' the dreadful news of Birchall's sentence she had 'wept freely and seemed heart-broken'. Reporters wrote that it was feared she would 'not long survive the terrible agony', and most now judged that whatever faults Mrs Birchall had dis-played in her support for her husband, they were forgivable, 'womanly' faults.

The Government Inspector of Prisons had prepared new in-structions for the authorities at Woodstock jail. Now he was a convicted murderer, Birchall's regime changed considerably. He was denied exercise in the jail yard. All potentially dangerous objects, such as knives, matches and steel pens, were removed from his cell, and most of his pictures were torn down and given to relic hunters. He was not required to wear prison garb, but was banned from eating hotel food. This last ruling might have been worse had it not been decided that, to avoid any chance of his food being adulterated, his meals must be specially prepared for him inside the prison. He was to be watched vigilantly at all times.

Despite these constraints, Birchall was reported to be keeping buoyant. On 2 October zealous pressmen wired the news to their editors that he had enjoyed himself that morning 'throwing a pebble at a crazy Dutchman in the jail yard, the Dutchman acting as retriever and returning the pebble to the cell window'. Birchall was also known to have a black cat living with him. Even so, it is scarcely likely that he felt as light-hearted as reports painted him to be. One of the more painful aspects of his new regime must have been that, from this point on, his wife's visits were very restricted. Their first meeting after the trial took place on 6 October. She was not allowed to touch him, leading a sentimental newspaperman to spell out for his readers that 'such a thing as a kiss was impossible'.

Now that he was confirmed as a ruthless killer, Birchall received the attentions of numerous poets, phrenologists, religious enthusiasts and other 'heartless cranks'. Of them all, he was most particularly irritated by the 'eminent psychologist', and effusive proponent of eugenics, Dr W. G. Bessey, who wrote in the press that Birchall's stout ears, furtive eyes and lascivious mouth all betrayed a plebeian strain in his blood, and concluded that he was a 'moral deformity' as a consequence of 'ill or unwise mating' amongst his forebears. Besides random articles of this sort, Birchall also now provided a benchmark for the press against which all other current Canadian murderers could be judged. Most were found wanting, though one killer from Quebec, who had chewed a wad of tobacco all through his trial and said he wanted to die, actually won the headline 'Cooler Than Birchall'.

Although many people, deranged or otherwise, were confident of Birchall's extreme criminality, commentators began a campaign as soon as the trial was over urging him to confirm his guilt in a confession. There was, it seems, a class of editorialist who perceived an uncomfortable gap between guilt beyond all reasonable doubt and guilt without any doubt whatsoever. Newspapermen who had thoroughly endorsed the verdict still wrote, therefore, that it was Birchall's duty to speak up, to 'relieve the minds of the jury'. In this atmosphere it was plain that any reporter who could secure a revelatory statement from the prisoner would score the most tremendous coup.

With this in mind, on Saturday 4 October, Mr Farrer, joint editor of the Toronto *Globe*, went to Woodstock to gather any gossip there might be about Birchall's explanation, since the trial, of events in the spring. Farrer found the second-hand material he sought, cobbled the stories together on the Sunday, and the next day printed an extended article under the descending headlines: 'Birchall. — Statements Made by the Doomed Man. — A Partial Confession. — He Implicates Another in the Crime. — The Mysterious Telegram. — He Admits That He Was an Accessory. — Fraud Charged Against Pickthall.'

Birchall's explanations, according to Farrer, had been

'gradually oozing out of him'. He was said to have claimed that he had had a plan in place with his one-time friend, Neville Pickthall, in which Pickthall was to pretend, using his own excellent brick farm, to be Birchall's manager, both on that property and on the adjoining hundred acres. After a couple of days of masquerade, Pickthall was to have handed Benwell a large sum of money to take to Birchall, supposedly representing the farm's profits for a month or two, and on the strength of this bounty it had been hoped that Benwell would either hand over his five-hundred-pound investment immediately, if he had brought the sum with him, or else would wire home for it at once. This scheme 'apparently did not involve murder', noted Farrer, 'though Birchall does not say how Benwell was to have been got rid of after he had been fleeced'. As Farrer understood it, Pickthall had for some reason 'funked' after meeting Birchall on his arrival in New York, perhaps because he found out there that Benwell hadn't brought the money with him.

After Birchall's incarceration, Pickthall had returned to Woodstock 'moody and reserved', on 1 April, reputedly picking up work thereafter as a farm labourer. His explanation to a local reporter for the entire period of his disappearance had been that he had gone away 'on the same old drunk'. Regarding Birchall's crimes, he 'knew nothing of the affair', though he did admit that he had applied to Macdonald for a pupil to work on his farm. 'Further than that,' he said, 'I did not go.'

After half-fingering Pickthall, Farrer's article moved on to a 'curious point' which, he wrote, was 'not brought out at the trial'. Birchall had told Pelly on 25 February that he had heard from the Stafford House in Buffalo that a letter and telegram were waiting for him there. In response, Pelly had suggested that Birchall wire the Stafford House to ask for the contents of the telegram to be sent on to Niagara. The 'curious point', as Blackstock had, in fact, briefly noted at the very end of his defence case, was that this first telegram from the Stafford House to Birchall was undoubtedly genuine, with a copy in the telegraph company records. It followed that unless Birchall was the author of the two messages to which this initial telegram referred, somebody really had been attempting to contact him in Buffalo. He himself, Farrer claimed, had hinted that these messages had been from a panicked Pickthall, sent from somewhere else in America, instructing Birchall to get rid of Benwell's luggage; but no proof of this remained. The telegraph office had failed, despite Birchall's request, to forward the contents of the mysterious original wire to Niagara because, Farrer wrote, it had not been paid to do so. The company had then destroyed this crucial telegram as being unclaimed, before any detective could secure it.

Farrer rehearsed a few last points, one unaccountable detail being that, while Benwell had owned a gold watch, neither this item, nor his gun, had ever been found. Farrer then went on to conclude that, all told, Birchall's hints did make a 'tolerably coherent story', but this was offset by the reflection that he was 'such an enormous liar', that, without corroboration, nothing he said was trustworthy. It should be added that in his analysis, Farrer was culpably unclear himself. In particular, he blurred the question of what it was to which Birchall had supposedly confessed. Farrer unblushingly wrote that, on the night of his conviction, Birchall had 'let it be understood there and then that he was guilty to the extent of having been an accessory before and after the fact'. This fails to address a critical question: an accessory, beforehand, to what? If Benwell's murder was premeditated, and if Birchall had been an accessory to that plan, then in law he was as guilty as the actual killer: he could, according to statute, be 'indicted, tried, convicted and punished in all respects as if he were a principal felon'. If, however, Benwell's murder had been unpremeditated, then, before the fact, Birchall was party only to an attempted swindle. As for his actions after Benwell's killing, the law stated that in punishment, 'Every accessory after the fact to murder is liable to imprisonment for life.' Farrer concluded his article by saying that, 'to sum up', Birchall had acknowledged, 'as has been said, that he was an accessory and therefore merits the sentence passed upon him'. Not only was there no confirmation of this claim, but if Birchall really wasn't Benwell's killer, then a precise understanding of what kind of an accessory he had been should have constituted the difference to him between life imprisonment and precipitate execution. Papers as far apart as the Woodstock *Sentinel-Review* and the London *Times* roundly condemned the *Globe* for printing a 'bogus confession'.

Birchall, once convicted, continued both to charm and to menace the public imagination. The press did not entirely lose sight of Pelly either. Newspapermen had intercepted him at the docks in New York on his way home, and as he waited to sail he was reported to have said of Birchall,

Poor fellow. I cannot but feel sorry for him. The verdict, however, was unquestionably a fair one. Oh, I can't think of that date—November 14—without a shudder. It has been a terrible experience, and one that I'll never forget as long as I live.

Pelly never afterwards admitted to any feeling of doubt about the jury's decision, or to concern about contradictions in the evidence.

Entries in Pelly's travel diary for 22 and 29 September, with somewhat heartless use of ditto marks.

Shortly after leaving her dock, his steamer, the *Majestic*, was hit amidships by the Hamburg Packet Company's vessel, the *Dania*, whose bridge was severely damaged, with three lifeboats 'smashed into splinters'. The *Majestic* lost one lifeboat and a little varnish, but carried on regardless. When Pelly eventually reached England, and his home in Saffron Walden, he stepped off an evening train to find a crowd of 'some thousands' had gathered at the railway station. His imminent arrival had been 'signalled by a *feu de joie*', and

he was received with prolonged and deafening cheers. The horses were unharnessed and the car was drawn to Walden Place by willing hands, preceded by the Excelsior Band playing 'Rolling home to dear old England', and men carrying lighted torches.

The town's windows had been hung with flags, 'the residence of Mrs. Bellingham was illuminated with coloured lights', and a triumphal arch had been erected at the entrance to Pelly's father's house, with the words 'Welcome Home' on the front. Crowds cheered all along the way, and the vicarage garden, 'hung with fairy lights', was soon full of people, who 'perambulated' while the band played 'a suitable selection'. Pelly gave a little speech of thanks.

On 11 October the Woodstock press was at last able to reveal the proposed inscription for Benwell's vault. With the

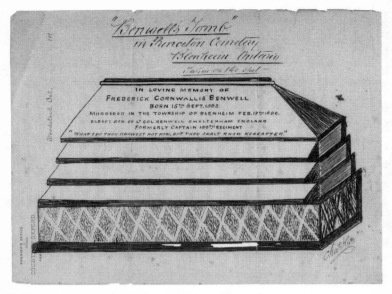

A Victorian pen-and-ink sketch of Benwell's vault.

trial over, and the case details fixed in law, he was to be described as having been 'Born 15th Sept. 1865', and 'Murdered in the Township of Blenheim Feb. 17th 1890'. There would also be a quotation taken from the Gospel according to St John: 'What I do thou knowest not now, but thou shalt know hereafter.' Benwell's younger brother, Charles, delayed his departure from Woodstock, even after these arrangements had been made, in the hope of finding work, 'but nothing apparently offered itself'. On 28 October, when he finally decided to leave, the Woodstock *Evening Standard* managed to interview him as he waited for his outbound train. When asked what he felt about the adequacy of the trial, he said he had been puzzled by the fact that the boots in which his brother's body had been found could not possibly have belonged to him. They had been the right size, but 'entirely worn out', and stained with rubber as though worn with overshoes. It was inconceivable that he would have donned footwear so 'shabby'. As to whether or not he thought Birchall had had a confederate, Charles Benwell said, 'Yes. At least there has always been a doubt in my mind.' If the Crown case was wrong, however, he said he thought it behoved Birchall himself to explain exactly what had happened on 17 February. He did also add that, while he had thought the defence very weak, 'There were certain points in it which I would like to have some satisfactory explanation of before it is too late.' The young man was by now leaning out of the window of his carriage. 'Just then' the train began to pull out of the station, taking Charles Benwell, and all his vague doubts, away.

While the *Globe* made capital out of its story of Birchall's supposed confession, his sympathizers began to organize a set of petitions appealing for executive clemency. It was understood that the Governor-General, who in such matters acted on advice, was 'always extremely reluctant to interfere with the sentence of the courts of justice'. Nevertheless, at least two petitions were widely circulated in Ontario. The first was based on a straightforward opposition to the death penalty. By the end of October it had reportedly been presented to several Toronto clergymen, 'every one of whom refused to sign it'. Even so, it was said to carry more signatures than the second petition, which questioned the viability of a verdict based wholly on circumstantial evidence, and objected to the fact that the press had 'inflamed and prejudiced the mind of the public' until an impartial jury had become an impossibility. Newspaper commentators were predictably caustic about this 'scandalous' and 'flagrant insult' to judge, jury and the press, and found support in various British papers for ignoring the pleas of the 'mad humanitarian' brigade. One English editorialist wrote approvingly of the Canadians that,

especially they have not yet learned from us that the more atrocious a crime is, and the better the social position of the criminal, the greater should be the anxiety of the whole array of benevolent busybodies to protect him or her from its consequences.

Two further petitions were hastily got up in England itself. Both included specific criticisms of the way Birchall's case had been handled by the Canadian justice system. The first noted that Birchall had always strenuously protested his innocence; that there was no direct evidence of his guilt; that the identification evidence had been dubious from the start and had altered over time; 'that the case was unduly prejudiced by the dishonest practices of Birchall (which must be admitted)', and that it had been further prejudiced by an unproven suspicion that there had been systematic murder of farm pupils in Ontario. Altogether, the Crown case had been unreliable, the verdict was unsafe, and an irrevocable punishment should not be inflicted. The second English petition, similar to the first, added the objection that 'No attempt has been made by the Government before the trial to discover whether and what other parties may be guilty as well as or more than the accused.' One Canadian paper responded wrathfully that these points were quite irrelevant, and that the English must not be allowed to 'paralyze' Canadian justice.

Mrs Birchall wrote, 'to the People of America', a letter begging for signatures on the petitions:

May I ask you to sign the petition for the commutation of my husband's sentence? I shall, indeed, feel deeply and truly grateful if you will help me to save him from the terrible doom that awaits him. Florence Birchall.

A Reuters correspondent wired ardently that 'this pathetic appeal is said to have touched the hearts of the people as no other has done in the history of the colony'. If this was less than believable reporting, it was true that Mrs Birchall's standing with the public at large had been raised by a long explanation of her behaviour recently printed in the *Globe*. Mrs Birchall's friends had let it be known that she had 'solemnly' declared that she had been as deluded by her husband as anyone else, and was now 'paying with a blighted life for having believed every word he told her'. Birchall had always seemed to have adequate money, and she had never 'heard a word against him'. They had gone to Canada on their first trip, after a speedy marriage, because he had claimed he'd been called there suddenly on business. Once they arrived, he had pretended to own various farms and horses, and had persuaded her that they were living off the profits of his businesses. Birchall had had many photographs of these farms which he had shown her, and she had naturally believed that they were his. When they returned to England, he had told her all his money was tied up in his Canadian businesses but that, when they were finally able to go back to Canada, the farms would realize a much bigger profit. In London he had been 'good and affectionate' and had 'kept proper hours'. He had had some sort of job in town, which he had told her was related to his Canadian affairs. If she had repeated his lies to Pelly and Benwell, she had done so in good faith. When, occasionally, she had discovered discrepancies in her husband's statements, he had somehow always managed to explain them away. She had been 'hopeless as it were in his hands'. Birchall had told her he was not guilty of killing Benwell, and she had believed him.

Plenty were busy claiming responsibility for Benwell's murder in Birchall's stead. One of the most entertaining of these confessions was sent to Osler from Massachusetts by a person using the name Mabel Morton. The Crown, Mabel declared, had made a terrible error: 'I expect you thought you were right, but you are very far from it.' Benwell had promised to marry her, 'but after he had ruined me he was cold and distant'. As though this were not bad enough, 'When I find I was about to become a mother I told Fred my worst fears, but he only laught at me.' Benwell had then informed Mabel he was going to America and would never see her again, at which she decided to take a steamer there herself, disguised as a man, by chance the very same steamer on which Benwell and Birchall had also travelled. Naturally enough, she had bought herself a pistol in New York, and she had also conferred there with Birchall, who had agreed to decoy Benwell to a lonely spot so that Mabel might frighten him into marrying her. When this ploy failed, in an Ontario swamp, she had shot her lover dead: Birchall might be wicked, she wrote, but he hadn't pulled the trigger. Another such letter, from 'J. B. Litchfield' of Buffalo, explained that Birchall was a fully paid-up member of a murder gang, with offices in London. Litchfield added gloatingly that Judge MacMahon and seven of the jurors at the trial were themselves slated 'to suffer death at the hands of the league' if Birchall should be hanged.

While these and many other missives were blatant fantasies, at last a letter turned up that troubled the public mind. One day the prison received a communication addressed simply to 'Reginald Birchall, Woodstock, Ont.' The envelope was

stamped 'Jackson, Michigan, Oct. 24th, '90, 4.30 p.m.',
though the letter inside was dated 5 October:

To Rex.—Well, Rex, my dear boy, I have been watching you
ever since that fateful 17th of February, and I see the Canadians
have got you in their clutches at last. Well, I must say that I am
sorry for you, although you know you are partly to blame as
well as me. You no doubt wonder where I am, and where I
went after leaving you. You can bet I made quick tracks out of
Canada, and have been around considerable. At present I am in
Jackson, Michigan, where I intend to stay until about the middle
of this month. I won't post this letter until the day I leave here,
for fear some stray detective might get the drop on me. By the
time you get this I will be where I will have naught to fear
from Canadian or American law. I see by some of your own
statements that you knew Benwell had a revolver. If you had
told me that he had a revolver this whole business never would
have happened, and you would have been a free man to-day.

To make a d__n long story short, and a bad one at that, let
me say that as soon as I left you I began to see it was not going
to be an easy job to get that fellow settled on a farm for even
two weeks or any length of time. I never got up to that old
rooster's with him, and I don't think I could have found him
any way. It would have been easy enough if you hadn't told
him you owned the place. We struck into that notorious
swamp just for fun to get a shot if we could see anything, and
while in there the devil seemed to come over me, and I told
him straight out that it was a clear case of swindle; told him
that the whole farm pupil business in Canada was a swindle,
and wanted him to chum in; as he was well connected with
the Old Country we could all make a big thing out of it by
using his name, and get a lot on a string, and that what he

would lose now would soon be made up again. Well, Rex, you ought to have seen him. Great Scott! didn't he get up steam! Threatened to shoot me on the spot, and he would too if I hadn't drawn my revolver. My blood was up. I reasoned with him and did all I could to get him around, but no go. We talked the matter over for perhaps half or three-quarters of an hour, sometimes quietly, sometimes otherwise. At last he jumped up, said he would expose the whole d__d lot of us, and started for the road. I followed, and knowing what exposure would mean, I settled it then and there. Now you know it all. I'm sorry I did it, and never thought of getting you into trouble of the kind you are now. Forgive me, Rex. His watch and revolver no one will ever see again. He didn't have much money with him. I should have thought that any darned fool of a lawyer might see that for you to kill him would spoil your chances of getting the boodle. I do hope the Canadian people will treat you fairly and at least will give you a reprieve. If so I will write you again and give you my address and will expect to get a letter from you. Please burn this as soon as you have read it, and don't give my true name to anyone. You have kept it to yourself well and I thank you. It would do no good now. I bid you a long farewell, but still hope to see you in this world once more. I hope you are prepared for the worst. The love of money and excitement has caused me much trouble, but I hope to do better in the days to come. Good bye, ever yours,

The Colonel

P. S.—I see that 'smarty' we met in London last January has been trying to get his say in too. If I meet him out here, he'll get a different box from the one that you offered him in the theatre that night, and he'll get it just as cheap too.

The 'smarty' was identified at once. On 9 October an interview had appeared in the Toronto *Mail* with a Mr Stevens, of
the Hope Coffee-house, Montreal, in which Stevens claimed
that the previous January, at Morley's Hotel, Trafalgar Square,
London, he had met both the Birchalls, a young man he now
believed to have been Benwell, and a bombastic, dislikable
man from the Southern States of America known as 'the
Colonel'. All of them had been staying at the hotel, and they
had been thrown together enough for the Colonel to have
vaunted a special lightweight railway car he was promoting,
and for Birchall to have bragged about his extensive theatrical
connections, claiming that he could secure free passes for
Stevens to any theatre in London. Stevens said he had turned
down the offer: as far as he was concerned, he had done what
he could to avoid his fellow hotel guests, consistent with being
polite.

The register at Morley's Hotel swiftly identified Birchall's
Colonel friend as Jared E. Lewis, and within a day or two a
reporter had tracked down Lewis to his office in Wall Street,
New York. Lewis could not have been more categorical in
denying any involvement in Benwell's murder. He said he
had met Birchall by accident and had known him only as long
as they had been staying in the same hotel, Birchall impressing
him as 'a devil-may-care sort of a man about town'. There
had been, he claimed, no talk of any sort between them about
'mutual business interests in any scheme', and it was plain the
confession letter was intended simply 'to mystify the case'.
Though others, in separate newspaper articles, were prepared
to denounce Lewis as a poker player, speculator, confidence
man and coward, British pressmen reported that his alibi for
February was watertight. 'Scores of friends' who had met him
in England 'every day during the first six months of the present

year' would readily testify that he could not possibly have been in Canada at the same time.

It would have been odd if this particular colonel really had written the letter. Whether it was genuine or concocted, its author was plainly, and with good reason, anxious to remain unidentified. The 'P. S.' leading instantly to Lewis would therefore appear to have been a deliberate and malicious red herring. It is notable, too, that if the original date on the letter, 5 October, is correct, then the 'P. S.' can only have been written as an afterthought, at least four days later, as the 'smarty' article didn't come out until the 9th. The Toronto *Mail* wrote that Birchall

laughed when he was told that a man by the name of Col. Lewis had registered at Morley's Hotel, and said that whilst the 'Colonel' might have registered under that name, still the name did not amount to anything.

Birchall did agree that he had met Stevens at Morley's, but after this grew 'very reticent'. According to the *Sentinel-Review* the next day, he also sought to confuse matters by saying 'that he knew several "Colonels" in London, for nearly every American there went by the title of "Colonel"'. 'The Colonel', in 1890, was certainly a conveniently commonplace alias. The *Mail* followed up its investigation into the letter's origins by writing that 'Birchall's solicitors have been pressing him to give some particulars of that individual, but it is said that he says he does not feel like going back on an old pal.' This colonel, therefore, was destined to remain a potent spectre.

If the letter was a fake, it was excellently conceived. It provided a neat and simple answer to the abiding question of how Benwell had ever been lured into the swamp in the first place, namely that he hadn't really been lured in at all: he and his companion had gone in for the fun of a spot of hunting. It also gave a sufficiently convincing account of how someone of Benwell's undoubted stiffness might have reacted to an invitation to join a criminal gang, and one whose object was not merely to rob other perfectly decent young Englishmen, but his own father as well. An old school friend of Benwell's wrote a letter to the New York *Morning Journal* at this time in which, though remembering Benwell fondly, the author described how 'his temper was of an extremely impulsive character. Quick to resent an insult where often none was meant, it often led him into schoolboy fights.' It was thus 'with the greatest difficulty' that he could be persuaded to give in, 'even when floored four or five times'. If Benwell was just the type to have pushed a conflict too far, the nature of his putative murderer, as portrayed in the 'Colonel' paragraphs, was not implausible either. It would have required someone with a real flair for deception to carry out a plan that kept Benwell not merely alive but acquiescent, and the character offered up by the letter did not have the stomach for the job. The instant press response, once Colonel Lewis had been ruled out of the picture, was to assume that Birchall had concocted this letter himself, though without the added proposal that it might have been essentially an accurate account by Birchall of his own actions. The warders at Woodstock jail, however, were adamant that no letter could possibly have been smuggled out without their knowledge. They refused to accept that Birchall could have composed it himself; and the person who had posted the letter in Michigan was never found.

If it was a fake, then two notable conclusions follow. First, the author was very canny. While there was no detail in it that could not have been derived from pre-existing newspaper reports, nor did it contain any obvious errors that proved it to be false; furthermore, it was an intriguing synthesis of available clues. There was, after all, a conspicuous failure to incorporate into its murder history the defence interpretation of all the injuries to Benwell's body, namely that he was killed after 17 February somewhere other than the swamp, and after some kind of fight. As Benwell's bruises were one of the strongest planks in Blackstock's argument, it might seem a failing to omit this evidence from a confession that was a calculated fake. The counter to this suggestion, however, is that a calculating author could well have thought it an advantage to keep any new explanation of events as close to the Crown's version of the story as possible. The nearer the letter remained to the narrative that had been established in law, the smaller the quantity of legally verified evidence that would need to be disbelieved. The second notable conclusion to follow, if the letter is understood as a fake, is that the author went to great lengths not simply to remove blame for the act of Benwell's shooting from Birchall himself, but to portray the murder as an act of the moment, and absolutely not planned in advance. According to the 'Colonel', Birchall was innocent not only of killing Benwell, but also of the capital charge of being an accessory to his murder before the fact. Whatever oddities the letter displayed, and whatever questions it failed to answer, when it was printed in the press it did strike many people as genuine, and led to a new burst of signatures on the clemency petitions.

As early as the middle of March, Birchall had declared that he would keep reporters guessing over whether or not he would issue some kind of public statement, but the impulse to explain himself did not crystallize until after his trial. On 4 October the press gleefully reported that he had decided to write an autobiography to make money for his wife, in order to balance the 'legacy of debt and dishonor' he would otherwise be leaving her. Many newspaper representatives rolled in to Woodstock to see what kind of deal they might strike with the condemned man. At least four New York papers, the *World*, the *Sun*, the *Herald* and the *Police Gazette*, contended for the prize; but in the end, after some sort of auction, it was a combined bid from the Toronto *Mail* and the New York *Herald*, at a total of one thousand seven hundred dollars, that won. The *Mail* now knew it had Canada's newspaper readers at its mercy, while the *Herald* planned to syndicate the autobiography through its New York and international editions.

From this point on, the *Mail* became conspicuously more partisan towards Birchall. Before buying the autobiography, the paper had thoroughly condemned the clemency petitions: 'The general feeling is that the petition is a libel on the jury that tried Birchall, and in fact a libel upon the law.' As for Mrs Birchall's letter begging for signatures, 'will it attain the object required? Not likely.' Once the paper had bought Birchall's autobiography, however, it got off its high horse and instead condemned the *Sentinel-Review*'s 'stage-thunder editorials' against the petition, informing its own readers smugly that the signatures so far gathered already covered two hundred feet of paper. The *Mail*'s change of heart was conspicuous, but it was not total. The paper later admitted that in order to avoid being accused of exerting improper influence, it had taken a decision not to print examples of the 'innumerable' letters that had poured in to the editor ever since Birchall's trial arguing that justice had committed a 'frightful error' in his case.

The pressure of events and revelations mounted as Birchall's execution date drew near. Mrs Birchall had confided to Pelly

ENCOURAGING CANADIAN LITERATURE.

SEEDLY (*entering office of the Mail Manager*) —" I have here, sir, a story of my Life I have just written and illustrated with pen and ink sketches. I've been a rather hard case, and I think it makes pretty interesting reading. I was an undergraduate of Oxford University, and you'll find the literary work good. You can have it, sir, for $1,400."

MR. BUNTING—" Have you ever committed a cold-blooded murder?"

SEEDLY—" Well—er—no, sir; I've never gone quite so far as that."

MR. BUNTING—" Exactly. Well, after you've done so, and been tried and convicted, I'll talk literature with you."

Grip *magazine satirizes the* Mail's *purchase of Birchall's autobiography.*

in Niagara that her husband did not get on well with his mother. If this was true, his imminent death provoked some sort of rapprochement, and the two of them were reported to be corresponding with great frequency. It was understood that his mother intended to visit him to say farewell, but at the end of October, news came from England that as 'the verdict was a great shock to her and reduced her to an extremely low condition of health', after rallying, she had had a relapse, being 'now too weak to do anything – even to write to her son. All idea of her going to Canada has been finally abandoned.'

Blackstock, Birchall's lawyer, also seemed to experience a violent reaction to the case. On 24 October a civil trial, Corlett vs. Mason, was held in Windsor with, as it happened, Osler prosecuting, Blackstock defending and MacMahon as judge. Blackstock cross-examined the plaintiff 'in a very abusive manner', leaving those members of the bar present 'shocked'. Osler reproached Blackstock and 'demanded the protection of the court towards the witness', but Blackstock ignored this intervention and proceeded to ask the man 'if he had been drinking'. MacMahon, unable to restrain himself any longer, told Blackstock 'such language must cease', whereupon Blackstock, 'his face flushed with anger, remonstrated against the judge's ruling'. MacMahon was unable to diffuse the situation, and Blackstock – reputedly only the third lawyer ever to do this in the whole history of Canadian jurisprudence – now announced that 'on account of the Judge's conduct', he refused to continue. He stalked out of the court leaving behind a stunned silence. Other defence counsel ran after him, but were unable to change his mind. Blackstock had abandoned the case for good, compelling the authorities to hold it over until the following spring. Though he was notoriously a 'very quick-tempered man', and would fairly soon thereafter spend periods confined in a mental institution, it is difficult to believe that the Benwell trial had no effect at all on Blackstock's furious response to Corlett vs. Mason.

At last the Inspector of Prisons grew impatient with the broadcasting of the confidential affairs of Canada's most famous jailbird. On Saturday 1 November, with a fortnight left until Birchall's scheduled execution, a new set of regulations was imposed on the prisoner. He was to receive no more newspapers, and reporters would no longer be allowed into the jail. All communications with him were to be passed through the hands of the county Crown attorney, Mr Ball, and Ball was also to vet each new instalment of Birchall's autobiography. On 4 November a letter writer, under the signature 'Fair Play', protested in the *Sentinel-Review* that no matter how decent Mr Ball might be, it was against the Canadian spirit to give the prosecuting attorney in a murder case the 'power of suppressing what might save a young man from the gallows'. This protest was in vain.

As the days rapidly passed by, the campaign behind the clemency appeal gathered momentum. Petition sheets had been replicated in great numbers and left in hotel lobbies and newspaper offices in the hope that as many people as possible would sign them. Estimates for the number of signatories from Woodstock ranged from two to three hundred. In Toronto, meanwhile, along with many ordinary citizens, about two hundred members of the Ontario bar signed their names, as did other 'influential people of the highest standing'. There was an entirely separate movement on Birchall's behalf in Montreal. Petitions there were signed not only by 'a great number of the leading advocates of the Province of Quebec', but by William Bennett Bond, third Anglican Bishop of

Montreal, the Roman Catholic Vicar-General, Marechal of Montreal, Mayor Grenier and other notable figures. One explanation given for this particularly impressive array of support was that the people of the lower province 'had not their minds so nearly made up when the trial started', and consequently had taken a more balanced view of the evidence that was actually presented in court. The *Sentinel-Review* responded irritably that the Montreal petition had been manipulated by a cartel of Catholics. Even if this was true, considerable popular feeling had been mustered, with a mass-protest meeting called to take place at the city's Victoria Ice Rink.

The English petitions had been signed by Birchall's mother, Birchall's half-brother Oswald, and other relatives and half-relatives. The name of Birchall's full sister, Maud, was absent, but there were many more signatories, a significant number of these being Oswald Birchall's lowly parishioners. Oswald himself had appealed to Colonel Benwell to sign the petition on the grounds that Birchall 'might not be the actual murderer', but this, the press divulged, had been a 'vain request'. Otherwise, several prominent English jurists had given their names to the cause, including Justice Hawkins, who had been counsel in the notorious Tichborne case, destroying, in cross-examination, many of the false witnesses for the Tichborne claimant. No accounts quite agreed on the numbers of signatories to all the petitions taken together, but the figure seems to have been in the area of ten thousand. The *Mail* wrote that it was 'about the largest petition asking for Executive clemency ever yet presented to the Dominion Government'.

15. Advanced Disorder

'I should like to know how many such scoundrels our universities
have turned out; and how much ruin has been caused by that
accursed system which is called in England "the education of a
gentleman".'

William Thackeray, 'A Shabby Genteel Story', 1840

Birchall's trial officially established that he alone had both
planned and committed Benwell's murder, and had done so
for profit. The *Globe*'s findings after the trial were that Birchall
admitted to having colluded with Pickthall and others in a
plan to swindle Benwell and his father, but that he granted
neither that the murder had been premeditated, nor that it
had been carried out by himself. The *Globe* did not scruple
also to report, more than once, but with no evidence, that
Birchall had privately confessed to the killing. By contrast, the
'Colonel' confession letter, whoever wrote it, was a formidable
attempt to persuade the public that Birchall was innocent of
any capital charge. Meanwhile, the various clemency petitions
simultaneously circulating, sought to avert Birchall's imminent
end through a popular appeal for his sentence to be commuted
to life imprisonment. In short, despite the trial verdict, there
was a complex battle still in progress to fix Birchall's story.

Against this contradictory background, Birchall himself
began to write his autobiography. He composed it at night,
and would read out the new passages to his death watch, only
going to sleep at around five o'clock each morning. There is

little doubt that the *Globe*'s contributions to the maelstrom of narratives were motivated in large part by competition with the *Mail*, which advertised that it would soon be printing Birchall's own chronicle in instalments, with any infringement of the paper's copyright liable to be prosecuted.

Birchall divided his autobiography into roughly two halves: his life up until he first visited Canada, and his life thereafter. He also took time, in preliminary remarks, to protest that he was writing about his 'very checkered career' only in order to 'add somewhat to the slender provision that I am otherwise able to make for my wife'. Besides this, he offered the work as a 'sad and solemn warning' to all young men who were naturally inclined to walk the paths of 'idleness and folly'. He noticeably failed to address a local Canadian readership, imagining instead an audience made up of young Englishmen rather like himself. He warned against the outpourings of those 'knights of the pencil' who had written so many newspaper columns of lies about him, and promised that his own picture of his shortcomings would be more accurate. He was at pains to deny that he had ever sought notoriety, and said that at those points in his life where he had attracted public attention, this had never been an end in itself, but rather the consequence of his 'utterly foolish acts and escapades'.

According to Birchall, he had grown up an idle boy but a jolly one. For some years he had been educated at home by his father, Revd Joseph Birchall, a scholar and an authority in ecclesiastical law, and a strikingly warm and indulgent man. At the age of twelve, however, and steeped in the Classics, Birchall had been sent away to Rossall, a public school near Blackpool. One month later, his father had died. 'I was completely heartbroken at the time,' wrote Birchall, 'and hardly

knew what to do.' After his father's funeral, he had returned
to the coast feeling deeply 'lonely' and 'moody'. Months of
mourning had been assuaged only by the pleasures of cricket
and football. Then, when Birchall turned fourteen, and was
at last beginning to flourish again, his guardians had made the
disastrous decision to move him to a different school, in
Reading. Here Birchall found the discipline to be 'fifty per
cent. lower in favour of the pupil'. Lawlessness this easy proved
irresistible, and so his new school had laid the foundations for
his later 'wasted and riotous career at Oxford'. In Reading he
had got drunk, smoked, stolen food, slacked, and acquired a
relish not merely for a 'loud and horsey style', but for the
'assumption of bogus authority'. Furthermore, he claimed to
have been in the vanguard of a reign of terror that culminated
in rebellion amongst the schoolboys and the eventual resig-
nation of the headmaster. As Birchall had done very little study
all this time, he had had to take the entrance exam to Oxford
twice, but at the second attempt he had got into Lincoln
College. There his life of 'advanced disorder' began.

Birchall explained that at Lincoln he had been told to attend
chapel thirty-two times a term, that is, four times a week, and
had been warned to be in his rooms by midnight; otherwise,
the college had expected him to arrange his studies for himself,
and that was the end of the matter. Chapel could be avoided
by signing a slate in the library, so he and his friends learned
one another's signatures and had instituted a rota whereby no
one even had to clock in at the slate for more than one week
a term. Faced with this much free time, Birchall warned his
readers of the horrible consequences for a young man freshly
arrived at Oxford of being seduced into borrowing money on
unlimited credit; and also of the dangers of the 'billiard sharp',
saying: 'There is only one effective way to deal with this

unwelcome personage and that is to "punch his head".' More positively, what he had loved about his Oxford life had been the outdoor fun: boating, camping, and absolutely anything that involved horses. Fox hunting he had specially enjoyed, besides all forms of driving: single, double, four-in-hand, tandem, unicorn – two abreast and one leading – whatever possible. He himself had set up the Black and Tan Club, whose members would drive to a village some miles outside Oxford, get wildly drunk, and then race back again to indulge in an 'all night sitting'. Though these adventures involved breaking numerous university rules, Birchall did deny the story that on one Black and Tan outing he had managed to kill a horse. This had been the act of an intoxicated friend of his, while the club rampaged back from Witney, the horse falling on a downhill slope and snapping its spine. Birchall added here that if he himself had treated all creatures as well as he treated horses, there could have been no complaints against him: 'A kind word to a horse is never lost.' He also defended the reputation of his bulldog, Bill, accused in the press of having killed a pig. 'I do not deny,' he wrote, 'that there may have been a certain feeling of respect for him existing at that time. I think myself that there was.' Still, the dog was innocent. Birchall had trained Bill to sit up on the box seat of a carriage, and the creature had ridden there on all his master's driving excursions.

Birchall's love of horses, not surprisingly, embraced a love of racing, on which subject, he noted, 'I could write forever, I believe.' To any reader afflicted by a similar interest, he recommended not betting at all; but if at all, only occasionally, and never by a system. Simply 'wait for the good thing and then plank it down when it comes'. He also wrote with relish about his love of the theatre. The life of an actor was dismally

unrewarding, but as a student Birchall had run wild with
travelling show folk, and in 1887 he had worked as an acting
manager, and then as a theatre manager in Burton-on-Trent,
annoying the stout folk of that town when he had tipped the
programming towards music hall and burlesque.

He moved on to reminisce about the pleasures of the
refreshment room at Oxford railway station, where one could
dally with the women behind the bar, and he defended the
right of a man to marry beneath him if he chose; though a
man who tried to use money to rise above his natural station
in life was a 'cad'. Birchall described the type of student who
actually worked as 'the smug, who spends his time in uppish
thought'. It is easy to imagine how infuriating he must have
been to anyone at Oxford so dreary as to wish to study. He
confessed to having cultivated the art of behaving in just such
a way that 'the serious ones of this earth, carefully exasperated,
have been prettily spurred on to unseemliness and indiscretion,
while overcome with an undue sense of right'. The good
spirits that spill out of these Oxford paragraphs may have gone
some way towards diffusing the impact, in his account, of
vicious fighting, drunkenness, rampage, destruction of property, horse accidents and general squandering of good fortune.
Yet the suspicion must have entered the minds of anyone
reading this work that Birchall hadn't told the worst of it
either.

Though he had paid little attention to study, he seems to
have had a magpie grasp of entertaining detail. He filled the
autobiography with his own illustrations of horses, dancing
girls and drunkards, some of which pictures, however, it
would seem he did copy from his supply of magazines. He
also littered his text with short quotations in the approved
Victorian manner, reproducing music-hall jokes, snatches of

A typically salacious drawing by Birchall, reproduced in his autobiography.

FROM A PEN-AND-INK SKETCH BY BIRCHALL,

ballads, Latin tags, sentences from Addison and so on. Along the way he mentioned his fondness for books. Like all school-boys, he had been 'forced to acknowledge the disagreeable existence' of such 'worthy gentlemen' as Virgil, Homer, Livy, Pliny, Plautus, Aeschylus, Thucydides and so on, but he could be as interested by Ruskin and De Quincey as by the 'ordinary yellow back or 25-cent shocker'. Still, it was more or less exclusively to the lighter authors that he had turned in jail. Birchall confided that he had discovered, from his life of habitual rowdiness, that it was best to read books in the dead of night, and best of all to read them just before dawn.

At Oxford, he noted, he had actually passed an exam in Holy Scriptures, and certainly echoes of the King James Bible often filtered into his own prose, especially when he was cross. When he wished to execrate his wife's detractors, for example, he wrote: 'How shall it be with you anon? Truly your day of reckoning will come, when for such vile and dastardly action you shall give account.' He also used high-flown language to comic purpose. Evidently he had been passed a press account of Pelly's return to Saffron Walden, as he submitted the event to an acid set of revisions. He imagined

the return of the wanderer, laden with spoil and witness fees, the sole and distinguished object of laud and honour, truly in the minds of this noble band of peasants a thing of beauty and a joy forever— onward they go, with banners waving, and crash of loudest braying from the village band, the hero bowing to the crowd, the carriage drawn not by horses or an elephant, but by the willing and demented power of these horny-handed sons of toil, eagerly vying with each other for the cigarette ends thrown them from his Excellency's carriage.

After considerably more in this vein, about the broken-hearted maidens Pelly had left behind in Canada, Birchall finished, 'Truly what littleness we have in our midst. Well may we say with the poet *In tenui labor* – verily the mountain has conceived and brought forth a mouse.'

Birchall had two important objectives as he contemplated the second part of his autobiography. First, he wanted to provide an account of his actions that would reinforce doubt in the public mind as to the legally established facts of Benwell's murder. Second, and in order for this counter-story to be persuasive, he needed to explain why, if innocent, he had omitted to prove it. These aims did not compel him to stick wholly to the truth, if his explanation is true at all, but taking human vanity into account, even his manifest lies may not be a reason to disbelieve the gist of his defence.

  Birchall, 'regarded from the artistic stand-point of the murder-fancier', had received sardonic credit in an English paper for a killing that was infinitely superior to 'the old-fashioned murders which used to shock and alarm a former generation', though this superiority derived partly from the 'peculiar conditions' of the era in which he had committed it:

the fierce competition for employment at home, and the wide-spread conviction that emigration with a small capital is a sure road to at least moderate fortune. The notion of advertising for victims with means, and personally conducting them across the Atlantic for the purpose of killing and robbing them, is scarcely one which would have suggested itself to anybody in the humdrum days of our grand-fathers. No scheme of the kind could then have been reasonably counted on as holding out the prospect of regular income.

Birchall did not wish to take credit for an inventive and modern system of murder, but he did vaunt what he claimed to have been the idea behind his intended theft. In his auto-biography he at last explained that he had had a ploy in progress that would have made his swindle pay dividends out of all proportion to anything the press, the prosecution, or even his ironical admirers had been able to imagine.

As he set about explaining the background to this plan, Birchall noted briefly that he had 'had some money to spare' after his marriage, and had been deceived by 'Fraud & Rathbone' into becoming a farm pupil, seduced by photo-graphs they showed him of fine farms. He had deposited £500 with them and had set sail with his new wife on 21 November 1888. He said that he had used the name Somerset, even in England, 'for a private reason and connection', but denied that he had ever attached a title to it, or that he had demeaned himself by taking active steps to avoid his creditors. Once Birchall had reached Woodstock, Macdonald had been kindly, being concerned that Birchall would 'find things a little rough'. This hardly covered Birchall's impression of the farm where he was taken: a 'human pig sty', with accoutrements that even the commonest jail conditions, he noted authoritatively, 'would give points to'. Naturally he had quit after a day. Birchall described Macdonald as devious, but did not blame him for the iniquities of the farm pupillage swindle.

After this false start, Birchall had been free to do as he pleased. He had made friends with Dudley and another ex-pupil called Overweg, and had spent his time chiefly in 'driving about', including to Pine Pond for picnics, though never to Mud Lake, never even 'within the swamp where the murder is said to have been committed'. Anyone who declared to the contrary 'told a wilful and corrupt lie'. Birchall claimed here that he had only ever received back from Ford & Rathbone the farmer's forfeited $125 bonus, though later in his account, in defending his wife, he remarked that she had believed his remittances from Ford & Rathbone, during the six months they lived together in Canada, to be the profits from businesses that he owned across Ontario.

On their return to the Old Country they had lived in the Stevenson household. Birchall had spent his first month back in England principally at the races, after which he had got a job as an advertising agent for Mayall's photographic company. His employment with them had 'expired' at the end of 1889, Birchall wrote, owing to 'a depression in trade'. With 'no occupation in view' after this job ended, he had 'cast about for some new idea', and had eventually 'planned out a great scheme which I thought would land me safely upon the shores of comparative affluence'. He wrote that he had spoken of it 'to others, who agreed and entered into it warmly'. Birchall claimed that he had received 'certain information that would have put us right' to make 'a pile of money'. All that had been needed was ready capital to work the scheme, money which, sadly, none of his partners in crime happened to possess. At this Birchall's mind had turned to his experiences with Ford & Rathbone, and he had decided 'there was a chance this way'. That said, 'Of course I could not work the thing single-handed, and so I arranged with others to "stand in," as the saying is.'

Birchall now explained a critical aspect of his plan, namely, how he had ever thought he could get away with such a risky international scheme. The simple answer to this was that actually he hadn't planned on getting away with the swindle at all: 'We intended to get the money from one or two men, and then in Canada nothing could be said to us, as we could not be held in Canada for fraud committed in England.' Birchall's gang would 'wait until we had brought off our *coup* and then repay the men with something over to appease them, and say farewell to them in good part. It was,' he wrote, 'a poor fraud, without doubt, but I thought so long as we repaid them afterwards it covered the fraud to a large extent, so far as my conscience, at any rate, was concerned.'

As for the *coup* itself: what was it? Birchall divulged that the 'certain information' that had sparked the entire adventure had been a tip off on how to realize a small fortune out of the 1890 Derby at Epsom. This race, run on 4 June, really had, according to the press, been extraordinary. Part way through, the top jockey Liddiard, riding the favourite, Surefoot, had suddenly found that he 'had his work cut out' to prevent his horse from 'savaging' the third favourite, an animal called Rathbeal. Surefoot was known for an 'erratic temper', but, even so, the fact that he went half mad trying to bite another runner, coupled with the finishing positions of the lead horses, caused the *Sporting Life* to conclude that 'the race was falsely run'. The second favourite, Sainfoin, did come in first, but the mass of spectators could hardly believe their eyes when Surefoot was beaten into fourth place. Who had 'nobbled' Surefoot, reporters did not go so far as to speculate, but even the international wire services implied that the race had been 'shunted':

The one hundred and eleventh Derby run at Epsom Downs today was as surprising in its results as any one of its predecessors positively can have been. Not in any of the similar events of recent years has the favourite been regarded as so sure a winner, and it is not recorded that any favourite has been so ignominiously beaten, comparatively speaking. Nobody thought of Sainfoin as a winner, though the bookmakers and the knowing ones believed he would run second, and backed him accordingly.

As the race began, the odds on Surefoot were ninety-five to forty, or very roughly five to two. The odds on Sainfoin were somewhat longer at a hundred to fifteen. Sainfoin had attracted a moderate amount of betting, but 'Surefoot had been backed to win to the extent of hundreds of thousands of pounds. Among his backers were large numbers of the aristocratic classes, and they suffered severely.'

There was a reason for wanting the money some months in advance of when the race was run. Had Colonel Benwell been persuaded to hand over five hundred pounds to Birchall in time for him to 'plank down' the entire sum on Sainfoin the day the Derby took place, then the rewards would have been respectable. However, the letter Birchall sent Colonel Benwell on 20 February shows that he set out to secure the money well ahead of time. The odds were much longer in the spring. Had Birchall been able to acquire these funds in time, say, to lay a five-hundred-pound bet on Sainfoin at the beginning of April, he could have done so at odds of twenty five to one, a bet that would have realized twelve and a half thousand pounds.

The risks Birchall took with Pelly and Benwell, and the baroque organization that lay behind whatever crime he was trying to commit, make much more sense for a profit on this scale, and it is all too easy to believe that Birchall would have liked to lift himself up out of the financial mire by such a means; but while it is perfectly easy to picture him on 5 June 1890, smoking a cigar, hunched over a newspaper in his cell in Woodstock, with the electrifying reports on the Derby spread out in front of him, there is no proof whatsoever that Birchall was privy to inside information about the race before it was actually run. Anyone could have claimed afterwards to have known in advance that the race would be bent. By his own account, one of Birchall's two favourite books of all — both about horses — was Hawley Smart's *From Post to Finish*. This novel, first published in 1884, opened by describing in detail a race being fixed to create just the result that would transpire in the 1890 Derby. Hawley Smart had been driven to turn out racing novels in order to offset his own dreadful losses at the track, so it is reasonable to take him as an authority on the dreams of gamblers. The whole novel was steeped in the idea that inside knowledge, correctly handled, made a man a king. If a betting racket funded by a farm pupillage swindle really does represent the truth of what Birchall plotted in London, then taken all in all, the plan begins to sound like a tremendously cavalier prank; and if one thing is certain about Birchall, it is that he specialized in cavalier pranks. Yet given Birchall's fondness for Hawley Smart's work, even if he had had no special knowledge about the 1890 Derby, he could

A CLOSE FINISH.

Another characteristic sketch by Birchall.

hardly have failed to wonder whether a crime such as this
novel described did not lie behind the race result.

Even if the whole matter of the Derby is dismissed as an
opportunistic fantasy, however, this does not confirm that
Birchall intended Benwell to die. Birchall repeated many times
in the autobiography that he wished to

state most emphatically, with all the force that my poor nature is
capable of, that the idea of murder was never for a moment thought
of or planned, and that it was a pure and simple fraud for the time
being.

'If it failed, it failed on its own merits,' he wrote, and then
added, with slightly more pride than he showed elsewhere,
'but as we had the thing down pretty fine it wasn't likely to
do that.'

To kick off this fraud, Birchall had put an advertisement in
the papers that had immediately been answered by T. G.
Mellersh of Cheltenham. 'He was a party who brought other
parties together,' wrote Birchall, and 'we got pretty confidential on such matters.' Mellersh wanted ten per cent of Birchall's

SITUATIONS VACANT AND WANTED.

GOVERNESS WANTED for Rectory; English, French, German, music, needlework; 35*l.*; experienced School Governess (cert.) 50*l.*—Mrs. Hooper's Governess Institute, Compton-terrace, Islington, London. Many vacancies; no booking.

HOLIDAY GOVERNESS REQUIRED, French preferred; music essential.—Miss Steel Johnson, Blandford House, Braintree.

WANTED, NURSERY GOVERNESS, or Mother's Help, for three children, eldest 13; must be Roman Catholic.—Write, stating salary and qualifications, to Mrs. C., Highlands, Stanford-road, Brighton.

A1.—A really first-class Opportunity.—A SALARY of 30s. per week, which can be increased from time to time to 3*l.* per week according to merit, can be secured in any part of England by a few hours' daily application only; many who have commenced in this way, and who are now giving the whole of their time, are in receipt of salaries varying from 200*l.* to 350*l.* per annum; a postcard applying for full particulars will convince any one of the bona fides of this advertisement.—Apply at once, by letter only, to 33, Standard Office, St. Bride-street, E.C.

ACCOUNTANT'S CLERK WANTED, at once; must be experienced in all branches of the profession.—Address, stating qualifications and salary expected, to A. B., care of Messrs. Street, 30, Cornhill, E.C.

AGRICULTURAL COLLEGE, Tamworth.—Scientific and Practical Training for Home and Colonial Farming; thousand-acre farm, corn mill and dairy; managed entirely by the College. Veterinary science, smith's work, carpentry, riding, shooting, fishing, and boating; terms moderate.

A Well-educated, respectable YOUTH WANTED in a Merchant's Office; small salary to commence to one who has learned the routine of office work—Apply, in own handwriting, stating age and how and where last employed, to W. E. 250, Messrs. Deacon's, Leadenhall-street, E.C.

CANADA.—Immediate OPENINGS for FARM PUPILS; excellent future prospects; board, lodging, and pay during pupilage; no exorbitant premium; particulars free.—Address H. Bevan and Co., 69, Finsbury-pavement, London.

CANADA. — University Man, having farm, WISHES to MEET GENTLEMAN'S SON to live with him and learn business with a view to partnership; must invest 500*l.* to extend stock; board, lodging, and 5 per cent. interest till partnership; highest references.—Address Oxon, Glen's, 579A, Strand, W.C.

CLERKSHIPS and SECRETARYSHIPS.—Metropolitan School of Shorthand (Ld.), 27, Chancery-lane; bookkeeping, business hand, type writing; gentlemen without business experience practically trained by chartered accountants. Grammar, languages, &c., by specialists. Prospectus post free.

COMPETENT ENGINEER WANTED; willing to invest up to 500*l.* in a private Company (Limited), and work as District Manager over a large area; liberal salary and commission on all contracts.—First apply by letter, S. W. P., Messrs. Deacon, Leadenhall-street.

DIRECTORS.—Gentlemen of business habits desirous of JOINING the BOARD of any sound undertaking may address Mr. A. Grace (in strict confidence), care of Messrs. Taylor and Co., 57, Walbrook, London.

Birchall's own farm pupillage advertisement: 'University Man, having farm, WISHES TO MEET GENTLEMAN'S SON.'

takings on any successful introduction, and after Birchall had chosen Pelly and Benwell from amongst a pile of applicants, Mellersh dictated Birchall's replies to the two young men. 'The Crown took possession of all the correspondence they could find between myself and Mellersh,' wrote Birchall, 'and much of it which showed that he knew of fraudulent transactions was suppressed by the Crown in order to shield him from the public indignation.'

Colonel Benwell had been 'simple and credulous' noted Birchall patronizingly: 'He asked me many questions, and I told him many lies.' Birchall refrained from saying a great deal about Frederick Benwell – *'de mortuis nil nisi bonum'* – but did write that Benwell had been terrified of his father. Birchall also sneered at the Pelly family, whom he said he had found to be living far above their station. As Pelly had paid his money up front, however, Birchall wrote that 'we didn't care a straw' about him. 'I was bound by the agreement to pay his board, lodging and washing, which I did, and was prepared to do at the rate of $5 a week, truly not a bad percentage in itself for the $800 he invested,' being, 'something like thirty per cent. per annum and a little over. I wonder what more he expected.' Pelly was to be kept busy until the Derby money came in, perhaps acting as Birchall's secretary. Birchall had intended that he be allowed to handle small sums, supposedly business profits, forwarded from an imaginary farm by Birchall's imaginary manager.

'Of course it must be distinctly understood by the reader,' said Birchall, 'that the scheme was all prearranged, and that of course it had been necessary to arrange to be able to show Benwell some property to satisfy him, and to execute a fraudulent deed upon, so that he should believe and be led to believe that it was mine, and mine alone.' While Pelly had been a low priority, it had been planned that Benwell would be kept occupied by the pretend manager, travelling about attending horse sales 'for show, and of course not finding any suitable for my purpose'. This, wrote Birchall, 'would have obviated the necessity of taking up residence upon a farm which I arranged to do first of all'. He claimed he had expected to receive the money from Colonel Benwell in a 'short time', and therefore believed he would only to need to sustain his fraud briefly. He then asserted that he had never really needed to enter into a fraudulent scheme at all, but that he had 'received such kindness at my brother's hands that I forbore to bother him for such a sum as we required'.

When Birchall and his party had reached New York they had checked in at the Metropolitan Hotel. 'I saw a couple of persons in the hotel, whose names I shall not mention, whom I recognized.' At Niblo's theatre in the evening, 'my wife retired early, and I went out during the middle of the piece to consummate a few arrangements upon which so much depended, and having done this I returned to the theatre'. After Pelly and Benwell had gone to bed that night, Birchall had continued his machinations, 'having other arrangements which kept me till a late hour'. He had also kept a secret appointment the next morning. The trip to Eastwood on 17 February had been 'fully arranged' in New York, though once again, 'emphatically', Mud Lake had been no part of the plan, 'which place I did not know of'. He explained that

the farm was not a hundred miles away from Pine Pond; and there are a couple of worthy persons who, if they would kindly come forward, could explain fully a great deal of what still remains unexplained. They were in the neighbourhood on the 17th of February, but I haven't seen them since, and shall probably never do so again.

He continued: 'I walked myself as far as I could', but he claimed that he had needed 'plenty of time to get back to catch the train going east, as I had said I should be back that night. I left the party where the road crosses from the straight road leading to Pine Pond'. Any evidence that he had gone further than that was 'bunkum'.

When Birchall had got back to Buffalo that night he had not wanted Pelly to know that he had been anywhere other than Niagara, 'as we told him the previous night we were going straight to the farm'. One of the questions at the trial had been how Birchall had persuaded Benwell to go further than Niagara. Birchall wrote now that he had given Benwell the impression that he owned a horse farm at Niagara and an ordinary farm near Pine Pond, to which Benwell had believed they were going that day. When Birchall arrived back in Buffalo alone, faced by Pelly, he had been 'forced to prevaricate in order to allay any doubts that might arise in his mind about the farm'. Altogether the easiest way for Birchall to organize his cover had been to say that Benwell had seen the Niagara farm, and that not only had it been unfit to be occupied at present, but on these grounds Benwell had struck off angrily on his own. 'I said this in order that Pelly should think Benwell was not going to stay with me, and that Pelly would then be my sole partner, as he couldn't understand Benwell being a partner too on the face of my agreement with him (Pelly).'

Once he, his wife and Pelly reached Niagara, Birchall explained, 'I went to the post-office and got letters from time to time, some of which I destroyed, and others were kept by the Crown for me.' He admitted that in the absence of these letters, he was slightly confused as to the exact timings of what followed, but 'as near as I can remember I received a letter on the Thursday after we arrived at the Falls, which was eminently unsatisfactory, although nothing was said about any such thing as murder'. That Thursday would have been Thursday 20 February. To take a charitable view, it would therefore be possible that Birchall had posted his letter to Colonel Benwell in the morning before then opening and reading the supposed incoming letter that contained 'unsatisfactory' news. Birchall did claim that he had sent his own 'flowery' letter because Colonel Benwell had 'directed me to write so soon as his son had seen the place'. Birchall had assumed that Benwell would 'jump' at the 'excellent and rare bargain' involved in apparently investing in the farm in question, and so had written off 'immediately, intending that both letters should go by the same mail to England as arranged'.

Despite the supposed first troubling letter from his cohorts, 'I took little notice of this; and later, not hearing further, I telegraphed at Pelly's suggestion to the Stafford House to see if there was any message there for me.' This event took place on Tuesday 25 February. Birchall simplified the story here. He himself had told Pelly that he had wired to Buffalo to ask whether any messages were waiting there for him. Birchall had got back the reply from the Stafford House to say that a letter and telegram had been received, and Pelly had suggested Birchall wire the Stafford House to ask the clerk to repeat the wire to Niagara. Without explaining how he had come to know its contents, Birchall continued, 'The letter at the Stafford House was merely the same as that I received at the Falls.' If so, whoever wrote it had been trying both of his likely addresses. As the telegraph office failed to repeat the telegram, 'I thought,' wrote Birchall, 'I would go and see after it.'

He explained the lost letter, purportedly from Benwell in London, containing checks for his baggage, in the following manner:

What I did assert was that a check for some bonded baggage was sent to me afterwards to see after two cases that were in the Customs office there; and I attended to this matter on receipt of a telegram telling me to get all Benwell's goods out of my possession, and send them away.

It begins to emerge from this, if Birchall is to be believed, that when he received communications from his co-conspirators concerning Benwell, he pretended to Pelly that they had been sent by Benwell himself. The checks had arrived in an envelope without a letter. Once again Birchall accused the Crown of destroying vital clues: 'I sought to produce some letters and envelopes I had received; but these were taken by Detective Murray,' and 'even now, after the trial they refuse to give them up, denying they have them'. It should be pointed out that if it is really the case that the Crown withheld evidence, there was no likelihood these documents would have been handed over later.

At last Birchall received news that 'at once told me there was something wrong. I determined to go to Buffalo to keep an appointment that was made, and therefore went to Buffalo the next day.' If the gist of this is true, then the information that Benwell was dead reached Birchall only on Wednesday 26 February. He had then 'found out all the particulars when in Buffalo, and my readers can well imagine the position in which I was placed'. He had been, he said, 'at a loss what to do, but I was bidden to have no fear about the matter'. Naturally enough, 'I said that I couldn't very well send away all Benwell's things without some authority to show Pelly, the result of which was the telegram signed "Stafford", which everybody has seen.'

Birchall returned to the Falls, 'fully determined to stand my ground, and feeling sure that whatever might take place would in no way affect me, save in the matter of fraud'. Stories in the press about a murder in Princeton had not previously drawn his attention, 'However, I was alert now.' To be on the safe side, 'My revolver I threw away when I heard of the murder, as I did not know what calibre the bullets were found to be in his head.' Had he kept his gun, said Birchall, the calibres would have proved not to match. The day after his unnerving trip to Buffalo, he read in the press that Benwell's cigar case had been found. 'I at once knew that identification would be established,' he wrote, suggesting that his supposed companions had not admitted this salient detail – broadcast at first only in the local press – when they persuaded him not to worry. 'I was in a great state of mind,' wrote Birchall, 'as I knew I had been seen with him in that neighbourhood, and hardly knew what to do. I made sure though that all would come right, and determined to go and see for myself, and hear further particulars.' He and Pelly had found that there were some hours before a train could take them direct to Paris, 'So I went back and told my wife who, with her dear loving nature, refused to let me go without her. I wanted her to stay behind, but she would not do so.' He did not mention in the autobiography that, soon after, she would provide him with a false alibi.

'Pelly at length appeared scared,' Birchall continued, a point that Pelly's own account amply verifies. He had so 'bothered' Birchall to be allowed to go to New York instead of Princeton that Birchall agreed. 'He told a cock-and-bull story about my trying to push him over the Falls and sundry other idiotic and childish ideas,' added Birchall, 'which, of course, were without a shadow of the truth.'

Once in Princeton he had been informed on all sides that the murder was understood to have been committed on Wednesday 19 February. He had been introduced to Dr Staples and Dr Taylor, who had assured him on this point, but who, at the trial, 'forgot so much' of their initial evidence. Birchall even claimed that Dr Staples had mendaciously reassured Bluett across the summer that his testimony would be in Birchall's favour. As for the actual identification, 'I was almost stunned when I saw poor Benwell dead, and I broke down and cried bitterly, Watson taking my arm kindly and assuring me he would do all he could for me.' This, in essence, Watson had confirmed in court. Of his interview with Murray, Birchall wrote that the government detective had also seemed persuaded that the murder had taken place on the Wednesday, and Murray's first press interviews confirmed this too.

Back in Paris, Birchall had told his wife that the body did belong to Benwell. She was 'naturally terribly distressed and fearful lest the blame be laid on me in any way', though 'even she did not know that I came further west than the Falls with Benwell'. Elsewhere in his account, Birchall wrote that 'she knew of no dishonest or dishonourable action of mine, nor had she any share or part in any of such actions'. Meanwhile, of his initial lies to Murray, some of which, of course, Mrs Birchall had actually confirmed, he wrote that 'hardly knowing what best to say, I make [*sic*] it up as I went along, and hence a good many of the conflicting statements I made'.

In Niagara, Birchall 'became aware' that he was about to be arrested, but as an innocent man, did nothing to destroy Benwell's baggage checks, keys and gold pencil. He explained how he had come to be in possession of the last item. In Buffalo, Benwell had compared the way that he and Birchall formed the letter 'B' at the start of their surnames, and this had led to them imitating each other's signatures. It was then that Birchall had borrowed Benwell's 'Conny' pen, knowing perfectly well that it was marked with his name. Birchall mocked the attempts of the detectives, once they had arrested him, to get him to speak under interrogation in Niagara, but was furious at their treatment of his wife. 'They gave her morphine to stupefy her,' he wrote, and she was 'grossly insulted by the officers'. He added, 'I cannot go into all the details here; my blood boils over as I write.' Pressmen had been less discreet on this point, reporting that although the Niagara police chief, Thomas Young, had had her examined in the proper manner by a female searcher at the point of arrest, when nothing incriminating had been found,

it is alleged that Detective Murray ordered Mrs. Birchall to be stripped again, and during this work she claims that she suffered great indignities, the door of the room having been left open so that the person in the next room, if he so desired, could take in the scene.

Whatever 'stripped' is taken to mean, it would indeed have been deeply humiliating for Birchall to imagine his wife exposed in a state of *déshabillé* to the gaze of Detective Murray.

After this distinctly selective account of events, Birchall was scathing about the trial in Woodstock. The court arrangements had been 'motley', 'unseemly', and 'grotesque', and would have shamed any 'civilized country'. He gave several explanations for why his case had failed. First, he said that he had been so certain he would go free that he had made inadequate provision for his defence. In part he blamed Detective Bluett for this, who 'would turn up with wonderful reports about the evidence he was getting, which, of course, exploded when touched'. There is some confirmation for this state of unwarranted confidence in the letters Birchall wrote immediately before the trial. In one, addressed to 'My Dear Old Friend', and signed 'Ever the Old Pal', he had said, 'I hope that when you get this you will have heard that all is well, and I know that you will be pleased to see me again.' His friend's nickname was *Vulpes*, or Fox, and Birchall pictured them one day soon, as of old, eluding the hounds together: 'Let us hope that we may again head away to some other spinney and there lie in peace, secure from all foes.' Oswald Birchall had also claimed, shortly after the verdict, that if his half-brother had for a moment led him to believe that there was serious doubt about its being 'Not Guilty', he would have gone to Canada for the trial.

Birchall's second explanation for the failure of his defence ran slightly counter to his first, and revolved around claims that Murray had both concocted false evidence, and concealed such evidence as tended to exonerate Birchall. 'During the time of my arrest a number of letters and papers were stolen from my boxes while in possession of the Crown, so I am unable to append many that I should have liked to,' he wrote. Birchall's letter to 'Mac' about farm pupillage, which Murray bizarrely reprinted in his memoir in 1904, but which had previously been lost to view, suggests there is truth in this claim. The Crown had put every obstacle in the way of letting the defence see copies of the evidence, Birchall added, constantly frustrating their attempts to examine such items as Benwell's clothing, and even preventing Birchall having access to his own lawyers. Birchall had been left unprepared for the 'mistakes' of Crown witnesses, and had had no evidence to hand with which to rebut them. In an October letter to a college friend, Arthur Leetham, now living in Montreal, Birchall explained that 'I was paralysed by the appearance of witnesses who swore positively to facts that never existed, and who had never in their lives seen or heard of me at all. Of course we could not get an unprejudiced jury. That was impossible from the start, and all the men who were inclined to be fair were immediately challenged by the Crown.'

A third explanation for Birchall's failure to avert a guilty verdict lurks in between his more direct comments on the case. If he was innocent of Benwell's murder, he was still likely to go down as a swindler, and, at more than one crucial moment, he had gambled on escaping the law completely. He wrote that, when he went to Princeton to identify the corpse, he had considered confessing his duplicity to Watson, the constable: 'I was undecided whether to tell the truth about being in Eastwood and confide in Watson about the fraud, and put him on the right track,' wrote Birchall, 'but on second thought I decided to let them find out everything for themselves.' This was taking a chance on the ineptitude of the rural police. With regard to the telegram that had come instructing him to get rid of all Benwell's kit and luggage, Birchall also wrote, 'This telegram has never been produced. I feared the Crown would seek at any rate to prove that I was an accessory, so I did not produce it at the trial, and did not give my lawyers any information concerning it, or to Detective Bluett.' Had Birchall admitted to some form of collusion with Benwell's putative real murderer or murderers, he would then have had to gamble on whether or not he could persuade his jury that the murder had been unplanned. Instead, Birchall must have calculated that his best chance of freedom lay in being acquitted of the direct charge of murder itself, leaving the murkier question of complicity out of the picture. He wrote that

I had fully intended to make a statement to the jury, but I was advised that if they were prejudiced, as it appeared likely that they would be, they would seek to make me an accessory, and, therefore, I should be no better off than if I made no statement. I think I should have done it all the same.

Given the nature of the jury deliberations, it is impossible to believe that Birchall could, in fact, have swayed them at the last minute. Near the end of his autobiography he suddenly launched into a disquisition on luck, writing that he believed in both good and bad luck as an 'existent motor'. This fatalism does seem, in an odd sort of way, to have buoyed him up as the odds against him grew ever worse.

On 8 November the Toronto *Evening News* wrote that, according to 'those who know', the only reason Birchall was refusing to confess to having killed Benwell was the dishonour involved in shooting a man from behind. The *Globe* got hold of the same story and added the disdainful comment: 'He is proud in his way.' While this little story was presumably an invention, the autobiography does confirm that Birchall respected a code of behaviour that would have ruled out betraying any partners in crime. It is a nice question whether or not this distorted adherence to a code of gentlemanly conduct might explain why he never fully indicted anyone else, but in the farewell letters he began to write in November, he continued to 'protest his innocence of the murder', saying to his friends, as a reporter paraphrased it, 'that had he told a straight story at first he would not now be in the shadow of the gallows. But he didn't, he lied to screen another and now that the end is near he would rather die than give that other away.'

It could be, of course, that there was no one else to indict; but, whatever the truth of this matter, Birchall went only a very limited way, in the autobiography, towards specifically implicating anyone else. 'I cannot mention any names, unfortunately, here,' he wrote,

and if I did it would do no good, as the parties to fraud, so far as lending their property was concerned, need never be exposed. The public have formed their opinion in their innermost minds on this matter, I fancy.

This remark was somewhat disingenuous, as Pickthall was clearly invoked in Birchall's paragraphs. His hint elsewhere in his narrative that, late into proceedings, he had been forced to come up with a plan of occupying Benwell with horse sales rather than having him live on a farm, also tends to confirm the idea that Pickthall 'funked' in New York. Yet, if these stray points really do lead to the idea that using Pickthall's farm had been part of Birchall's original plan, they do not obviously lay Benwell's murder at Pickthall's feet; and, on this matter, Birchall was completely silent. He even went so far as to suggest that he was not entirely sure what had happened to Benwell. 'How to account for Benwell's boots I am utterly at a loss,' he wrote at one point. 'The boots at the trial certainly were not the ones he had on when he was with me.' As for Benwell's missing possessions, his revolver and gold watch, Birchall wrote that 'doubtless' they would 'appear later on, and it will be interesting to know whence, for I do not for one minute believe they have been destroyed'.

As regards the confessional 'Colonel' letter, Birchall said only that it had not been written by him, and that although he had 'endeavoured to find the sender', he had failed. It is difficult to glean from this whether he wished the confession to be believed or not, but as for making a confession himself, he remained unequivocal throughout. 'I pleaded "not guilty" at the trial and I meant it.' He did not intend, 'for any sum of money', to invent a confession, and since he had 'made up quite enough' in his lifetime already, he had decided, he said, to stop. Typically, it is possible to believe the essence of this remark even while realizing that his autobiography is full of elisions and lies. Birchall went to the lengths of commissioning a legally attested document to repudiate any further bogus confession that might be attributed to him after death, so determined was he not to be thought ever to have caved in on this matter.

On Thursday 5 November Mrs Birchall, and Blackstock's law partner, Mr McMurchy, arrived in Ottawa to present the clemency petitions to Sir John Thompson, the Minister of Justice. McMurchy, who told a reporter he found the Birchall case 'heartrending', was given leave to mention the salient points for the defence 'in a conversational way'. He brought out the fact that Benwell's stomach had been empty when he was killed, though there had been five places where he might have eaten breakfast on the journey he took the morning of 17 February. He mentioned that Charles Benwell had 'utterly refused to admit' that Benwell had owned the 'dilapidated' boots in which he had been found dead, adding also the fact that they had had no mud on them, though, around Eastwood, 17 February had been a muddy day. He noted that Benwell's money, watch and revolver had never been recovered, and said that Birchall's possession of a single lead pencil of Benwell's was not grounds for execution. He submitted that 'public opinion hanged Birchall before he was tried', so that no juryman who read newspapers could have come to the case unprejudiced, and alluded to the 'immense', and, by implication, unbiased Montreal petition as evidence to this effect. He mentioned the unfairness of the fact that the Crown had had unlimited resources in preparing the prosecution. He then broke down the evidence to show that there was no solid proof that Birchall had ever entered the swamp. He also urged the idea that Birchall's actions after 17 February suggested innocence much more strongly than they did guilt. The 'Colonel' confession letter was not mentioned, but McMurchy did hand over an affidavit, signed by James Langstaff, an employee at the Thompson House in Woodstock, swearing that Alice Smith and another witness, Helen Fallon, had listened in to the trial by telephone before giving evidence themselves. Though Alice Smith was a star witness for the Crown, Helen Fallon was the more crucial of the two to McMurchy's argument. She had been one of the witnesses who claimed to have seen two men walking into the swamp at midday on 17 February, and was billed as the last person, apart from his killer, to have seen Benwell alive. The Toronto *Mail* thought this affidavit might have 'considerable weight', besides alerting the justice department to this 'rather novel use of the "Scoopograph"'. It was 'altogether likely', the paper said, 'that Justice MacMahon will not allow any more telephone transmitters in a court-room where he is sitting'.

McMurchy finished by asking that 'most careful and solemn consideration' be given to what he had said. The *Globe* reported that there then followed 'a very affecting scene, recalling some historical pictures of a woman pleading before a sovereign power for the life of a lover or husband'. Mrs Birchall presented Sir John Thompson with the petitions, said that she fully believed in her husband's innocence, that 'time would show how true this was', and added that if Birchall were executed, 'her life would be blighted and two honourable families ruined'. Sir John was noncommittal in reply, but told them that they should not expect a decision before Saturday.

On the Friday the *Mail* printed the first instalment of Birchall's autobiography right across its front page, where every subsequent instalment would begin, calling the work 'one of the most intensely interesting stories of real life that has ever been published'. As these first paragraphs rolled off the presses, Birchall was still at work on the last ones. The

Toronto Presbytery reacted with grave displeasure. Revd Dr Kellog felt 'exceedingly pained' that the words of a condemned criminal would be 'served up to his children at the breakfast table', while Revd J. Neil 'did not know of anything that would exert a worse influence on young people than reading such a book as that'. The *Mail* reported their disquiet and carried on regardless.

That afternoon a press dispatch reached Woodstock announcing that the Cabinet Council had already reached a unanimous verdict against Birchall. Mrs Birchall and her sister 'burst into tears but would not at first believe the news', which was not due for another twenty-four hours. Mrs Birchall visited her husband in jail without telling him what had happened. When she returned to her hotel, however, she found official confirmation that the verdict had been reached early. Subsequent reports suggested that the decision had actually been taken without delay, before she had even left Ottawa. Mrs Birchall, her face 'wet with tears', returned with her sister to the jail. At the sight of both women crying, the turnkey, Mr Forbes, himself 'could not keep back the tide'. When Mrs Birchall broke the terrible news to her husband, he, too, was 'completely unmanned for the time being'. It was 'upwards of an hour' before he regained 'his marvellous composure'. The Toronto *World* told its readers that Mrs Birchall 'went through the ordeal with wonderful nerve, but when she reached the hotel what had appeared at first to be a dream vanished and the stern realities of the situation drove her into hysterics'.

16. The Greatest Show on Earth

That heaving chest ! – Enough – 'tis done!
The bolt has fallen! – The spirit is gone –
For weal or for woe is known but to One! –
– Oh! 'twas a fearsome sight! – Ah me
A deed to shudder at, – not to see.
R. H. Barham, 'The Execution', 1840

In 1890 Canada had no official hangman. As a result before Birchall's sentence was even pronounced, therefore, a motley assortment of characters had begun to apply for the position of his executioner. The press took great delight in publishing their letters. One of the earliest came from a man who declared politely that he would have 'much pleasure' in doing the job. Another wrote to the sheriff's wife:

Mrs. perry if you want a man te hang burchill i take the chop (signed)＿＿＿
Wilmot township
    Dun Dee Postoffice
Write back as soon asyou like to let me knows.

An accomplished 'death artist' wrote from England offering to 'treat the subject' by any means desired, 'electricity, guillotine or gallows', and yet another applicant was bold enough to state his terms:

DEAR SIR,- I will do the job on the 14th next month for eighty dolars an ralerode fair. Let me no soon.

Yours truly,

_____ Norwich.

A different arrangement came to the mind of a local farmer, who, gambling on the value of Birchall's execution memorabilia, offered to hang him 'for $50 and "find" the rope'. More expensive, meanwhile, was the deal proposed by a man who wrote to Birchall directly to say that he would willingly be hanged in his stead for the sum of a thousand dollars.

The aim of a skilled hangman is to cause instant death by dislocating the victim's neck. The letters that so amused the press were funny in a chilling sort of way because they suggested a lack of professionalism on the part of the applicants. What was not amusing was the prospect that the hanging might really prove as inept as these letters were illiterate. In all its history the county of Oxford, Ontario, had had only two previous convictions for murder. In one of these cases the man concerned had been incarcerated for life in an asylum for the criminally insane. In the other, which had occurred in 1862, the murderer had been a blind man named Cook, who, during a drunken quarrel, 'with a random blow struck his wife on the head and fractured her skull'. She had soon died, after which he was hanged in public outside Woodstock jail. This judicial exercise had been 'of a very revolting character', as 'when the trap-door fell the rope was too long, and Cook's head was torn completely from his body'.

When pressmen began to calculate the remainder of Birchall's life not in weeks but in days, and when they started to provide their readers with detailed progress reports on the arrangements for killing him, the Presbyterian Ministers' Association in Toronto finally lost patience. There were members of the public who held the view that a judicial murder was no less of a murder than any other kind, but 'the brethren' objected only to what they feared might be the low nature of the executioner, on the grounds that

this supreme act of justice should be rendered in circumstances giving it the greatest possible solemnity. That there should be selected for this purpose a man of no reputation, sometimes a man of hardened, debased character, possibly even worse than this, is fatal to the whole purpose as a moral impression.

At least they soon knew who it was they were actually arguing about. On 25 October the press was able to announce that a hangman had now been selected. It was unclear whether his name was Thomas Ratley, Radclive or Ratcliff, but he was said to be a middle-aged Englishman with a day job as a steward at the Sunnyside Yacht Club in Toronto. It was claimed that he had assisted at many hangings in England, and he had recently performed three, unassisted, in Canada, 'when the gory and ill-omened Juggernaut of justice' had been 'dragged forth to crush out a guilty life beneath its cruel wheels'. His known subjects had been a man who had murdered his 'putative' wife, a man who had murdered his paramour, and a man who had murdered his paramour's husband. Ratley was presented to the public, with less than complete conviction, as 'one who, it is claimed, will do the job without bungling'.

In the days immediately before the scheduled execution there were press representatives coming into Woodstock on every train, until the hotels were packed with reporters 'waiting for the day of doom'. Some even had the gall to climb up on the roof of the jail. Prison officials, with mute contempt, cleared their ladders away and left them to jump for it.

All day on Wednesday 12 November the jail was in a commotion, with everything 'being put in a bright and clean condition ready for the execution'. The able-bodied prisoners were made to work hard 'with whitewash and scrubbing brushes cleaning up the gloomy interior walls and corridors', while Birchall himself was forced to change day cells. Reporters speculated that this was to prevent him taking advantage of a concealed means of suicide. Many expected him to cheat the gallows, as the phrase had it, not least 'in order that his widow may not go through the world with the stain of having been the wife of a felon who perished upon the scaffold'. A second good reason for moving him was thought to be the decision to spare him the sight of the instrument of death being erected in the jail yard.

With almost no time left, Birchall was galvanized by the need to arrange his affairs. He had much business to complete, but surely his most outré act that day was to sign an agreement, negotiated for him by his day guard, the sheriff's grandson, George Perry, with H. S. Morrison & Co. of the Musée Theatre or Wonderland in Toronto. Wonderland was a ten-cent waxwork museum full of 'artistic and wonderful spectacles' that advertised itself with the particular claim that its 'chamber of horrors is as horrible as it can be, and is well worth a visit'. This chamber offered 'living heads and busts swinging in mid-air, apparently in lively enjoyment of their situation'. Birchall, for the sum of a hundred and fifty dollars, agreed to give the museum 'the coat, vest and trousers' he had worn on 17 February, 'and also authority solely to exhibit a cast of his head, bust and figure'. It was agreed that George Perry would hand over Birchall's clothes, and a selection of his sketches, the very next day.

On a less fantastic note, Mr Finkle made his way to the jail that Wednesday to draw up Birchall's will. In this document the prisoner left all his wealth to his wife, whether 'in possession' or 'expectancy'. The sums involved, as far as the press could discover, derived only from the sale of his autobiography and the deal he had struck with Morrison's Wonderland. What precisely Birchall had in 'expectancy' no one knew, though it was widely reported that he had claimed he would 'fall heir to considerable property in the spring'. The timing makes it seem probable that he referred to an inheritance due to come to him on his twenty-fifth birthday, in May of 1891. It had been reported months before that Birchall had sold out his expectations when he left university, but a different possibility, arising out of the described terms of his will, is that his entire swindling operation had been designed to ameliorate immediate debts and to tide him over for a year, when the balance of a paternal inheritance would come his way. If, in truth, there was nothing left of this money, then he would seem to have been deliberately deluding his wife.

In the will, Mrs Birchall was listed as executrix, and two further executors were appointed, Mr Forbes, the prison turnkey, and Arthur Leetham. Leetham was known to Birchall as 'Ghost', a title he had acquired at Oxford through 'his powers of making himself appear and disappear so unexpectedly'. Leetham, who had been one of Birchall's closest college friends, had first written to him in Woodstock jail at some point in October. In the reply that Leetham received to this communication, Birchall had said:

You can have but a small idea of what a bright ray of sunshine your letter brought to me in the midst of all this gloom. I was almost at a loss to realize that it was a letter from one of the old old firm, pure and unadulterated, without the prejudice and hatred that have pursued me all along. Indeed it was welcome in every sense of the word, and made me completely happy last night, in the midst of all my troubles.

In a subsequent letter, soon after, Birchall made a pathetic appeal to his friend:

If ever you pass through Woodstock, old chap, pause for a few seconds by your old pal's grave, which you will find in the cemetary here. No doubt it will be found without difficulty, and if it's only just to give a passing glance, or to chuck a stone upon it just for 'Auld Lang Syne,' then again, I shall hope that when you return to England, if you happen to see any of the old firm, you will tell them that I was brave to the end.

Leetham 'thoroughly' believed 'that Birchall did not do the actual killing'. He had immediately passed these letters to the press, presumably in the hope that their publication would sway those people who contemplated adding their signatures to the clemency petitions. When the petitions failed, however, Leetham decided that real friendship required him to go to Woodstock to see Birchall through his very last days. Of all Birchall's other friends, it was widely reported that Dudley, too, had attempted to make contact, sending a telegram to Mrs Birchall from Point Edward, Ontario, in which he begged for five dollars to enable him to come to Woodstock, so that he could say farewell to his friend. If this was true, the appeal certainly failed.

Mrs Birchall's veiled but dainty appearance, her night-time hysterics and frequent recourse to opiates, had been much discussed in the press throughout the case, but she had so far avoided attempts by newspapermen to speak to her. On the Wednesday morning, however, the *Mail* printed a brief interview with her that appears to have been genuine. The reporter observed that 'she was looking wretched and completely cast down'. When he asked why she had not fled to England weeks earlier, she supposedly replied, 'My life is blighted and the future seems so full of clouds, but to leave the poor lad here all alone, I could not do it.' In response to a further question, about the enormous cost of attempting to defend Birchall, 'Mrs. Birchall's eyes filled with tears.'

Yes, but what did it matter if I could save him or prove to him I was doing all I could? There is the $1,500 received by the poor fellow for his writing, and my lawyers, Messrs. Blackstock and MacMurchy, were so kind and so liberal, that though they could have taken it all they refused. I hate the money, it is the price of his life.

What she can have thought about Birchall selling his clothes to a waxwork museum it is painful to speculate.

Mrs Birchall's last meeting with her husband was set for the Wednesday evening. She stayed with him for four hours, and was finally led away, 'her frail form shaken by a storm of tears'. The New York *Herald* had its own version of how this meeting ended:

one long, lingering embrace and look, and Mrs. Birchall was led out of the cell and dark stairway to look upon her husband no more

*The press imagines a last kiss
between husband and wife.*

in this life. She was driven to her hotel, where she passed the night
in hysterics.

Whether or not this was true, she rapidly formed the resolution
to ask to be allowed to see Birchall yet one more time. So it was
that reporters who had crowded into Woodstock's telegraph
offices on the Wednesday night to transmit lengthy columns
on the couple's last meeting, found twenty-four hours later
that they had to concoct the story all over again.

Birchall, true to form, hardly slept on the Wednesday
night. In the weeks since his trial he had become especially
fond of his death watch, Colour-Sergeant Thomas Midgely,
another Englishman, and presumably the same Thomas
Midgely whom the prosecution witness, Alfred Hayward, had
been unable to recognize across the court room at the trial.
In his autobiography, Birchall praised Midgely greatly and
described how 'very soon we were the best of friends'. It
seems likely that Birchall slewed his timetable to stay up half

the night not only because he valued the quiet of the small hours, but because he found Midgely and the black cat together to be the most congenial company regularly available to him. It wasn't until that Wednesday night that Birchall actually finished his autobiography. In a note on the final restrictive prison regulations that had been imposed upon him, he wrote grimly, 'I should have thought my life was a sufficient penalty to pay for anything.' Despite the fact that one of these new regulations had barred him from reading any newspapers, he did claim in his last paragraphs to have seen in print 'about half' the already serialized instalments of the autobiography that he was only now completing. There must have been some truth in this, as at the very end of the work he responded to press criticisms that were already forthcoming about the beginning of it. In particular, comments on his undue sarcasm led him to reply: 'My poor pen could never scathe the objects of my feeble railings with force sufficient to show them their contemptibility of bloated self-esteem.' He had also been accused, after his autobiography started to come out, of heartlessly failing to mention his mother. He rectified this at the end by stating simply that 'She was always the kindest and best of mothers to me, and I cannot for one moment attempt to express my feelings with regard to her in this work.'

The one person, besides himself, about whom he had written more than any other, was his wife. Repeatedly, and for many a long paragraph, he had protested her ignorance of his deceits, and therefore her innocence of any involvement in them, calling all who doubted her 'despicable hounds', and declaring that, even as he wrote, she continued to repose in him 'wholly faithful trust, such as only so guileless and pure a being and loving angel as she is can give to a man situated as I am at present'. He claimed to have described his farm to her in such fine detail – and claimed that she had so longed for a home of her own – that Pelly had been fooled into construing her enthusiastic dreams as deliberate deception, Pelly becoming in this process her 'brazen and systematic would-be detractor', and a 'human viper' into the bargain. Birchall acknowledged 'the true comfort that she has been to me in my sorrow', as well as 'the utter sorrow and grief I feel for having blighted her life as I have', but eventually, even in this inspiring matter, he ground to a halt: 'I cannot bear to speak on this very tenderest subject.' He asked his readers to excuse him writing further on a topic that aroused in him 'such complete suffering and pain'.

As he drew to a close, Birchall noted that writing his little book had been 'on the whole to me a terribly sorrowful experience to go through'. Despite the attacks he had made on many individuals, he closed graciously, lifting words from the general confession in Holy Communion: 'Those who have wronged me in thought, word, or deed, I most cordially forgive and forget, and having said this I am about finished.' He was not totally finished, though:

I am now upon the eve of Death, which, let me say, I do not fear. For my poor wife and my relatives, the idea of the disgrace I bring upon them is heavy to bear; indeed it is always hard to part.

After these, again, adequately suitable closing sentiments, Birchall still stumbled on. The Revd Mr Wade, who had become 'a dear friend', had gone to the jail that night to sit out the hours with Birchall, Midgely and the cat. Birchall felt moved to add an encomium to his spiritual adviser, whom he considered blessedly free of cant, and appended to these praises a few lines of verse that implied a faith many had doubted he possessed:

> But though we two be severed quite
>   Your holy words will sound between
> Our lives, like streams one hears at night,
>   Louder because it is not seen.

Birchall also turned to verse to express the wish that he might escape being utterly extinguished on the gallows:

> So unto Death I do commend my spirit,
>   And time which is in league with Death, that they
> May hold in trust and see my kin inherit
>   All of me that is not clay;
> Embalm my voice and keep it from decay,
>   Then I will not ask to stay,
> Nay rather start at once upon the way
>   Cheered by the faith that at our mortal birth
> For some high reason beyond Reason's ken
>   We are put out to nurse on this strange earth
> Until Death comes to take us home again.

Both quotations were taken from the work of Alfred Austin, soon to find himself amongst the ranks of the English throne's most undistinguished poet laureates. These lines, slipped in at the end of Birchall's text, did cast over his writing a soothing note of respectable passion; but, on the whole, the voice Birchall had embalmed in his autobiography was not only defiantly high spirited, but defiantly shifty.

Seemingly as an afterthought, he added one last paragraph

that contained a 'Farewell!' to his friends, thanks to his publishers, and a quaintly formulaic sign off:

If this little work has done no good it cannot do any harm, and at any rate those who have read it may warn their children in time and season to beware of the follies and sin that led to the writing of this book and the untimely fate of the writer.

Reginald Birchall, Nov. 12, 1890.

Whatever hour of the morning it was that Revd Mr Wade finally left the prison, Birchall then slept until one o'clock in the afternoon of Thursday 13 November, his last full day. He must, therefore, have been asleep during the arrival, at eleven o'clock that morning, of Thomas Ratley, the executioner, who had come to supervise the finishing details of the scaffold. Ratley had already announced himself to the world that day by means of a lengthy and widely reported newspaper interview. He was frankly unashamed of his work, and refused to wear a mask, believing, 'I am but an instrument in the hands of the law.' He explained that he always took a look at his subjects before killing them in order to judge their size and their nerve. 'The murderer who dies bravely is a harder man to kill than the fellow who is half dead with fright in anticipation of the end,' he confided, adding that he thought Birchall would be an easy case because he was 'craven-hearted'. Ratley said that he had deduced this from the fact that Birchall had been too much of a coward to commit suicide.

He went on to reveal that he didn't believe in the trap-door method of hanging, calling it 'the old system', and said that in designing the Woodstock gallows, he had required the scaffold to be built extra high to facilitate the use of a longer than usual rope. He had had the rope stretched, he explained, to thirty-six feet, and was reckoning that a ten-foot drop for the three hundred and fifty pound iron weight now sitting in the jail would satisfactorily jerk Birchall up into the air. When the reporter asked a question about the rope, he was shocked that Ratley immediately produced it to show him. It was one-inch diameter Manila, and a 'Grim, Black, Ugly, Strangling Cord'. When the reporter expressed confusion about the excess height of the gallows, Ratley was happy to explain:

Every inch of that rope is worth $1 to me. You have no idea of the number of relic hunters who desire to procure pieces of a rope with which a man has been ushered into eternity.

If he was right in his calculations, Ratley stood to make four hundred and thirty-two dollars from the rope alone. He added that he had already agreed to sell a foot's length, plus Birchall's gallows clothing, which was 'a prerequisite' of his by agreement with Sheriff Perry, to Madame Tussaud's, 'for her exhibition in London, England', and in a later interview he set the figure of this agreement with Madame Tussaud's at two hundred dollars. Ratley would express irritation, in yet another interview, that Birchall had been allowed to sell some of his garments to Morrison's Wonderland. The usual fee for a hangman was about fifty dollars, but the peripherals in the Birchall execution apparently stood to make Ratley about ten times as much again.

Once Birchall had woken up on the Thursday afternoon, Ratley seized the chance to take a look at him: 'the prisoner turned and faced his executioner at the door. They both eyed each other for a moment, and then the hangman turned and walked down the stairs.' In theory Ratley, from this one unfriendly glance, was able to judge Birchall's 'weight and build and thus arrange his ropes and fixtures' with such precision that he could ensure the breaking of Birchall's neck.

The scaffold was set up in a corner of the jail yard. It consisted of two uprights made out of seventeen-foot timbers that were buried several feet in the ground and steadied with braces, and a cross-piece on top that was morticed into the jail wall. Added to this structure there was a simple system of ropes and pulleys. Word leaked out of the jail that Birchall had seen workmen carrying pieces of the scaffold into the yard, and had commented, 'that's a very crude looking affair'. He had later asked his guards to draw him a picture of the finished mechanism, and had been disconcerted by the 'weird-looking' instrument they produced, working at the mathematics to see whether the hangman could possibly have made his calculations correctly. One of the items found in Birchall's day cell when it was cleared out had been a pile of papers covered by trigonometry problems. He had the right sort of mind to be able to assess the hangman's grasp of the science of instant killing. The taller trees around the jail were full of spectators that afternoon as Ratley gave his mechanism a dry run. When he had let the weight fall, he declared, 'It will just go off like one-two.'

While Ratley made his preparations in the jail yard, Birchall, from his cell, continued to organize the last details of his own existence, including making a list of the clothes that he wanted to wear for the execution. Though he wished to be buried in a stiff linen shirt, for the hanging he asked for a shirt of white flannel, with a turn-down collar, and a black silk four-in-hand tie, to avoid any chance of lending resistance to the rope. He also planned to wear a black saque coat, a black waistcoat, dark checked trousers and patent leather shoes, prompting the headline in one paper, 'A Dude to the Last'. As well as these arrangements, Birchall organized for a variety of small gifts to be distributed to his friends inside and outside the jail and, in characteristic late-Victorian style, wrote messages to all the people he cared about on the back of copies of his own photograph.

At some point during the afternoon the Bishop of Huron came to give Birchall spiritual consolation, then at eight o'clock in the evening he received what really was his final visit from his wife. A clutch of reporters waited hour by hour outside the jail for Mrs Birchall to re-emerge. When 'the electric lights had left the streets in darkness save for the dull glow from the windows of the telegraph offices and hotels', the town at last subsided into 'midnight quietude'. Still, queues of 'tired newspaper men' remained at the telegraph offices, waiting to file their 'last pages of copy', in which most of them would freely describe the weeping and caresses they imagined to be taking place inside the jail. Suddenly they were startled out of their fatigue by news that a messenger had just left the jail at a run. He proved to be searching for the deputy sheriff, John Perry, who himself then made for the jail as fast as his legs would take him. A rumour quickly spread not only that Birchall had after all succeeded in killing himself, but that Mrs Birchall had died with him. It took some time for all the reporters in town to discover that the problem had actually been Ratley, who had been required to spend the night at the jail, and who had arrived at the prison door wildly drunk, threatening to 'clean out' the institution. The deputy sheriff was faced with the job of quietening him down. Partly because of the extra copy generated by this incident, that night the town's telegraph offices never closed at all.

Besides a few hardy reporters waiting for Mrs Birchall to come back out of the jail, there were night officers patrolling the prison walls, while half a dozen linemen from the Canadian Pacific Company worked frantically to run a wire from a neighbouring telegraph pole into the jail yard. The Great North Western Telegraph Company had already strung its own wires, but the Canadian Pacific had only received permission at midnight to set up a contending service. Both companies planned to have an operator stationed in the yard for the execution, so that word could be cabled to England at the very moment of the drop. It would be a public competition to see which company could get the news across the Atlantic the fastest.

Reporters predicted that, after her final jail visit, Mrs Birchall would be 'placed under the influence of opiates' that would 'carry her in unconsciousness into widowhood', and she does indeed seem to have chosen to be drugged. Birchall himself, by contrast, decided not to take any sleep that night, but passed the time smoking and chatting to his friends within the jail, who slunk in at various points to say goodbye. For the very last time, Revd Mr Wade sat up with the condemned man all through the night. 'If left alone,' wrote the *Globe*, 'the chances are he would have broken down. His guards themselves partly guessed this, and were anxious to avert it.' Reporters found that 'one and all' of the guards and jail officials 'had grown fond of the man despite his desperate crime. His spirit of camaraderie had won them all.' Though the leave-takings were hushed, amidst what was otherwise a 'death-like quiet' in the prison, Ratley, for two long hours, remained drunkenly talkative. The jail functionaries who could not contain him were highly relieved when at last he stretched himself out on a sofa and 'fell asleep with his unfinished cigar in his hand'. The jail clock loudly struck the hours as night wended towards morning.

★

At about six o'clock, Birchall, who was still dressed in his clothes of the day before, changed for his execution. At seven he was shaved. When the barber asked him how he felt, Birchall replied, 'Like this', and warmly shook the man's hand. A few favoured reporters had been allowed to spend the night inside the jail. One of them told his readers that

Birchall must have been well liked during his confinement, because constables and guards, with years of experience and hardened by constant intercourse with criminals, moved softly in and out of the corridor, with heads bent and tear-stained cheeks.

Birchall was given a breakfast of poached eggs, toast, canned raspberries, canned peaches and coffee, but he took very little.

The hanging was scheduled for eight in the morning. The *Sentinel-Review* had urged decency on its readers:

Parents should keep their boys at home till 9 o'clock. The sight of small boys climbing telephone poles, walls and trees will not be an edifying one or creditable to home influences.

Woodstock's men of religion had also fretfully urged their congregations to keep away. However, as the London *Times* had noted sniffily after Birchall's trial, it was perfectly clear that 'ignoble appetites' burned 'quite as fiercely in the breasts of Canadian farmers as in those of the *proletaires* of the corrupt capitals of Europe'. In consequence, from an early hour that morning, 'a great crowd' gathered outside the jail walls 'clamouring for admission'. Amongst those who were refused, many 'climbed up into the neighbouring trees', or on top of the unfinished walls of the adjacent new court house, determined to view the 'grewsome sight' by whatever means possible.

Leave to attend the hanging inside the jail yard was by ticket only. At half past seven, about 'half a hundred reporters', and a hundred or so other men, were finally allowed in. The gallows had been built in the darkest corner of the yard where no grass grew. The pressmen were dismayed by the horrible details that confronted them; by the weight, a 'sexagonal block of iron', by the way the rope was greased at the noose, and by the fact that the entire contraption for killing Birchall 'appeared to be as simple a contrivance as an ordinary swing'. There was hoarfrost on the ground, and the spectators in the yard 'stood about kicking their toes' to counter the extreme chill. The prisoners whose cells overlooked the yard pressed their faces – 'gaunt, dirty unshaven faces' – against the bars on their windows, and young boys could be seen shaking the winter leaves from the trees as they climbed to the highest branches that would carry them. The whole picture was unutterably 'gloomy', and when dawn broke the scene within the jail yard 'frightfully contrasted with the brightness that reigned without'. As the waiting pressmen 'assembled in front of the instrument of death', in the semi-darkness 'was heard that strange, subdued noise, that murmur which yet is silence, those sounds without words, that betoken the presence of an absorbed and anxious crowd'.

The suspense lifted slightly when Ratley walked out of the jail. He was smoking a pipe, and showed 'no traces of the liquor he had consumed the night before'. As he installed the rope into the scaffold, checked the pulleys and raised the weight, 'notebooks flashed from pockets', but when he disappeared back inside the jail again, the anxiety in the crowd only increased. While they waited, many reporters scribbled the details of their own states of mind. They had ceased even to murmur. 'The sudden closing of a distant door caused a perceptible thrill through the assembly.' Several men 'grew pale from emotion and expectation', and 'each second as it passed seemed an hour'.

Inside the jail, Ratley changed from his corduroy jacket into a dark Prince Albert coat, then he went and stood, leather strap in hand, at the bottom of the winding staircase that led up to the condemned cell, 'waiting for the signal which would give him absolute control over the body of Reginald Birchall'. Birchall had requested that the two executors of his will, Mr Forbes and Arthur Leetham, be present for the hanging. Leetham later admitted, 'the idea was very revolting to me', but he complied nevertheless. Just before Birchall left his cell, he turned to shake Leetham's hand and then suddenly bent forward and kissed him. Leetham was caught completely by surprise and started to cry. When Birchall stepped out of his cell, he walked straight to Ratley, and 'dumbly held out his hands'. Ratley, however, 'slipped round behind Birchall, pulled his arms behind him and used the strap to pinion him at the elbows'. It was the custom to leave the wrists free at a hanging so that they could be checked after the drop to see if the victim still had a pulse.

There had been much speculation that Birchall would make a speech from the scaffold. He was asked one last time if he would have anything to say, but replied that he wouldn't. With this point established, there were no further grounds for delay. Birchall once more looked to Leetham, and George Perry, reading the glance, gave permission for Leetham to support Birchall and remain with him to the end. 'Yes,' Birchall said, 'take hold of my arm, old man, and walk with me as we used to in the old days together.' George Perry took

Birchall's other arm, and Birchall whispered his thanks to him for all his kindness 'during their connection'. The hanging was already a few minutes behind schedule. A solemn procession of prison officials now led Birchall out of the jail. Revd Mr Wade, in a white surplice, walked at the front. Birchall and the jail functionaries walked behind him. Ratley 'walked behind them all'. They passed through a line of 'terror-stricken prisoners' before stepping out into the yard. Birchall, according to several reporters, 'remained stationary for a moment and surveyed the crowd with a partial smile'. The New York *Herald*, borrowing the notorious slogan of Barnum's circus, could only conclude from his singular poise that Birchall's belief 'that he was the greatest show on earth' had 'robbed death of half its terrors'.

Constables with long poles were standing round the gallows and now ushered the crowd back 'in smothered words' so that Birchall might not hear. Revd Mr Wade, meanwhile, had immediately begun to read out the Order for the Burial of the Dead from the *Book of Common Prayer*: 'I am the resurrection and the life, saith the Lord: he that believeth in me, though he were dead, yet shall he live: and whosoever liveth and believeth in me shall never die.' As he made his way through these familiar words, there was 'agony' in Wade's voice, and 'he broke down again and again'. The suspense this induced, while he struggled to continue, 'seemed terrible to the crowd'.

One correspondent, from Ottawa, was clearly especially appalled by what he found himself witnessing. Birchall looked 'so young' to him, and displayed such 'undaunted courage', that it was hard to hold in mind that he had shot a friend in a lonely swamp. 'The solemn tones of the Anglican service,' wrote the correspondent, thrilled everyone there with a horror that hardly let them realize the tremendous importance of that in which they were taking part. They felt an overpowering pity for the black-haired, white-faced young man standing on the threshold of eternity.

'It is not possible', he continued, in his attempt to describe Birchall, 'to imagine the expression of his face.' Then in a bizarre choice of words he added: 'It was not despair, but he had strung his whole being up to die game.' This facile pun at first seems in appalling taste, but the writer's state of awful anticipation perhaps made everything about the experience seem to spiral in on itself.

Revd Mr Wade somehow reached that part in the burial service usually to be read while 'the Corpse is made ready to be laid into the earth'. Falteringly he intoned, 'Man that is born of woman hath but a short time to live, and is full of misery. He cometh up, and is cut down, like a flower; he fleeth as it were a shadow, and never continueth in one stay.' The *Mail* noted that as Wade concluded the 'pathetic appeal for mercy', he 'turned his head away from the gallows'. If 'the suspense was terrible to the witnesses', it was also plain that 'no human knowledge' could say how terrible it was 'to the man standing alone there on the green sward'. Birchall once more

turned to his friend Leetham and kissed him. Their lips remained intact for several seconds and though there was no outburst or any external signs of emotion it was evident to everyone present that the parting was accompanied by the intensest agony.

At the words, 'earth to earth, ashes to ashes, dust to dust', Birchall stepped up to the scaffold and Ratley pinioned him below the knees. As he did so, Birchall was 'twisting his head from side to side like a bird', and seemed to examine 'the pulley and the noose and the weight' as though seeking to understand the 'peculiar mechanism' of the gallows. Though Birchall had stated that he would say nothing, the Ottawa correspondent was struck by the fact that he made his silence 'a silence that seemed by the intensity of his purpose to be a silence concentrated a hundred times'.

The burial service was almost complete. Revd Mr Wade spoke the words, 'blessed are the dead which die in the Lord: even so saith the Spirit; for they rest from their labours'. Birchall then whispered a request to George Perry, which led to Wade stepping forward. 'Birchall, kissing him quietly on the lips, straightened up as if he had drawn strength from the consolation given him.' He said, 'Good bye, Mr Wade, God bless you,' and in the waiting crowd, 'everyone knew death was at hand'.

Reporters disagreed afterwards as to who initiated the gesture, but Birchall and Ratley now shook hands, before the hangman pulled a black hood over Birchall's head. Ratley then positioned himself beside Birchall, ready to catch him should he give way too soon. 'Many people turned their face from the gallows or directed their eyes to the ground,' but the two telegraph cable operators, who were leaning, machines in hand, against the jail wall, stared fixedly at the weight, poised to notify England the moment the drop occurred. More telegraphers were lodged inside the jail, and sat on a bench, 'fingers on keys', waiting for the deluge of copy.

'The sublime words of the Lord's Prayer rang out upon the keen and frosty air,' and whether at 'Thy will be done', 'Deliver us from evil', or 'Amen', there was a ghastly click. The weight 'dropped with the rapidity of thought' and sank 'six or eight inches into the ground'. Birchall's body shot out in a sideways arc before hurtling more directly upwards, almost to the height of the gallows cross beam. He did not immediately die. The rope was too long and the knot had been misplaced. Convulsions passed through his body 'from the neck downwards' as he slowly strangled. Arthur Leetham, Revd Mr Wade and George Perry began to sob. 'The body swayed to and fro till the hangman caught and steadied it. But it still continued writhing and the chest vainly heaved.' A reporter noted that 'almost everyone in the crowd held a watch'. At the end of two minutes Birchall's pulse was still running at sixty.

News of the hanging was sent thousands of miles across the submarine cables, and was displayed on newspaper bulletin boards in London, 'within a fraction of three minutes'. Only at six and a half minutes, however, did 'the muscular contractions of the body' cease to 'horrify' the crowd. Reporters agreed that there had been fifty-one convulsions before Birchall was pronounced dead. At last his body swung 'limply to and fro, the face ever turning towards the spectators'. Those who could bear to look found that the rope had lifted one side of the hood, to reveal half of a faint smile that lingered on his countenance. He was left to hang a few minutes more, to be certain of no mistakes.

Author's Postscript

In the spring of 1891 Pelly heard through intermediaries that Florence Birchall had threatened to sue him for libel, on what grounds he didn't know. This action never materialized, but Pelly was sufficiently alarmed to write to the legal authorities in Woodstock asking for the return of the various letters that Birchall had written him, several of which had been submitted in evidence at Birchall's trial.

A century later these and other letters about the case, along with various sepia photographs of court-room scenes and of the swamp, plus a copy of Birchall's autobiography, lay tied up with pink ribbon in a desiccated envelope in the attic of one of Pelly's grandsons. Pelly's private memoir, meanwhile, had remained in the possession of his elderly daughter, who for many decades left it half-forgotten under a heap of obsolete bank statements at the back of a spare-bedroom cupboard.

Pelly's daughter is my father's mother. The story of how her father, my great-grandfather, became entangled in a murder case was first told to me some years ago round the lunch table of a Pelly cousin. The version of events given that day was brief and extremely inaccurate. Benwell's killing, for example, had been solved through the discovery of an initialled handkerchief, while Pelly had survived being murdered on a bridge over the Niagara Falls because he had had a vision of an angel warning him to turn back. I was intrigued despite the implausible details, and became all the more so when I understood that the lives of nearly everyone present at that lunch, including my own, really did depend upon the fact that Birchall had failed to cast Pelly into the whirling Niagara rapids.

I would like to make special mention of the kindness with which, from that day on, my Pelly relatives, some of them writers themselves, have helped me to take up a story that is a peculiar inheritance of theirs no less than of mine.

Acknowledgements

For their broad guidance, detailed help or in some cases plain hard work on research questions, and on the writing and putting together of this book, I would like to thank Fred Belinsky, Ann Cooke, Gina Cowen, Ashley Drees, Katharine Gowers, Patrick Gowers, Timothy Gowers, Eric Griffiths, Derek Johns, Sadakat Kadri, Madeline Meckiffe, Richenda Miers, Juliette Mitchell, Thorsten Opper, David Pelly, Adrian Poole, Simon Prosser, Peter Alan Roberts, Frank Sharp, Helen Small, George Tiffin, Ida Toth and Natasha Walter. I am grateful above all to Timothy Gowers and Helen Small, who were extraordinarily generous in the time they gave to each page of my prolix first draft.

My thanks go also to St John's College, Cambridge, for awarding me a Harper-Wood studentship, thereby funding my original research in Canada; and to Trinity College, Cambridge, for sending me to the University of Chicago for a year, where Robert A. Ferguson put discipline into my early thinking on the subject matter of this book.

I would also like to thank the curators, archivists, librarians, editors and other dedicated staff who helped me at the Archives of Ontario, the Bodleian Library, Oxford, the British Newspaper Library, Colindale, English Heritage, Lincoln College, Oxford, the William Morris Gallery, the National Trust, the Oklahoma State University Special Collections and University Archives, the *Oxford English Dictionary*, the Public Record Office, the Toronto Public Library, the Woodstock Public Library, Ontario, the Woodstock Museum National Historic Site, Ontario, the York University Law Library, Toronto, the University of Illinois at Chicago Special Collections, and the University of Western Ontario Archives. At the last of these, my thanks go specially to Stephen Harding, who, shortly before I finished this book, to my great excitement and not negligible fear, located a box of original materials on the case in the archive's holdings, sending me a blizzard of emails to describe the photographs and other, peculiar artefacts he had found.

In quite another sphere, for their dauntless support over the past three years, without which I don't know where I would be, may I thank from the heart my family and all my friends. They are too many to list by name, but I would mention very particularly Tanglewest and Raymond, whose dotty interest in this project kept me going through some of the darker moments of my life.

Notes on Sources

The facts of the narrative unfolded on these pages were established principally through cross-referencing both original press reports on the Birchall case, and the two slightly contradictory accounts of the same events contained within the 1933 memoir of Douglas Raymond Pelly.

Replicas of all materials relating to this subject hitherto held privately by members of the Pelly family, including numbers of letters, and sections of Pelly's memoir and travel diary, can now be found at the University of Western Ontario Archives: the J. J. Talman Regional Collection, Douglas Pelly fonds. In its Louise Hill collection, the same archive has a separate holding of original materials and photographs arising from the case, while further letters, telegrams, artefacts and photographs can be found at the Woodstock Museum National Historic Site, Ontario.

There are many broad references in the text to local Ontario newspapers, to the Toronto press and to the American press. The specific titles in question are: the Woodstock *Sentinel-Review* and the Woodstock *Evening Standard*; the Toronto *Daily Mail*, *Evening News*, *Globe*, and *World*; and the New York *Herald*, *Sun*, and *Tribune*. Other titles substantially consulted were the New York *Herald, London Edition*, the London *Times*, and the Ottawa *Evening Journal*.

There are three other main sources for this book: Birchall's autobiography, the 1890 pulp novel *The Swamp of Death*, and Detective Murray's memoir. After serializing Birchall's autobiography on its front pages, the Toronto *Mail* immediately published it as a fifty-cent book in pink paper covers, with the main text sandwiched between the newspaper's own account of Benwell's shooting and its report on Birchall's strangulation. *Birchall: The Story of His Life, Trial and Imprisonment as Told by Himself*, survives in two editions: the first and the sixth, though the sixth is almost certainly really the second, dressed up to look like a bestseller.

Fraser's pulp novel, *The Swamp of Death: or, The Benwell Murder*, was published in at least three editions. The anonymous Toronto version was brought out by the Rose Publishing Company in 1890 with a newspaper account of Birchall's execution added in at the end. The first American edition, credited to Hawkshaw, was published as part of its Globe Detective Series by the Eagle Publishing Company, Chicago. This edition seems to exist now only as a title advertised in the back of other works in the Globe series. In 1891 or 1892, however, Eagle rented or sold on the plates for the book in a job lot of titles that went to a second Chicago reprint and pirate publisher, M. A. Donohue. Donohue issued *The Swamp of Death* as number ninety-one in its Flashlight Detective Series; a set of one hundred novels that sold at a single title for a quarter, three for fifty cents, and seven for a dollar.

Detective Murray's *Memoirs of a Great Detective: Incidents in the Life of John Wilson Murray*

A souvenir pamphlet from the Wonderland waxwork museum.

was first published by Heinemann, in London, in 1904. The next year saw both a New York and a Toronto edition, and these credit Victor Speer, a Canadian magazine and newspaper writer, with having compiled the work. It seems probable that Speer took an active hand in converting Murray's reminiscences into readable form.

Other original sources or reference works consulted during the writing of this book are either indicated in the text itself, or are noted, by chapter, below:

A Sort of Travelling Gentleman Farmer

Dryden, John, *Ontario: Premier Province of Canada. Description of the Country – Its Resources and Development – Glimpses of its Scenery – Attractions for Tourist, Sportsman and Settler* (2nd ed.), Toronto, Warwick & Rutter, 1897

Wright, Charles, and Fayle, C. Ernest, *A History of Lloyd's: From the Founding of Lloyd's Coffee House to the Present Day*, London, Macmillan, 1928

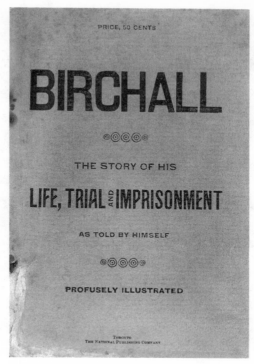

PRICE, 50 CENTS

BIRCHALL

◉◎◉◎◉

THE STORY OF HIS

LIFE, TRIAL ᴬⁿᵈ IMPRISONMENT

AS TOLD BY HIMSELF

◉◎◉◎◉

PROFUSELY ILLUSTRATED

TORONTO
THE NATIONAL PUBLISHING COMPANY

Birchall's pink-wrappered autobiography.

A Greater Nuisance

Kludas, Arnold, *Great Passenger Ships of the World Vol 1, 1858–1912,* trans. Charles Hodge, Cambridge, Patrick Stephens, 1972–4

Haws, Duncan, *Merchant Fleets: White Star Line (Oceanic Steam Navigation Company),* Hereford, TCL Publications, 1982

The Unfortunate Unknown

Rutherford, Paul, *A Victorian Authority: the daily press in late nineteenth-century Canada,* Toronto, University of Toronto Press, 1982

Sotiron, Minko, *From Politics to Profit: The Commercialization of Canadian Daily Newspapers, 1890–1920,* Montreal & Kingston, McGill-Queen's University Press, 1997

Big Difficulties

Tugby's Illustrated Guide to Niagara Falls, Niagara, Thomas Tugby, 1889

Mitchell, Sally (ed.), 'Telegraph and Telephone', *Victorian Britain: An Encyclopedia*, New York, Garland Publishing, 1988

Heaton, J. Henniker, 'Postal and Telegraphic Progress under Queen Victoria', *Fortnightly Review* 67 (June 1897)

[Head, Sir Francis Bond,] *Stokers and Pokers: or, The London and North-Western Railway, The Electric Telegraph, and The Railway Clearing House*, London, John Murray, 1849

Kipling, Rudyard, 'A Song of the English', 1893. See *A Choice of Kipling's Verse made by T. S. Eliot*, London, Faber & Faber, 1941

A Swell, Sharper and Deadbeat

Burke's Peerage (51st ed.), London, Harrison and Sons, 1889

Ryder, Tom, *History of the Coaching Club, 1871–2000*, London, J. A. Allen, 1999

Chester, Lewis, Leitch, David and Simpson, Colin, *The Cleveland Street Affair*, London, Weidenfeld & Nicolson, 1976

McCaughan, Margaret M., *The Legal Status of Married Women in Canada*, Toronto, Carswell, 1977

Terrible Domestic Calamity

Brown, Lucy, *Victorian News and Newspapers*, Oxford, Clarendon Press, 1985

Read, Donald, *The Power of News: The History of Reuters 1849–1989*, Oxford, Oxford University Press, 1992

Morison, Stanley, *The History of the Times, Vol. lll: The Twentieth-Century Test, 1884–1912*, London, The Times, 1935–

Gernsheim, Helmut and Alison, *Queen Victoria: A Biography in Word and Picture*, London, Longman's, 1959

Plunkett, John, *Queen Victoria: First Media Monarch*, Oxford, Oxford University Press, 2003

Stevenson, David, *Fifty Years on the London and North Western Railway, and Other Memoranda in the Life of David Stevenson*, London, McCorquedale, 1891

Kelvin, Norman (ed.), *The Collected Letters of William Morris, Vol. II, 1885–1888*, Princeton, Princeton University Press, 1987

Morris, May, *William Morris: Artist, Writer, Socialist. Vol II: Morris as a Socialist*, Oxford, Basil Blackwell, 1936

The Christian Socialist: A Journal for Those who Work and Think, monthly, 1887–1890

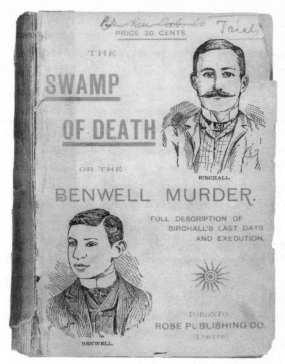

The 1890 Canadian edition of The Swamp
of Death.

Outrivalling the Detective Tales of Fiction

Higley, Dahn D., *O. P. P.: The History of the Ontario Provincial Police Force*, Toronto, The
    Queen's Printer, 1984

Lighter, J. E. (ed.), *Random House Historical Dictionary of American Slang*, New York, Random
    House, 1994–7

'A. P. G.', *All About Typewriters and Typewriting*, London, Horace Marshall and Son, 1903

Morton, Arthur E., *Type-Writing and Type-Writers; or Aids to Rapid Writing: and How to Select
    a Machine*, London, Thomas Poulter and Sons, 1890

*An American reprint, circa 1892, with
incorrect title and irrelevant cover picture.*

Installed for the Summer in a Villa by the Sea

Cullen, Tom, *Autumn of Terror: Jack the Ripper and his Crimes*, London, The Bodley Head,
1965

A Little Deluge of Literary Slops

O'Connor, Richard, *The Scandalous Mr. Bennett*, New York, Doubleday, 1962

Hoppenstand, Gary (ed.), *The Dime Novel Detective*, Bowling Green, Ohio, Bowling Green
University Popular Press, 1982

Moran, Richard, *Executioner's Current: Thomas Edison, George Westinghouse, and the Invention
of the Electric Chair*, New York, Alfred A. Knopf, 2002

The Curtain Rung Up at last

Guillet, Edwin C., 'The Swamp of Death; a Study of the Evidence', 1944. (Unpublished MS held by York University Law Library, Toronto.)

More Stimulants

The Revised Statutes of Canada 1886, Vol. II, Ottawa, 1887
Blackstock, C. M., *All the Journey Through*, Toronto, University of Toronto Press, 1997

Advanced Disorder

Mortimer, Roger, *The History of the Derby Stakes*, London, Cassell, 1962

Picture Credits

Chapter 1 *A Sort of Travelling Gentleman farmer.* **p.3** Pelly at Cambridge: *circa* 1886. Private collection. **p.16** Mr and Mrs Birchall, copy print by Westlake of Woodstock. Courtesy of the J. J. Talman Regional Collection, the University of Western Ontario. Chapter 2 *A Greater Nuisance.* **p.24** The *Britannic* crash: 'Just After the First Blow', *Illustrated London News*, 11 June 1887. By permission of the British Library: Ld 47. Chapter 3 *The Unfortunate Unknown.* **p.39** The road leading into the Blenheim Swamp: 1890. Private collection. **p.41** Where the murder was committed: 13 March 1890. Private collection. **p.50** The corpse, photographed by Westlake of Woodstock, 23 February 1890. Courtesy of Woodstock Museum National Historic Site. **p.51** 'The Murdered Man', Woodstock *Evening Standard*, 26 February 1890. Courtesy of the J. J. Talman Regional Collection, the University of Western Ontario. Chapter 4 *Big Difficulties.* **p.58** The Lower Suspension Bridge, *Tugby's Illustrated Guide to Niagara Falls*. Niagara: Thomas Tugby, 1889. Private collection. Chapter 5 *A Swell, Sharper and Deadbeat.* **p.90** Mrs Birchall. Courtesy of the J. J. Talman Regional Collection, the University of Western Ontario. **p.90** Mrs Birchall: syndicated newspaper engraving, March 1890. Private collection. Chapter 6 *Terrible Domestic Calamity.* **p.100** Illustrated title page, R. M. Ballantyne, *The Battery and the Boiler, or, Adventures in the Laying of Submarine Cables*. New York, Thomas Nelson & Sons, 1882. Private collection. **p.120** Reginald Birchall as a student. Courtesy of Woodstock Museum National Historic Site. **p.122** Lincoln College Order Book, 9 December 1887. Courtesy of Lincoln College, Oxford. Chapter 7 *A Wreath of Mildew.* **p.127** Princeton inquest: 'Niagara Falls Murder', New York *Herald*, London Edition, 23 March 1890, p. 1. By permission of the British Library: shelf mark A.2a. **p.146** Murray and others in the swamp: 13 March 1890. Private collection. Chapter 8 *Outrivalling the Detective Tales of Fiction.* **p.150** John Wilson Murray, copy print by Westlake of Woodstock. Courtesy of the J. J. Talman Regional Collection, the University of Western Ontario. **p.167** 'F. A. Somerset' and Dudley, 1888/9. Courtesy of the J. J. Talman Regional Collection, the University of Western Ontario. Chapter 9 *Installed for the Summer in a Villa by the Sea.* **p.178** 'The West Corridor with Birchall's Cell', 'The Gaol Looking North' and 'Birchall's Day Cell. Birchall Night Cell', Woodstock *Sentinel-Review*, 14 November 1890, first ed., p. 2. Archives of Ontario, N 124, reel 27. **p.182** Reginald Birchall. Courtesy of the J. J. Talman Regional Collection, the University of Western Ontario. **p.183** Reginald Birchall: syndicated newspaper engraving, March 1890. Private collection. **p.190** Frederick Cornwallis Benwell: copy print by J. Zybach & Co., Niagara Falls. Courtesy of Woodstock Museum National Historic Site. Chapter 10 *A Little Deluge of Literary Slops.* **p.204** Hawkshaw the Detective [John Arthur Fraser], *A Wayward Girl's Fate*. Chicago: M. A. Donohue, 1889. Private collection. Chapter 11 *The Curtain Rung Up at*

Last. **p.212** 'The Benwell Tragedy', Woodstock *Evening Standard*, 11 September 1890. Courtesy of the J. J. Talman Regional Collection, the University of Western Ontario. **p.216** Woodstock's town hall square, postcard circa 1890. Courtesy of Woodstock Museum National Historic Site. **p.218** 'Birchall in the dock pleading "not guilty" ', 22 September 1890. Private collection. **p.226** Pelly giving evidence: 22 September 1890. Private collection. Chapter 12 *An Exhibition of Weakness.* **p.243** Osler, copy print by Westlake for the Woodstock *Sentinel-Review.* Courtesy of the J. J. Talman Regional Collection, the University of Western Ontario. **p.243** Blackstock, copy print by Westlake for the Woodstock *Sentinel-Review.* Courtesy of the J. J. Talman Regional Collection, the University of Western Ontario. Chapter 13 *Having Murder in your Heart.* **p.280** The jury, copy print by Westlake for the Woodstock *Sentinel-Review.* Courtesy of Woodstock Museum National Historic Site. **p.281** 'Two Fine Photos', Woodstock *Sentinel-Review*, 5 November 1890, p. 3. Archives of Ontario, N 124, reel 27. Chapter 14 *More Stimulants.* **p.295** Douglas Pelly's travel diary, 22 and 29 September 1890. Private collection. **p.296** Victorian ink sketch of Benwell's vault. Courtesy of the J. J. Talman Regional Collection, the University of Western Ontario. **p.308** 'Encouraging Canadian Literature', John Wilson Bengough for *Grip*, 8 November 1890 (vol. XXV, No. 19, p. 296). Courtesy of the Toronto Public Library. Chapter 15 *Advanced Disorder.* **p.317** 'From a pen-and-ink sketch', Reginald Birchall, *Birchall: the Story of his Life, Trial and Imprisonment.* Toronto, The National Publishing Company, 1890, p. 20. Private collection. **p.324** 'A close finish', Reginald Birchall, *Birchall: the Story of his Life, Trial and Imprisonment.* Toronto, The National Publishing Company, 1890, p. 26. Private collection. **p.325** 'Situations Vacant and Wanted', *London Evening Standard*, 6 December 1889, p. 8. By permission of the British Library: Ld 15. Chapter 16 *The Greatest Show on Earth.* **p.348** The last kiss: 'An Interview with his Wife', Woodstock *Sentinel-Review*, 14 November 1890, 2nd ed., p. 4. Archives of Ontario, N 124, reel 27. Notes on Sources. **p.370** 'Birchall Relics', souvenir pamphlet. Courtesy of the J. J. Talman Regional Collection, the University of Western Ontario. **p.372** Reginald Birchall, *Birchall: the Story of his Life, Trial and Imprisonment.* Toronto, The National Publishing Company, 1890. Private collection. **p.374** Anon. [John Arthur Fraser], *The Swamp of Death: or, The Benwell Murder.* Toronto, Rose Publishing Company, 1890. Courtesy of the Toronto Public Library. **p.377** Hawkshaw the Detective [John Arthur Fraser], *The Swamp of Death; or, The Benwell Mystery.* Chicago: M. A. Donohue & Co., nd [1891/2]. Courtesy of the Robert Cotton Collection, Special Collections and University Archives, Oklahoma State University.

Every effort has been made to trace copyright holders and we apologize in advance for any unintentional omission. We would be pleased to insert the appropriate acknowledgement in any subsequent edition.